MW01032599

THE SECRET OF THE GRAND HÔTEL DU LAC

KATHRYN GAUCI

First published in 2020 by Ebony Publishing
ISBN: 978 0 6487144 1 5

Copyright © Kathryn Gauci 2020

This novel is a work of fiction based on real events.
Except for those names and institutions in the public domain,
all the characters and organisations mentioned are either a product
of the author's imagination or, if real, used fictitiously without any
intent to describe actual conduct. Any resemblance to real persons,
living or dead, is entirely co-incidental.

This book is dedicated to the bravery of the men and women of the Resistance in the Jura/Franche-Comté region of France, and to the passeurs who smuggled hundreds of Jews and others fleeing Nazi-occupied France across the border into Switzerland.

CONTENTS

'Whatever happens, the flame of the French Resistance
must not be extinguished, and will not be extinguished.'
Charles de Gaulle 1940

Here everyone knows what he wants,
what he does when he passes my friend.
If you fall, a friend will come from the shadows to take your place.
Tomorrow, black blood will dry under the sun on the roads.
Sing, companions, on the night of Liberty we hear.
My friend, do you hear the muffled cries of the country
that is in chains?
'The Partisans' Song'

ZONES OF OCCUPATION, EASTERN FRANCE

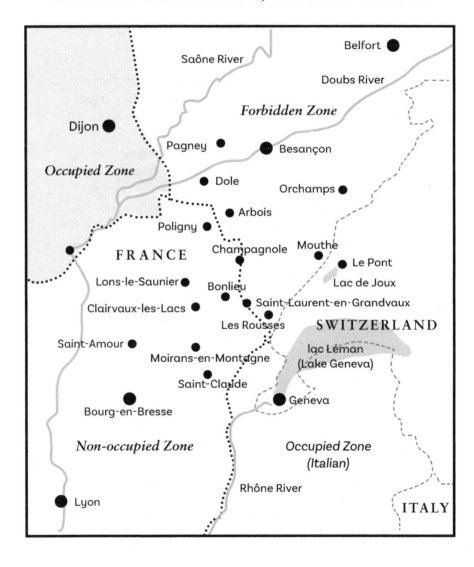

CHAPTER 1

Christmas Eve 1943: The Haut-Jura, France.

The silence was eternal. At least that's how it seemed to Guy Maxwell, stranded in a wooden hut in the middle of a forest. He'd been there, huddled on a bed of straw under a thick layer of blankets for days — maybe even longer — it was hard to tell. He'd lost all sense of time. He dragged himself up off the floor, wiped the condensation from the small window pane with the cuff of his jacket, and peered out into the forest. The snow was falling, silently and gently, covering the forest floor in thick drifts that glistened in the ethereal glow of moonlight. His eyes fell on the fir trees, their boughs bending under the weight of a thick layer of snow. He was reminded of the village where he grew up as a child in England, except that at this time of year the fir trees would be adorned with colourful lights and shiny silver stars. He looked at his watch. It was almost midnight. Maybe Christmas had come and gone. Somewhere in his scrambled thoughts he'd imagined he would be back in England spending this time with Elizabeth. Now he wondered if he'd ever see England again — or Elizabeth for that matter.

A searing pain shot down his side and left leg, forcing him to lie down again. He covered himself with the blankets and tried to keep warm, aware of the silence that cocooned him like the mist that shrouded the forests in winter. Except for the persistent ringing in his ears, there wasn't a sound to be heard. He covered his head with the blankets, trying desperately to block it out. Was it the explosion that caused the ringing? He couldn't be sure of that either.

When he opened his eyes some hours later, it was dawn. The ringing was still there and his vision was blurred. A man sat in the corner watching him. Startled, Guy quietly moved his hand under the blankets in search of his pistol.

'If this is what you're looking for,' the man said, holding the gun.

'You won't need it. You're in safe hands.' He put the gun on the floor.

The man introduced himself as Raymond — a friend. He also added that he was a doctor.

'Where am I?' Guy asked.

'In the mountains: not too far from Moirans-en-Montagne, but far enough to be away from the Germans who are combing the area as we speak.' He reached into his jacket, pulled out a small silver flask and handed it to Guy. 'Drink: it will do you good.'

'I hope it's something strong,' Guy replied. 'I'm in agony.'

He took one sip and gave a nod of thanks. He recognised it as Genepi, an alcoholic drink similar to absinthe made from mountain herbs that the people of the Franche-Comté drank for medicinal purposes as well as pleasure. He felt its effects immediately. A few more mouthfuls and the pain diminished slightly.

Raymond asked to look at Guy's wounds and pulled the blankets away. Guy shifted uncomfortably on his straw bed. For the first time, he saw how seriously injured he was. The clothes he had been wearing the day he received his wounds had been replaced by someone else's; a few sizes too big, but clean. Raymond asked Guy to turn over. He wanted to check the area below his left lower shoulder blade where the bullet had penetrated. Guy winced.

'Thankfully you were out to it when it was removed,' Raymond said, referring to the bullet. 'No serious damage and no sign of gangrene. Now show me the leg.'

The leg was still a mess, but Guy was assured, that too would heal.

'I need to clean it a little more. You'd better grit your teeth; it will hurt.'

He placed a container of water on the floor next to Guy's makeshift straw bed and took out a tin from his backpack containing medical supplies. First, he cleansed the area where the bullet had penetrated, gently sponging away the dried blood that had congealed around the wound. Then he applied a fresh bandage and started on the right side of his torso and the leg. The leg worried him the most, he said. Guy had third degree burns from the top of his thigh to the middle of his calf and it looked a mess — red raw and blistered — like the left side of his face. Even Raymond's soft touch did not stop Guy from wanting to scream out loud. Instead he bit tightly on his jacket.

'That's enough for today,' Raymond said, covering the area with a thin layer of ointment. 'You'll be fine soon. Hopefully, after a couple of days, we can move you to somewhere more comfortable. In the meantime I'll leave you these pills. They'll ease the pain, but only take one at a time and no more than three a day.'

He put the medicine tin in the backpack and brought out a large flask of chicken broth and a brown paper package tied with string.

'Merry Christmas.' He smiled as he handed them over. 'I can't offer you Christmas pudding so I hope this will suffice.'

The package contained several thick slices of bread, half a smoked sausage and hard cow's cheese. The sausage had been smoked over the wood from fir trees — a local tradition — and the aroma was mouth-wateringly intense. Until that moment, Guy hadn't realised how hungry he was, and tucked into it with relish, even though it hurt when he chewed. Washed down with the broth, it was the best Christmas meal he'd ever had.

'That's a good sign.' Raymond laughed. 'Now I know you'll pull through.'

On hearing it was Christmas day, Guy knew how long he'd been holed up in the room. At least three days. Three days without food and water and wounds that could have turned bad at any moment. Three days of sleeping on a cold stone floor with only a bed of straw and a few blankets to keep him warm. No wonder he was famished.

'Where is this place?' Guy asked.

'It's used by foresters and hunters. Hardly anyone comes here these days. Not since the occupation. The Maquis use it as one of their hideouts. It overlooks the gorge. You're safe but as soon as that leg gets a little better, we'll move you on.'

'What happened?' Guy asked. 'How did I get here? All I remember is that after the *parachutage* we headed to the Ledoux Farm and were in the process of hiding the contents of the containers in the outbuildings when a lookout arrived to say the Germans were coming. There was no time to escape. All we could do was prepare ourselves for the onslaught. Minutes later the farm was surrounded and there was a hail of gunfire. We knew that if we stayed we stood no chance, so we made a decision to escape through a window and head for the forest. No sooner had we started to make a run for it than I was hit. Then I heard a loud explosion. The next thing I knew, I was here. I didn't even know for how long until you just told me it was Christmas day.'

Guy took another mouthful of bread and sausage and lay back down on the straw. It hurt too much to sit up.

'The others,' he asked, 'tell me they're alright.'

Raymond reached for Guy's mug and refilled it. 'I'm sorry to tell you that only you and André survived. The other maquisards all died at the scene. Monsieur and Madame Ledoux were taken to Gestapo Headquarters at Lons-le-Saunier and I don't like their chances of returning alive. André is in hiding at the moment. It was he who saved you. Apparently the Ledoux kept a container of gasoline hidden behind the cowshed. That's what caused the explosion. It blew the shed to smithereens when it was hit. You are both lucky to be alive.'

Raymond reeled off the names of those who had been either killed in action or executed straight after. Apart from André, the *chef de réseau* — head of the local network in Saint-Claude, two other names were not mentioned — Guy's radio operator, SOE agent "Vincent", known in the field as Paul-Emille, and Claude Favre, another maquisard.

'Paul-Emille: what happened to him?' Guy asked.

'I don't know. Do you recall if he was with you at the farm? There were two other sheds where the Ledoux kept their animals. Maybe he was also captured and taken to Lons-le-Saunier but I am sure our sources would have said something if there had been someone else.'

Guy rubbed his temples. 'I can't recall. It's still all a blur. Are you sure you identified all the bodies?'

Raymond nodded. 'We assumed we'd accounted for everyone.'

Guy had an anxious look. On hearing there were two others missing, Raymond also became worried. It was one of the Maquis' first rules that after any combat, regardless of how small or large the operation, everyone was to be accounted for.

'Think hard,' Raymond urged. 'Did all the men accompany you to the farm?'

'Now it's coming back to me — all except Paul-Emille and Claude Favre. André asked Favre to go ahead and keep a lookout while we collected the containers and hid the parachutes. Paul-Emille left with him.'

'Was that usual, especially when you needed as many hands as possible to distribute and hide the contents of the containers?'

'It wasn't unusual for Paul-Emille and I to part ways straight after a drop.'

'Why is that?'

'Sometimes it's safer to part ways. Besides, I wanted him to transmit to London straight away to let them know the drop had been a success.'

'And do you think that's what he did?' Raymond asked. 'I mean, it wasn't exactly what you would call a success, was it? The farm was ambushed. Someone knew the men would be there.'

'What are you suggesting?' Guy asked, growing angry at the line of questioning.

'I'm not suggesting anything, but we do have to find him and make sure he's alright too. You know we must account for everyone. The survival of the Maquis depends on this. Where would he have gone?'

Guy looked at him. 'I can't tell you that.'

Raymond sighed. 'My dear friend, I'm trying to help you. I am trying to help *us*. He may be lying dead in the woods somewhere, but one thing is for sure, one way or another, we will account for him — dead or alive.'

'What about Favre?' Guy asked. 'Where is he? I'm surprised André didn't mention him.'

'He may simply have forgotten because he was not at the farm. I'll check it out. Favre wasn't the one who alerted you all that the Germans were on the way. That was a young man by the name of Pierre Jonval. He was a lookout, and we found his body at the farm too.'

'Then Favre might be lying dead in the woods too,' Guy replied.

'You may be right. Let's pray that isn't the case.' Raymond paused for a while, watching Guy drink his broth. 'You asked how you got here. I'll tell you. After André brought you to my house he said he was disappearing for a while until the heat died down, just in case anyone talked. He didn't say where he was going or when he would be back, but he did ask me to take care of you. My son and I brought you here. We are the only ones who know where you are. When you've recovered enough to walk, you will be moved to a safe house. That's all I know at the moment.' He looked at Guy's straw bed on the floor. 'I'm sorry it's not the most comfortable of lodgings, but you are safe. That's the most important thing.'

Raymond packed away the empty flask, leaving the rest of the food for Guy to eat later.

'When can I expect you again?' Guy asked.

Raymond shrugged. 'I hope tomorrow or the day after. When I return, I will give the signal.'

'You mean whistle the song?'

'Yes — *Cette chanson est pour vous*. You know the reply; the next line.' He handed him a slip of paper — a crude map containing fir trees, dashes and crosses. At the top was a compass.

'Just in case something happens to me, I want you to have this. You are here, due north of Saint-Claude and east of Moirans-en-Montagne.' Raymond tapped his finger at a point on the map and at several crosses. 'These represent safe houses and Maquis camps. The nearest is over five kilometres away: quite a walk, so I don't expect you'll be going anywhere soon. Study it and then destroy it. If you do go on alone, remember to give the signal when you come to a safe house.'

Raymond picked up his backpack and slung it over his back. Before leaving, he handed Guy another box of cartridges for his gun, and a flashlight. They shook hands and he left. Guy pulled himself up from the floor, but by the time he looked out of the window Raymond had gone. Only the fresh imprint of skis remained as a reminder that Guy had received a visitor. With the snow still falling, they too would soon disappear. He lay back on the bed, checked his gun was still loaded, and put it by his side underneath the blankets. The pain was returning again and he took one of Raymond's little white pills. It worked wonders. Within a few minutes he was asleep.

The following day was the same as the last. The hut was cold and damp. The temperature outside dropped to sub-zero, and the softly falling snow soon turned into a blizzard. After finishing the last slice of bread and cheese, washed down with a mug of cold tea, he stood up and tried to walk in the confined space of the room. Much to his relief, the pain in his leg had eased, as had the buzzing in his head. After five minutes, he lay back down again. Guy Maxwell was a fit man. In his student days at Oxford, he'd been a highly respected canoeist having twice taken part in the Oxford and Cambridge boat race at Henley-on-Thames. He was also an avid hiker, mountain climber and a first-class skier. If he had the good fortune to survive the ambush, then he could recover quickly. Now was not the time to hang around, cooped up in a hut in a forest. He had work to do and he knew he must force himself to walk again as soon as possible. An hour later he did the same thing — up and down. This time it was for longer. He did this every hour until he could walk for a full fifteen minutes at a time. When the pain returned, he took another of Raymond's pills and continued. By the time the sun went down, he was exhausted and settled down under the warm blankets mulling over the events of the night of the drop. Someone had betrayed them. That much was clear:

but who? They had been so careful. Under the influence of the pills, combined with the sheer exhaustion at pushing himself so hard, Guy fell into a deep sleep again.

The next day the blizzard eased. He heard a noise outside and grabbed his gun. When he peered through a chink in the wooden door, he was relieved to see it was only wolves. He counted four altogether, loping and sniffing around the cabin as if they sensed someone was inside. The largest one, the leader of the pack with thick, glossy fur, pawed and scratched at the door for several minutes. Guy remained motionless but the wolf knew he was there. There was intelligence in his eyes: one born out of the wild, scanning the surroundings for danger or opportunity. He had seen their determination before, when a pack broke into a cowshed, devouring the calves. The sight had haunted him for weeks after. After a while they retreated back into the forest, their movement as graceful as any dancer.

Sometime during the early hours of the morning, he awoke again, this time with a start. He was sure he heard a noise outside. It sounded like a twig snapping. Under normal circumstances it would have meant nothing, but in the silence of the forest every sound was magnified. There it was again. This time it was closer and his instinct told him it wasn't the wolves. He reached for his gun and quietly looked out through the window. The moon was on the wane, wrapped in the soft gauze of snowfall and it wasn't easy to see. Maybe it was a fox, or even a deer. Then he heard it again, right outside the door. He cocked his gun, pressed his body flat against the wall next to the door, and waited. The room was in total darkness and his senses were heightened. After a few minutes, he heard the soft click of the door latch. Guy stood behind the door and aimed. He had a visitor and it wasn't Raymond.

CHAPTER 2

February 1944: Baker Street, London.

Elizabeth Maxwell approached 64 Baker Street with a spring in her step. She had been called to a meeting by her liaison officer, Vera Atkins, assistant to the head of F Section of the Special Operations Executive, the section responsible for agents working in France. Elizabeth had been back in England for just over six months now and apart from her initial de-briefing, had not been asked back to Baker Street. That meeting had gone well. She'd told them everything she could about her three months in France working undercover as a courier for Guy Maxwell's Belvedere network. Guy and Elizabeth had returned to England together. They met in France while on assignment and fell in love. Neither of them had expected it and if anything, both had fought against their emotions, fearing it could compromise their mission. In fact, they had hidden it so well that when they decided to get married on their return to London, it was a surprise to everyone. Most of their friends were happy for them. After all, agents were aware they were living on borrowed time, and love and affection of any sort was to be grabbed while it could. The only people who weren't happy were the people at Baker Street. Guy Maxwell was one of their best agents and they couldn't afford for him to get tangled up in a love affair.

Elizabeth walked up the stairs and passed another agent on his way out.

'Elizabeth, how lovely to see you again,' Andy Pickard said, giving her a friendly peck on the cheek. 'I haven't seen you since the wedding. Where have you been hiding yourself? And how's that husband of yours? Keeping out of mischief I hope.'

'I'm hoping that's why I've been called here,' Elizabeth replied, 'so that they can give me some good news about his return.' She tapped her watch. 'I'm afraid I can't talk now. I have a meeting in five minutes and you know what they're like if you're late.'

Andy asked if she would like to join him for a drink in the pub afterwards. She agreed.

'I'll be waiting.' He laughed. 'Don't stand me up, will you?'

When she reached the third floor, Vera was already waiting for her. With her was Colonel Maurice Buckmaster, Head of F Section and Vera's own boss. The two worked closely together and were known to stay back late into the night in the signals room, awaiting the decoded transmissions sent by agents in the field. Vera was a tall, imposing figure with short, wavy hair, always conservatively dressed, usually in brown or navy tailored suits. She often appeared rather cold and formal and was not a woman to be side-tracked by small-talk. She told you only what you needed to know and nothing more. Yet, for those who knew her better, she was highly efficient and, once she decided you were an agent, she took a great deal of care in your well-being. Elizabeth always thought she was one of the few in SOE who could be trusted. Vera shook Elizabeth's hand and asked her to take a seat. After offering her a cigarette, she opened the file in front of her.

'How have you been?' she asked.

Elizabeth replied that she had taken a nursing position at St Thomas' Hospital since her return from France. She told them she'd thought of returning to Devon but decided that due to the bombing, her nursing skills would be put to better use in London.

Colonel Buckmaster commended her conscientiousness.

'Thank you, sir. Yesterday we received a visit from the King and Queen. It can't have been a pretty sight but the patients appreciated it.'

Vera gave her one of her rare smiles. 'I'm sure they did,' she replied.

There were a few minutes of awkward silence while Vera sorted through several papers while smoking her cigarette — Senior Service, her favourite brand — with the Colonel looking on over his glasses. A secretary brought in a tray of tea and biscuits. Along with the fact that Colonel Buckmaster was present, Elizabeth realised it was a sign she would be there for a while and wondered if Andy Pickard would still be waiting for her in the pub.

'I won't beat about the bush, Elizabeth,' Vera said. 'Have you heard from Guy?'

Elizabeth stared at her for a moment. The look on both of their faces frightened her. She knew in an instant that something was wrong.

'No, I've heard nothing. I came here expecting you were going to give me the good news that he had returned safely back from France.'

Vera threw a concerned glance at the Colonel. He moved away to look out of the window, allowing Vera to take control of the meeting.

'I don't have to tell you, this conversation is not to be repeated,' she said to Elizabeth in a stern voice. 'The thing is, we've lost contact with him. Perhaps I should rephrase that. We believe the Belvedere network may have been penetrated by the Germans. The radio operator sent a signal omitting his security check. That was sometime in mid-December. We thought it might have been accidental as it was only a few days before an airdrop and this particular signal was coded — urgent. We were to cancel that drop zone immediately as it was deemed unsafe and use another. New co-ordinates were relayed to us shortly after. When we received another signal a few weeks later from another radio operator in another network, omitting his security check, we started to worry. The thing is, because no-one has heard from Guy we have to operate on the basis that something has gone terribly wrong. The last plane delivering a drop to the region was shot down on the return to England and we didn't receive a transmission from Belvedere saying the drop went according to plan. So you see, we have no idea what really did take place that night. In fact, we've lost all trace of Belvedere completely.'

Elizabeth felt a chill run down her spine. Vera wouldn't tell her if London had sent back messages, only that they thought something was wrong. Her stomach churned, but outwardly she kept a cool composure. Her training kicked in immediately: don't show your emotions.

'Why are you telling me this?' she asked.

This time the Colonel spoke. 'You know we took a dim view of the two of you getting married so soon after you returned from your last mission. Purely for practical reasons, you understand — nothing personal. We don't approve of intimate relationships in the field. It could compromise not only the agent, but the network and our entire mission.'

Elizabeth bristled. 'But it didn't, did it, sir?'

Buckmaster coughed. 'You are quite right, and I commend you on the fact that the two of you kept it a secret.'

'Is that why you didn't send me on another assignment? You knew I wanted to return. I wanted to serve my country as much as the next person — married or not.'

'Quite so,' Vera said, sensing the tension in the room. 'But the truth is, we didn't send you because we didn't have the right mission for you. And the fact that Guy was sent was because he was head of Belvedere. There were other couriers out there he could use. No need to send another.'

Elizabeth knew she'd never get the truth out of them anyway.

Vera continued. 'We didn't invite you here today simply to impart worrying news: we invited you because, regardless of the outcome, we would be derelict in our duty if we didn't get to the bottom of all this. Good heavens, we are all hoping there has been a simple mistake somewhere and we are worrying for nothing.'

'What would you like me to do, ma'am?' Elizabeth asked. 'I don't see how I can help. I was aware when Guy left that I probably wouldn't hear a thing until he returned.'

'We have an assignment for you. We want to send you to France again,' Vera replied.

She took another Senior Service out of the packet, lit it and sat back in her chair waiting for Elizabeth's response. It had come as a shock and Elizabeth needed a few minutes to think about it. Those minutes seemed like an eternity. The clock on the wall ticked loudly and the sound of traffic in the street below seemed deafening. In the meantime, no one said a word. Vera poured them all a cup of tea and passed the biscuits around while they waited for her response.

'Were you planning to send me back to the Jura?' Elizabeth asked, stirring her tea.

'Yes,' Vera replied. 'We want you to make contact with the Resistance there and try and locate Guy and any other members of Belvedere.'

Elizabeth wanted to ask what happened to their rules about married couples. They had conveniently put all that aside for the time being.

Vera read her mind.

'Colonel Buckmaster and I believe that if anyone can make contact with Guy, it's you. You know the terrain, have contacts in the Resistance there, but more importantly, you know him better than anyone else — how he thinks, the sort of disguises he uses, etc. We believe only you can anticipate his moves.'

'When did you plan on sending me back?' Elizabeth asked.

'Sometime in the next few weeks; we can't tell you exactly. The question is, will you accept or not? If you need another day to think about it, that's fine. You must be sure of your decision. You can't afford to let your heart rule your head. If your decision is no, then this discussion ends and we will expect you to uphold your duty with regards to the Official Secrets Act.'

Once the reality sunk in that Guy was in danger, there was no possibility that Elizabeth would refuse their request. 'I accept,' she replied. 'Will I be sent as a courier again?'

This time Colonel Buckmaster continued the conversation. 'We've had a good look at your file and although you were an excellent courier, we noted that during your training, you also excelled in radio transmission. Miss Atkins and I discussed the possibility of you transmitting and we both agree that, due to the delicate situation, you would be more valuable working alone, which means giving you your own radio. You will be our eyes and ears and we will be relying on you to keep us informed.' He looked at her over his glasses. 'Are you comfortable with that?'

Elizabeth nodded. 'Yes sir.'

'Good girl,' Buckmaster replied. 'Now, if you will excuse me, I have other business to attend to. Miss Atkins will take it from here.'

He shook her hand firmly. 'I have every confidence in you.'

'Thank you, sir. I won't let you down.'

Buckmaster looked across at Vera and smiled. 'You were right about her.'

When the two were alone, Vera got up from behind her desk and pulled a chair up next to Elizabeth.

'Now,' she said with a smile. 'Let's have a little chat, shall we?'

CHAPTER 3

It was late afternoon when Elizabeth left 64 Baker Street. She knew she had to get to the Red Lion before the blackout came into effect. It was bad enough trying to escape the constant bombing raids, but trying to navigate the streets, either on foot or in a vehicle, was equally dangerous. Dimmed headlights caused terrible road accidents and people tripped up or fell down stairs in the darkness. Every day the hospital was filled with such casualties. She had fallen down a flight of stairs herself a couple of months earlier and almost broke her leg.

Approaching the pub, she saw several men piling sandbags against the wall. The glass windows had shattered so many times that they were now boarded up. It was a desolate sight, yet inside she could hear people singing. The war was not going to stop people enjoying themselves and, as usual, the Red Lion was packed. A pianist was playing, surrounded by a group of men and women giving a rousing rendition of a Gracie Fields number. She spotted Andy Pickard at the bar. He waved her over.

'What will you have?' he asked.

'The same as you.'

He ordered half a pint for her and they moved away from the bar to a quieter part of the room.

'I'd almost given up on you.' Andy took a sip of his beer. 'How did it go?' Her face gave her away. 'Is it Guy? Has something happened to him?'

She stared into her glass, wondering whether to tell him the truth. Andy was familiar with Guy and Elizabeth's work in SOE. They had flown out from Tempsford at the same time. He was working near Lyon while she headed further north towards Dole and they both used the same safe house for a few nights.

'I wish I could tell you,' she said with a heavy sigh. 'I don't know too much myself, suffice to say they offered me another assignment and I'm taking it.'

'Good Lord! You too.'

Elizabeth looked at him and realised he too had been called to

Baker Street for another "little chat" as Vera and Buckmaster liked to call it.

'So you've been offered a job too. When do you leave?'

'In a couple of weeks, I imagine. They said it was urgent. This time they're dropping me off in the Loire. What about you?'

She told him she was heading back to the Jura.

He shook his head. 'I believe a few other agents have also been asked to fly out again. There must be something big going on. Whatever it is, they're keeping it close to their chest. How long are you expecting to be away?'

'I don't know. Until the job is done, I suppose. I have to go away for a few days to do some more training. Maybe we will fly out together.'

Elizabeth asked what he'd been doing since she last saw him.

'Working with the bomb squad,' he replied. 'My scientific and engineering background has come in useful.'

Elizabeth gave him a concerned look. 'That's highly dangerous. I can't tell you how many people have been brought to the hospital trying to defuse unexploded bombs.'

'I also repair damaged electrical wires and ruptured gas mains. I've seen enough corpses to last a lifetime. It makes a mission in occupied Europe look like a walk in the park.' Andy smiled.

'Don't say such things. That's not funny.'

He apologised. 'I'm sorry. It was rather tactless of me, wasn't it?'

The pub was getting rowdier. The pianist asked for requests and someone suggested a Flanagan and Allen song. A large woman wearing a thick, grey flannel coat and a matching hat, with a pheasant feather neatly tucked into the rim, came over shaking a tin. She had a strong cockney accent.

'Would you like to donate to a good cause?' she asked. 'We're raising money for a Spitfire.'

Andy reached into his pocket and pulled out a few shillings. 'An excellent cause,' he replied.

'That's very kind of you, sir. Quite a few of the pubs are doing it. We have to do our bit don't we?' She turned to Elizabeth who was looking in her purse. She'd just spent most of her pay on the rent.

'Sorry it's not much more,' she said apologetically, dropping sixpence into the tin.

The woman thanked them and moved to the next table. No sooner had she gone than someone else came over. This time it was a young boy selling raffle tickets. He had four left.

'First prize is a jar of pickled eggs. Second prize, a pint of beer, and the rest of the money goes to the homeless shelter.'

Once again, Andy reached into his money and gave him a few pence. 'I'll take the four: two for me and two for the lady.'

The boy ripped them from his booklet and returned the empty booklet and money back to the publican. Ten minutes later the raffle was drawn. An elderly couple won the eggs and Elizabeth, the pint of beer. Everyone cheered. The publican brought over the beer which she divided between herself and Andy, and the music started up again. This time it was a Vera Lynn number — *It's a Lovely Day tomorrow.*

Andy smiled. 'Let's hope it really will be a lovely day tomorrow.'

They had almost finished their drinks when the air raid sirens started. It was the third that day. An air raid warden poked his head around the door telling everyone to get to a shelter immediately.

People hurriedly put on their hats and coats and started to leave.

'Have you got your gas mask with you?' Andy asked.

Elizabeth pointed to the large bag she'd been carrying.

'Come on then, let's get a move on. We'll go together. The Underground isn't far from here.'

'Won't you be needed?' Elizabeth asked.

'They gave me the day off — for my visit to the doctor.' He was referring to 64 Baker Street.

Outside it had started to rain. Tracer bullets and searchlights lit up the night sky like a fireworks display and the rhythmic rise and fall of air raid sirens together with the sound of ack-ack guns pounding away at German planes caught in the light, was blood-chilling. Elizabeth pulled up her collar to keep her warm, looped her arm through Andy's, and together they made a quick dash to the entrance of the Underground, just as the bombs started to fall. The ground shuddered and the sound of bomb blasts mixed with screams of the people scurrying into the bowels of the earth was still hard to bear, even after all this time. The platforms were already packed. Hundreds of people were jostling for a space, trying their best to make themselves as comfortable as possible with their blankets and pillows, thermos flasks and sandwiches. They managed to squeeze into a space between two families. With no blanket of their own, Andy took off his coat and draped it over Elizabeth's shoulders.

'It's going to be a long night. No doubt you'll have a busy day ahead of you at the hospital tomorrow so you'd better try and get some sleep.'

It had been a long day, and now the reality of her conversation with Colonel Buckmaster and Vera Atkins was beginning to sink in. The war was still raging, Guy was missing, and she was about to be flown into the unknown. At that moment the future looked anything but rosy. She laid her head on Andy's shoulder, covered herself with his coat and, mentally exhausted, closed her eyes to try and get some sleep.

In the morning, the all clear was given and everyone poured out into the street. The dust was choking and firemen were busily putting out fires with water and sand. At the end of the street they could see a row of shops with the front blown out and ambulances were trying to get through the debris to reach the wounded.

'Can I walk you home?' Andy asked.

Elizabeth thanked him, but said she was going straight to the hospital.

'Under the circumstances I'd rather keep my mind occupied,' she replied.

They parted ways, both wishing each other luck on the next assignment.

The following day, Elizabeth left the hospital heading in the direction of her apartment when a black car pulled up a few metres in front of her. A woman got out and stood on the pavement waiting for her. It was Vera Atkins.

'Good evening, Elizabeth.' She opened the back door and indicated for her to get in.

When Elizabeth asked where they were heading, Vera simply said she was taking her back to her apartment and would wait outside while she gave her half an hour to get her things in order: she was being taken to one of SOE's holding facilities.

'What about the hospital?' Elizabeth asked. 'I'll have to hand in my notice.'

Vera smiled. 'It's all taken care of. No need to worry.'

The driver parked the car outside the apartment and Vera took a cream-coloured envelope from her handbag and handed it to her.

'That should be more than enough to cover the next six months' rent,' she said. 'I'm sure you will be well and truly back home before then. And just in case you aren't, I will make sure the place is secure until you return.'

Elizabeth took it graciously. Now she wouldn't have to worry about storing their few belongings.

'Don't be long,' Vera shouted out after her. 'We don't want to get caught up in another air raid.'

Elizabeth lived on the second floor. She and Guy had moved in together when they returned from France. They didn't have much in the way of possessions but it was filled with memories. She packed a small bag with a few items of clothing, an almost empty pot of cold cream and a red lipstick in a cardboard refill. It seemed frivolous given the circumstances, but like many women, it lifted the spirits. Besides, she knew Vera wouldn't let her take them to France with her, so she'd use them while she could.

Lastly, she picked up a silver-framed photograph from her bedside table. It was of her and Guy on their wedding day, standing on the steps outside the registry office. It was the happiest day of her life. She touched his face with her fingertips. *I know you are still there, my love, and I will find you.* She took one last look around the room and left. The apartment on the ground floor was occupied by her landlady, Mrs Perry. Elizabeth knocked on the door. Mrs Perry was surprised to find her standing in the hallway with her bag.

'You leaving?' she asked, wiping her hands on her pinafore. 'Everything alright? Would you like to come inside and have a cup of tea?'

Elizabeth apologised. 'I'm afraid I can't. I'm in a hurry. I've come to tell you I'm going away — to stay with friends in the country. I may be gone for quite a while.' She gave her the money. 'This should cover the rent for the next six months.'

Not wanting to enter into a conversation, she said goodbye and left.

'Good luck,' Mrs Perry called out as Elizabeth opened the front door. 'Look after yourself.'

Minutes later Elizabeth was driven away, leaving a surprised Mrs Perry standing on the doorstep watching her. The car headed out of London into the countryside. They arrived at Ashton Manor in Surrey just as the air raid sirens sounded. London was about to suffer another heavy bombing.

During the next two weeks Elizabeth spent much of her time under the close scrutiny of her instructors, either in the manor or at a cottage surrounded by bushes and hedges to keep out the prying eyes of anyone who might accidentally walk by. With her were four other agents due to fly out at the same time. Andy Pickard was one of them. Most of the time was spent perfecting her coding and Morse code skills. The rest of the time was making sure she remembered all she had been taught previously: the use of guns and explosives, silent killing techniques, lock picking, disguises, etc.

At the end of this intensive training, Elizabeth was taken to a flat in Orchard Court and briefed on her assignment. She was told she would be parachuted into an area near the town of Auxerre in Burgundy the next day. There she would be met by members of the Resistance working with another sub-network that SOE deemed still safe. There were long discussions about Elizabeth's previous contacts with the Belvedere network. As a courier she'd moved around a lot and Vera wanted to know if there was anyone she could contact: anyone at all whom she considered safe and who had little or no idea of her role there. Elizabeth had a razor-sharp memory and she mentioned half a dozen names, all of them with connections to various Resistance groups throughout the region from Belfort to Geneva.

Vera Atkins told her Guy was still using his old code name "Daniel" and his cover name was Daniel Bardin, an antiques dealer from Paris. She then handed her a photograph of a woman and asked her to take a good look at it. Elizabeth studied the face closely. The woman was in her early twenties. She had exotic looks, a sensuous mouth and dark brown eyes framed in long dark lashes which gave the impression she was studying you rather than the other way around. Her hair was dark brown, naturally wavy, and cut just below the jaw-line — a beautiful woman who probably had a string of admirers. Elizabeth recalled being cautioned about looking too glamorous as it would be out of place in the rural area where she was being sent, but this woman didn't need make-up and fancy hairdos to be glamorous. She was a natural beauty.

'She's certainly attractive,' Elizabeth said. 'Who is she?'

'Guy's courier — agent "Mireille". She goes under the name of Amelie Rousseau, a cosmetics saleswoman.'

Elizabeth suddenly felt a pang of jealousy which she was careful to keep from Vera. She could easily see why they'd listed her occupation as a cosmetics saleswoman. She was certainly beautiful enough to be one.

'Like the rest of Belvedere, we have no idea where she is, but it's possible she may be in hiding.'

'What makes you say that?'

'Because the last transmission we received mentioned that Guy was thinking of sending her on an errand. Whatever he was doing, I don't think she was there at the time of his disappearance.'

Elizabeth had one last meeting with Vera the next day before flying out to France later that night. Because she was already known to certain members of the Resistance and agents in the field, it was decided that she would be travelling alone under her old identity — Marie-Élise Lacroix. To SOE, she would still be known as agent "Lisette". Vera asked her to repeat her cover story once more. Elizabeth knew it by heart: so much so that in her mind, she already was that person.

'Marie-Élise Lacroix, 10 rue de la cité, Lyon. Occupation, children's nanny; father, Henry Lacroix — deceased; mother Sophie, a seamstress,' Elizabeth answered.

Vera was pleased. Elizabeth had passed her tests with flying colours. It made her realise what a good agent she'd been and how they should have used her in the field again before now but she would never admit that. She handed her the new identity papers, travel documents and work permit, ration cards, and a sum of false French money. Then she gave her a will to sign. It was a sombre moment as it served to remind Elizabeth this with not a game. She signed it and handed it back, along with her wedding ring. Vera put in a brown envelope and attached it to the will.

Next, Vera personally checked all the clothes she would be wearing to see that they were French: buttons, labels, etc. She was given French cosmetics which included a new lipstick and mascara and presented her with two special gifts; a silver powder compact engraved with the initials, M.E.L. — Marie-Élise Lacroix, and a lace-trimmed cream handkerchief embroidered with the same initials in the corner in gold silk. From the moment she landed on French soil until the time she returned, all communications between them would now refer to her as Lisette. Elizabeth Maxwell ceased to exist.

During their last minute heart-to-heart chat, Elizabeth was given her own pistol — a Ballester-Molina — and offered a cyanide tablet which she hid in the back of a sterling silver brooch styled in the shape of a flower with furled petals. In the raised centre, purposely made to hide the cavity at the back for the cyanide pill, was a deep-pink tourmaline. Vera double-checked the safety catch at the back and pinned it on Elizabeth's lapel herself. Elizabeth smiled, making a comment about a thing of such beauty hiding something so lethal. Vera did not smile.

'There,' Vera said, flicking a few flecks of cotton from Elizabeth's lapel. 'Don't lose it.' She stepped back and lit up a Senior Service. 'Now, is there anything else you want to ask?'

Elizabeth asked that she be informed if there was any news of Guy, good or bad, to which Vera agreed. She also promised to send out periodic good news letters to her family, letting them know she was well. This was common practice for all the agents.

It was a cold, damp, miserable evening when the two women stepped outside the sandbagged, red-bricked building into the same black car that had taken her away a few weeks earlier. They headed south to a cottage near the airfield in Sussex. During the drive, they said very little, each one wrapped up in their own thoughts.

At that moment, Elizabeth's reception committee in France was being alerted by a BBC message inserted in the *messages personnels*, of the arrival of the plane carrying agent Lisette later that night. When they reached the cottage, Elizabeth was given what the agents referred to as "the last supper" — a final good meal accompanied by a glass of wine — before being taken to the airfield. This time the car windows were blacked out as a precautionary measure in order that no agent would be able to pinpoint the airfield if captured and tortured. The car circled the perimeter of the airfield a few times and came to a stop on the tarmac near the waiting plane. Its engines were already running.

'Good luck, my dear,' Vera said, shaking her hand.

Until this moment, Elizabeth had been so happy at the thought of returning to France that she'd been living on a high. Now, listening to the sound of the aircraft's engine and knowing that in less than ten minutes she would be crossing the English Channel, her stomach tightened.

Vera patted her shoulder. 'You'll be fine, my dear.'

Elizabeth took a deep breath, turned around and climbed into the plane. The pilot welcomed her. He had no idea who this attractive young woman was or what her mission was, but he could tell she was more apprehensive than she made out.

'The forecast is for good weather tonight,' he said with a cheerful smile. 'We'll have you there in no time.'

Elizabeth took her place and as the plane started to taxi down the runway she caught sight of Vera waving her farewell. Minutes later they were airborne.

CHAPTER 4

March 1944: Somewhere near Auxerre, Burgundy.

At around 02:30 a.m. on a clear moonlit night, the pilot received the prearranged signal in Morse code from his contact on the ground and responded by blinking back the appropriate code letter. When he saw the drop-zone lit with three landing lights, he flashed a light in the cabin warning Elizabeth she should prepare to jump. Seconds later the hatch opened and Elizabeth, accompanied by six containers of arms and supplies for the Maquis, parachuted into the darkness. She landed in a clearing surrounded by woods, about fifteen kilometres from Auxerre, where she was met by members of the Burgundian/Franche-Comté Maquis hiding out in the Morvan woodlands.

When the chief of the group introduced himself as Maurice, the contact name Vera had given her, and greeted her as Lisette, she breathed a sigh of relief. The landing had gone well and she was in safe hands. After accounting for the six containers and burying the parachutes, the group hurriedly made their way to a farm belonging to the family of one of the maquisards. The farmer's wife served Elizabeth a hearty meal of rabbit stew accompanied by red wine, while the other maquisards checked the containers. They were extremely happy. Sten guns, Bren guns, ammunition, explosives, plus tins of food and a few bars of chocolate, which would be distributed to the Maquis immediately. Most of all, Elizabeth's radio transmitter was fine.

After a good night's sleep, she gave Maurice a wad of money from SOE and thanked her hosts for their hospitality. She left the farmhouse soon after daylight, taking a sixteen-kilometre bicycle ride to the small town of Montbard. Thankfully, the weather was mild with only a slight breeze. In Montbard, she left her bicycle at a certain point near the walls of the château as Maurice had instructed, took her bag from the small wire basket at the front, untied her suitcase with the radio transmitter from the rack at the back, and walked down the hill to the train station to catch a train to Dijon. Montbard was only a small town but she had expected to see people going about their daily business. Instead, she found it oddly quiet. In the silence she was aware of her wooden heels clattering loudly on the cobblestones. At any moment she half expected someone to look out of the windows to see who the stranger was in their midst, but the windows were shuttered and the few shops in the main street closed.

When she reached the station, she found the ticket office open. A man in a black suit and wearing a railway cap was warming his hands in front of a tiled heater. It was the stationmaster and he looked agitated when he saw her. Elizabeth put down her heavy suitcase and took some money out of her bag.

'I'd like to buy a ticket to Dijon.'

The man eyed her with suspicion.

'I'd like a ticket to Dijon,' Elizabeth repeated, this time a little louder. 'I believe the train leaves at 12:30.' She looked at the large round clock on the wall. 'In ten minutes.'

The man looked at her suspiciously. 'Who are you?' he asked, his eyes narrowing to a squint behind his wire-rimmed glasses.

This time it was Elizabeth's turn to look surprised. 'I beg your pardon. I don't see what business that is of yours. Are you going to give me a ticket or not?'

'You're not from here, are you?' the man asked. 'I know everyone around here but I haven't seen you before.'

Elizabeth was beginning to feel uncomfortable. The last thing she wanted to do was to attract attention.

'You're quite right. I'm not from around here. I'm passing through. Look, what is this? Is everything all right? The place is like a ghost town. What on earth has happened?'

At that point, Elizabeth was aware of someone sobbing in an adjoining room. The sign on the room read "LEFT LUGGAGE".

'Are you sure everything's alright?' she asked again, her eyes glancing towards the closed door.

'Don't you know what happened last night?' the man asked.

'No. I wasn't here. Tell me.'

'There was a *rafle*. The Germans made one of their surprise raids in the middle of the night. They had a list.'

'What sort of list?'

'Jews and men to be sent to work in Germany: I don't know what else. They forced everyone out of their homes and made a thorough search. Ten men were rounded up, put on trucks and driven away.'

The sobbing in the next room grew louder and the man became even more nervous. His eyes darted towards the room. It was clear to Elizabeth that he was hiding someone in there.

'I'm a friend,' she said. 'You don't have to worry. Tell me who you have in there. Maybe I can help.'

At first the man was reluctant, but Elizabeth was persistent. He opened the door and let her through. A woman holding a small child was cowering in the corner behind a couple of suitcases and several large boxes. The child looked to be no more than two years old. Elizabeth assured the terrified woman she meant her no harm.

'Who are they?' Elizabeth asked.

'My wife and daughter. My wife's Jewish. No-one here knows and she's not registered as a Jew.' His eyes were moist with tears. 'Somehow or another, Blanche's name was on that list. I don't know how, but they must have found out. We managed to hide here until they'd gone.'

'What are you going to do?' Elizabeth asked. 'You can't stay here now. They'll be back and they'll come for you too. You know that.'

'We have nowhere to go.'

At that moment, they heard the sound of approaching vehicles coming down the hill. A car followed by two motorcycles with sidecars. The Germans were back. They stopped at a house half-way up the hill and started banging on the door.

'*Bon sang!*' the man exclaimed, wiping the sweat from his brow. 'Damn it! That's my house.'

The woman started to cry again, rocking the child to and fro.

Elizabeth urged them not to panic. 'The train will be here in five minutes. Please give me my ticket — and make sure you all get on the train yourselves.'

'We can't leave. We have no money.'

Elizabeth could see that the man was so shaken he wasn't thinking clearly.

'Pull yourself together,' she said sharply. 'You must get out of here straight away. It's too late to leave the village by road. Most likely they have all exits blocked off. She pulled out some money from her bag and gave it to him. 'Get yourselves a ticket and take this. It will see you through. But for God's sake, get out while you can.'

In the distance they could hear the train approaching. At the same time, the Germans left the house and headed towards the station. The stationmaster started to shake.

'Listen to me,' Elizabeth said sternly, her hand firmly on the man's shoulder. 'This is what is going to happen. There's not a second to spare. Get your wife and child while I go to the far side of the platform and keep them occupied. In the meantime, hide behind the building in the opposite direction. When you see them talking to me make a quick dash and get on the train. It's your only hope. Now go — and keep out of sight until the moment is right.'

Elizabeth took her gun out of a secret compartment in the bottom of her bag along with a sharp double-edged knife, slid them inside her belt and quickly walked to the far end of the platform. The Germans entered the station just as the train came to a standstill. She positioned herself in full view at the far end of the platform. Her heart racing, she approached one of the carriages. A uniformed German officer called out for her to stop. She put her heavy suitcase down and turned to face two men striding towards her, one of whom had a machine gun aimed on her.

'*Papiere, bitte.* Where are you going?' one of the men asked, examining her papers.

'Dijon,' Elizabeth replied politely, giving them one of her most charming smiles.

'What is the purpose of your trip?'

'I'm going to stay with my aunt for a few weeks. She's ill.'

When she pulled out her identity card and travel documents, she accidentally dropped a photograph. The second man picked it up.

'Who is this?' he asked.

'My fiancé.'

The man showed it to his colleague who examined it thoroughly. As he did so, Elizabeth spotted the stationmaster and his wife and daughter making a dash to get on the train.

'He's an engineer working for the Führer in Germany. I always keep it with me,' she continued, trying to keep their attention.

The second man eyed her suitcase. If they opened it, they would see clothes lying on top. If they looked further, she would have to shoot them and make a run for it. Another soldier called out that they'd searched the ticket office and there was no one there.

'Who gave you this ticket?' the first man asked.

Elizabeth laughed as if it was a silly question. 'Why, the man in the ticket office of course. I think he was in a hurry. After he handed me my ticket, I saw him leave the station. He headed that way.' Elizabeth pointed down the hill. 'He seemed in a hurry.'

The men looked at each other.

'Thank you. You may go,' the man replied.

They turned on their heels and headed for the exit with the first man barking out orders in German to his colleagues. Elizabeth picked up her suitcase and got on the train with only moments to spare. As the train pulled out of the station, she saw the Germans get in their vehicles and head in the direction she'd pointed to. Her heart thumping loudly, she leaned against the wall for a moment and gave a huge sigh of relief. Making sure no-one was around, she quickly put the gun back in her bag, took out her powder compact and dabbed a little powder on her flushed cheeks. She'd had a lucky escape but not one she wanted to repeat.

The train was already filled to capacity but she managed to find herself a seat in a compartment filled with nuns. She put her suitcase on the rack and sat down. Thankfully, no-one was anxious to strike up a conversation. Elizabeth couldn't get the stationmaster and his wife and child off her mind. Their anxiousness made them unsuitable for a life on the run, yet she had seen first-hand how quickly people changed when their lives were at stake. All the same, she wanted to help and decided to see if they were alright. She asked her travelling companions if they would mind her suitcase while she went outside for a cigarette, and left the compartment, heading towards the front of the train. In the next carriage she spotted the ticket collector entering a compartment closely followed by two plain-clothed men who she knew would be Gestapo. It was hard to tell if they were heading this way or towards the front. She managed to pass them without being seen as they were already pre-occupied with some unlucky traveller. The stationmaster was in the next carriage. Thankfully his daughter was asleep and his wife had stopped crying. When he saw her face behind the glass sliding door, he left the compartment to join her.

'With a bit of luck we may reach Dijon without the Gestapo checking you out,' Elizabeth whispered. 'They're preoccupied with someone in another compartment.'

She asked if he had any idea where they would go. The man shook his head.

'Head for *l'église Saint-Michel*. It's off rue Vaillante. Ask for Father Albert. He'll look after you. The church has three doors and you must enter the one on the right, which is the oldest. It bears the date of 1537. Wait by the door until he approaches you. Rest assured you will be in safe hands.'

The man gave Elizabeth a firm handshake. 'I can't thank you enough. I don't even know your name. What is it?'

'It's not important. I told you, I'm a friend. I think you'd better get back to your wife before we attract unwelcome attention. Good luck.'

Elizabeth made her way back to her seat. On the way she passed the ticket inspector who asked to check her ticket. He gestured to her to return to her seat. Fortunately, the Gestapo were still preoccupied with the same man to take notice of her. Ten minutes later, they arrived in Dijon.

Exiting the crowded station, the gendarmes and plain-clothed Gestapo were checking all papers. She noticed the stationmaster huddled behind a group of people being questioned. He was holding his daughter in his arms and his wife stood close by. While the Gestapo were occupied detaining people and herding them away at gunpoint to waiting trucks in the nearby street, they grabbed their chance and walked out of the station into the concourse unhindered. It was a small step but they'd made it. She hoped for their sakes, their luck would not run out.

After answering a few questions to a young gendarme, mostly about why she was in Dijon to which she replied she was visiting an aunt, she left unhindered and took a twenty-minute walk to a small hotel overlooking a park. The family who owned it were sympathetic to the Resistance and were known to have hidden Allied airmen whose planes had been shot down. It was a golden rule that none of her clandestine guests stayed more than three days in order not to arouse suspicious neighbours. The Genot family had been helping escapees since the French government signed the armistice. Madame Genot was a tall, middle-aged woman with a sharp mind and a head for business which she put to good use for acquiring things on the black market to help those in need. For those who knew her well, she was always open and warm and someone they sought solace in when times were hard. Her softer side belied her toughness and it was not wise to cross her, as some people had discovered to their detriment.

She recognized Elizabeth's face immediately even though it was almost a year since she was last there and her hair was styled differently. At that time, on orders from SOE to the network, Elizabeth had helped two Frenchmen out of Dijon and taken them to a place where they were flown out of the country to liaise with General de Gaulle in London.

'How long will you be with us?' she asked.

'Only one night. I need to get to Dole.'

Elizabeth omitted to say that Dole was not her final destination and Madame Genot didn't ask, but she did offer a piece of advice.

'If you are planning on going by train, you may want to rethink. There have been a lot of transports recently and the station is heavily guarded.' She recognised a flash of concern in Elizabeth's eyes. 'I finish early this evening. Would you like to join me for a stroll through the park? Let's say at around 7:00 p.m.? Maybe we can have an aperitif somewhere.'

Elizabeth knew this was a cue that Madame Genot wanted to impart information and she readily agreed.

CHAPTER 5

At 7:00 p.m. sharp, Elizabeth met Madame Genot in the foyer. She was wrapped up in a calf-length, dark grey astrakhan coat with a matching pillbox hat which sat neatly at an angle on her carefully manicured hair. She had her Pekinese dog with her on a lead. Elizabeth felt rather plain in her presence. She wore her only suit but had managed to give it a lift with a pretty silk scarf and her beautiful brooch. When the time was right, she would treat herself to a new wardrobe.

They headed through the scenic park of Jardin Darcy and sat on a bench near the fountain where Madame Genot unleashed her dog to allow him to play for a while. Elizabeth knew the area well. Two streets away was the infamous 9 rue Docteur Chausseur, a beautifully curved block of apartments designed in the modernist style which was requisitioned by the Gestapo during the early days of the occupation. In the beginning, *Feldkommandantur* Von Rothberg and his staff occupied the Hôtel de la Cloche, but two months later, during the first summer of occupation, a handful of Gestapo officers and their secretaries discreetly appeared in Dijon taking up residence in the opulent building. At that time, Dijon had been declared an open city and many of its residents fled south.

Madame Genot filled Elizabeth in with a few facts, warning her that things had worsened since she had last seen her. Ludwig Kraemer, whom the Dijonnais nicknamed "Stucka", had replaced the 32-year-old Willy Hülf, who apparently had never tortured anyone. At first, the Gestapo's main mission was limited to intelligence and to supervise customs officers in the region but she pointed out that had now changed.

'Kraemer has at his disposal, several officers and non-commissioned officers. Worst of all, he has recruited a large handful of French collaborators. These people are no better than thugs. Do you know that the denunciation of a Resistance member can pay up to 70,000 francs: much more for the chief of a network?' She shook her head in despair.

In her briefing, Vera Atkins had warned Elizabeth of the rise of the

Milice and Madame Genot confirmed this.

'The Milice is managed by a man called Gaston Ducas, an odious character who struts about like a peacock in a German uniform. Last year it is estimated that there were nearly a thousand collaborators in the prefecture of the Côte-d'Or Department and Bourgogne/Franche-Comté region. Eight hundred alone in Dijon! I am ashamed of my countrymen.'

Elizabeth listened carefully. Things were much worse than any of them in London had suspected.

'The torture chambers in 9 rue Docteur Chausseur are located in the basement cellar of the building,' continued Madame Genot. 'I've heard there is a room with a bathtub and some sort of openwork tables attached to the wall. There the unfortunate souls are made to undress and lie on one of the benches with their feet and hands firmly tied. They gag their mouths with a towel and bandage their eyes and the victim is tortured. If they survive, they are returned to the cellar and attached to a ring on a chain hanging from the ceiling or wall, making movement impossible. I cannot tell you the amount of tears I have cried over this.'

Her description was so vivid Elizabeth could only conclude she'd known some of the victims personally.

'I've heard of men who, after being condemned to death, still haven't talked. They are hit in the chest and stomach with some sort of wooden plank fitted with pins. It's so barbaric that after each stroke the blood spurts freely. Then they are thrown into a bathtub filled with ice water while their executioners hold their head underwater: just long enough to prevent suffocation. This miserable test is repeated fifteen times. The list of torments inflicted on such men is unbearable.' Madame Genot dabbed her eyes. 'Then they are either deported or executed without any other form of trial. It is impossible to say how many. People just simply disappear and that's the truth.'

A group of German soldiers appeared along the pathway. Madame Genot instinctively called her dog over and secured his lead. The men passed, bidding them a good evening in French. She suggested they head for a nearby bar to have their aperitif and on the way started to talk about the Milice, warning Elizabeth to be careful.

'I have no idea where you are heading or what you are doing,' she said to her, 'but you must take care. It is said that the Milice now numbers over 35,000 members. These men are paid according to their age. Some say it's anything from 2,800 to 4,500 francs per month. On top of this, they are able to eat in the Gestapo canteen cheaply every day. Naturally, the salary is attractive to them. Life is hard. Even so, they cannot sleep easily in their beds because when this war is over the Resistance will swoop. Of that I am sure.'

'It can't be long now,' Elizabeth said. 'The Allies have already made inroads into Italy.'

'That's so, but the Germans are putting up a strong resistance. They are not going to give in without a fight.'

'Madame Genot,' Elizabeth said as they neared the building. 'What do you know about the deportations? I heard they've increased and that many leaving from here are sent to Germany. Is that correct?'

'That's true. Here, Lyon, and Besançon. These are the central points in the region of the Cote-d'Or, the Jura and Franche-Comté. But once they leave, it's hard to trace where they end up so I can't tell you any more than that. Why do you ask?'

'I'm trying to locate someone and I have no idea if he is alive or dead.'

'Where and when did the person go missing?'

'I'm sorry, at the moment I have no idea.'

'Then I cannot help you,' Madame Genot replied.

'Surely there are lists of names of those who arrive here and are interrogated? And what about those deported?'

Madame Genot laughed. 'I suppose there are, but none that we've been able to lay our hands on yet. Finding your friend will be like looking for a needle in a haystack. It will be almost impossible if a prisoner leaves Dijon under the hush-hush *Nacht und Nebel,* Night and Fog policy. At least that's what we think it's called. If that's the case, you will never find him. The German Minister of Justice has established special courts to deal with their cases in response to the increased activity of the Resistance. Those condemned under the policy are either shot or spirited away. Many of the trains that leave for the camps are blacked out. I have contacts in the rail yards but not even they would know who were on those trains.' She gave a deep sigh. 'For the sake of your friend, you had better hope he didn't meet such a fate.'

After listening to Madame Genot, Elizabeth felt utterly depressed. She had never underestimated the task she'd been given but the thought that Guy could have simply disappeared through such an operation was more than she could bear.

The proprietor of the bar welcomed the women with an effusive kiss on both cheeks.

'What will you have to drink?' he asked, clicking his fingers at someone behind the bar to bring a fresh bowl of water for the dog.

Madame Genot ordered a *vin rouge*. Elizabeth's mind was far away and when she didn't answer, Madame Genot answered for her. 'My friend will have a cognac.' Seeing the distant look in her eyes, she told the proprietor to make that a double.

'I told you all this to help you,' she said, watching her dog thirstily slurp his water from the silver bowl on the floor next to the table. 'Any information is useful, wouldn't you agree?'

Elizabeth thanked her. No matter how hard her task would be to find her husband or anyone else from the Belvedere network, she was grateful. The problem was where to start. Madame Genot was right: it was like looking for a needle in a haystack.

'Is there anything you want to ask?' Madame Genot said. 'Anything at all I can help you with?'

'There is one thing, and it has nothing to do with why I am here. I met a man evading a raid. He was hiding his wife and child. It appears he hadn't told anyone she was Jewish. As a consequence, she wasn't registered as a Jew. When he realised the Gestapo were on to them, he hid. The thing is, I am worried about them. I don't think they will last long on the run.'

'Who are they?'

'I don't know their names. I gave them some money and told them to look for Father Albert.'

At the mention of the priest, Madame Genot's eyes widened. 'I'm afraid he was caught some months back now. He was sent to a camp somewhere in Germany and hasn't been heard of since.'

Elizabeth's face paled. It wasn't a good start to her assignment. 'What have I done?' she asked helplessly.

'Did you send them to the church?'

'Yes. They would have got there about the same time I arrived at your hotel.'

'Drink up, my dear. There may still be time to find them before curfew.'

She scooped her dog up in her arms and deposited several coins in a small saucer for their drinks. Outside the bar, she told Elizabeth to

40

go back to the guest house but Elizabeth insisted she go with her.

'No. I am better off alone. No-one will bother a lady alone taking her dog for a walk. Tell me, what do they look like?'

'They are both thin,' Elizabeth replied. 'And they have dark hair.'

'That applies to most of the population. I need more.'

Elizabeth struggled to remember something different. Neither of them stood out.

'The woman was wearing a dark brown coat, the man a dark suit. Oh yes, the child, she's about two years old. You will recognise them because of her. She was wearing a pale blue coat with a knitted hat. I think the hat had a pompom. Yes, that's right: a darker shade of blue.'

'That's enough. Now go home.'

They parted ways and Elizabeth headed back through the park which was now becoming occupied with Germans taking their girlfriends for a walk. Back in her room, she sat by the window for well over an hour waiting for Madame Genot to return. It was now two days since she'd left England and the reality of what she'd walked into was catching up with her. Before long she fell asleep. Waking with a jolt in the early hours of the morning, she undressed and got into bed. No doubt she would find out what happened in the morning. It was then that she noticed a note had been slipped under her door. On it were two words — ALL FINE.

Elizabeth breathed a huge sigh of relief. 'Thank you, God,' she muttered to herself. 'Thank you.'

Elizabeth wasn't particularly religious but since being given the assignment she found herself praying far more than she had ever prayed before. She'd confided about this to another woman who was about to be flown into France during her training.

'It never hurts to have God on your side.' The woman laughed.

God had heard her prayers this time but even she knew there would be times when God would turn a deaf ear and she would need to rely on her wits. For the moment at least, she would savour a good night's sleep.

In the morning there was a knock on the door. Madame Genot had brought her breakfast: real coffee — a rare treat reserved for special guests and bought for an exorbitant sum on the black market — home baked bread, two eggs, and cheese. It smelled delicious. She saw the note she'd left on the bedside table, picked it up and put it her pocket.

'It turned out fine. They were sitting at the back of the church waiting for the good Father. When I told them he was no longer in Dijon, the woman started crying. You were right. They are of fragile mind. They begged me to help.'

'Where are they now?' Elizabeth asked.

'At a safe house but they can't stay there for long. I've urged them to leave the child in an orphanage and either go into hiding themselves or try to flee the country. Fleeing the country is the most difficult option as the money you gave them won't last very long. Naturally they don't want to leave without the child, but I had to lay the cards on the table. Now is not the time for sentimentality. If the child is in an orphanage under a new identity, it will at least have a better chance of survival. Escaping France is almost impossible with a small child.'

All of a sudden Elizabeth lost her appetite. She pushed the tray away.

'Eat up,' Madame Genot snapped. 'You cannot help them by starving yourself. Besides, food is too precious to be wasted.' She pushed the tray back towards her. 'We will do our best. The rest is in God's hand.'

Elizabeth sighed. *God's hand. If he really cared, he would stop all this suffering.*

'I haven't come here to talk about these people,' Madame Genot said, a little irritated. 'I wanted to let you know there's a bus leaving for Dole at eight o'clock this morning. It might be a good idea to get it. I know the bus driver. He will look after you.' She turned to leave but before doing so, jerked her head towards the breakfast tray. 'And if you don't feel like finishing your breakfast now, wrap it up and take it with you. You'll soon be hungry again.'

Elizabeth glanced at her watch. She had over an hour to get ready and get to the bus station. Madame Genot was at the reception desk arranging a vase of flowers when Elizabeth appeared. Elizabeth started to take a few notes from her purse but Madame Genot reached out to stop her.

'You can repay me by staying safe.' She smiled. 'Good luck my dear.' She gave her two kisses on the cheek and turned her attention back to the flowers.

An hour later, Elizabeth was on her way to Dole.

CHAPTER 6

The bus ride to Dole took almost three hours: twice the normal time due to several checks at roadblocks and a noisy exhaust and an engine that threatened to break down at any moment. It didn't help that it was also filled to capacity and overloaded with a mountain of luggage on the roof. During one spot-check, they were held up for half an hour while every passenger's luggage was searched. Thankfully, the bus driver — Madame Genot's contact — must have expected this and had hidden her suitcase next to his seat. Three people were hauled off the bus and bundled into two waiting cars.

By the time Elizabeth reached Dole she had a splitting headache and felt quite sick. She found a bench and finished off the rest of her breakfast — a slice of bread and one of the eggs. It settled her stomach but her head was still pounding. She checked the bus timetable for her connection to Lons-le-Saunier. She had a two-hour wait and decided to find a café or bar away from the gazing eyes of the German police and Milice who patrolled such places on a regular basis. There was little on the menu and she made do with ersatz coffee made of barley. It was bitter and she was grateful for the jug of water provided to wash it down.

The time went by slowly but it gave her a chance to think the situation over in her mind. Guy was on her mind all the time. She knew SOE were worried, and rightly so, but deep down Elizabeth felt sure he was safe. It was just one of her gut feelings that made no sense at all but usually turned out right. Vera Atkins and Colonel Buckmaster were concerned the network had been infiltrated, yet Elizabeth's instincts told her that if it had, she was convinced Guy would have smelled a rat. He had a nose for traitors. If he had gone silent, then there had to be a good reason. He was one of their best agents, with a knack of staying one step ahead of his enemy. The whole time she had worked with him, he had amazed her with his ingenuity. Vera had warned her to be prepared for the worst but she brushed it off. She couldn't have done the job if she thought he was dead. She had to believe: that alone would drive her to find out the truth.

Before she left England she had discussed her first transmission with Vera. London wanted to hear from her as soon as she landed to verify all was well but Elizabeth asked for an extension. Transmitting was always fraught with danger and she didn't want to put her hosts at risk so she asked for a delay of three to four days to give her time to get settled. She assured them that if they hadn't heard from after that time, they would know something had gone wrong. Now she had only today — tomorrow at the latest.

It was early evening when Elizabeth arrived in the market town of Lons-le-Saunier, capital of the Jura Department in Eastern France. Because of its geographical position, being equally placed between Besançon, Dijon, Bourg-en-Bresse, and its close proximity to Switzerland, it had quickly established itself a centre for the Resistance. It was near here that she first arrived when she was flown to France to act as a courier in Guy's Belvedere network a year earlier, and she knew it well. When France fell to the Germans, Lons-le-Saunier was in the free zone, but its proximity to the Jura Massif in the east made it an ideal area for escape routes through the Swiss border and the place was riddled with Nazi spies and double agents. Even so, she was relieved to finally be in home territory.

A light rain was beginning to fall when she stepped off the bus and two taxis were parked nearby, waiting for last minute customers before the curfew. One called out to her but she ignored him and walked on. It was far too dangerous to catch a taxi. Elizabeth was shrewd enough to know that if the drivers were in the pay of the Gestapo they would give away her destination at the drop of a hat. Consequently, she decided to walk. It took well over half an hour before she reached her destination, a small villa situated in a quiet leafy street on the outskirts of the town. Like most of the houses in the street, it was designed in the Belle Époque style with deep blue shutters and decorative wrought iron balconies. The house was set back from the road by a high wall. In the centre was a large iron gate flanked with decorative urns spilling with ivy.

Elizabeth pushed open the gate and rather than knock on the front door, followed a narrow gravel pathway through the shrubs towards the back of the house. Here the garden opened up onto a wide lawn surrounded by more shrubs, several trees and rose bushes. A heavily pregnant woman was carrying a basket of washing inside the house. When she reached the steps of the terrace something made her turn and look around. She almost dropped the basket in fright.

'*Bon Dieu*! Marie-Élise! Is it really you?' Juliette Dassin cried out. 'You gave me a fright.' The two women embraced each other. 'Where have you been? It's been so long.'

Hearing her mother's voice outside and wondering who the visitor was, a young girl sheepishly appeared at the door. Elizabeth held her arms out and picked the child up, kissing her affectionately.

'Angeline, my little angel: I've missed you!'

The dark-eyed child recognised her instantly. '*Tante* Marie-Élise,' she beamed. 'You came back after all.'

'Have you been a good girl for your Maman while I was away?' Elizabeth smiled.

The child wrapped her arms around Elizabeth's neck and giggled. 'Of course.'

'Come inside out of the rain,' Juliette said. 'You'll catch your death of cold.'

Juliette ushered Elizabeth into the kitchen and pulled up a chair for her in front of the warm stove. She asked her daughter to set the table while she poured out a glass of red wine for them both.

'*Santé*,' she said, raising a glass. 'You cannot imagine how happy I am to see you again. We've been so worried.' She glanced at her daughter setting out the soup spoons next to the bowls. 'We can talk later,' she whispered.

'Pregnancy suits you,' Elizabeth said. She smiled. 'How far are you?'

'Seven months,' Juliette ran her hand gently over her stomach. 'It's already kicking.'

Elizabeth didn't need to ask if her husband, Pierre, was well. Her happiness spoke volumes.

'And you?' Juliette asked. 'I see you have no ring. Is there still no man in your life?'

'Not at the moment,' Elizabeth said, hating the fact that she couldn't share the news about her and Guy being married.

Juliette's face reddened. 'I'm sorry, I shouldn't have asked. It was quite insensitive of me. It's just that when I see how you are with Angeline, I know you will make a good mother. Maybe when this war

45

is over and you return to England.'

'Maybe.'

Juliette quickly changed the subject. 'Let's eat. You must be starving.'

She served up their meal; a watery soup consisting of barley and cabbage in a beef broth. Afterwards, Elizabeth tucked Angeline into bed. It was something she'd done many times during her last assignment and it was often accompanied by a story. Tonight there would be no story but she did watch her while she said her prayers.

'Will you still be here when I wake up?' Angeline asked.

Elizabeth saw the look of concern on her pretty round face. 'Of course, my darling. Now go to sleep. I'll see you in the morning.'

She pulled the coverlet over her and kissed her on the forehead.

When they were alone, Juliette was anxious to know how Elizabeth had been. 'How long is it since we saw you last? Over eight months?'

'Eight months exactly; you have a good memory.'

Juliette was one of the few people who knew Elizabeth was an SOE agent. Her husband, Pierre was the *chef de réseau,* the chief of a Resistance network in Lons-le-Saunier and the nearby region of Baume les Messieurs. It was an area he knew well, as his family were wine producers from Château-Chalon. The whole family were involved in the wine business, one of them producing the coveted *vin jaune*, for which the region was known.

'How is Pierre?' Elizabeth asked.

'He's fine, thank God. The Germans have given him an *Ausweis*, a special permit to move around and sell the family wine to the local wine shops. Naturally he has to make sure they have a good supply for themselves. At least he has escaped the dreaded *Service du travail obligatoire* (STO). Many able-bodied men who did not report have either been shot or deported to Germany. The Compulsory Work Service has only served to alienate the people more. Many have fled to join the Maquis and who can blame them.' Juliette went on to say she saw less of Pierre than ever as he used his work as a cover to liaise with the Resistance and the Maquis. 'In fact he will be here tonight. He'll be so happy to see you again.'

'Tell me Juliette, have you or Pierre kept in touch with the others?' By *others* Elizabeth meant Guy, and his radioman, Paul-Emile, and the courier, Amelie.

'I know Pierre saw them just before Christmas. After that, I'm not sure. I remember at the time being worried because he seemed on edge. When I asked what the matter was, he told me he thought that the Gestapo might be on to them. It didn't surprise me — the Gestapo are always after us, but when I pressed him for more information he refused to say any more, saying he didn't want to worry me unduly as I might lose the baby. I was not worried for me, but for Angeline. He assured me he would tell me if something bad had happened and we needed to hide. His words scared me, but as long as he came home, I felt reassured that everything was fine.'

Elizabeth didn't like what she was hearing. This was around the time London lost contact with them. Pierre was not a man to be easily ruffled. He was always level-headed, calm and steady. It was one reason he was chosen to be the *chef de réseau*.

At that moment they heard the front door open. Juliette jumped up.

'It's Pierre.' She ran to greet him. 'Darling, we have a visitor. You'll never guess who it is.'

Pierre entered the room, apprehensively at first, but when he saw Elizabeth, his face lit up.

'This certainly is a wonderful surprise.' He embraced her warmly. 'And you look so well. Whatever you've been doing, life has been treating you well. You're not as skinny as the last time I saw you.'

Elizabeth smiled. He was still as observant as ever. Juliette chastised him playfully for being so rude, but Elizabeth knew he was right. She *had* gained weight since being in England. Food was rationed there also but it was not as harsh as in France. Like Juliette, Pierre did not question what she'd been doing since they last met as he wasn't aware she'd been back to England. Everyone had their secrets these days. All the same, looking too healthy could draw unwanted attention.

'This calls for a celebration,' he said, 'and afterwards perhaps you can enlighten us on why you are here.'

He brought out a bottle of *vin jaune* which they kept hidden behind the bookshelf. Elizabeth told them she had the radio with her and needed to contact London as soon as possible and asked if he knew of a safe place to transmit from. Pierre told her that *Abbé* Henri from the nearby Catholic Church could help as he belonged to the Resistance. He asked Juliette if she would fetch him. The light rain earlier in the evening had now settled into a steady downpour. She wrapped herself up in a heavy coat, grabbed an umbrella and left immediately. When he was sure his wife had gone, Pierre topped up Elizabeth's glass and moved his chair closer to hers.

'What's the real reason you are here, Marie-Élise?' he asked.

'I need to find Daniel and Paul-Emille as soon as possible.'

Pierre took out a pipe and tobacco pouch from his pocket. She studied him carefully while he filled the bowl loosely with tobacco and pressed it lightly down with his thumb. He added a little more and pressed down again, as if deliberately stalling for time. Finally, he lit it with a match and drew, emitting wisps of smoke from the side of his mouth. At the same time, he crossed his legs in a nonchalant manner and gazed at the burning logs in the stove.

'Something's wrong isn't it?' she asked.

After a few minutes that seemed like an eternity he sat back in the chair, shook his head and let out a deep sigh. 'Where do I start?' he replied, as much to himself as Elizabeth.

She felt her heart pounding in her chest. She always knew she would have to face this moment and mentally prepared herself for the worst.

'You can start at the beginning,' she said calmly. 'I gather whatever you're about to say must be bad as you obviously kept it from Juliette.'

'There was an incident,' he said, trying carefully to choose the right words.

'Pierre, please don't take me for a child. I am here to do a job. For God's sake, stop beating about the bush.'

'Please promise me you won't breathe a word of what I am about to tell you to Juliette.'

'I promise, although you may find that she understands more than you give her credit for. Just tell me what's been going on.'

'As I said, there was an incident. It took place a few days before Christmas. I wasn't there but word went around straight away that a collaborator had infiltrated the network. During the months leading up to this, the Milice and collaborators intensified their activities. Deportations and executions were happening at a terrifying rate and as a consequence, we'd been extra vigilant.

'All I know for sure is that Daniel and Paul-Emille went to a drop zone after receiving a signal from London that several containers of ammunition and explosives were to be dropped that night. It was verified on the BBC earlier in the evening. They were with a group of maquisards headed by André. From what I gathered, the drop zone was changed a couple of nights earlier. I have no idea why they did that. I can only surmise they got wind the area was unsafe for some reason or other.'

Elizabeth already knew that. It was verified by Vera Atkins and Colonel Buckmaster. However, she was not at liberty to tell them she'd been in England and heard it straight from the horse's mouth, or that they were extremely worried about Belvedere. To do so would only create panic. She had to tread carefully: a step at a time.

'I was in Poligny,' he continued, 'delivering wine to my uncle, when I heard what happened. Someone recognised my van outside the wine shop and came to tell me. We immediately closed the shop and went to a safe house where there was a gathering of a few members of the Poligny Resistance. Among them was the mayor. It was he who received the call. He informed us that at sometime in the early hours of the morning, the Germans surrounded the Ledoux Farm near Saint-Claude in a surprise ambush.'

Pierre took a long drink and relit his pipe which had a habit of going out. Elizabeth took a cigarette from her case and leaned over for him to light it. Her hand was shaking.

'Then they set fire to the farm.'

Elizabeth felt her throat constrict. 'Did they take anyone hostage?' she asked, trying hard to contain the emotion in her voice.

'Monsieur and Madame Ledoux were brought here to Gestapo HQ and questioned, but eight maquisards died at the scene. Their bodies were taken and displayed in the square in Saint-Claude along with a large placard stating that they were traitors — enemies of the Reich. Everyone in the village was rounded up and forced to look at them. It was a terrible sight.'

'You said the dead were maquisards: what about Daniel and Paul-Emille?'

'They were not among them.'

Elizabeth had prepared herself for the worst but on hearing that Guy was not one of the dead, she felt as if a great weight had been lifted from her.

'So they're safe then?'

'If only it was that easy. The truth is we don't know what happened to Daniel. I know André escaped. He's gone underground for a while until they find out who talked, but I did hear that on the night of the ambush he was seen at the doctor's house in Villards-d'Héria. This person said he appeared to be helping someone but couldn't be sure who it was as the weather had turned bad and visibility was limited.

He described him as almost carrying the man.'

'Surely someone must have questioned the doctor,' Elizabeth replied.

Pierre shook his head. 'The Gestapo raided all the villages within the vicinity straight away. They wanted to be sure no-one got away. The doctor's house was one of the first on their list just in case anyone was injured and went to seek help. When they hammered on the door, it was his wife who answered. She made some excuse about them being in Champagnole and presumed they had not returned because of the curfew. She kept her nerve even though she was held at gunpoint while they searched the premises. In the end they left, telling her that both her husband and son must report to the police station in Saint-Claude on their return.'

'Did they?' Elizabeth asked.

'Yes. They were questioned at length by the Gestapo. They stuck to a story about picking up medical supplies and because of the difficulties with permits and queues, were unable to get back in time. It seems they believed them because they let them go, but a few days later the house was raided again and they were dragged away at gunpoint. The son was released after being roughed up, but the doctor was sent to Dijon.'

The situation sounded very bad, but at least Daniel's name was not mentioned among those caught or killed at the farm. The clock chimed eleven o'clock and Pierre looked anxious.

'Juliette will be back any moment and I'd prefer it if we didn't talk so openly in front of her — especially about the deaths or those deported.'

Elizabeth gave him her word. 'What about Paul-Emille and the other maquisard — Claude Favre?'

Pierre turned his gaze to the floor again. 'Paul-Emille was captured as he entered his house near Clairvaux-les-Lacs. They were waiting for him.' Elizabeth felt her throat tighten. 'Claude Favre was picked up the same night in his village. They were waiting for him too.'

Elizabeth stubbed her cigarette out aggressively in the ashtray and stood up, pacing up and down the room. Paul came up behind her and put a firm hand on her shoulder.

'*Bon sang!*' she cried. '*C'est terrible.*'

Her eyes filled with tears and she shook with emotion. Pierre handed her his handkerchief.

'I'm so sorry, Marie-Élise. It's been a terrible few months for us all. I had no idea you were unaware of all this. You used to be so close to everyone in the Belvedere circuit.'

Elizabeth longed to tell him Guy had returned to France without her but she couldn't. *Say as little as possible until you find out what happened to Daniel* Vera Atkins had told her. *Don't trust anyone.*

'What else do you know?' Elizabeth asked, wiping away her tears.

'In total, fifty-eight people were sent to Dijon. They were either kept in the prison or at Gestapo HQ. Most were then deported to camps in Germany. Monsieur and Madame Ledoux were sent away also. A few were sent to Avenue Foch in Paris, including Paul-Emille, and I'm afraid to say we don't know what happened to him. Claude Favre managed to escape as he was being transferred from Dijon. We don't know what happened to him either.'

'How did you get to know who was sent away?'

'There's a German here in Lons-le-Saunier–a secretary by the name of Klaus Schubert. He works at the German High Command. I got to know him because of the wine deliveries. Occasionally I make sure he gets a bottle of the very best wine. When I asked him for a special favour — to show me the list of deportees — he said he would only show me a copy in return for several bottles of Frances's finest wines. I told him I couldn't even lay my hands on them myself as the Wehrmacht had plundered the best. "Then we don't have deal, Herr Dassin." He gave an arrogant shrug and called someone to show me out of the building. Naturally I gave in, asking him to give me a few days to see what I could do. "I knew you would see sense," he said with a smirk. I wanted to kill him with my bare hands. I returned with his gifts a few days later and, true to his word, he showed me the list. I recognised most names on it. The meeting lasted no longer than five minutes.'

'One more thing,' Elizabeth said. 'What do you know of a woman called Amelie Rousseau?'

'Amelie, Daniel's courier?'

'Yes, that's her.'

He smiled. 'You know Daniel is a bit of a dark horse. He never says much, but I think he thought highly of her. I only met her once. By all accounts she is an excellent agent. Why do you ask?'

'It's just that you haven't mentioned her at all, and as she belonged to Belvedere, I wondered what happened to her.'

Pierre looked surprised. 'I thought you'd know her, especially as she is a courier like yourself.'

Elizabeth refused to be drawn on why she had been replaced by another agent. She was still smarting over it. How could she tell him that SOE deemed her a liability because she'd married the leader of Belvedere? It was laughable when women all over France had joined the Resistance: wives, lovers, mothers, sisters… Did their emotions get in the way of their work? But in the end, they *had* called her and she suspected they realized the error of their ways.

'Where was she when the raid took place?'

'I don't know. Daniel mentioned something about sending her away on an assignment. I don't know anything more. He had a few things on his mind besides arming and training the maquisards.'

Elizabeth asked what they were.

'He'd established a new escape route using a family of smugglers known locally as *passeurs*, in la forêt du Risoux in the Jura, and lac de Joux in Switzerland, because there had been a series of bad incidents around Les Rousses and several escapees and resistants were caught. The resistants were shot and the escapees deported. With more escapees needing help because of the Gestapo and Milice crackdown in the area, he had to do something.'

Pierre paused and Elizabeth waited patiently for his next revelation. 'I believe Amelie and Paul-Emille were in a relationship and I don't think Daniel approved.'

Elizabeth felt her cheeks redden. She thought of the times she and Guy had made love in haylofts and fields, and the secret glances of affection they'd given each other, especially in the face of imminent danger which happened almost on a daily basis. Why would he be upset about that? Lots of agents conducted *affaires d'amour* in the field.

Their conversation was cut short when they heard footsteps approach the back door. Juliette was back with Father Henri.

'We'll continue this conversation another time,' Pierre said.

As soon as Juliette entered the kitchen, she noticed Elizabeth's eyes. They were full of sorrow.

'Is everything all right?'

'Everything's fine,' Elizabeth replied, biting her lip, determined not to let her emotions get the better of her.

The room was filled with tension and Pierre stepped in quickly to stop his wife asking any more questions.

'Marie-Élise, let me introduce Father Henri. You will be in good hands. Paul-Emille has used his services on several occasions.'

Juliette said they would wait up until she returned but Elizabeth insisted they get some sleep. She had no idea how long she would be and didn't want to bother them unnecessarily.

'We can talk in the morning,' she replied, as she handed the priest her precious suitcase to carry for her. 'You two get some sleep.'

It took less than ten minutes to reach the church. Thankfully, the streets were deserted and the shutters and curtains firmly closed. Father Henri was a young man in his mid-thirties. He told her he'd joined the Resistance in the early days. His parents' house near Paris had been bombed during the invasion and they were both killed, but his brother, who was outside when it happened, was unhurt and escaped to England to join de Gaulle's Free French.

'I am grateful Britain has given refuge to my brother and the General so if there is anything I can do here to help the agents, I will do it. I know it won't be long now before the invasion. When it happens, France will be ready.'

Father Henri radiated gentility and calm, and Elizabeth did indeed feel safe in his company. He unlocked the church door and offered to help her with the wiring, saying he'd helped other radio operators before her in addition to Paul-Emille, and he was sorry to hear he'd been caught. When they were done, he went into the sacristy leaving her alone to transmit.

This was her first transmission and she was nervous, but, as soon as she tapped out the first letters, she felt fine and quickly regained her confidence. It didn't take long for her to let London know she was safe and well and to give them an update on the situation, including the fact that Paul-Emille — agent Vincent — was caught entering his safe house after the drop. It was almost an hour later when she received a reply.

RECEIVED GOOD LUCK

Elizabeth took off her earphones and gave a sigh of relief. Her first transmission had gone well. She packed up the radio and Father Henri escorted her back to the villa.

'I am at the church every day,' he said, 'should you need me.'

She shook his hand and they parted ways. Except for several candles burning in the kitchen, the Dassin's villa was in darkness. Pierre and Juliette had retired to bed. Elizabeth took off her jacket, now damp from the rain, and picked up a plate of cheese and bread Juliette had thoughtfully left out for her in case she was still hungry. She sat down on the couch and, in the silence of the night, hungrily polished it off before curling up and falling asleep.

Elizabeth woke up in the morning to see Juliette already at the stove cooking breakfast. The smell of fried eggs mixed with last night's tobacco which still lingered heavily in the air. She sat up and stretched out her arms.

'I slept like a log.'

'I can see that,' Juliette replied. 'But you didn't have to sleep here. I made a bed for you.'

'I was so tired I must have just drifted off.'

'Come and eat this before it gets cold. Afterwards you can take a wash. There's enough hot water.'

She wiped her hands on her apron and served up the eggs. Angeline was already seated at the table waiting eagerly. Pierre joined them.

'I am assuming all went to plan,' he said, breaking a piece of bread and dipping it into the deep orange yolk. 'Juliette and I were wondering what your immediate plans are. You are most welcome to stay with us for a while.'

Elizabeth thanked them but she said she preferred to find a base to stay. It would be safer.

'Did you have anywhere in mind?' Juliette asked.

'Yes. I'd like to stay in the old cottage in Clairvaux-les-Lacs. If it's still available, that is.'

Pierre made no comment, but the expression on his face spoke volumes. She knew he would argue against the idea, given that Paul-Emille had been taken from there. A few minutes passed before he replied.

'I have to go to Champagnole today to drop off some wine. I could detour and take you.'

Elizabeth could tell he wasn't too happy. She wasn't even sure if it was the right thing to do herself.

CHAPTER 7

The Menouillard family owned a large tract of farmland seven kilometres outside Clairvaux-les-Lacs, on the Rive du Lac Road, the road which led to Villards-d'Héria where André was last seen approaching the doctor's house. The property bordered the forest on one side and the Grand Lac on the other. They also owned a large sawmill next to the forest, along with several other small cottages which were mostly occupied by seasonal itinerant loggers and farmhands who worked for the family. Since the German occupation, these were seldom occupied.

The Menouillards belonged to the Resistance. Their eldest son, Sylvain, was a soldier who lost his life fighting the Germans during the first week of the war. As a consequence, the family could not accept the French surrender by their government and called them traitors. It wasn't long before Monsieur Menouillard began helping people escape across the demarcation line between the *zone occupée* and the *zone libre* — the occupied and non-occupied zone — which was less than thirty kilometres away. Before long, the farm became a hideout for escapees, particularly Jews and downed airmen, and anyone else fleeing the tyranny of occupied Europe. As a result of their work, they soon became known to the intelligence organisations in London, in particular SOE. Elizabeth knew them well as it was in one of the Menouillard's cottages that she had occasionally operated from with Guy.

She asked Pierre to drop her off at the bridge on the outskirts of Clairvaux-les-Lacs. He knew the Menouillards well and insisted on taking her there, particularly in light of what she was carrying, but Elizabeth declined. She wanted to make her own way to the farm. Sabine Menouillard was outside feeding swill to the pigs when the dogs started to bark loudly. In the distance she saw a smartly-dressed woman walking down the long driveway carrying a suitcase and large bag. She put down the bucket and squinted over her glasses wondering who it was. As the woman got closer, Sabine realised.

'*Bon Dieu*!' she muttered under her breath. 'Good God! It can't be!' She called out to her husband. 'Armand, come quickly. You'll never guess who's here.'

Armand opened the farm door immediately, half expecting unwelcome visitors and was shocked to see Elizabeth.

As with the Dassins in Lons-le-Saunier, she was given an enthusiastic welcome, but unlike Juliette and Pierre, the Menouillards knew she had returned to England.

'We thought we'd never see you again,' Sabine said.

She was wearing her farm clothes: an old cardigan over a thick woollen dress, and her wellington boots were caked in mud and manure which gave off a powerful odour. Wisps of fine grey hair protruded from under a brown felt cloche hat so old it had lost its shape. Armand on the other hand, smelled of a combination of sawdust and woodchips, bits of which were embedded in his pullover and thick beard. Their rough and tatty attire belied the fact that the Menouillards were wealthy landowners — salt of the earth country people — and it was rare to find them dressed in anything other than farm clothes, unless they were going to church, a wedding, or a local feast.

Armand took her suitcase and bag and carried them inside while his wife plied Elizabeth with a multitude of questions.

'Marie-Élise, what on earth brought you back again?' she asked. 'You're crazy. You should have stayed in London. Things are even worse now than they were when you left. Haven't you heard?'

'Yes, I know,' Elizabeth replied. 'That's precisely why I'm here.'

In the farmhouse, Armand placed the luggage by the door and pulled out a chair at the table for her while his wife took out a set of keys from her pocket, searched for the right one, and unlocked a store-cupboard in which she kept a tin of real coffee. She said she was saving it for a special occasion and now was one of them. When Elizabeth asked why it was kept under lock and key, she said a worker had stolen the last tin and it was outrageously expensive to replace.

'Thieves!' she said scornfully, referring to the worker. 'You can't trust anyone these days.'

Armand shrugged his shoulders and ignored her. 'What brings you back, Marie-Élise? It must be serious for them to send you into the field again, especially after the last time.'

He was referring to two of several incidences. The first one was when Guy and another member of Belvedere and two maquisards were driving along a quiet country road and came across a German patrol on the lookout for maquisards. One of the maquisards was killed in the crossfire. The Belvedere agent was wounded when he threw a grenade at the Germans, which blew up their truck enabling them to escape. The agent died from his wounds shortly after. It sparked a series of reprisals in the area and innocent people were executed. They all went into hiding for a few weeks until things died down. The second incident took place a few days before she and Guy were due to return to England. They were picked up in a bar in a village outside Lons-le-Saunier by the Gestapo and interrogated at their headquarters. Guy was beaten up and suffered a few cuts and bruises to the head, and Elizabeth was punched and slapped around the face several times and threatened with rape. Luckily, this was a mild interrogation to what could have taken place, but they stuck to their cover stories and were released the next day. They never did find out the reason why they had been picked up and put it down to just another surprise *rafle*: being in the wrong place at the wrong time. Unfortunately for Elizabeth, she was three months pregnant and suffered a miscarriage. It was something she kept to herself. Not even Guy knew she was carrying his child. It was also another reason why she jumped at Vera Atkins's offer to get back in the field: she had a score to settle.

'When did you arrive?' Sabine asked, carefully pouring the coffee into three elegant porcelain cups usually reserved for special occasions. 'We usually get to hear of any drops and as far as we know, there hasn't been any for a while.'

'A few days ago. I was dropped elsewhere and made my way to Lons-le-Saunier by bus and train. Pierre Dassin dropped me off just outside the village. I wanted to surprise you.' She smiled.

'You did that alright. But a lovely surprise indeed,' Armand replied. He gestured towards the suitcase by the door. 'If you're carrying what I think you are, you're damn lucky not to have been caught.'

Elizabeth didn't need to be told that. She said a prayer every time she walked down the street with it.

'I'm sorry I've landed on you without prior notice. It couldn't be helped. The thing is, I need somewhere to stay and I was wondering if the old cottage was still free?'

Sabine glanced at her husband as she handed them their coffee. It smelled delicious and it tasted even better.

'Of course,' she replied. 'It's yours for as long as you want, but are you quite sure you want to stay around here? I mean, it's become extremely dangerous. We weren't joking when we said things have worsened since the last time you were here. Many people have been killed, deported, or simply gone missing. The Wehrmacht and the SS have stepped up their raids and they're aided by a growing Milice and collaborators. They are the worst of all.'

'London has always been grateful for your help,' Elizabeth said, 'but more than that, I trust you both and if I am going to feel safe anywhere, it's here with you.'

Sabine reached across the table and squeezed Elizabeth's hand reassuringly.

'Thank you. We're here to help in any way we can, but I'm sure you understand that it would put our minds at rest if we knew the reason why you came back again.'

Elizabeth came straight to the point. 'London is worried about the Belvedere network.' She was careful not to show her own personal anxiety for her husband. 'They haven't heard from Daniel or Paul-Emille in a while. Pierre filled me in on what's been happening, especially about Paul-Emille and it confirms our worst thoughts. The thing is, he says he has no idea what happened to Daniel — or André for that matter?'

Armand finished his coffee and prepared to light his pipe. 'We expected something terrible would happen at some time or other,' he said. 'It was the swiftness of what took place and the devastating consequences that shook us. We were also taken in for questioning and spent three days in the jail in Rue de la Chevalerie without food or drink. Now and again we'd be hauled out of the cells and taken to Gestapo HQ to be interrogated. When we were freed, we realised we were the lucky ones. Everyone else had either been executed or sent on elsewhere.'

Sabine nodded in agreement. 'Every time I think about it, I shudder. I think the only thing that saved us was that Paul-Emille moved into the village about a month earlier. It was there that they went looking for him, not here.'

'You mean Paul-Emille was staying with you?' Elizabeth asked, surprised.

'Yes. Daniel asked if he could stay. He was here for a while.'

'Then why did he leave? Why move to Clairvaux when he had a

perfectly safe place to stay?' Sabine threw another quick glance at her husband.

Elizabeth, astute as ever, noticed. 'I need to know everything, no matter how small. It may hold a clue.'

Sabine sighed. 'We may be wrong but we think it was because he was seeing the other English woman.'

Elizabeth's eyes widened. 'What! You mean...'

'Yes — Amelie — Belvedere's new courier. I think he wanted to keep the affair from us. I can't think of any other reason he'd move. He was quite happy here and it was safer to transmit than from Clairvaux where detection vans regularly passed through.'

'A very attractive woman,' Armand added. 'By all accounts, she had quite a few admirers.'

Recalling the photograph she'd been shown, Elizabeth could well imagine that.

'How long had this affair been going on?'

'We're not sure,' Armand replied. 'She arrived here a couple of weeks after Daniel. Paul-Emille was already here then. She was staying at a safe house in Clairvaux.'

Elizabeth wanted to clarify the situation. 'Do you mean they were actually having an affair or was it just a flirtation? This job is dangerous as you well know and sometimes people play around to let off steam.'

'It was more than a flirtation.' Sabine smiled. 'My dear Marie-Élise, do you think we are blind? We were in love like that once you know.' She looked at Armand. '*And* a little reckless too.' Her smile faded. 'But we did not have the Germans breathing down our necks.'

Elizabeth felt confused. Given SOE's many warnings about not putting yourself in a compromising situation, she wondered what Vera Atkins and Colonel Buckmaster would say if they knew. It was one reason she and Guy had been so careful to try and conceal their love. She had yearned to come back with him and serve her country but their marriage had put a stop to it. Sometimes she wondered if they just should have carried on the way they were, keeping their affair a secret. How unfair life was.

What Sabine said next, shocked Elizabeth even more.

'As I said, we are not blind. We also saw the way you and Daniel used to look at each other, even though you hid it very well.' She paused, observing Elizabeth cheeks redden. 'Marie-Élise, I never thought we'd be having this conversation but you may as well know, Daniel told us you'd got married. It was one of the first things he said when he returned and we asked after you. We weren't surprised at all and hoped for both your sakes, the war didn't ruin it for you.'

Elizabeth was lost for words. 'I don't know what to say. Daniel was quite upset when SOE refused to send me back into the field with him. After a long discussion, we decided it was best not to mention it to anyone here in France. I didn't want him worrying about me when his life and that of others was in danger. He had a job to do and that is what took precedence.'

'The thing is,' Armand added, 'we didn't expect to see you here again. None of us did. At least not until the war was over. We can tell you though; Daniel said we were the only ones who knew.'

Elizabeth shook her head. Part of her was happy he'd told their trusted friends they'd married, yet another part wondered why. The question was soon answered.

'He said he wanted us to know in case anything happened to him. He was afraid that after the war, London might cover their tracks and he knew you would come looking for him.'

Elizabeth felt a chill run down her spine and took a deep breath to gain her composure. Sabine poured her a glass of water. 'You're scaring me. Please tell me he's not dead.'

'We told you,' Armand continued. 'We don't know. We only know he went missing after the raid on the Ledoux Farm. Thankfully, no-one has found his body and our sources tell us his name was not on any deportation list.'

'But what if *was* caught and disappeared under the Night and Fog policy?'

'We don't think so. Someone would have recognised him and got word to us.' He paused for a moment. 'Is that why they sent you, because of Daniel?'

'It's likely the network has been compromised, and maybe others too. There was no time to send someone here who doesn't know how Belvedere operates. I know the area well. More than that, I know how Daniel works. I couldn't say no. I can't sit and wait out the war not knowing.'

Elizabeth fought back her emotions about Guy which she'd tried so hard to hide. She was sent back into the field because she was a good operator and both Colonel Buckmaster and Vera Atkins realised she was the only one with any chance of finding him.

'The courier, Amelie, have you any idea what happened to her?' Elizabeth asked.

Armand shook his head. 'From what I gather, Daniel sent her away shortly before the raid. At least we think he did. He never mentioned it again and we never saw her after that, so we presumed she'd left.'

'Do you know where to?'

'She travelled all over the Jura: sometimes to Burgundy, other times to Switzerland. All we know is she didn't return.'

It had been a few days since Elizabeth arrived back in France and she was exhausted. The combination of being on the move with very little sleep and the tension she'd been under, carrying a suitcase with a transmitter inside, had put her under immense pressure. She needed a clear head to digest the situation. Sabine could see this and suggested she take her to settle in at the cottage. They could continue the conversation later.

The old stone cottage was just as she'd remembered it. Being a worker's cottage, it consisted of two simple rooms — a kitchen/living room and a small bedroom, large enough to hold a single bed and a side table. The low ceiling was a mixture of uneven beams, darkened over the years by wood smoke, and from which hung several hooks. A wicker basket hung from one of them, a copper jug another. The others were for hanging rabbits and game birds until the aroma developed and the flesh matured. The furniture was sparse and rudimentary. In the centre of the kitchen stood a table so old that the wood had mellowed with age and the top incised with a multitude of scratches and knife cuts from years of use. Around it were four spindle-legged chairs which Armand had crafted from wood from the nearby forest. There was a stone sink and one tap. On one side of the room was a fireplace built over a raised firebox with a pair of cast iron andirons, a crane and chain trammel hooks on which to hang a cooking pot. Next to it stood a pair of bellows and tongs. It was Guy who first taught Elizabeth to build a proper cooking fire. Her first attempts were unsuccessful and she smiled to herself when she thought of the times she'd almost smoked them out of the house. There was a skill to making a good fire Guy had told her, and in the end she mastered the skill well enough to cook stews and even roast a suckling pig. Standing here once again, those memories burned brightly in her heart.

Sabine put a set of sheets and towels out for her and checked the electricity was working and that there was enough kerosene for lamps and the portable stove. Elizabeth put the suitcase with the transmitter on the table and asked Sabine if it was fine to transmit from here.

'Of course: you are quite safe here, you know that. Just make sure you keep it well hidden when you're not using it. We could be raided at any time. I suggest hiding it in the woodshed next to the outhouse where the toilet is.'

She left, saying dinner would be served around seven.

When she was alone, Elizabeth put a pot of water on the stove to wash herself with and stepped outside to sit on the steps and survey the countryside while it boiled. The beauty of the French countryside belied what the French were going through. Amid the tranquillity was an acute sense of fear. Every word, every gesture, had to be made with care. The freedom of the France she'd known as a young girl growing up in Burgundy seemed a lifetime away. Her father was a lawyer, her English-born mother a teacher, and her childhood had been one of privilege: holidays in the Swiss Alps and summers on the Riviera with her paternal grandparents. Then her father died and things steadily collapsed. Times were hard and the money was running out. War was on the horizon. One day a letter arrived from her English grandmother, Granny Elizabeth, who she had been named after, informing them that she was seriously ill and wanted to see her daughter and granddaughter one last time before she died. Elizabeth and her mother left France for Devon immediately. A month later, war broke out and Granny Elizabeth died soon after, leaving the house to her daughter, and all hope of returning to France seemed doomed until Elizabeth came to the attention of Vera Atkins. When she accepted the assignment to work with Belvedere, she told her mother she was returning to France but was unable to say where and in what capacity. Her mother knew Elizabeth was headstrong and, unable to convince her otherwise, wished her well. This time, Elizabeth thought it better to not tell her at all.

During her first assignment, Elizabeth had lived at a safe house outside the village of Syam some six kilometres from Champagnole. Strategically positioned, the safe house was actually a small château owned by the Delatour family. Set in large grounds, it had acres of farmland and employed a stream of itinerant workers and was ideally suited as a base from which to liaise with maquisards in the

Department of the Doubs, an area in the Bourgogne/Franche-Comté region of Eastern France named after the Doubs River. Belvedere worked with all the groups in Ornans, Pontarlier, Montbéliard, Belfort and Mouthe, the latter being important for escape routes through la forêt du Risoux. The Risoux was a dense forest of firs and spruces on the edge of the Swiss border in the Haut-Jura. The Maquis were extremely active and a major part of Elizabeth's work involved making frequent letter-drops to these groups concerning supplies sent by England or notifying the *passeurs* of those needing help to get into Switzerland. Guy was based further south, in the area of Saint-Claude. What divided the area was the main road between Dijon and Geneva, an area the Germans kept a close eye on. At the start of the German occupation, the Delatours turned the château into a temporary orphanage for both French orphans and those of foreign Jews. Being an aristocratic family, they were also well-connected with the mayor of Champagnole and other notaries in the area and used their contacts alongside the Swiss Red Cross and the Swiss Children's Help Society to make sure the children were safe. On more than one occasion, Belvedere arranged for some of the older ones to escape across the Swiss border.

This time, Elizabeth decided against making the château her base. She wanted to be nearer to where Guy operated and the Menouillard Farm was known as one of the best safe havens in the area. From here she would span out in search for Guy and the rest of the Belvedere network. Guy had used this cottage during their time here and it held special memories for her, not least because it was here that they fell in love, and here, in the small cramped bedroom, that they first made love. Sitting on the stone steps looking out across the fields, she could picture him as clearly as if it was yesterday, walking along the path, gun in one hand and a brace of pheasants slung over his shoulder.

The years of a healthy life, playing sport, skiing and hiking, had done wonders for him. He was in the prime of his life with a good body to show for it. Elizabeth was smitten at once but quickly realized that Guy was a loner who kept to himself and as such, would probably never share the same feelings. It was not until a few weeks later that she discovered he had fallen for her too.

They were returning from a drop zone late one night with several other maquisards. Everything had gone according to plan until a German patrol neared the area. The men scattered into the woods and fields. Elizabeth lost her way and fell into deep ditch full of brambles. Guy was ahead but when he heard her cry out, he turned back to save her. Unfortunately, armoured cars and motorcycles were coming over the hill and he was forced to jump into the ditch with her. The Germans passed close by and at one point the convoy came to a standstill while several Germans scoured the area. Elizabeth's heart beat wildly as she and Guy steadied their pistols in readiness to shoot. Fortunately, they stayed well-hidden and were not discovered and the convoy moved on.

Elizabeth let out a deep sigh of relief. 'That was a near miss.'

What happened next surprised her even more than the Germans approaching. Guy pulled her into his arms and kissed her long and hard on the mouth — a kiss so full of passion that she thought she would faint.

'From now on I'm not letting you out of my sight,' he said, unfurling his arms from around her slender body to put his gun away.

He pulled her up, and stamping down the brambles with his boots, carried her out of the ditch. Her legs and arms were covered in scratches but she hardly noticed. All she recalled was the passionate kiss. So he *had* felt something for her after all. This tender moment was not mentioned again until a few weeks later and Elizabeth concluded it was simply something that happened in the heat of the moment. The combination of fear and adrenalin made people do crazy things. Then one night after a meal at the cottage which involved consuming copious amounts of a particularly good wine that Pierre had managed to secure from the family *cave* in Château-Chalon, he pulled her aside as the other members of the Maquis were leaving, saying he had something important to discuss with her. He wore such a serious look that Elizabeth thought something was wrong. Had she messed up one of her courier jobs? She hoped not.

When they were alone, he pulled her into his arms again. As before, there were no words, just the same intense feeling they'd experienced that night in the bramble ditch. Hungry for each other, they soon ended up in bed. It was a night of passion that would forever be etched in Elizabeth's mind and it sustained her through those miserable weeks and months after he returned to France without her.

The water was boiling. She poured it into a large tin bowl, undressed, and sponged her tired body with a block of green olive oil soap Sabine had thoughtfully left her. The warm soapy suds on her bare skin were sheer luxury after days of wearing the same clothes. Afterwards, she wrapped herself in a towel and lay down on the bed, breathing in the refreshing scent of soap combined with woodsmoke and the earthy smell of the land that seeped through the walls, and fell asleep.

CHAPTER 8

It was dark when Elizabeth woke up and the warmth of an early spring day had evaporated leaving a cool chill in the air. She switched on the bedroom light, anxiously watching the overhead bulb flicker for a few minutes like fireflies in the night until it eventually settled into a warm, orange-tinged glow, and then took out a clean set of clothes from her bag; a camel-coloured woollen skirt and olive green ribbed pullover. The last time she had worn these was in London when Vera Atkins offered her the assignment. Tidying her hair in the mirror, she thought how long ago that seemed: another world away. She imagined them in the office in Baker Street, pacing the room, anxiously awaiting news from France. She could visualize it. *"Have you heard from agent Lisette today,"* Colonel Buckmaster would be asking, only to get a *"Sorry, sir. Not today."* Colonel Buckmaster would huff a little and Vera would assure him all was fine. It was a ritual. Elizabeth would report to them tomorrow. For the moment she wanted to see what else the Menouillards knew. And she was hungry.

The path to the farm, some five hundred metres away, was little more than a dirt track. Elizabeth knew it well but with only a half moon, she still needed her flashlight. The path bordered a field on one side and the edge of the forest on the other. When she rounded the bend, the farmhouse and outbuildings came into view. In the distance was lac de Clairvaux, stretching across the horizon like a black watery mirror streaked with silver ribbons. As soon as she approached, the dogs started barking, running towards her and wagging their tails as they had done earlier. Their friendliness was due to the fact that they already knew her. In reality, they were excellent guard dogs with a penchant for baring their teeth and growling menacingly at unwelcome strangers. It was because of the dogs that the Resistance had managed to evade many surprise visits from the Germans by scattering into the woods at a moment's notice.

Armand was sitting by the fire in his favourite chair watching Sabine cut slivers from a dense pork Morteau sausage produced on the plateau and in the mountains of the Jura. She handed Elizabeth a slice on the end of a sharp knife.

'What do you think?' she asked. 'Armand was given two yesterday in exchange for a truckload of timber.'

Elizabeth closed her eyes, savouring the conifer and juniper-smoked meat that exploded in her mouth. *'C'est merveilleux,'* she exclaimed. 'How I've missed this.'

'We have another surprise,' Sabine added and handed Armand the key to the store cupboard.

He returned with a bottle of *vin jaune* which, like the coffee had been securely locked away from would-be thieves, imaginary or otherwise.

'A gift from Pierre,' he said as he uncorked the bottle, 'and a good one at that. The family managed to hide it from the Germans in one of their secret *caves*. We were saving it for a special occasion.'

'Santé, Marie-Élise! Welcome back.'

The wine trickled down her throat smoothly, producing a warm afterglow. Like the sausage, it was simply wonderful. Over dinner, Elizabeth broached the subject of Amelie. 'Can you tell me more about her, apart from the fact that she's beautiful?' She smiled. 'I was shown a photo of her in London so I think we all agree on that point. '

'She's clever,' Armand said.

'Wily,' Sabine added. 'As cunning as a fox that one and quick to sniff out when something's amiss — like those dogs.' She gestured towards the door where the dogs were sitting on an old carpet chewing on bones. 'It was not only Daniel who trusted her. Everyone else did too. It's just a pity Paul-Emile had to fall head over heels for her.'

Elizabeth looked confused.

Armand frowned at his wife. 'Let's not keep focusing on Paul-Emille and Amelie as a couple. They were both responsible agents and none of us know why the raid took place that night.'

'Except that the Germans *must* have known there was a drop and knew exactly where to cast their net,' Elizabeth replied. 'Tell me, do you think Amelie is still alive?'

'My instinct tells me, yes,' Sabine answered.

Elizabeth looked at Armand, waiting for his reply.

'Mine too,' he said, after giving it some thought.

Elizabeth persisted with this line of thought. 'Let's look at our options then. The first is that she found out what took place and went into hiding in case the Gestapo were looking for her. The second option is that she escaped into Switzerland, most likely using one of Belvedere's own escape routes.' She paused for a moment. 'Which begs the question, if she did, why didn't she contact London and let them know? It would have been easy from there. But it's been a few months now so I think we can rule that option out.'

Sabine got up to clear the table in readiness for dessert. 'If she didn't contact London, then she's either dead or...'

'In hiding,' Elizabeth said, finishing off Sabine's sentence.

She asked for a pen and piece of paper and made a list of possible safe houses between Burgundy and Switzerland while Sabine replaced the Morteau sausage in the centre of the table with a crock-pot filled with plums in eau-de-vie which had been left to macerate over winter.

'Are you going to check every single one?' Sabine asked, as she spooned out a good-sized serving of fruit into small bowls. 'You've got quite a few there.'

'I must. Someone must know where she is — and Daniel too.'

'And André,' Armand added.

'Three people cannot simply disappear and no-one knows anything. It's impossible,' Elizabeth said.

She took a small bite of plum. The juice was so potent she felt her cheeks glowing.

'If there's anything we can do, let us know,' Armand said, picking up the bottle of *vin jaune*. It was almost empty. 'Who's going to have the last drop?'

'After such a delicious meal, I think the chef deserves it,' Elizabeth replied.

Sabine was already a little tipsy, but she gladly accepted. She raised her glass towards Elizabeth. '*Bon chance, mon amie*. You will need it.'

*

The sleepy village of Clairvaux-les-Lacs was just as Elizabeth remembered it. The shops were still open but there was hardly anything to sell. The bakery in the main street now closed an hour after opening due to the early morning rush to get what few loaves they were able to bake, and there were no sweet pastries or beautifully

68

decorated cakes any more. Those days had long gone. Everything vanished in the first hour. Only the grocery store had things left: a few tins, dried pulses and the odd vegetables on otherwise empty shelves. One or two shops were still doing business, but it could hardly be called a roaring trade. The seamstress on the edge of the village was one of them, but with little fabric on sale and ration cards needed, her work mostly consisted of reworking existing clothes — taking in dresses and suits at the waist for those who had lost weight because of the hardships they all endured, or adding a pretty collar and cuffs for a special occasion.

Another was the cobbler who did a robust trade repairing existing shoes because, like the seamstress, few had the money to buy new ones. And then there was Mitzi, the hairdresser. Even though there was a war on, women wanted to look good. It made them feel better. And for those who had no money, Mitzi was only too happy to put it on tick: they could pay her after the war. There was also another reason Mitzi stayed open. She belonged to the Resistance and it was in her rented apartment over the salon that Amelie had lived while she was in Clairvaux.

The church clock struck 12:00 p.m. — lunchtime. Elizabeth decided to have a drink at Bistrot Jurassien in the square. She propped the bicycle against the wall and peered through the window. Except for an old white-haired man sitting in the corner, the place was empty. She entered, took off her coat and hung it on a hook by the door and sat at a table near the fire.

'Bonjour,' she said to the white-haired man and the bartender as she took off her headscarf and ran her hands through her hair.

'Bonjour,' they replied, in a manner that made her think she'd intruded on something.

The waiter came over to take her order. He was also old. In fact, it was obvious that there were hardly any young men around at all. Elizabeth ordered a red wine and asked if the owner, Madame Dumont, was in.

'It's her day off,' the waiter replied.

'Do you expect her in tomorrow?'

The waiter lifted his shoulder in a heavy shrug and made a pfff sound. 'Perhaps.'

Perhaps seemed a strange answer and the waiter walked away before Elizabeth could ask anything else. She sipped her wine in silence, listening to the crackle of logs on the fire and mulling over the notes she'd made the night before. There were two people she needed to speak with. One was Madame Dumont, a member of the Resistance, and the other was Mitzi, but the hair salon was now closed. She would have to come back tomorrow.

Elizabeth noticed the white-haired man had a mangy-looking dog snoozing on the floor by his side and there was an accordion on the chair next to him. She wished he'd play something — anything — to break the silence. After a while, she got up to leave.

'It's very quiet,' she said as she placed a few coins on the table.

The bartender asked if he could pass on a message to Madame Dumont.

'Just tell her a friend called. I'll come back another day.'

She put on her coat and was just about to walk out the door when the white-haired man mumbled something. He stared straight ahead and Elizabeth saw he was blind.

'Excuse me,' Elizabeth said. 'I didn't catch what you said.'

The man stroked his dog. 'Didn't you hear? They shot two of our young ones last night. The Milice found them plastering anti-Vichy posters on the walls after curfew. They ran off but the Milice alerted the Germans and they were discovered sometime later in the woods: gunned down in cold blood. Bastards! They didn't even bring them in for questioning.'

Elizabeth felt her blood run cold. 'I'm sorry. I had no idea.'

'That's why it's so quiet,' the bartender said, wiping the counter with a cloth. 'Everyone's afraid.'

Elizabeth thanked them and left. Outside, she took a few deep breaths, grabbed her bike and peddled back to the farm in case the Germans had decided to search the farm and cottage. Thankfully, she had been careful to hide the suitcase with the radio among a pile of logs in the woodshed. When she reached the bridge at the edge of the village, she saw a convoy of armoured vehicles and motorcycles in the distance, heading her way. Her papers were in order but she didn't want to risk being stopped by the Germans if they were out to round people up. She jumped off her bicycle, dragged it down the embankment and hid underneath one of the stone archways under the bridge. Minutes later, the convoy rumbled by in the direction of Lons-le-Saunier. When it was out of sight, she scrambled back up again and peddled away as fast as she could.

Armand was in the house comforting a terrified Sabine. He had a deep gash in his cheek which was beginning to swell and blossom into a purple bruise. Blood trickled through his beard and down his neck.

'I heard what happened,' Elizabeth said, 'about the two boys. Do you know what took place? Were they killed on your property?'

The questions tumbled out.

'Yes, we know who they were, and no, it didn't take place in our woods otherwise I would have got far more than this,' Armand replied, pointing to his cheek. 'It happened near Cogna.'

'Who were they?'

'One of them was from Clairvaux — Jean-Michel Dumont. The other was from Cogna.'

Elizabeth's hand flew to her mouth. 'The son of Monique Dumont, the owner of Bistrot Jurassien?'

Sabine nodded. 'Yes. Her son was about to turn twenty and he knew he would be sought out for the *Service du travail obligatoire*, so he ran away over a week ago to join the Maquis. The other was the same age. They were inexperienced. Apparently, they came back after dark to plaster posters around Clairvaux when the Milice surprised them. They tried to make an escape but were caught hiding in the woods. At least that's what they say. There were no witnesses except the Germans and the Milice, so who can tell what really happened?'

'How did they know who they were?'

Sabine started to curse. 'They didn't have false papers. That was another mistake.'

'What did the Germans do with the bodies?'

'They photographed them and dragged them to the village square,' Armand said. 'Then they went to inform the families and took them in for questioning. They called for reinforcements and searched the woods in case there were other maquisards, which is why they came here. The soldier in charge hit me with the back of his pistol and threatened to kill us both if we didn't talk but there was nothing to tell. We didn't know anything until one of the villagers who works at the sawmill reported this to me just after you left. Fortunately, they believed us.'

The dogs wouldn't stop growling. Whatever took place had obviously upset them too. Elizabeth opened the door to let them out. Armand's cut was worsening by the minute and the blood continued to flow. Elizabeth's medical training kicked in and she fetched a bowl of hot water and a cloth.

'Sit down. Let me clean this before it turns nasty.' She gasped when she saw how bad it was. 'It needs sewing or you'll end up with a bad scar.'

Sabine fetched a medicine box and handed her a needle and silk thread for sutures. After sterilizing the needle, she set about sewing the skin together.

Armand was a large, sturdy man with thick-set features who'd suffered several bad injuries throughout his fifty-five years, but even he winced and gritted his teeth when Elizabeth set about sewing the wound. Sabine squeezed his shoulder watching on and trying hard not to show any emotion. After eight stitches, a dressing was applied.

'Keep it dry for at least two days,' Elizabeth said. 'If the dressing becomes wet from blood or any other liquid, it must be changed. Call me and I'll do it.'

It wasn't safe to venture to Clairvaux again that day. The thought of what Monique Dumont was going through in Lons-le-Saunier sent shudders down her spine. She was an important connection for Belvedere. Bistrot Jurassien was considered one of the safest places for letter-drops in the area. Now all she could do was hope she wouldn't be blamed for her son joining the Maquis. If so, it was highly likely she would be deported immediately — or worse. Elizabeth returned to the cottage to inform London she was setting out to look for Daniel and agent Mireille who she was sure, were still alive. London replied immediately. She was to proceed with caution.

CHAPTER 9

The funeral cortege meandered slowly through Clairvaux-les-Lacs to the cemetery in the Rue de Sapins. Elizabeth walked arm in arm alongside Sabine at the back with the rest of the women while Armand walked in front with the pallbearers carrying the casket containing Jean-Michel Dumont's body. The sky turned from a cloudless dove-grey to a deep graphite, threatening another spring shower. A cold wind started to whip up from across the lake carrying the pungent smell of incense through the street which mingled with the fragrant blossoms of the cherry trees whose branches spread across the road in a cloud of pink petals. Elizabeth pulled up her collar and pulled her headscarf low over her forehead with her gloved hand. All heads were bowed, not only out of respect, but because the villagers were only too aware of the Gestapo's presence viewing them with suspicion from the comfort of their cars parked in the square and near the cemetery. No-one was in doubt that they were making a note of all those in attendance. All the shops were shuttered and it seemed to Elizabeth that everyone was there, including any collaborators who would not want to make their identities known by not appearing to show respect to the dead boy.

The mourners passed through the cemetery gates and gathered around the grave to watch the casket gently being lowered into the earth. The priest read from the bible and said a few prayers. Elizabeth glanced over her shoulder and spotted two men in dark overcoats wearing broad brimmed hats watching at a distance over the wall. *Bastards*, she thought to herself. *Even in death they continue to bother us*. Monique Dumont's mother left an open jar of honey by the graveside to attract flies which the villagers believed held the souls of the deceased, and the priest gave the sign of the cross. Superstition and religion still played a big part in their lives, even in wartime.

After the funeral, the mourners filed past Monique Dumont to pay their respects. She stood erect, shoulders back, defiant against the Gestapo who watched them like a hawk. Neither would she shed a tear in front of them. That would mean they had won and her boy would have died in vain. She was too proud for that.

When it was Elizabeth's turn to pay her respects, Monique kissed her on both cheeks.

'Hello Marie-Élise. They told me you'd returned,' she said in a low voice.

'Monique, I am so sorry,'

'Don't be sad. He did not die in vain.' Monique was conscious of others waiting to pay their respects. 'Please come to the wake. You will be most welcome.'

The mourners made their way back to Bistrot Jurassien where a table of food was waiting for them. A large photo of Jean-Michel had been placed in the centre next to a vase of flowers. Monique kissed the tips of her fingers and tenderly placed them on her son's lips. She held them there for a few seconds, fighting back the tears.

'My son is a hero,' she said to everyone. 'He preferred to die rather than give his life to our hated oppressors.'

The mourners clenched their fists in the air and erupted into cheers. The blind accordionist played the first few notes of the Marseillaise and everyone started to sing. They were so loud that that two Gestapo men sitting in a black Citroën in the square outside heard it and got out to see what was going on. Through the window everyone could see them making their way towards the bistro. Refusing to be intimidated, they kept singing. Armand nodded to two other men and they went outside to confront them. Sabine edged closer to Elizabeth, fearing a backlash, but the backlash never occurred. Minutes later the men returned. Whatever they'd said worked and the mourners were left alone.

When the Marseillaise ended, the accordionist entertained them with other songs with a more jolly air. For the moment the defiance was over and the Gestapo returned to the car.

'I don't know what he said,' Elizabeth whispered to Sabine, 'but it worked.'

Sabine gave a shrug. 'They are still there and they will have made a note of everyone in here. Let's hope they don't come looking for you.'

'My papers are in order. I have nothing to worry about.'

Sabine raised one eyebrow and gave a little half-smile. 'We are playing a dangerous game.'

The wake lasted little longer than an hour. The villagers didn't want to push their luck.

Monique pulled Elizabeth aside. 'Come and see me the day after tomorrow. We can talk then. The other boy's funeral will be taking place in Cogna and they will be too busy watching them to bother us.' She indicated to the men sitting in the Citroën.

The guests dispersed and Sabine and Elizabeth climbed up on Armand's logging cart which he'd parked in the yard behind the bar. Another couple joined them. The cart clattered over the cobblestones and headed for the lake. At a point near the bridge, they noticed the same Citroën that had been parked outside the bar earlier. The men asked to see everyone's papers. One of them seemed more focused on Elizabeth than the others. Outwardly, she appeared confident and friendly: inwardly her stomach churned. The man scrutinized her papers in great detail, at one point holding them to the light. The others remained silent and apprehensive.

'Occupation?' the man asked.

'I'm a children's nanny.'

'Where are you staying?'

Elizabeth couldn't lie. 'At the moment I'm with Monsieur and Madame Menouillard.'

The man glanced at Sabine and Armand and stared at her for a few seconds before replying. 'They don't have any children so why are you staying with them?' He smirked, waiting for her reaction.

'That's true, but they do need people to help in the fields. It's hard to find employment as a nanny these days, and I need to eat so I am prepared to do anything.'

The man handed back her papers and waved her away with the back of his hand. He watched them as they rode way, then got in the car and headed in the direction of Lons-le-Saunier.

Everyone heaved a sigh of relief but Sabine commented that they would be back. She needed to take care.

*

Monique ushered Elizabeth into the salon at the back of the house, a street way from Bistrot Jurassien. The house was one of the oldest in the village and had belonged to her parents when they were alive. Elizabeth remarked on the beautiful view from the salon which overlooked the garden and rooftops of the lower section of the village towards the lake.

'I always loved this view. It's a perfect place to watch the changing seasons.' She turned towards her old friend and said again how sorry she was to hear about the death of her son.

'I begged him to wait until I could get him a new identity but he was afraid they would come for him. He'd heard of early morning *rafles* in other villages. They were plastering anti-German and Vichy propaganda notices when they were spotted by the Milice. Instead of giving themselves up they ran away. They didn't stand a chance.' Monique handed Elizabeth a small glass of her mother's home-made cherry liqueur. 'Anyway, I prefer not to dwell on it. Tell me about yourself. Where have you been? You look wonderful.'

Elizabeth avoided telling her she'd returned to England. Instead she said she'd been on an assignment elsewhere.

Monique smiled. 'I'm sorry, I shouldn't pry. It's just that I wondered what had happened to you as no-one mentioned you. I'm glad to see you're safe.'

Elizabeth wasted no time in saying why she wanted to see her. 'I heard about the raid on the Ledoux Farm and the subsequent *rafles*. The thing is, no-one seems to know anything about Daniel, André, and Amelie. I need your help. What do you think? Are they still alive or dead?'

Monique carried her glass to the window and looked out over the rooftops. 'It was a terrible time: January even more so. Several thousand people were deported after big raids on the 17, 22, 27 and the 31 of January, but we have no idea if they were connected. I'm sure Sabine and Armand have told you all that. I'm not sure what else I can add. The Germans have really cracked down.'

'You didn't answer my question. Do you think they are still alive?'

Elizabeth could see Monique was deliberating over what to say.

'Monique, if you know something, please tell me.'

Monique returned to her seat and offered Elizabeth a cigarette. After lighting one for herself, she sat back in the chair and exhaled slowly.

'Amelie — she's still alive — or at least she was a few weeks after the raid. I never got to know her as I did you, and I always wondered why she replaced you. I thought something bad had happened to you. Don't get me wrong. She was a nice girl, but you fitted in so well.

Amelie was a bit of a loner and I think some of the villagers viewed her with suspicion.'

'You said she was alive; how do you know? Did you see her?'

Monique pinched her lips together in an effort to recall the exact date. 'I think it was sometime between the raids of the 17 and 22 January. Yes, that's right.' She leaned forward a little. 'I don't want this conversation to leave this room,' she said in a low voice, even though there was no-one else around. 'I promised her I wouldn't breathe a word.'

'You have my word,' Elizabeth replied.

Monique relaxed a little. 'She knocked on my door in the middle of the night: gave me the fright of my life. I thought it was the Gestapo coming for Jean-Michel.'

'Why on earth would she do that?'

'She said she needed my help. She knew the Gestapo were watching her apartment and there was something in it she needed to get. She didn't want to contact Mitzi personally as she too was being watched. I told her I'd see what I could do and asked her to come back the next day. She was here less than two or three minutes. I had no idea where she was staying.'

'What did she want?' Elizabeth asked.

'A list of names written on a scrap of paper which she'd rolled up and pinned inside the hem of the lace curtain.'

Elizabeth smiled. A clever ruse which she herself had used on several occasions.

'It was so well-hidden I would never have found it if I hadn't known where to look.'

'Did you recognise any of the names on the list?'

Again, Monique looked uncomfortable. 'There were about fifteen and I didn't recognise any of them. Maybe they were aliases. I couldn't be sure.'

Elizabeth wanted to know how Monique got into the flat if the Gestapo were watching.

'That was easy. I went to the salon and told Mitzi I needed to get into Amelie's flat. It was she who suggested how to do it. She washed my hair and seated me in full view of the window where I could be seen by any passers-by and after putting my hair in rollers allowed me to move to the dryer which was out of view. From there I slipped out the back and up a flight of stairs and entered the apartment through a back door, while she kept watch. I was there no more than a few minutes.'

'Did Mitzi ask what you were looking for?'

Monique shook her head. 'No. We don't ask too many questions. It's safer that way.'

'And then what happened? Did Amelie return that night to collect it?'

'Yes. It was about four in the morning and I was beginning to think something had happened to her. This time I asked her in. She looked anxious and her face was drawn. I gave her the list and offered her something to eat. She was grateful and polished off the food in no time. I had the feeling she'd not slept or eaten well in days. Before she left, she begged me not to tell anyone about the list or that she'd seen me.' Monique sighed heavily. 'I've betrayed a trust, haven't I?'

Elizabeth put a reassuring hand on her friend's knee. 'No, you haven't. It's possible she's in great danger and if there are collaborators in our midst, then its natural she wouldn't want it to go any further — for your sake also.'

It was lunchtime and Monique asked if she would like to stay for a bite to eat. Elizabeth gladly accepted. Monique was an exceptional cook, and it would give her a chance to glean a little more information about what had been happening in the area. Monique had used her culinary skills to run Bistrot Jurassien for a few years until the death of her husband, from pneumonia, the previous winter. Now she ran the bar. Apart from weddings, funerals, and a few religious feasts, her culinary skills were put on hold.

Monique served a mouth-wateringly delicious potato gratin with smoked sausage and morels and a generous amount of melted Comté cheese. How much better people in the countryside ate compared with city dwellers. They ate it with a straw-coloured wine from Pierre's family vineyard in Château-Chalon.

Elizabeth told her she'd stayed with the Dassins in Lons-le-Saunier.

'He's a good man,' Monique said. 'I'm so grateful he can still look after us, but he's lost too many friends just lately, and he's putting on a brave face. I hear his wife is expecting again. He's very protective of her. God bless them both.'

An image of Juliette playing with Angeline flashed through her mind as she recalled Pierre's fear of her getting to know what was really going on. She wondered how long it could go on for. After they'd finished a second helping of gratin, Monique said she had something else to tell her. She went to the bookcase and took a large book from the top shelf. Hidden among the pages was a sheet of buff-coloured paper which looked as if it had been torn out of a notebook.

'I found it on the floor in the hall after Amelie left. She must have dropped it when she put her coat back on. I thought she might have realised and come back for it, but she never did.'

Elizabeth's eyes widened. It was a hand-drawn map with rough pencil markings showing what appeared to be two winding roads, the smaller one joining the larger one at a junction. On the left side were a series of upside down U-shapes dotted with simplistic drawings of fir trees, and among them were four X's. There was also a curved line marked with slashes which suggested a train line. Another line of intermittent dashes meandered through the trees, and next to two of the crosses were letters and numbers — G.1 and G.2. Next to another were three small wavy lines on top of each other. Elizabeth was stunned. How could Amelie be so careless?

They tried to determine what the markings stood for but it was not easy.

'Obviously these two are roads and this particular spot is a junction.' Monique pointed to a spot near the centre of the page. 'And the upside down U's must be mountains with woods or forests.'

'This could be a train line,' Elizabeth added, 'and I think the three wavy lines represent water. We used it during our map-making training.'

'Then it must be a lake,' replied Monique. 'What else could it be?'

Elizabeth agreed. The region was also filled with waterfalls and rivers, but they ruled them out.

'So if it's a lake, it must be in this area — and not far from a train line.'

Monique laughed. 'Do you know how many lakes there are around here?'

'They are not all surrounded by woods and forests though.'

The map had several fold marks and stains on it. Elizabeth held it to her nose.

'It smells of tobacco — Gauloises.'

Monique burst out laughing again. 'Almost every man in France smokes them, especially Resistance fighters. They are considered patriotic and an affiliation to our French heartland values.' She picked up her own packet and lit another and made a tutting sound. 'Marie-Élise, you will need more to go on than that.'

Elizabeth ignored her. 'Take a look at this,' she said.

Monique peered over her shoulder. Next to the wavy lines was a small t. It was smudged and barely visible due to a brown stain. 'It doesn't have two horizontal bars so it can't symbolize the Cross of Lorraine.'

'It could denote a religious cross: maybe a church.'

'Take it with you,' Monique said. 'If anyone can make sense of it, it's you.'

After days of speculation, Elizabeth finally had something to go on, however tenuous, and she thanked her and promised not to breathe a word about it to anyone — not even the Menouillards — although she did think they might have been able to help.

'Another thing,' Monique said as Elizabeth prepared to leave. 'You may want to pay a visit to Mitzi. She may be able to answer more of your questions.'

'I intended to do that but thought I'd wait a few days until things quietened down and the Gestapo stopped hanging around.'

CHAPTER 10

April 1944. Clairvaux-les-Lacs.

Elizabeth spent the next few days poring over the local maps to see if anything matched Amelie's rough drawing. At first, she wondered if the X's were Maquis camps, but decided against it as she couldn't believe Amelie would carry a map around that might make them a target if the map fell into the wrong hands. Convinced that the three wavy lines symbolized water, she looked at the lakes in the area. It couldn't be the Grand Lac de Clairvaux because the position of the mountains didn't fit. Maybe it was the Petit Lac? She ruled that out too. Neither did she think it was the lac de Chalain or lac d'Ilay. They were too big, although they did have mountains to one side.

One thing bothered her greatly. Surely Amelie must have realised she accidentally dropped the map in Monique's house. If so, why didn't she go back for it? And why did she carry a map like this in the first place? Elizabeth had already memorized it. Why didn't Amelie? Carrying such a thing could have untold consequences. Perhaps she wasn't as clever as everyone made out, but then, everyone lets their guard down at some time or other.

Elizabeth's head thumped with studying maps for almost two days, and her neck ached. Seeing it was a beautiful day, she decided to go for a bike ride to clear her mind. She put Amelie's map in a tin container and hid it in the woodshed along with the transmitter. Cycling along the winding driveway towards the main road, she passed Armand directing two trucks filled with logs towards the sawmill, an indication that the logging activities had started up again after the heavy winter and spring rains.

'How's the cut?' she asked, noticing he wasn't wearing the bandage any longer. She took a closer look and told him she'd be round later in the evening to take the stitches out.

Cycling through the countryside was one of the joys of being in France and today was a perfect spring day: cloudless blue skies and warmth that lightened the soul. She had no idea where she was going and set off in the direction of Moirans-en-Montagne, passing the Grand Lac and the Petit Lac that sparkled in the sunshine like a cracked mirror. All she wanted to do was to shed the turmoil of the last few weeks and lose herself in the beauty of the countryside. It wasn't difficult to do. The Jura was beautiful at any time of the year, but particularly in spring when the green meadows were flecked with a profusion of wildflowers: the blue-violet of the Field Scabulous which always reminded her of thistles, and bright pink Rosebay Willowherb, whose scent lingered in the air and could be tasted in the local cheese. Most of all, her favourite was the yellow Gentian which the villagers harvested to make into a liqueur drunk as a digestif.

As a child, Elizabeth had travelled for miles exploring the small villages with their centuries-old churches and market places. She'd missed that in London. When she returned to work with Belvedere, she relished being able to use her cycling skills as a courier. It was nothing for her to cover thirty or forty kilometres a day. It kept her fit and as Guy said, gave her a good set of legs into the bargain.

Before long, the meadows gave way to woodland and dense forest filled with spruce and pines, and here and there, piles of timber lay stacked at the side of the road. For most of the winter they had lain under the thick blankets of snow that cloaked the Haute Jura for as far as the eye could see. Now they were ready to be picked up and taken to one of the many sawmills in the area. The pleasant ride was almost marred when a German truck passed her near Charchilla, almost five kilometres away from Moirans-en-Montagne. It had the tarpaulin down and the six soldiers riding in the back waved to her.

'*Guten Tag, schöne Frau. Gute Fahrt.* Enjoy your ride.'

Whether it was the beautiful day or she just didn't want to antagonise them, she waved back. Only when she reached Moirans-en-Montagne did the harsh reality of war bring her back to earth again. The square was filled with Wehrmacht vehicles and two tanks, and soldiers patrolled the town. She was asked for her papers and then allowed to go on unhindered. Outside the town, she turned left into the mountains and decided to stop at the side of the road to eat her hard-boiled egg, cheese, and slice of bread. It was past midday and the sun was warming up giving her cheeks a rosy glow. She folded her cardigan into a pillow and rested her head on it. A stream of white clouds floated across the blue sky and nearby, a choir of bees hummed in a sea of wildflowers — hypnotic and soothing. She could easily have drifted off, but a sudden thought flashed through her mind. Pierre had mentioned André had been seen carrying someone to a doctor in Villards-d'Héria and she recalled a signpost with the name of the village just outside Moirans-en-Montagne. It wasn't that far away. The doctor was deported but the son was still here. Maybe — just maybe — the wife and son might be able to shed some light on that fateful night of the raid on the Ledoux Farm. It was worth a try. She clambered back on her bike again and rode off in the direction of the village.

Villards-d'Héria was a sleepy village surrounded by beautiful forests, and like most villages in the region at this time of the day, there was no-one around except for an old man sitting on a bench in the square. He had both hands firmly clasped over a shepherd's crook and eyed her with curiosity. She asked him where the doctor's house was.

'Over there.' He nodded his head in the direction of a row of houses by the church. 'But if it's the doctor you're after, you won't find him. The Germans took him away.'

'Actually it's his wife I want to see. Does she still live there?'

'She does, poor woman, but she's not herself these days.'

Elizabeth thanked him and went over to the house. She knocked on the door several times but no-one answered. It was definitely the right house: the plaque was still on the door — Dr Raymond Berger. It was only then that she realized she had not known his name. She took a few steps back to survey the place. Something caught her eye. The curtain in a window on the upper floor moved. There was definitely someone inside and she wasn't going away until they opened the door. She knocked again. This time more loudly. After some minutes, the door opened, but only slightly, and a woman with the eyes of a frightened rabbit peered at her. After checking that she was indeed Madame Berger, Elizabeth assured her she was not here to cause trouble. She just wanted a word with her. The door opened a little wider — just enough for Elizabeth to slip inside. She was shocked to see the state of the woman standing before her. She was skin and bones and her face bore a haunted look.

'Who are you and what do you want?' Madame Berger asked. 'I don't know anything.'

'My name is Marie-Élise. I'd just like to ask you a couple of questions. It won't take long.'

She was ushered into the drawing room and told to take a seat. Madame Berger sat down opposite her with her hands folded on her lap and waited for Elizabeth to continue.

'First let me say how distressed I was to hear what happened to the good doctor.'

The doctor's wife's face remained unmoved. Elizabeth looked at her with pity. She had probably never smiled again since the day her husband was taken away.

'The thing is,' Elizabeth continued, 'I'm trying to locate a good friend of mine who went missing after the raid on the Ledoux Farm. I know many people died or were deported afterwards but no-one seems to know anything at all about my friend. There are no records of him being deported and his body has never been discovered.'

'Are you a relative?' Madame Berger asked. 'Or his girlfriend?'

Her direct question threw Elizabeth and she paused to take a deep breath. 'I'm a friend, that's all — a close friend.'

'What do you want to know? I told you, I don't know anything. My husband never discussed his work with me.'

'I was told that on the night of the raid on the Ledoux Farm, one of the maquisards, a man called André, came to your house sometime in the early morning. He had a man with him who was badly injured. Is this correct?'

Madame Berger's hands started to shake. 'That's right.'

'Can you tell me what happened?'

'It was during the early hours of the morning. We heard a knock on the door.'

Elizabeth could tell the woman was distressed and hated herself for adding to her misery.

'Every time you hear a knock in the night, you fear the worst; the Gestapo — Milice — or some other hateful person with the devil in his heart. Raymond looked out of the window and told me to go back to sleep: it was only a maquisard. How could I sleep? A man doesn't come to your house in the middle of the night for nothing! When he opened the door, there were two of them: André and another man. I'd seen André before, but I had no idea who the other man was. Both men were injured, but the second one more so. Raymond took them into his surgery and asked me to fetch our son. At the time he lived in the village. The men were so anxious that I should not be seen that

I had to go the long way around. The weather was terrible, cold and icy and beginning to snow. Even though I wrapped up well, I was still chilled to the bone. When I returned with my son, André came out of the surgery and took him aside so that I couldn't hear what they were saying. I saw the look of concern on my son's face. "There was a raid on a farm not far away. The other man is seriously injured," my son said to me. "They've taken his clothes outside and hidden them until we can burn them. I don't want you to worry, Maman, so please go to bed and get some sleep. We'll call you if we need you."

'A few hours later, the Gestapo arrived. They raided all the villages within the vicinity and being a doctor's house, we were one of the first on their list just in case anyone was injured and came to seek help. When they hammered on the door, my husband asked me to open it. He told me to tell them he'd gone to Champagnole to get medicines with our son and would be visiting relatives while they were there. Most likely they had not returned because of the curfew. In the meantime, they hid the man and themselves outside. I was held at gunpoint while the premises were searched. I had no idea what they would find in his surgery, but fortunately they'd cleaned it up so well and there was no trace of what took place earlier. In the end the Gestapo left telling me that my husband and son must both report to the police station in Moirans-en-Montagne on their return. I was shaking like a leaf.

'After they'd gone, my husband and son came back inside carrying the injured man back into the surgery. I went to bed but couldn't sleep a wink. In the morning my husband came into the bedroom to speak with me. He looked terrible. He told me they were still trying to save the second man, but having to hide outside had not helped the situation. When I asked what his injuries were, he shook his head despondently replying that he was shot and suffered severe shrapnel and burn wounds from an explosion. He was alive, but only just.'

Elizabeth felt a lump rise in her throat and she had difficulty breathing. Madame Berger saw this and got up to fetch a glass of water before continuing.

'My husband saw the look of fear on my face. I was so scared the Germans would come back. They always did after a raid like that — and I panicked.'

Elizabeth's eyes widened. 'What do you mean — you panicked? What did you do?'

'I told him he couldn't keep the man here. What if someone saw them? I couldn't think straight. My son heard our raised voices and came in to the room. "Maman, the man is too ill to be moved." In the end I calmed down and they promised to move him the next day.'

Elizabeth didn't like what she was hearing. Madame Berger was not the sort of person to cope with stress and she had second thoughts about being there. If the Germans got wind someone had been asking questions, she would buckle.

'What about André? Was he still here as well?'

'No. My husband patched him up and he left soon after he dropped the man off — just before the Germans arrived.'

'And did they move the stranger the next day as you asked?'

Madame Berger nodded and her face bore a look of guilt. 'Yes. My husband and son begged me to change my mind, especially as it snowed heavily the next day, but I was too afraid for them. It was past midnight and I remember watching them both wrap the man in blankets and put him on the sled. He was still unconscious. Then they took their skis from the hallway and left. I regret it now but I will have to live with it. I always wondered what happened to him.' Her eyes seemed to ask for Elizabeth's forgiveness. 'I did it for my family, you understand. I am sure you would have done the same in my situation.'

Elizabeth knew it would be hard for someone with such terrible injuries to survive if he was exposed to the cold Jura winter. Knowing that, she feared she was coming to a dead end.

'Did you actually see the man?' she asked, trying desperately to glean more information no matter how small.

'Yes. When my husband and son were elsewhere, I went in to the surgery to take a look for myself.'

'Can you describe him?'

'It was difficult as there were lots of bandages. I think he had dark hair; slightly wavy. Obviously, I couldn't see his eyes, but I do recall he had long dark lashes — and a slim moustache.'

'How tall was he?'

'That's a difficult one.' Madame Berger thought for a moment. 'I remember his feet reached the end of the examination table so I would say, he was tall — almost two metres.'

Elizabeth felt her heart race and, tenuous as this information was, she experienced a glimmer of hope. Guy did have dark wavy hair *and* he was noted for his deep brown eyes framed by long dark lashes. The height fitted too. When he left England he also had a moustache, but then, he had been known to have a beard at times too.

'Do you know where your husband and son took him?'

Madame Berger shook her head. 'They didn't tell me. After my husband was taken away by the Germans, my son and I never spoke about that night again. I'm sorry. That's all I can tell you.'

Elizabeth told her she'd been an enormous help and she didn't blame her for being scared and wanting the man gone. She had some sympathy for her predicament and if anything, felt sorry for her. She could see she was a gentle, kind-hearted woman, but the stress of living under occupation took its toll on everyone. She asked if she might have a word with her son. Maybe he would be prepared to tell her more. Madame Berger's anxiousness flared up again.

'He doesn't live in the village any longer. He rents the apartment above the pharmacy in Moirans-en-Montagne where he works, but at the moment he's in Lyon. He told me he was going to try and obtain pharmaceuticals and other things which are in short supply. I don't know how long he'll be away. I can tell him you called. What is your address? Maybe he can contact you.'

Elizabeth was reluctant to give her address. 'Please don't put yourself out. I'll call again in a few days.' Madame Berger saw Elizabeth to the door. 'Oh, one more thing,' she said, as she picked up her bicycle. 'What is your son's name?'

'Antoine.' She reached for the handlebars blocking Elizabeth's way. 'You won't tell anyone about our conversation will you?'

'I can assure you I will be discreet,' Elizabeth replied.

On the way back to Clairvaux, Elizabeth cycled past the pharmacy in Moirans-en-Montagne. It was indeed closed. There was a tobacconist and wine shop next door and she went in to inquire when it would reopen.

'He's gone to Lyon,' the man said. 'He goes every week to stock up. He should be back in two days' time.'

Elizabeth cycled away, relieved that at least he corroborated Madame Berger's reason for her son's absence. Back at the cottage, she pulled out the map again. She had already pored over the area many times but after what she's just learned, she couldn't envisage a man with such severe injuries being transported too far away. If the injured man was Guy, he must have been taken somewhere nearby. Hanging on to a thread of hope, she scrutinized the area around

Villards-d'Héria and the Ledoux Farm. She also knew from Vera Atkins where the drop had taken place that night. Working within a radius of ten to fifteen kilometres, something jumped out at her. There was a small lake near Villards-d'Héria — Lac d'Antre — and it was surrounded by mountains. Her heart raced, yet the more she compared the local map to Amelie's, the more she decided it could not be the area. In the first place, there was not a junction, and secondly, there were no train-lines. She'd come to a dead end. Frustrated, she went over to the Menouillards to join them for dinner. Seeing the look on her face, Armand went to get another bottle of wine.

'This will help take your mind off things.'

He was right. It had the desired effect. Before she accepted the offer of a top-up, she wanted to take out his stitches. Armand grimaced and downed another glass.

'It's healed beautifully,' Elizabeth told him. 'In a week or so, you won't see a thing.'

CHAPTER 11

A few days after the funerals of Jean-Michel and his friend, the German presence in Clairvaux relaxed but no-one was in any doubt that collaborators were still keeping an eye out for them. Outwardly, it was business as usual: in reality, the villagers distrusted their neighbours even more. Elizabeth decided it was time to visit Mitzi and made an appointment to have her hair done. Mitzi was thrilled to see her back again and shut up shop in order for them to talk freely. She was still involved with the Resistance and the first thing she wanted to know was when the Allies would be landing. By now it was common knowledge something would happen, but few knew when or where. After assuring her it would be soon, Elizabeth wasted no time in asking what happened around the time of the raid.

'It was as much a surprise to me as it was to everyone,' Mitzi replied, lathering Elizabeth's hair in the bowl. 'Things seemed to be going well.'

'Were you aware they didn't find Daniel's body at the farm?' Elizabeth asked.

'Yes, I heard.'

'His name has not been found on any deportation list either.'

Mitzi towel-dried Elizabeth's hair and moved her over to the mirror. 'I don't know about that, but it wouldn't surprise me. They do move people without recording their names you know. Maybe he gave them another name.'

Elizabeth had already thought of that. 'If he did, he would have used another identity.' She didn't want to tell Mitzi about the doctor and his son. 'Who's in charge of the false papers in the area these days?'

'As far as I know, it's the same people you used to deal with: Didier in Champagnole and Bernard from Chaux-du-Dombief near Saint-Laurent-en-Grandvaux, but I heard he's moved again.'

'And neither of them was caught up in the round-ups?'

'No. Maybe because they live further afield. The Resistance and maquisards around here still use them. There are others in Saint-Claude and Lons-le-Saunier but I have no idea about them. It was Didier who was arranging a false identity for Jean-Michel. Didn't Monique tell you that?'

Elizabeth shook her head. She hadn't thought to ask her and maybe Monique didn't think it was important.

Elizabeth really wanted to know about Amelie. 'What can you tell me about Amelie? I'm trying to find her and I believe she rented the apartment above the salon.'

'That's right. I didn't see too much of her though. She was away most of the time. When she was here, she would often come and see me. I used to style her hair for her and in exchange she would give me manicures and pedicures. She was good company and an excellent beautician. Occasionally she and I went to the bar for a drink, but apart from that she kept to herself — that is when she didn't spend the evenings with her friend, Paul-Emille. I can't tell you anything else except that I missed her after she left.'

'Did she tell you she was leaving?' Elizabeth asked.

Mitzi stood back a little to check Elizabeth's hair. 'She said she might be going away for a while, but as she was always away, I didn't think anything of it. Naturally I expected her to return, even after the raid, but she never did. I suppose she got wind the Germans were looking for her too. They came here and searched the place the same night the raid took place at the Ledoux Farm, but she never left any incriminating evidence. She was clever like that. Even so, they still watched this place like hawks for a while. I was lucky not to have been rounded up as a suspect myself. I often wonder what happened to her.'

'I gather she was having an affair with Paul-Emille,' Elizabeth said. 'Did they meet here?'

'He stayed in a house near the bridge and came to see her whenever she was back in the village. Occasionally he came here even when she wasn't here. She asked me if he could have a key.' Mitzi smiled. 'I'm not sure how long the affair had been going on but I could tell they were very much in love. Paul-Emille was arrested as he was entering his house. They were waiting for him. I dread to think what would have happened if he was here that night.'

'Do you know if they found his radio?'

'I doubt it. He would have hidden it somewhere, but not on the premises. I know that because Amelie said he was always careful and even she didn't know where he kept it.'

'Do you remember the last time you saw her?'

Mitzi folded up the towel, laid down the hairbrush, and showed Elizabeth the back of her hair with a small hand mirror. 'I remember it well. She didn't seem to be her usual self. She had dark hair but she asked me to lighten it — considerably. When I told her it wouldn't suit her, she snapped at me and just asked me to do as she asked. Then she told me something which at the time seemed insignificant. It was only later — after the raid — that it bothered me. She and Paul-Emille had had an argument. She told him she suspected someone had it in for her and he thought she was imagining things.'

Elizabeth's ears pricked up. 'How do you mean?'

'Amelie had admirers, but Paul-Emille also had his own admirers. He was a handsome man you know, and charming too. There was this one young woman from the village of Patornay; her name is Liliane but everyone knows her as Lili. She used to follow him around. Love-struck she was.'

Elizabeth was surprised at this latest revelation. Why hadn't Sabine or Armand mentioned it? 'Why didn't he just tell her he wasn't interested?' she asked.

'Maybe he did, but she was what you would call...' Mitzi made a circling gesture next to her temple with her hand. 'We called her Liliane. *Pauvre Lili, elle est simplette*, people used to say. You know, a bit simple.'

Silly as it appeared, something about this latest revelation rang alarm bells with Elizabeth.

'Why would Amelie let a thing like that bother her?'

'Because she thought the girl was following her. Paul-Emille thought she was being overly sensitive, but she was deadly serious. As far as I know it was the only thing they argued over. I even heard them myself one night. I went upstairs and asked them to keep the noise down. Paul-Emille picked up his jacket and left, almost knocking me over. They both apologised the next day.'

'Mitzi,' Elizabeth said in a low voice. 'People in our position can't afford to have enemies – crazy or not! I don't blame her for being upset. Did she tell Daniel?'

'I don't know.'

Elizabeth offered to pay Mitzi for her hair but she refused. 'If I can be of any more assistance, let me know.'

*

The cottage door was locked and the radio was on the kitchen table ready to transmit. Elizabeth went over her encryption one more time and at the allocated hour started to communicate with London. Nervously, she tapped out her signal, being careful not to make any mistakes and including the all-important security check.

BELIEVE D AND M ALIVE LISETTE

Shortly after midnight an answer came and she deciphered it.

SENDING TWO FFI PACKAGES ADVISE COORDINATES EXERCISE EXTREME CAUTION

London also sent her a coded message to give to the Resistance chiefs in the area. The invasion was imminent. She knew that would indeed make them very happy, especially Pierre, who was now her main contact in Lons-le-Saunier, and the Menouillards. Elizabeth pulled down the antenna, packed up the transmitter, and hid it back in the woodshed. The warmth of the day had cooled and while waiting for London to reply, she'd made a small fire. In no-time at all, the cottage had warmed up nicely. She boiled herself a cup of ersatz coffee and sat by the hearth, poking the fire with an iron poker. The glowing embers twirled in a fiery dance, occasionally shooting out wisps of smoke into the room. A comforting smell of woodsmoke drifted through the house like fragrant incense. Uppermost in her mind was Guy. Madame Berger's description could very well fit Guy. *Dear God, let him be safe*, she said to herself. She pictured him walking through the door at any minute, taking her in his arms and smothering her with kisses. *See, I'm safe after all. You worried for nothing.* She finished her coffee, silently cursing Vera Atkins and Buckmaster for not sending her back with him, then quickly pulled herself together. *No good crying over spilt milk. Get on with the job in hand. That's why they sent you.*

In the morning she opened the shutters and saw Armand walking along the path with a basket. Pierre was with him. He greeted her with a friendly kiss.

'This is a lovely surprise and couldn't have been timelier. I was going to contact you,' she said.

Armand pulled six brown eggs and a loaf from the basket and

Elizabeth offered to make them breakfast. Pierre accepted, but Armand said he'd already eaten and had far too much work on to hang around chatting. He left, saying he was expecting more logs to arrive at any moment.

'What brings you to Clairvaux at such an early hour?' Elizabeth asked as she started to gently whisk the eggs in readiness for an omelette.

'It's Juliette. She's in labour. I wondered if you'd care to come and stay with us for a few days — just until the birth.'

Elizabeth stopped whisking and looked at him anxiously. 'I thought she wasn't due for another month.'

'That's what we thought. Perhaps the doctor got the dates wrong.'

'Is she in pain?'

'Yes. And she's scared. I think this is going to be a difficult birth.'

Elizabeth's thoughts flashed to the pharmacy. Uppermost in her mind was Antoine. Seeing him was her top priority. If she went to Lons-le-Saunier, God knows how long she could be there. Maybe it was a false alarm and the baby wouldn't come for another few weeks. That sort of thing was common.

Pierre could see the hesitation on her face. 'I know you've got important work to do and I wouldn't have bothered you if it wasn't serious, but Juliette asked for you because you're a nurse.' He paused for a moment. 'And we trust you.'

She finished cooking the omelette and slid it onto a plate. 'Eat up first and we'll get going.'

CHAPTER 12

Elizabeth took the opportunity to catch up on what Pierre had been doing while they were driving back to Lons-le-Saunier. He was heartened by the news that General Charles de Gaulle had announced he was taking command of all Free French forces, thinking that it would unite the various Resistance forces who were prone to acting on their own impulses and putting everyone at risk. When she told him of the impending arrival of the two French operatives, this particularly pleased him and he assured her he would arrange a meeting with the local Resistance groups as soon as possible. They were in dire need of assistance and arms since the round-ups of the last few months.

'I've been thinking about you since you left,' he said. 'Wondering if your investigations were beginning to bear fruit.'

'I believe so. I'm following a few leads at the moment although the pieces of the jigsaw are not coming together yet.'

'How do you mean?'

'When I last saw you, you mentioned André was observed carrying someone to the doctor's house sometime after the ambush at the Ledoux Farm.'

'Yes, that's right.'

'It puzzles me why you never found out who it was. Did anyone make enquiries?'

Pierre threw her a sideways glance. 'I'm not sure what you're getting at. Everyone kept their heads down after that — at least until things quietened down. Some of our men went to offer condolences to Madame Berger. When she was asked about André she didn't say a word. He wasn't the only one arrested in Villards-d'Héria; a few more were taken in at the same time and all were deported, so it could have been one of them who saw them.'

Knowing how badly Madame Berger had reacted to Elizabeth's visit, she quickly understood why she hadn't told a soul. Probably she was the only one who knew the full story — and Antoine.

'Did you know her son, Antoine, was there that night?' Elizabeth asked.

Pierre pulled the van up at the side of the road. 'Spit it out! What's bothering you?'

'Did you or did you not know Antoine was there that night?'

Pierre shook his head. 'No. How did you find that out?'

'This is between you and me, but I paid her a visit yesterday. She still bears the mental scars of what took place and was reluctant to talk. However, when she saw I meant her no harm, she confided to me that her husband had asked her to fetch her son and together they patched André and the stranger up. André's injuries weren't so bad and he left soon after. The Gestapo did indeed raid the place but didn't find them because her husband and son had hidden the stranger outside. After the Gestapo left, she became scared and pleaded with her husband to get him out of the house, which they did the next night. She has no idea who he was or where they took him. All I can tell you is that both the doctor and his son acted together. As you know, Antoine is still working in Moirans-en-Montagne as a pharmacist. I called by but he'd gone to Lyon.' She paused for a minute. 'And it might be wishful thinking, but from her description, I think the stranger could be Daniel.'

Pierre stared out of the van window. '*Merde!*'

'Antoine is one of us,' he replied after it had sunk in. 'I trust him with my life.'

'Then why did he never tell you this?' Elizabeth asked. 'If it was Daniel, then he helped the head of Belvedere and never said a word!'

'I'm as shocked as you. All I can say is that he would have had his reasons. If what you're saying is true,' he looked her into the eyes, 'then he must have been sworn to secrecy.'

He lit up a cigarette and Elizabeth wound down the van window to let in some fresh air.

'I was going to visit him,' she said, 'until you arrived.'

Pierre started to apologise. He told her he would take her back to the farm straight away if that's what she wanted. He would manage with Juliette the best he could. Elizabeth could see he was upset. She put a hand on his knee.

'No. It can wait a few days. For the moment, Juliette needs us so we'd better get a move on.'

He pulled her hand to his lips and kissed it before driving off again. 'I promise you, we'll get to the bottom of this.'

By the time they arrived in Lons-le-Saunier, Juliette's waters had broken and she was in severe distress. The doctor had been called but hadn't arrived and the local midwife was busy elsewhere. Instead, two neighbours were attempting to help and a terrified Angeline was providing pressure on her mother's back. Elizabeth's nursing background kicked in again, but unlike Armand's gash, she knew this was not going to be easy. She had delivered enough babies to know when a problem presented itself. She put her arm around Juliette's shoulder and tried to calm her down.

'You did right to call me,' she whispered to Pierre, 'but these women are making things worse. Get them out of here — and bring me bowls of hot water, towels, and a freshly washed apron.'

Pierre did as she ordered while Angeline was sent to her room with her doll.

'Is she going to be alright?' Pierre asked, returning to the room with everything she'd asked for.

Rather than give him false hope, Elizabeth chose not to answer. She quickly put on the clean apron and washed her hands.

'I need to check her. It's up to you if you stay here or not, but if you do, make yourself useful and try and comfort her.' She moved Juliette into a better position in order to examine her. Pierre could tell by the look on her face, it wasn't good news.

'It's a breech,' Elizabeth said. 'Feet first: I'm going to have to turn it.'

Juliette continued to scream and both Elizabeth and Pierre did their best to try and calm her. At one point, she started to lose consciousness. Pierre bathed her forehead with a hand-towel, while whispering words of comfort in her ear. 'We are here for you, my darling. Stay strong.'

'Not long now,' Elizabeth said, beads of sweat beginning to trickle down her forehead. 'Take deep breaths. We're almost there.'

Half an hour later, the baby arrived. The birth was traumatic but the child was alive.

'It's a boy.' Elizabeth smiled. 'A healthy boy.'

She cut the cord, bathed the child and wrapped it in a towel and placed it on a barely conscious Juliette's chest. Pierre was silently shedding tears.

'How can I ever thank you?'

It was not over yet. The placenta was taking longer to come out than usual and she rubbed Juliette's belly with circular movements, constantly checking to see what was happening. She had lost a lot of blood and Elizabeth feared an infection. Silently she prayed. *Please dear Lord, save her.*

After some time, the placenta finally came away. Elizabeth set about bathing Juliette with warm water laced with soothing herbs and the metallic smell of blood was soon replaced by the scent of lavender and chamomile.

'She needs lots of rest,' she said to Pierre as she wiped her hands, 'but she's going to be fine.'

Juliette was weak but lucid enough to know her child was alive. Her joy and relief were palpable, but she was exhausted. She touched his face gently, smiled and closed her eyes. Pierre took the child from her and held it in his arms.

Elizabeth looked at him and caught her breath, recalling the miscarriage she'd had.

'Do you have a name?' she asked.

Pierre shook his head and laughed. 'Juliette was convinced it would be a girl.'

'Well you have all the time in the world. For the moment let's introduce Angeline to her baby brother — and then maybe we can celebrate with one of your finest wines.'

It took a couple of days before Elizabeth felt confident that Juliette would make a full recovery. Money was tight but Pierre wanted to savour the joy of his son's birth and be there for his wife for a few days before going back to work again. With neither of them having parents nearby, he was grateful to have Elizabeth there to help. She cooked and cleaned, and both she and Pierre took turns sitting with Juliette until she was able to get out of bed.

It was Easter, and Elizabeth decided to go into town to buy flowers for her. It was also an excuse to get out of the house. She couldn't get Antoine out of her mind and needed to return to Clairvaux as soon as possible. She'd given Pierre a few days to arrange meetings with several local Resistance leaders and after that she would leave. Time was also running out before the full moon too and she had to locate a good landing site before then. There was a lot to do and to make matters worse, the telephone lines in the area had been down for three days making communications difficult, even though they mostly used letter-drops.

The beautiful weather had brought people out of their homes. The cafés were beginning to fill and people were promenading, albeit under the watchful eyes of the Germans. After buying a small bunch of red tulips, she found a table outside le Grand Café du Théatre in the centre of town and ordered a glass of wine. It was noticeable to everyone that there was an exceptional amount of German traffic heading west through the town: convoys of trucks, armoured vehicles, and cars filled with both German officials in uniform and men in smart civilian clothes. It signalled something was seriously wrong and she wondered what it could be. Just as the waiter arrived with the wine, she saw three plain-clothed Germans get out of a black Citroën and approach the café. No-one was to leave until they'd checked everyone's papers. Elizabeth recognised one of them as the same man who'd stopped and checked their papers in Clairvaux. She hoped he'd go to the other side of the café, but it wasn't to be.

'Your papers, please, Mademoiselle.' At first, Elizabeth wasn't sure if he recognised her but then she knew the Gestapo better than that. 'Ah, the children's nanny,' he said, giving her the same smirk he'd given her before. 'What brings you here? Did you find employment after all?' He glanced at the roses on the table.

Elizabeth smiled sweetly. 'Yes I did, thank you.'

'And where would that be?'

It was hard to conceal where she was staying as she knew it was likely he would check on her. He already knew where she stayed in Clairvaux.

'I'm staying with a family for a couple of weeks. The wife had a difficult birth and needs help. After that I shall look for other work.' She paused. 'I came into town to buy her flowers.'

'Address?'

Elizabeth dreaded this question and told them the truth.

He recognised it. 'Oh, Dassin the wine merchant!'

He handed her back her papers and moved on. For the moment he had more to occupy himself with. A man had tried to escape through a back door but had been caught and was being dragged through the crowd at gunpoint. The men shoved him roughly into the back of the car as the café patrons looked on in silence. After they'd left, the patrons resumed their socializing, albeit less happily than before.

Elizabeth paid the waiter and left. She needed to warn Pierre.

'I'm careful,' he replied. 'Besides, there wouldn't be a house in the town that has not been subject to their surprise visits.' He pointed to a large cupboard. 'That's where I keep a few bottles of the finest Château-Chalon wine. It's amazing how a few bottles of those can bend even the hardest men.' Elizabeth wasn't too sure about that. 'I have some good news for you,' he added.

'Is the telephone working?'

He frowned. 'No, the lines are still down, but I've had a message from Father Henri. We've arranged a meeting tonight with three of the Resistance chiefs.'

At some point around midnight, Pierre and Elizabeth made their way to meet Father Henri at the church. They found him in a highly agitated state. He informed them that there had been *rafles* around Saint-Claude and wondered why Pierre hadn't been warned. It was put down to the telephone lines being down. Because of this news, they went to a different safe house a few miles outside the town. The other men were already waiting for them. Elizabeth was familiar with these rendezvous as she'd been privy to quite a few during her time with Belvedere. These Resistance chiefs were relatively new, having replaced those who had been killed or deported, but that didn't make them any less effective. "Brando" worked in the water department in Lons-le-Saunier, and was a good friend of the Dassins: "Max" was a clerk in the municipal offices at Orgelet, and the other, "Gavroche", a maquisard from the village of Saint-Amour. All were highly skilled in subversive work, cunning, and admired by their men. No-one wasted time getting down to business, but the first news they had to impart was not encouraging. In the few days she'd been in Lons-le-Saunier, the Germans were in the process of another crack-down. This time it was much worse than previous.

Brando spoke first and what he said filled Elizabeth with dread. The *Groupes Mobile de Reserve* — Vichy paramilitary groups, together with the *Sicherheitsdienst des Reichsführers* – the German Secret Intelligence agency of the SS, based in Lyon, had instigated a surprise attack in the Haute Jura, in particular the area around Saint-Claude. What frightened her most was that it involved Klaus Barbie whose reputation was already known to the hierarchy in the Resistance. It was said that he personally tortured adult and child prisoners, earning him the nickname of the "Butcher of Lyon". The stories that reached them filled everyone with dread. Max said he was seen heading to Saint-Claude. Few knew what he looked like, but one of Max's men had been interrogated by him personally at the Hotel Terminus in Lyon and had managed to escape.

Unknown to Elizabeth, while she had been tending Juliette, there had been a *rafle* in Saint-Claude on Good Friday, two days earlier. Martial law was established and a curfew imposed from 8:00 p.m. to 6:00 a.m. Several people had been arrested, including foreign Jews. The next day the Germans scoured the countryside and executed twenty people.

Pierre paced the room cursing that none of his informants had personally contacted him. Now Elizabeth realised why there was so much activity in the town earlier that day. The worst was yet to come. It was Easter Sunday and while the people in Lons-le-Saunier were at church services, in Saint-Claude, the day had quickly descended into what was to be known as Bloody Sunday. It was not just Saint-Claude: the Germans were establishing martial law in other towns and villages too.

These events dampened the news Elizabeth gave them about the impending invasion and the arrival of the two French operatives, but they had no choice but to continue with the job in hand. They needed a good drop site away from the German patrols in the region. Brando suggested a place not too far away from the Menouillard's farm but after careful consideration it was deemed to be too near the raids. In the end they decided on a field near Saint-Amour. The men gave her a list of supplies which she went through in fine detail and said this would be passed on. At 3:30 a.m. the meeting ended and they all went their separate ways. Returning to the house, Elizabeth told Pierre Juliette was strong enough to do without her now and she was returning to Clairvaux straight away. He offered to drive her there but she refused, thinking it would attract less attention if she caught the bus.

CHAPTER 13

It was late afternoon when Elizabeth stepped off the bus in Clairvaux. She was approached by a German soldier demanding to see her papers. After lengthy questioning she was allowed to go and headed to Bistrot Jurassien to find out what was going on. There, she found a despondent Monique behind the bar talking to Mitzi. Several German soldiers sat at the tables playing cards and chatting. One of them called for more drinks. Monique took them over to the table on a tray and Elizabeth noticed no-one attempted to pay.

She returned and put the tray on the counter with a loud clatter. 'Bastards,' she hissed under her breath. 'I would like to poison the lot of them.'

'What's happening?' Elizabeth asked. 'I heard there have been more raids.'

'That's an understatement,' Mitzi scoffed, ignoring a German who was getting drunker by the minute and making eyes at her. 'This lot,' she indicated the men, 'are with the German Kommandant here. They've requisitioned all the hotels and public buildings, including a school where prisoners are locked up. And two officers have installed themselves here in Bistrot Jurassien. They're occupying the two spare rooms upstairs — so be careful what you say. Walls have ears.' She laughed sarcastically.

'It's a good job you weren't here earlier,' Monique said. 'They rounded everyone up this morning. Half a dozen were shot — more as an example of what would happen if we didn't comply.'

'Do I know any of them?' Elizabeth asked.

'They particularly targeted the old mayor and the councillors and have replaced them with their own cronies. And they've locked up my old bartender too, poor soul. He wouldn't hurt a fly.'

'What about the Menouillards? Are they safe?'

'Yes, thank God. And as you see, Mitzi and I are doing a good job of playing the innocent women.'

The soldier who had been eyeing Mitzi came over and attempted to chat her up. At that moment a German officer came down the stairs from the apartment and, seeing what the soldier was up to, gave him a dressing down in front of everyone and threatened to deal with him severely if he did it again. Embarrassed, the soldier returned to the table with his tail between his legs. The officer apologised to the women, clicked his heels and left.

Mitzi gave a little half-smile. 'How gracious they can be if they choose to. Butter wouldn't melt in their mouths.'

Elizabeth spent the evening with the Menouillards who were relieved to see her back safe and sound. They were able to paint a clearer picture of what took place in the area. One of the foresters who brought logs to Armand's sawmill was visiting his relatives in Saint-Claude when the Germans marched in. On their arrival, they set about putting posters up saying that they were *ensuring the safety of the locals against terrorists who have shown harmful and dangerous activity in the region.* Then on Easter morning, when the population were preparing to go to church, they informed everyone that all the men between 18 and 58 years were to assemble in the Place du Pré no later than 10:00 a.m. Those failing to comply would be shot on sight. The forester managed to escape and hide in an old tomb in the churchyard just as the round-up began. From there he could see what was taking place.

The atmosphere was heavy. A table had been set up in the middle of the square and several officers, one of whom was Klaus Barbie, went through a list, sorting a crowd of almost two thousand men into various groups. It was evident by the scenes some of them were making, that many thought they had been tricked into thinking the Germans were only looking for troublemakers. Those who gave the most trouble were mown down mercilessly by heavy machine guns which surrounded the square, bullets ricocheting from stone walls and rocks. A large group in the middle were chosen for deportation and taken to the school where they would spend the night until they could board a special train the next day. It was all over by 7:00 p.m. and the bloody Place du Pré emptied. The forester came out of hiding at dark and, more by luck than anything else, escaped the village and spent the night in the woods. The next day he caught a glimpse of the special train filled with deportees snaking its way through the countryside. Large banners hung across the top of each carriage saying *Terrorists of the Haute Jura*, striking fear in the hearts of all the villages it passed through.

Armand and Sabine knew Elizabeth's time in Lons-le-Saunier would have entailed more than taking care of Juliette and they asked if everything went according to plan. She took them into her confidence and told them of the new drop zone which they agreed with. As usual, they offered their assistance, which she gratefully accepted.

'Just be careful,' Armand warned her. 'I know you've work to do but the crackdowns are getting worse. What happened in Saint-Claude will happen elsewhere, mark my word.'

Elizabeth left the farmhouse just before midnight. Armand offered to escort her back to the cottage, but she refused. It was a beautiful night and she needed to think. Antoine was uppermost on her mind and she hoped he'd not been caught up in the raids. The moon was in its waxing phase and she could barely see a thing. Thankfully she had her small flashlight with her. Rounding the edge of the wood she heard a rustle and stopped in her tracks to listen. She realised she didn't have her gun with her. Seconds later a deer appeared out of the darkness of the trees, stopped on the pathway and looked at her for a few seconds before trotting away fearlessly. She breathed a sigh of relief but it was a reminder that she must be careful to carry her gun more often.

She headed to the woodshed and pulled the suitcase out of the wood pile and took it back to the cottage to set up ready to transmit. She tapped out the latest news about the raids and the chosen drop zones and using her maps, gave them the coordinates. Last of all, she mentioned she was still following up the two important leads on Daniel and Amelie. A few hours later she received a reply telling her the drop was being set up and she would be advised nearer the date. Again, she was cautioned to proceed with care.

*

Moirans-en-Montagne was twenty kilometres away from Saint-Claude and even less from Villards-d'Héria, but it didn't stop Elizabeth cycling there despite the occasional roadblocks and checks. This time the pharmacy was open. Inside, the pharmacist was tending to a woman with a small child. She hung back a little until he'd finished. He placed several bottles of medicines and pills in a paper bag for the woman and escorted her to the door. When she'd gone he put the CLOSED sign on the door and locked it.

'Marie-Élise Lacroix, I've been expecting you,' he said. 'Let's go into the back room.'

She followed him into a small room which doubled as a storeroom and a parlour. He wanted to know if she'd been followed or told anyone she was there. When she said no-one knew, he relaxed a little.

'How did you know who I was?' Elizabeth asked.

He smiled. 'My mother described you well.'

'What else did she say?'

'Everything: she may not be herself these days but she has a good memory.'

Elizabeth spoke about the recent round-ups. She wanted to know if they'd been caught up in them.

'One man was deported from Villards-d'Héria but that was all, thank the Lord.'

Antoine Berger appeared to be in his mid-thirties. Tall and good-looking with chestnut hair and an olive complexion, he struck Elizabeth as a quiet, gentle man — the studious type who would avoid trouble at any cost. He was not wearing a wedding ring which made Elizabeth wonder if he was married. That question was answered when he said he lived alone in the apartment over the pharmacy.

He studied her carefully. 'Who are you?' he asked. 'Who are you really?'

'As I told your mother, I am trying to find a man called Daniel Bardin who disappeared after the raid on the Ledoux Farm. I have reason to believe he did not die that night and neither was he deported.'

'Why do you want him?'

The way he replied gave Elizabeth hope. 'So he is alive after all?' Antoine did not reply. 'I have a message for him. An important message and only I can deliver it to the head of the Belvedere network himself.'

It had taken a leap of faith for Elizabeth to say that. She was exposing her hand but as she saw it, she had no choice, and time was running out.

'I am a friend of Pierre Dassin.' She noticed the telephone. 'You can telephone him if you want. He will verify it.'

'I believe you,' he replied. 'I only use the telephone for emergencies. The lines are tapped.'

'Now can you please tell me if the man you helped the night of the raid was indeed the man I am looking for?'

Antoine nodded.

'Did he die of his wounds?' It was one of the hardest questions Elizabeth had ever asked.

'No. He was in a very bad way and for a while it was touch and go, but he pulled through.'

The sense of relief Elizabeth felt was so enormous that for a moment she could not speak. The months of not knowing finally bubbled to the surface and she thought she would burst into tears.

'When I was called to my parent's house, I had no idea who he was,' Antoine said. 'That's the truth. All my father told me was that he was an important man and we would be killed if the Germans got wind we'd helped him. When my mother asked us to get rid of him, I still didn't know who he was. It was only in the hours before my father was arrested for the second time that he told me the name.'

'Why didn't you tell Pierre or anyone else in the Resistance?' Elizabeth asked.

'Because at the time my father asked me not to: no-one was safe and the fewer people who knew, the better it was for everyone — even in the Resistance.'

Elizabeth looked confused and the questions tumbled out. 'Where did you take him and why would Daniel not want his friends to know he was alive? It doesn't make sense.'

'André guessed someone must have betrayed them. My father patched his wounds up and he left, leaving us to watch over the man I later discovered was Daniel. André never said where he was going at the time, but we knew he'd gone into hiding until things blew over. When Daniel recovered, he too asked me not to say anything. So you see, I was honour-bound, and before you ask, yes, I trust Pierre. He's a good man.'

A few minutes passed while Elizabeth digested this news. Antoine watched her, waiting for her reaction.

'Where is he now? I want to see him. Can you take me to him?'

Antoine shifted uncomfortably in his chair. 'I'm afraid that's not possible.'

Elizabeth felt as if she would explode. 'Why not?' Her voice expressed anger. 'It's important that I see him.'

Antoine tried to calm her down. 'I told you. I am sworn to secrecy.'

Elizabeth jumped out of the chair. This time she had her gun in her satchel and it crossed her mind to hold him at gunpoint until he was more forthcoming. The only reason she didn't was because he had looked after Guy and as much as it irked her, if he was sworn to secrecy, she had to respect that.

Antoine refused to budge. 'I will pass on your message. I'm sorry, that's all I can do for you at the moment. If I do, I want you to give me your word that you won't breathe a word of this to anyone — not even Pierre. If he asks me about this conversation, I will deny it.'

Elizabeth threw her hands in the air. 'Fine.'

Antoine looked relieved. For the moment this conversation was over. 'Can you call back in three days' time?' He opened the door and stood back to let her pass.

'One more thing,' Elizabeth said. 'What do you know about a woman called Amelie — Amelie Rousseau?'

'The name doesn't ring a bell. What does she look like?'

Elizabeth went on to describe her beauty and exotic looks. He shook his head.

'Sorry. I can't help you there. I'm sure I would remember a woman like that.'

Elizabeth was not sure whether she believed him or not. At the beginning of the meeting, she'd thought Antoine a gentle, quiet person who'd avoid trouble at the drop of a hat. Now she'd changed her mind. He was as tough as old boots as Guy used to say about certain people, and she could see why he'd been entrusted with this secret. He put the OPEN sign back on the door and bade her good day. Several customers were waiting outside.

'In three days' time,' Elizabeth whispered. 'Same time.'

He nodded. 'I'll be waiting for you.'

She cycled away, the happiest she's been in months.

CHAPTER 14

For three whole days Elizabeth stayed at the cottage, deliberately not going anywhere in case of random round-ups and roadblocks. The last thing she wanted was to attract trouble when so much depended on her going back to Moirans-en-Montagne. To occupy herself, she made herself a new dress with a few metres of left-over pale pink cotton that Sabine had given her. The weather was beautiful and she sat on the doorstep finishing it off with embroidered wine-coloured rosettes on the cuffs and neckline. The days passed slowly and it gave her time to think. She went over and over the plans for the upcoming airdrop in her mind until she knew them off by heart. Every now and again her thoughts drifted back to Amelie's map. She was still no wiser about it and began to wonder if Amelie hadn't deliberately dropped it to throw anyone off her scent.

When the time arrived to visit Antoine, she had butterflies in her stomach. She had no idea how the meeting would go, but a part of her hoped he would take her to see Guy. What they were doing was highly dangerous, yet she felt like a teenager going to meet her lover. In anticipation, she styled her hair in soft waves, put on the mascara and lipstick Vera Atkins had given her, and dabbed her face lightly with the soft powder puff before slipping into her new dress. She looked in the mirror and felt pleased with herself. Her cheeks were rosy and she looked healthy even though a combination of living on adrenalin and cycling long distances had made her thinner. She'd arranged to meet Antoine at one o'clock. There was still plenty of time. She checked herself in the mirror again and realised that in her excitement she'd forgotten to wear her brooch. It was something she wore at all times — just in case. She picked it up and fastened it to the dress. The deep-pink tourmaline in the centre which hid her cyanide capsule matched the embroidered rosettes beautifully. She fingered it warily: such a small thing separating her between life and death.

Last but not least, she picked up her pistol which she'd been cleaning the night before, and rather than hide it in the hidden compartment at the bottom of her bag, wrapped it loosely in her cardigan and put it in the wicker basket at the front of her bicycle. She was always worried that with the Germans escalating their searches they might look too closely at her bag so it wasn't always a good idea to keep it there. She wheeled the bicycle along the path and had only gone a few metres when she suddenly stopped in her tracks and turned back. Something told her to let Armand and Sabine know where she'd gone just in case anything went wrong. She took a piece of paper and wrote a sentence saying that as it was a lovely day, she'd gone for a ride to Moirans-en-Montagne. She left it on the kitchen table. There was no mention of the appointment with Antoine. With a mixture of optimism and apprehension, she cycled away to meet him. This time she didn't encounter any Germans at all. It was as if they'd left the area. How wrong she was.

As soon as she entered Moirans-en-Montagne she noticed a few people hurriedly running through the streets in the opposite direction to where she was heading. When she turned into the square, she saw several cars parked near the pharmacy. German soldiers were climbing out of the back of trucks cordoning off the area while smartly-dressed men in plain-clothes, who Elizabeth took to be Gestapo, piled out of the cars with a determined look on their faces. She jumped off her bicycle and stood back in the recess of a tailor's shop door to gauge what was happening. Only a few people bravely lingered around to watch the unfolding events, fearing the same *rafle* that had taken place in Saint-Claude was happening to them; the rest ran to their homes and bolted the door.

She watched on and to her horror, quickly realized they had deliberately targeted Antoine's pharmacy. A few of the plain-clothed men entered the premises while soldiers stood outside with machine guns. The tailor spotted her in the doorway.

'Come inside. There'll be trouble if they catch you watching them.'

Elizabeth asked what was going on, but he had no idea.

'They just arrived out of the blue,' he said in a low voice, beckoning her to get inside.

Elizabeth started to wheel the bicycle inside when they heard a shot coming from the pharmacy. She put her hand to her mouth in horror.

'Oh my God!' she blurted out.

The tailor quickly pulled both her and the bicycle inside and locked the door. They continued to watch the scene unfold from behind three tailor's dummies in the window. Several more men ran inside the pharmacy and those that had stayed to watch were rounded up and herded to one side. After a while, one of the men came out and said something to a Wehrmacht officer who promptly sent two soldiers inside with a stretcher. When the men came back out in the street, they were carrying the body of a man. From across the square, Elizabeth could see straight away who it was — Antoine.

She felt her legs turn to jelly and reached for a stand behind the dummies to steady herself. The tailor quickly pulled up a seat and gave her a glass of water. After half an hour, the plain-clothed men left the premises and drove away, leaving a soldier to cordon off the pharmacy. Elizabeth looked on in dismay. It was impossible to go over there now and find out what happened. All she could do was pray Antoine had the good sense not to leave anything incriminating behind.

'I have to get going,' she said to the tailor, and thanked him for the water.

He tried to persuade her to stay a while longer but she refused. She needed to get away from there as soon as possible. He unlocked the door and checked the street to make sure the Germans had gone. She thanked him and cycled away as fast as she could. About two kilometres outside the town, she heard a vehicle approaching in the distance. An open-top car was coming behind her. Fearing that she would certainly be stopped, she rode at a more leisurely pace as if she had all the time in the world. The car slowed down and as it passed, she saw it was the two plain-clothed men she'd seen at the pharmacy. At first, she thought they were driving on but then they stopped about a half a kilometre in front of her. Her instincts were telling her something was wrong and she slowed down even more. There was nowhere to run and hide. On both sides of the road was a low stone wall and beyond that, fields. The nearest woods were at the far side of a freshly-ploughed field.

As she neared, both men got out and stood at the side of the road waiting for her to approach. The passenger, who appeared to be the older of the two, pointed a gun towards her indicating for her to pull up at the side of the road. With a pounding heart, she got off her bicycle and walked the last few metres towards them.

'Where are you going?' the man with the gun asked in perfect French.

'I'm just out for a ride. It's such a beautiful day,' Elizabeth replied, innocently.

Neither man reciprocated her smile. 'Your papers, please,' the man said.

She took her bag off from across her chest and handed it to them. The driver took it from her, put it on the back of the car and started to look through it. He called the man with the gun over and showed him her identity card. A discussion ensued and although Elizabeth understood a little German, their voices were so low she couldn't hear what they were saying, but she knew this wasn't another normal identity check. The man with the gun turned to her and ordered her leave the bicycle by the side of the road and get in the car. She did as she was told and when she turned her back on them to lay the bicycle down in the grass, pulled her cardigan with her pistol out of the basket. When she turned around, she fired a shot at the man with the gun knocking him backwards against the driver. In a split second, Elizabeth fired a second time, this time at the second man as he was trying to get his gun out of his holster. She ran forward to check them both. The driver was dead but the first was still writhing on the road. Elizabeth aimed at his head and shot him again.

The day was quickly turning into a nightmare. She looked around to see if anyone had seen them but there was only an eerie silence punctuated by birdcalls. She had to act fast before someone came. A myriad of thoughts raced through her mind. She could get on her bicycle and ride away, in which case someone might come along at any moment and associate her with the scene of the crime, or she could attempt to make it look like an accident. She decided on the latter. She put her cardigan on to protect her dress, opened the passenger door of the spacious car and with enormous difficulty managed to drag the first man onto the luxurious leather seat, pushing his legs roughly inside the car. Then she did the same with the driver. Thankfully, he was smaller and slimmer than the first. She hurriedly took off her bloodied cardigan and threw it on the seat next to them, but what should she do with the two guns — two perfectly good Walther P38s. They would come in handy and she made a split decision to hide them under a pile of rocks behind the stone wall. All being well, she would come back for them another day.

Praying that no-one would appear, she began to pull up dry clumps of grass from the side of the road, took off the petrol cap to the fuel tank and began to stuff the dry grass into the pipe. With her heart pounding and sweat trickling down her forehead, she picked up her bag and took out a cigarette lighter, grabbed her bicycle and straddled it, ready to cycle away. Before she did so, she flicked the lighter and carefully lit the short length of dry grass that she'd left exposed out of the fuel pipe. The flame caught quickly. Without a moment to spare, she cycled away as quickly as she could. Seconds later she heard a loud explosion and the sound of chunks of flying metal landing on the road behind her. Without stopping, she looked over her shoulder to survey the damage. The car was engulfed in fire. Bright orange flames danced amid a cloud of billowing black smoke. Thankfully the road took a steep decline and within a few minutes she had managed to cover a couple of kilometres: well away from the scene.

At the bottom of the hill was a small junction with a narrow road used by loggers. It would take her twice as long to get back home but it was safer to go that way than to stay on the main road. The road was furrowed with dried mud making it hard to cycle and when she reached the safety of the forest, she was forced to walk. Two hours later, the forest petered out into farmland and she could see Clairvaux in the distance. She was shaken and exhausted but at least she was alive.

Nearing the farm, she saw Armand in his truck heading towards the gate.

'Thank God!' he cried out. 'We saw your note and you had us worried.'

He told her he already knew about what took place in Moirans-en-Montagne. That was when he went to the cottage to tell her and found her note.

'We need to talk,' Elizabeth said. 'I'll come to the house this evening.'

Since leaving the cottage in the morning, she had been sustained by adrenalin, but on returning, the adrenalin had turned to exhaustion and despair. When she got off the bicycle, her legs almost gave way. Inside the kitchen, she collapsed on to the chair, arching her stiff back. Elizabeth was a fit woman but the pain in her calf muscles was excruciating and she had blisters on her feet from walking through the forest in her sandals. She took off her dress to wash herself and noticed several spots of blood. Her hands shook visibly as she sponged them away. Thoughts raced through her mind. The Germans could have killed her on the spot, but then they would never have had the satisfaction of presenting a prize catch to Gestapo HQ. Whichever way she looked at it, her instincts told her that if she'd gone with them, they would have tortured her and either executed her or deported her. There *was* no other option but to kill them. When she thought about Antoine, it had distressed her so much she burst into tears. How could such a thing have happened? He had been so loyal to Guy. With his untimely death, she had no idea what she would do next.

CHAPTER 15

It was dark when Elizabeth arrived at the farmhouse and she was surprised to see they already had another visitor — Pierre. The look of concern on his face echoed Armand's.

'I came as soon as I heard. Were you there when all this happened?' he asked, referring to Antoine and the pharmacy.

'I'd only just arrived so had no idea how it happened. The Germans were already in the square. I heard the shot and saw his body being taken away. After that I fled as soon as I could.'

Pierre had brought several bottles of wine with him. One was already empty. Armand opened another and poured her a drink.

'We also heard there was an explosion not far from the town. Did you see it?' Armand asked.

Elizabeth took a long sip of wine. It felt good.

'Yes. I saw it.' She grinned.

The room went quiet. Sabine, Armand and Pierre looked at each other.

'I think we'd better start from the beginning, don't you?' Armand said.

Over the next few hours and after getting their assurance that this would remain a secret between the four of them, Elizabeth confided everything to them: the fact that she'd learnt Guy was still alive and the map dropped by Amelie late one night at Monique's house.

'I knew it,' Sabine said. 'I knew that girl was a smart one.'

Armand shook his head. 'You should have told us all this before, Marie-Élise. Four heads are better than one.'

At that moment, the telephone rang. Another coded message and the look on Armand's face told them something bad had happened again.

'That was one of our men. Madame Berger has been taken to Lons-le-Saunier. She's at Gestapo HQ.'

This was something Elizabeth had dreaded and she blamed herself. She picked up her glass and drank the wine in one go. Pierre refilled all their glasses. It was going to be a long night. He asked if he could make a telephone call to Lons-le-Saunier. They listened while he spoke in more coded sentences to Father Henri asking him to check out what was going on. There was little to do but wait. In the meantime, Elizabeth told them about the incident with the men and the car. After weighing things up, they all agreed she'd done the right thing. But she'd been lucky. Had someone seen her, they could all have been in trouble.

When she brought up the subject of the map, this really did come as a surprise. It was too far to go back to the cottage and get it and besides, her legs were still aching and the wine had gone to her head. She knew it off by heart anyway and drew them another. A few locations were discussed but as no-one could agree, they were none the wiser. Overcome by tiredness, Sabine suggested Elizabeth sleep the night at the farm. Pierre too as it was well past curfew.

Shortly after dawn, Pierre received word from Father Henri that Madame Berger was to be deported that morning. Sabine knocked on Elizabeth's door to deliver the bad news. She felt numb.

'It's not your fault,' Sabine said. 'Don't beat yourself up.'

After breakfast, Pierre continued to Moirans-en-Montagne on the pretext of delivering wine. He would return later in the day on his way back to Lons-le-Saunier and update them with any news. In the meantime, Elizabeth returned to the cottage and went straight to bed. She needed to clear her head.

When Pierre returned, he told them that Antoine had been betrayed by the man who owned the bar next door. The same man she'd spoken to a few days ago. They'd had a falling out over something insignificant and the man was overheard speaking to the Milice in a telephone booth. The word was now out about the bar owner's collaboration with the enemy and Pierre assured them he would not live to see the next dawn. As for Antoine, he took his own life rather than be tortured, and most probably, executed. His mother was taken because he died before the Gestapo had managed to obtain any information from him. They refused to believe she knew anything about her son's resistance work. None of this made Elizabeth feel any better but she had to admit, this was the reality of the life she now lived.

For the next few days, Elizabeth kept a low profile taking walks by the lake or through the forest to clear her head, and she avoided Clairvaux as the Germans were still installed there. After a week, she had fully recovered and was back to her old self and went to retrieve the two guns she'd hidden. It wasn't difficult to find the spot. There was a small crater in the road where the car had blown up. Apart from a few small pieces of charred metal in the grass, the wreckage had been cleared away. Luckily there had been no reprisals in the area.

In two days' time there would be a full moon and she must now concentrate her energies on the airdrops and prepare the welcome committee for the men from England. During her next transmission to London, she received notification that the drop was on and there would be two planes arriving this time. Their precious cargo of arms, munitions, and the two important Frenchmen would be dropped by parachute. The weather was expected to be fine and they anticipated no problems. The day before, accompanied by Armand, she left the cottage for Saint-Amour. Pierre was already there to greet them along with Gavroche, the maquisard chief of the area, and Brando, the resistant from the water department in Lons-le-Saunier, along with several other members of the Maquis. They spent the night and the following day hiding out at the Château d'Angerville. As the sun slipped over the horizon on the evening of the drop, they received the long-awaited coded message over the BBC telling them the two planes were on their way.

After curfew they headed across the fields to the drop zone. They couldn't have wished for a better night. The warm night air was sweetly fragrant with the perfume of blossoms and wildflowers, yet the tension was palpable: a mixture of fear and excitement. The group took up their allocated positions and waited. Their senses were heightened: every sound, every shadow, was cause for concern. Elizabeth leaned back against a tree and looked up. The moon hung like a silver ball in the night sky surrounded by a myriad of twinkling stars. It was hypnotic, but they were at their most vulnerable and no-one could afford to let their guard down. Every now and again, Pierre and Elizabeth checked the guards keeping watch over the nearby narrow country road.

Just after midnight, they heard the tell-tale drone of a low flying Halifax and the lights were flashed from the field. Seconds later, the first plane roared over the tree tops, dropping the Frenchmen

115

and several containers. Even after so many drops, this was the part Elizabeth dreaded the most and she always found herself holding her breath. To her, the sound of the aircraft was deafening. The reception party greeted de Gaulle's men effusively. At the same time the containers were quickly picked up and taken into the woods. It took less than three minutes. They had another ten minutes to wait before the second plane arrived and it was far too dangerous for their newly arrived guests to hang around, so it was decided that Pierre and half a dozen men would escort them to the château while Elizabeth stayed behind with Gavroche and his men. The second plane was later than planned but there was no mistaking the approaching drone of the Halifax's engines. The codes were flashed once again and from a height of just over 400 feet, it dropped its precious cargo of fifteen canisters. Seconds later it disappeared, heading back towards the English Channel. Both drops had gone to textbook perfection. The canisters, containing an assortment of guns, ammunition and explosives, were all retrieved in good condition, their guests were safe and sound, and there wasn't a German in sight. Elizabeth and Gavroche headed back to the château where the welcome party was in full swing with wine supplied by Pierre.

The Château d'Angerville had been unoccupied since the war and, always fearful that the Germans would requisition it, the Resistance were careful to hide away in one of the many rooms and attics should anyone pay them a surprise visit. Thankfully, it was surrounded by a moat and Gavroche's elderly uncle and his wife who lived nearby kept an eye out for them.

Pierre, Elizabeth, and de Gaulle's men left the men to their carousing to find a quiet room where they could talk without being interrupted. The older one, Colonel Robert Navarre, a former Legionnaire in his late forties, had been with de Gaulle for the last two years. He was a tough-looking character, built like an ox and with hands that looked as if they could strangle you without the slightest effort. The other, Lieutenant Jean Arbez, looked about ten years younger and had an athletic physique and was well-tanned. He reminded Elizabeth of Guy. He had led Allied and French soldiers over the Pyrenees before joining up with de Gaulle's Free French in Algeria. Both men were experts in counterinsurgency and the blowing up of strategic infrastructure and they had been sent specifically to help train the Maquis, now known as the *Forces Françaises de l'Intérieur*, French forces of the interior

(FFI), something they were badly in need of and one of the things Guy was involved with prior to his disappearance.

Elizabeth took a liking to them straight away. She felt their presence and the fact that de Gaulle was sending his own men to France would lift the morale of the maquisards enormously. There was plenty to discuss and the meeting went on through the night. Discussions about the proposed Allied invasion were high on their list as it was expected to take place sometime in the next few months. After they'd finished, Colonel Robert, as everyone called him, gave Elizabeth a present from London — another French lipstick: this time a deep shade of garnet. With it was a bottle of matching nail polish. Elizabeth smiled when she thought of Vera Atkins choosing the colour. She knew that with Vera's attention to detail, she would have known exactly which colour was the most fashionable and which suited her complexion the best. One of the canisters contained chocolate and tinned food, tobacco and cigarettes, and whisky: well-deserved presents for the men, which Pierre would distribute later. The following day, Armand returned to Clairvaux alone and as Pierre would be with Colonel Robert and Jean Arbez for a few more days, Elizabeth caught the bus to see Juliette.

Spending the day with Juliette was very much a welcome change from the events of the past few days. Juliette had recovered well from the difficult birth and was her usual happy and cheerful self. They sat in the garden and talked while the baby, who had been named Louis, slept peacefully and Angeline played with her dolls. Mostly they talked about domestic things: sewing and knitting patterns, especially for Louis and Angeline, and what was available in the shops in Lons-le-Saunier. After lunch, Juliette insisted on baking a chocolate cake for her to take back home. Pierre always gave her his share of chocolate sent over by SOE or which he'd acquired through exchanging wine, and like Sabine, Juliette put it aside for a special occasion. The special cake was to thank Elizabeth for her help in delivering the baby. Such a scene of peaceful domesticity was rare for Elizabeth these days and she thoroughly enjoyed herself. At no time did Juliette ask about her work even though she knew that what she was doing was dangerous. Sometimes it seemed to Elizabeth that she knew far more than she let on but, by not acknowledging it, any fear she had was safely locked away and she was able to carry on as normal. She also wanted to cushion Pierre from his resistance work. When he came home at the end of the day, he was often tired and anxious, but under Juliette's love and care, his worries faded. For all French women, it was an enormous strain to think that every time their menfolk left the house they might never return.

After the cake had cooled and been iced, Juliette placed it in a box and tied it with a red ribbon, and with Louis in her arm and Angeline by her side, stood at the gate and waved her goodbye. She caught the bus back to Clairvaux and arrived without being asked for her papers once. In Clairvaux, she went to Bistrot Jurassien to catch up with Monique. The Germans were still there but for the time-being had stopped harassing the villagers. Monique was behind the bar when she entered and took her aside to ask if everything was fine.

'As fine as can be,' Elizabeth replied.

'I have some news for you. Guess who came to Clairvaux the other day?'

'I have no idea. Who?'

'*La simplette!* Lili — the simpleton who took a shine to Paul-Emille.'

'What on earth did she want?'

'She wanted Mitzi to dye her hair.' Monique saw the look of surprise on Elizabeth's face and nodded. 'Yes, that was my reaction too. Mitzi came over to see me after she's gone. At first, she was angry with her and refused to do her hair because she left Clairvaux without paying her last bill. Apparently, it was quite a bit. Lili apologised and to Mitzi's surprise, took enough money out of her purse to pay off her debt and for what she was about to have done. She also showed her a diamond ring and said she was getting married to a garage mechanic from Dijon.'

'Did she say anything else?'

'She asked how everyone was but Mitzi thought her rather vague. In fact she thought the only reason she'd returned was to brag about her engagement more than to see her old friends. Otherwise she could have gone to a local hairdresser in Champagnole. The only other person she asked after was Amelie, which Mitzi thought odd as she always thought she was jealous of her.'

Elizabeth was not only surprised; she was concerned. 'What was Mitzi's reply?'

'That she hadn't seen her in months — which is true. All very odd don't you think?'

'Extraordinary!'

Monique twisted her index finger against her temple. '*Pauvre Lili.* I pity the poor man she's going to marry.'

Elizabeth changed the subject. 'Did you hear about Antoine Berger?'

'I did, poor man.'

'His mother has been deported. I feel like it's my fault for sticking my nose into things.'

Monique's reply was brusque and to the point. 'Don't talk like that. We will see many more lose their lives before the Germans leave. It's a cross we have to bear.'

She asked about the map and Elizabeth told her it was still a mystery. Two German soldiers entered and inquired what was on the evening menu to which she replied roast pork with sauerkraut, beets, and apple pie.

They were happy with her reply and after a short discussion in German about Monique's cooking being far superior to the old man's who owned the bistro down the road, they decided to dine there.

Elizabeth pricked her ears up when Monique said roast pork.

After they'd sat down, Monique whispered in her ear. 'The Germans love pork and they supplied me with two pigs themselves. Who am I to complain? I've put a little aside for myself.' She excused herself to go into the kitchen to prepare the food. 'Come and see me tomorrow, around eleven. It's market day. We'll go to a café for a drink. It will be a welcome change of scenery for me.'

Elizabeth dropped Juliette's cake off at the Menouillards where they enjoyed it together accompanied by a glass of amber-coloured Marc du Jura, a powerful and fragrant brandy made by Pierre's family. The desolate mood of Antoine's untimely death was momentarily lifted with the success of the parachute drops and the arrival of Navarre and Arbez. Afterwards, Sabine pulled out her sewing and sat at the table cutting out fabric for a new dress for a relative, while Armand smoked his pipe and read in his favourite chair. At one point, he turned on the radio and tuned it to the BBC's *Radio Londres* — the French broadcast.

"*Ici Londres! Les Français parlent aux Français*...This is London! The French speaking to the French..." It always began with the same message — "*Before we begin, please listen to some personal messages*".

They listened to the personal coded messages which bore no relevance for them — they had already sent and received theirs — but

119

which had so much meaning for thousands of others. It gave them a great sense of connection that they were not alone and thousands were working towards their freedom. *"Sylvia's got a black cat"*, *"There is a fire at the bakery"*, *"Jean has cut his hair"*, *"The wine harvest promises to be a good one this year"*, and on and on.

When it was finished, he turned it off. 'Maybe one day soon, we will hear the most important message of all.' He was referring to the impending Allied landing.

Elizabeth assured him he wouldn't have long to wait.

CHAPTER 16

After examining her new pink dress to make sure there were no spots of blood she'd missed, Elizabeth decided to wear it to meet Monique. As soon as she slipped into it, she thought about the two dead men's heads resting on her chest as she heaved them into the car. It gave her an odd, distasteful sensation and she anxiously brushed away imaginary marks from her breasts with her hands. She was sure she could still smell blood on her even though she'd washed the dress and hung it out to dry amid sprigs of dried lavender. Guy used to tell her things like that played havoc with the imagination and he was right. In an effort to cheer herself up, she painted her nails and put on her new lipstick. It looked good against the healthy, tanned complexion she'd acquired from all the bike-riding.

She was early and decided to wander through the market in case she spotted anything to take back for Sabine. There may have been a war on but the market was still doing a brisk business. While there was a limited supply of fresh vegetables, all of which were at inflated prices, there were plenty of other stalls, mostly selling bric-a-brac: wicker baskets and items made out of wood or iron, etc. Not too many people were buying, but with the sun out it gave them an excuse to mingle. Elizabeth spotted a white cotton tablecloth edged with hand-made lace which she thought would make a lovely gift for Sabine. When she asked the price the stall-owner quoted her an exorbitant figure but after a bit of haggling, reduced it by half. She bought it. While she waited for it to be wrapped, she felt a strange sensation that someone was watching her. She looked around and spotted a woman wearing a drab, calf-length brown coat, floral headscarf and sunglasses standing at a stall on the other side of the road looking at her. Elizabeth paid for the tablecloth and headed towards the stall where she'd seen the woman but she was nowhere to be seen. She scanned the crowd in the hope she might spot her. It was useless. The woman had vanished.

The church clock struck eleven and she headed to the café to meet Monique. The café overlooked the lake. It had a veranda with bright yellow awnings, marble-topped tables and wicker chairs. Bright red and white geraniums cascaded from window boxes either side of the entrance. There were quite a few patrons, all enjoying the warmth of the day and the view of the lake which looked like a silver-blue mirror in the bright light of the late morning sun. Monique was already there, sitting at a corner table reading a newspaper. She had with her a bunch of flowers that she'd bought at the market and was taking them to her son's grave after their rendezvous.

'You look lovely in that dress,' she said, folding away the newspaper. 'And I do love the shade of your new lipstick. It matches the embroidery on your dress.' Her eyes fell on the silver brooch with the deep-pink tourmaline. 'Most exquisite. You are quite the chic Parisienne today.'

Elizabeth noted that Monique was still wearing black after the death of her son. Even so, she was immaculately dressed and whilst it may have been a black outfit, it was impeccably made in fine materials: a silk blouse with lace ruffles on the neckline and cuffs and a woven cashmere skirt of the highest quality, no doubt purchased in Paris or Lyon before the war.

Monique ordered them both an aromatic aperitif drink from the Haute-Doubs, flavoured with aniseed. 'How good it is to get away from Bistrot Jurassien for a while.' She glanced at the package Elizabeth was carrying. 'Did you find anything nice at the market? One can pick up quite a few bargains these days.'

Elizabeth told her about the tablecloth for Sabine. 'You know, the strangest thing happened when I was there. I felt as if I was being watched by a woman at another stall. When I looked again, she'd vanished.'

Monique raised a neatly pencilled eyebrow. 'Did you get a good look at her?'

Elizabeth described her.

'How odd. She sounds like someone I saw the other day.'

Elizabeth was relieved. For a moment she thought she was getting paranoid.

'Yes, she was here the same day as *la simplette* and was wearing those exact clothes.'

'Then you got a good look at her too,' replied Elizabeth.

'Well not really. I was at Bistrot Jurassien and I saw her from the window. She was standing near the fountain and had her back to me. She caught my eye because of the headscarf. It must have been silk because with the sun on it, it had a beautiful sheen and the flowers looked lovely — shades of purple and lilac on a brown background. The coat might have looked drab, but the scarf was certainly not. In my opinion it looked expensive. Not the sort of scarf most women around here would wear.'

Elizabeth smiled at how observant Monique was: a great asset to the Resistance.

'I didn't think any more about it as we do have lots of tourists and hikers coming through Clairvaux, especially now the weather has picked up, but now that you mention it, I've just thought of something else. She seemed to be staring at the building opposite.'

'Mitzi's hair salon?'

'Yes, that's right.'

'Was Lili having her hair done at the same time?' Elizabeth asked.

'You know, I believe she was.'

They both looked at each other. 'I've got a strange feeling about this. Do you think she was looking for her?'

'Can we really jump to that conclusion on so little?' Monique asked. 'It's not much to go on is it?'

Elizabeth apologised. 'I have a tendency to suspect everyone these days.'

'That's understandable. I'll keep my eyes open. If I see her again, I'll let you know.'

They left the café around midday. Monique said how much she'd enjoyed herself and then headed in the direction of the cemetery. Elizabeth started to walk down the hill towards the bridge but then decided to go back to the market just in case the woman was still there. It was lunchtime and several stalls were packing up. Others decided to stay a few hours longer in the hope they could make a few more francs. As she neared the square, she felt it again; that strange sensation of being watched. All of a sudden, she caught sight of the same woman. This time she was making her way towards the church and as she neared the church door she glanced over her shoulder and realised she had been spotted. Elizabeth picked up her pace. The woman hurried into the church with Elizabeth hot on her tail. When Elizabeth entered the church, it was empty. *Damn! Where has she gone?* She walked down the aisle to see if there was anywhere to hide, and spotted a small side door ajar. It led to a narrow side-street. At the far end she caught a fleeting glimpse of the woman turning into the main street and took off after her. Elizabeth was extremely fit but she was no match for the woman. She reached the corner just in time to see the woman step on a bus parked half-way down the street. It was useless to try and catch up. The bus was already moving on.

Damn, she muttered to herself again. An old man out walking his dog was coming towards her.

'Excuse me, Monsieur, the bus that just left, do you know where it was going?'

'Saint-Laurent-en-Grandvaux,' he replied.

Elizabeth wondered what to do next. The bizarre episode drew her to only one conclusion. She *had* been followed after all. But if she had, why, and why would she follow *la simplette* also? It didn't make sense. She walked to the bus stop and looked at the timetable. There were three buses going to Saint-Laurent-en-Grandvaux: one in the morning, the one that had just passed, and one in four hours' time. *Was she really considering catching the next bus to Saint-Laurent-en-Grandvaux when she didn't even know if the woman was going there?* Feeling utterly despondent, she considered waiting for Monique to return but decided against it as talking to her about this immediately after her visit to her son's grave would be too stressful. Instead she walked home, pondering what to do next.

That evening, Elizabeth went to visit the Menouillards where they happily polished off the remains of Juliette's chocolate cake. Sabine was thrilled with the tablecloth, saying she would bring it out for the next special occasion, adding that she hoped that would be when they discovered the whereabouts of Daniel. This time, Elizabeth didn't hold back and told them about the mystery woman and the conversation with Monique.

Sabine knitted her brows together, a habit of hers when she was deep in thought. 'I wonder if it was Amelie.'

Elizabeth thought about it. 'That crossed my mind too, but she doesn't know who I am or what I look like. Besides, if she was following me, why was she following *la simplette* too? It's not as if we're connected. And if she is still around, why hasn't she made herself known to her trusted friends?'

Neither of them could answer that. Armand said that bus route originated in Lons-le-Saunier, and depending on whether there were roadblocks and searches, it was usually on time. He thought it highly likely that it was the same bus driver on this route.

The following day, Armand took Elizabeth into Clairvaux and waited with her until the bus came. When it pulled up, she asked the driver if he was the same one who came through the day before. He was. She went on to describe the passenger he picked up and asked if he knew where she'd got off. At first, he said he couldn't remember. Elizabeth persisted, asking him to please try and recall: it was very important. He was wary. There were others on the bus and her questions attracted unwanted attention. Elizabeth saw this and said she was in the same café as the woman and noticed she'd left her purse behind. She took her own out to show him, pretending it belonged to the woman. In the end he said he'd stop at the same place she got off and as she had no idea where that was, she paid for a ticket to Saint-Laurent-en-Grandvaux, took a seat at the back of the bus and waved to Armand. She was to call him as soon as she returned.

The bus wound its way through the picturesque countryside passing through small villages and hamlets flanked in parts by rolling fields on one side and dense forests on the other. By the time they reached the village of Bonlieu she was the only passenger left on the bus. Elizabeth had cycled along this road before but wasn't as familiar with it as other areas. She did know however, that unless the bus detoured, there was only one more village between Bonlieu and Saint-Laurent-en-Grandvaux — Chaux-du-Dombief — a sleepy village and home to one of Belvedere's best forgers who now worked and lived near Champagnole, some twenty-five kilometres away.

All of a sudden, the bus came to a halt at a point in the road where there was not a building to be seen anywhere. On one side were thickets of brambles behind which were a patchwork of fields and woods, and on the other, a dramatic Jurassic landscape of rocks and dense pine forests which soared across the mountain range as far as the eye could see.

'This is it,' the driver said. 'This is where I dropped the lady.'

Elizabeth looked surprised. 'Are you sure? There's nothing here.'

The bus driver looked irritated. 'It's not my place to ask why people get off where they do. Are you getting off or not? Make up your mind. I'm already twenty minutes late.'

Elizabeth almost decided to continue to Saint-Laurent-en-Grandvaux but quickly changed her mind.

'What time are you returning?' she asked.

'In two hours. If you're catching the bus back, stand over there by those logs. I won't miss you.'

The bus disappeared and Elizabeth looked around for signs of habitation. There was nothing. No rooftop, no smoke signalling a dwelling: nothing at all and she wondered if she'd made a mistake. But the driver seemed convinced this was the spot where the woman got off. She decided to walk back towards the village of Bonlieu. Maybe there was a farm she could ask at? But what was she to ask without alerting attention to herself? She had only gone a few yards when she spotted a couple of hikers coming through a clearing in the trees. The couple, who appeared to be in their mid-fifties were wearing hiking clothes, a backpack and carrying hiking poles. It never failed to amaze Elizabeth that even though there was a war on there were still lots of French people who carried on as if things were normal: taking holidays by the beach or hiking through the countryside were just two of their many pastimes.

She slowed down until they caught up with her and exchanged greetings.

'Excuse me, could you tell me where I am?' Elizabeth asked. 'I'm looking for a friend's farm and seem to be lost.'

She made up the name of the farm, hoping the hikers weren't locals. The woman eyed Elizabeth carefully from underneath the wide brim of her straw hat. Fortunately, she had chosen to wear a pair of chocolate slacks, cotton cream shirt, and flat walking shoes rather than her pretty pink dress which would have looked completely out of place.

'We can't help you,' she said. 'We're not from around here.' Elizabeth noted that the woman had a Parisian accent.

'Maybe they can help you at the hotel,' the man added.

Elizabeth looked surprised. 'Which hotel?' she asked, thinking they must be referring to one in the village.

The man pointed. 'It's down there: next to the lake.'

She looked in the direction where the man was pointing and could see nothing. 'How do I get there?'

'Over there,' he said, pointing further along the road. 'There's a signpost. You can't miss it.'

She thanked them and they went on their way, quickly disappearing over another wall and across the field. Elizabeth walked on in the direction the man had pointed to and soon found the wooden signpost pointing to a narrow dirt road leading off the main road. The sign said Lake Bonlieu, but there was nothing about a hotel. She started down the road in the hope that the woman was right, and besides, she really didn't have too many options. She had two hours so it was worth checking it out. It was a beautiful day for a walk and the least she could do was to make the most of it. The road meandered through a large tract of farmland passing over a small bridge under which ran a babbling brook.

Near the bridge, something caught her eye — a neatly folded cream handkerchief with a lace trim peaking out of the grass. She bent over to get a better look. Her heart skipped a beat. *Surely not! She was imagining things.* When she picked it up, she knew immediately who it belonged to. The embroidered initials in the corner could only mean one thing — A.R. — Amelie Rousseau. It was exactly the same handkerchief Vera Atkins had given her. The same one she gave all her girls. Elizabeth's mind raced. She had not felt such a sense of elation since Antoine Berger told her Guy was alive. She wanted to scream with delight. Finally, persistence and instinct were paying off. Sabine was right. The mystery woman had to have been Amelie. God willing, whatever was going on would soon be solved.

With newfound optimism and a spring in her step, she continued along the road, soaking up every aspect of her surroundings. What was so striking was the forest itself. From the road she was aware of its height, but now she was closer, the cliff-face soared into an almost vertical forested escarpment of intense shades of green. Rounding the bend, she came across a red-roofed building approached through a gate with the name, *Le prieuré*, worked into the wrought-iron in a neat sweeping curve across the top. Further along, she saw what she had been looking for — the hotel. Beyond that, at a spot where the road ended, she caught a glimpse of the lake, a shimmering vibrant turquoise in the afternoon sun, peeping out between the vibrant green trees.

It was not the beautiful lake that made her stop in her tracks, but the hotel. It was completely unexpected. Set against the dramatic backdrop of the cliff face in a garden of undulating lawns interspersed with rose bushes and hydrangeas, it was a blend of Jura farmstead and elegant Franche-Comté city elegance. The building appeared to have three stories and was long rather than tall with a steep sloping roof, ideal for winter snowfalls. Several of the first floor windows opened up onto narrow balconies just wide enough to accommodate a small table and two chairs and the entire facade was painted a warm butter-yellow with shutters in a faded rose-red. In the bright afternoon sun, it had an old-world charm to it. The name of the hotel also bore an element of grandeur — the Grand Hôtel du Lac. For a hotel in the middle of nowhere, it certainly lived up to its name.

She decided to take a closer look but suddenly stopped in her tracks. The front of the hotel had a wide terrace with a view of the lake and on the terrace several people were dining under the shade of yellow umbrellas. She recognised several of the uniforms — Wehrmacht officers. In an instant, the elation turned to dread. A car approached her from behind and she stood aside to let it pass. It was an open-top Mercedes and in it was a smartly dressed, uniformed man accompanied by a glamorous blonde woman who looked like a film star. The woman lowered her sunglasses as the car passed, caught Elizabeth's eye and smiled. Elizabeth was too stunned to return the smile. The car drove past the terrace into a carpark and parked next to several other smart cars. Elizabeth squeezed the cream handkerchief tightly. Inadvertently, she had entered the lion's den and unless she wanted to draw attention to herself, she had no option but to go on. Taking a deep breath, she boldly walked towards the terrace and into the hotel.

CHAPTER 17

The woman behind the reception desk eyed Elizabeth over the top of her glasses.

'How can I help you?' she asked. 'If it's a room you're after, I am afraid we are fully booked at the moment.'

Elizabeth explained that she was taking a stroll by the lake and only wanted to dine there.

'In that case, please take a seat over there and someone will attend to you as soon as possible.'

She pointed towards a lounge filled with leather-bound chairs and velvet couches, interspersed with potted palms in decorative jardinières. Elizabeth took a seat, picked up a French edition of *Signal* magazine lying on a coffee table and flicked through it while quietly taking in her surroundings. On one wall was a large propaganda poster put out by the Vichy regime telling people to spend their holidays in the country. From where she sat she had a view of the terrace through the open French doors and a clear view of the lake in the distance with several people strolling along the bank as if they hadn't a care in the world. Clearly some people took notice of such posters, choosing to think life went on as normal. A smartly attired waiter moved about from table to table with the adroitness of the best Parisian waiters, serving the finest wines, coffees and cigars. Every now and again peals of laughter drifted into the room.

The receptionist came over with a glass of fresh lemonade on a silver tray, placed it on the table in front of her with a serviette. She handed her a menu with the name of the hotel set in a gold frame under which was the head of a stag, and asked if she would care to peruse it while waiting for her table. She scanned her eyes down the beautifully printed page, wondering what Monique would say to such *délices de la table*. Starters included Trout Purée in Pastry Shells, Cheese Ramequins, Herb Pie, and Spring Soup; Mains consisted of a variety of meats and fresh fish with an assortment of seasonal vegetables, followed by mouth-watering desserts rarely seen on any bistro menu these days; *Tourte de Frangipane*, and an assortment of marzipan, turnovers, macaroons and custards. As befitted a hotel of such elegance, there were no prices. Elizabeth knew it wouldn't be cheap and hoped she had enough money with her. This was not the place where ration cards would be required.

The couple who had passed her in the car walked onto the terrace and sat at a table which had obviously been reserved for them. Two Germans on the next table stood up and saluted the man. After five minutes, the maître d' came over to inform her that her table was ready. Knowing that she would probably attract attention being a woman on her own, Elizabeth held her head high feigning a confidence she wasn't too sure about. A French couple on the next table bade her a good day as the maître d' pulled out a chair for her. With a flourish, he flicked open a white napkin and dropped it into her lap, asking if he could get her a drink while she was deciding on the menu. She needed to keep her wits about her at all costs and rather than anything alcoholic, ordered another lemonade.

Elizabeth ordered the Spring Soup followed by grilled trout. It was not uncommon anywhere in France for good hotels to be frequented by Germans, but there was something sinister about this place and she couldn't put her finger on it. As often happened, one only needed to scratch away the veneer and dig a little deeper to see what was really going on. Lake Bonlieu was fifteen kilometres from Saint-Laurent-en-Grandvaux and until the whole of France was occupied, the train line running through Saint-Laurent-en-Grandvaux had been the dividing line between the occupied and non-occupied zones. Strategically, it was on the route de Genève — the main road from Dijon, Champagnole, and through Morez in the Forbidden Zone on the Swiss border. The Wehrmacht moved along this road at all times, radiating out into the countryside in the event of any problems caused by the Resistance. It was also one of the main roads the Belvedere network intended to target leading up to the invasion of France, so Elizabeth could hardly be surprised by the presence of such a diverse group of high-powered Germans.

The couple that attracted her attention the most was the one in the car. By the look of his insignia, he was an *Obergruppenführer*– a high ranking general of the SS, or as Guy used to tell her, a jumped-up stormtrooper. Whatever he was, he was certainly good-looking. It was hard to tell, but Elizabeth thought he must be in his early forties. Tall with blonde hair, a healthy tanned complexion and a good physique, his companion couldn't get enough of him. In looks, she was his equal: also tall with wavy shoulder-length blonde hair and from what Elizabeth could recall as she observed her in the car, grey-blue eyes. Interestingly, she also wore the same fashionable coloured lipstick that Elizabeth had received during the last drop. Vera Atkins had certainly done her homework. Every now and again the woman stroked the man's hand whilst talking to him; a small flirtatious gesture which appeared to delight him enormously. She wore a cornflower blue dress with a low cowl neckline and around her neck was a strand of pearls which she twirled around her fingers playfully. Elizabeth noted she also wore a wedding ring.

After finishing the main course, she decided to forego one of the tempting desserts in order not to miss the bus back. She had no idea where the mystery woman in Clairvaux had gone and it seemed pointless to hang around. The waiter presented the bill and asked if she could pay at the reception desk. As expected, the meal cost a small fortune. London would not look too kindly on her going on a wild goose chase and spending the equivalent of a French factory worker's weekly salary on a single meal. The same woman was still behind the reception desk and asked if she'd enjoyed her meal. Elizabeth asked to give her compliments to the chef. It was then that she took the handkerchief out of her bag.

'I found this as I was walking along the lane,' she said. 'Someone must have dropped it. Ordinarily I wouldn't have bothered to pick it up except that it's particularly beautiful and probably cost quite a lot of money. It has hand-embroidered initials in the corner and may even have been a gift, in which case the owner would be distressed if she knew she'd lost it.' She opened her hand to reveal the initials and a section of the lace. 'I wondered if perhaps you had a guest with such initials.'

The woman put on her glasses attached to a gold chain around her neck and took a long look. 'No, I'm sorry. I can't help you. Maybe the owner didn't come here. She could have gone to the lake. Not everyone calls in here, you know.'

Elizabeth sensed the woman did not want to continue being questioned and turned her attention to someone standing behind her — the blonde lady.

131

'Madame Lombard, what can I do for you? Did you enjoy your meal?'

Elizabeth moved aside and the woman asked if Claudette, the hotel's beautician, was able to bring forward her appointment for a manicure and pedicure.

'I know I'm not booked in for another half an hour, but Herr Krüger needs to leave before then, so if Claudette could possibly fit me in now, I would appreciate it.'

It was then that Elizabeth noticed a sign on the desk listing various guest services. Along with sporting activities such as supplying fishing tackle to fish in the lake, and towels for swimming, there was one for a beautician — facials, massages, manicures and pedicures. Clearly life went on as normal at the Grand Hôtel du Lac.

'I'll just check for you.' The woman picked up a house telephone on the wall behind her.

In the few seconds it took to make the call, the blonde lady had scribbled something on a notepad lying on the desktop, torn it off, and thrust it into Elizabeth's hand.

The woman put the receiver down. 'She'll be with you in five minutes.'

'Thank you,' the blonde lady replied. 'I know the way; I'll wait for her in the Beauty Salon.'

She walked off down a corridor and disappeared around a corner. Elizabeth quickly glanced at the note. On it was written — Ladies Room. She screwed it up and stuffed it in her trouser pocket. The woman behind the desk saw her hesitate.

'Is there anything else I can help you with?' she asked.

'Can you direct me to the Ladies Room, please?'

She pointed to the corridor where the blonde lady had gone. 'Turn left at the end.'

Elizabeth set off along the carpeted corridor lined with a collection of deer heads of varying sizes, photographs of the lake, and a large painting of Mont Blanc. When she turned the corner, she saw three doors. On the right was a glass door that appeared to lead into the vegetable garden, another at the very end had a brass plate with the words — Beauty Salon: By Appointment Only — and the one on the right, set back in an alcove, had a gold silhouette of a lady's profile on it which Elizabeth took to be the Ladies Room. She stopped for a moment to listen. The only sounds were coming from the terrace through an open window. She was not taking any chances and took a slim knife from the heel of her shoe. The knife had a sliding blade contained in the handle which opened automatically with the press of a button. She pushed the door open.

The blonde was applying lipstick in the mirror and Elizabeth was careful not to let her see the knife. After she'd finished applying the lipstick, she slipped it back in her bag and at the same time quickly drew a revolver out and pointed it towards Elizabeth.

'What are you doing here?' she asked. 'What do you want?'

Elizabeth could see the woman was angry and tried to deflect the situation. 'You're not going to use that are you? The noise will attract a lot of unwanted attention. I'm sure you don't want that.'

'I asked you what you are doing here.'

'I was taking a walk and I came across the hotel and decided to have a meal.' She paused for a few seconds wondering if the woman really would use the gun. 'I could ask you the same question. What is a French woman doing with a German — and someone so important? What did you say his name was — Herr Krüger — Herr *Obergruppenführer* Krüger?'

The woman raised her gun to the level of Elizabeth's chest. 'That handkerchief — where did you find it?'

'I don't see how it's any of your business.'

'It belongs to me.'

'And are your initials A.R?'

'I am telling you, that handkerchief belongs to me. Hand it over.'

Elizabeth stood defiant. 'I don't believe you. If it was yours you would have said something at the desk.' She saw the woman falter and in a quick movement knocked the gun out of her hand. It spun across the room and landed on the floor. The woman made a dash to grab it but Elizabeth was too quick for her and put her foot on the woman's hand, at the same time bringing the knife up to the side of her neck.

'Leave it or I'll kill you.' She brought her leg up and pushed her on to the floor, picked up the gun and pointed it at her. 'Now tell me who you are and why the handkerchief is so important to you.'

The woman rubbed the back of her head which had hit the wall with a thud while Elizabeth locked the door and went through her bag, emptying out the contents. A comb, small mirror, lipstick, powder compact, and a silver cigarette case clattered on to the marble sink. With them was an identity card.

'Odette Lombard!' exclaimed Elizabeth. Address Champagnole. 'O.L. does not equate with A.R. I think you'd better start talking, don't you?'

The woman gave a half-smile. 'I don't know who you are but if you don't let me go, someone will come looking for me.'

Elizabeth knelt down and pressed her knife into the woman's neck. She winced when she felt the pressure of the blade on her neck. 'No more warnings,' Elizabeth hissed. 'I will make it look like suicide and will be away from here before anyone finds you.' The end of the knife nicked the skin producing a spot of blood.

Elizabeth could tell by the way the woman's chest rose and fell that she was scared.

'All right you win.'

Elizabeth pulled her up off the floor and pushed her onto a plush chair next to gilt-framed mirror. The woman smoothed down her blue dress and composed herself.

'That handkerchief is not mine, but it was meant for me. I was supposed to pick it up.'

'Where?' asked Elizabeth.

'Near the bridge.' Elizabeth had been careful not to say where she found it which made her think the woman was telling the truth. 'I know you saw me with the German, but you have to believe me, it's not what you think. I'm French and I would never sell my soul to the Nazis.'

'That's not what it looked like to me,' Elizabeth replied, sarcastically.

'Please believe me. Do you think I care about them?'

Elizabeth thought about how handsome the *Obergruppenführer* was, and how she had shamelessly flirted with him. Power and looks went a long way in occupied France.

'Why were you supposed to pick up the handkerchief?'

'It meant I had a message to pick up from someone.'

'Someone in this hotel?'

'Yes. I was to pick up the message and pass it on to someone in Champagnole.' The woman wiped the trickle of blood from her neck. She was visibly scared. 'If you breathe a word of this to anyone, you have signed my death warrant.'

'Who does the handkerchief belong to?'

'Please don't force me to reveal another woman's name.'

Elizabeth took her own handkerchief out of her bag and showed it to her. She knew it was a gamble but one she was prepared to take.

The woman's eyes widened when she saw them side by side.

'The same handkerchief but different initials: a strange coincidence wouldn't you agree?' Elizabeth said, and put it back in her bag after the woman had taken a good look at it. 'Now, Odette, let's start again — from the beginning this time. Who were you supposed to meet?'

'Claudette the beautician; she works here. I don't know her too well, but I come here to deliver and pick up messages every now and again and give information on the movements of the Wehrmacht or SS. Anything I can pick up from my relationship with Krüger. I'm a courier working with the Resistance. That's all.'

'Are you telling me Claudette the beautician is your contact?'

'Yes.'

Elizabeth had hoped Odette would mention Amelie, but at least she was making progress, although where this would lead, she still wasn't sure. To be sure she was genuine, Elizabeth asked her to name someone in the Resistance in Champagnole. Odette gave her a name she didn't recognise.

'Not good enough,' Elizabeth replied, matter-of-factly. 'Let's try again.' She scrutinized her identity card. 'If you are working for the Resistance, I am presuming this is a forged document. Who forged it?'

'Are you seriously expecting me to give you the name of a forger?' Odette said.

'Odette, I don't play games. I have shown you that I have the same handkerchief as the woman you were to meet. In my book, that counts for a lot, wouldn't you say? I will ask you again. Give me the name of the forger who made this card.' Elizabeth waved it in front of her. 'He's obviously a good one. You have my word I will not betray you.'

This time, she gave a name Elizabeth recognised. Bernard, the forger from Chaux-du-Dombief: the same one Belvedere used.

'How do you know him?' Elizabeth asked.

'The Resistance uses him. He forged my identity card for me and changed my surname to Lombard to make it look as if I was married.'

Elizabeth let out a sigh of relief. She handed Odette her gun back and told her to put it away.

Odette thanked her. 'What's all this about anyway?' she asked, her hands still shaking.

'It may come as a surprise to you, but we're both working for the same side. I need to find someone called Amelie as soon as possible. Is she here?'

'I've already told you; my contact is Claudette and I should be meeting with her now. Maybe she knows her.'

Elizabeth extended her hand. 'I'm sorry if I scared you, but I need to meet this Claudette as soon as possible. It's urgent.'

'Follow me,' Odette replied.

CHAPTER 18

Odette entered the Beauty Salon with Elizabeth following. The room was small and pristine, with a massage table and chair in the centre. To the side was a screen next to which stood a table filled a large vase of colourful flowers and an array of bottles and jars of lotions and creams and nail polish. A dark-haired woman wearing a short-sleeved white cotton jacket sat at a desk near the window, writing notes in a diary. She had her back to them and didn't bother to look up as she spoke.

'Take a seat, Odette. I'll be with you in a moment.'

'Claudette,' Odette replied in a low voice. 'We have a visitor.'

'I told you, I'll be ...' When she looked up and saw Elizabeth, she jumped out of her chair and at the same time reached for a gun underneath a towel. The gun had a silencer attached to it.

Elizabeth noticed the floral scarf draped over the back of the chair. There was no mistaking who the beautiful woman was — agent Mireille — Amelie Rousseau, and now beautician Claudette at the Grand Hôtel du Lac. It was a face Elizabeth had memorized down to the last detail, except that in the flesh she was even more beautiful than her photograph. Elizabeth wanted to laugh, partly out of relief that Claudette was actually the elusive Amelie and was really working as a beautician in the hotel, and partly because she shouldn't have been surprised. Vera Atkins *had* told her she was posing as a cosmetic saleswoman. Amelie continued to point the gun until Elizabeth took out her own handkerchief and showed it to her along with hers.

'It's okay,' Elizabeth said, casting her eyes on the gun, 'you won't need that. We are working for the same people, wouldn't you agree?'

Odette looked uncomfortable. 'Do you have anything for me? I can't keep Herr Krüger waiting too long.'

In the heat of the moment, Amelie had almost forgotten about her appointment with Odette. 'No. You can go. I'll contact you when I need you again. Thank you for coming.' Odette turned to leave.

'Odette,' Amelie said, 'not a word to anyone about this, okay?'

Odette nodded.

When they were alone, Amelie relaxed. 'How are Vera Atkins and Colonel Buckmaster?' she asked.

'Waiting to hear from you,' Elizabeth replied, with a hint of sarcasm.

Amelie took a cigarette from her silver cigarette case and offered her one.

'How did you find me?'

'I saw you following me in Clairvaux. Then I traced you to here, although I must say, I didn't expect to find you in such salubrious surroundings. Neither did I expect to find you associating with the mistress of a high-ranking German, even if she has a false identity.' She paused for a moment, giving Amelie time to let it all sink in. 'I've known you were alive for a while. I also know Daniel is alive too.' Elizabeth was careful not to show too much emotion.

'Who are you?' Amelie asked, drawing on her cigarette. 'I heard someone was making enquiries about us, but I wasn't sure if it was London or someone impersonating a British agent.'

Elizabeth took her identity card out of her bag to show her. 'I will level with you. My name is Marie-Élise Lacroix. London sent me to find out what happened to Belvedere. That's all you need to know. I will only divulge my code name with Daniel. He will vouch for me as soon as he sees me so the sooner you take me to him, the better it will be for all of us.' Amelie checked the card and handed it back. 'And not only were we given the same style of handkerchief, but you are wearing the same shade of lipstick I wore when I arrived,' Elizabeth added. 'Another parting gift from Vera to us both.'

After almost six weeks, Elizabeth had finally come face to face with agent Mireille and she knew she had to gain her trust or it was possible she might simply disappear again.

'Amelie, you have to tell me what happened. Is Daniel safe and why haven't you contacted anyone?'

'Daniel's safe: that's all I can say at the moment.'

Elizabeth walked over to her. 'I know what happened the night of the raid on the Ledoux Farm but London needs to know what's going on. *I* need to know. What has happened that you couldn't even tell us whether you were alive or dead? Don't you realise they are worried? Don't you even realise how many lives you've put at risk by going underground?' Amelie remained quiet and Elizabeth threw her hands up in the air in exasperation. 'I don't get it, really I don't. If you needed help, you only had to contact London. And what about the friends you have here? Why keep them in the dark too? Apart from that, the Maquis needs help. Do I have to go on?'

Amelie listened. 'I know what the maquisards need. I don't need to be given a lecture on that,' she replied curtly.

Elizabeth pleaded with her. 'I have to see Daniel. You must arrange a meeting. Whatever it is you're hiding I need to know, as I must report this to London. You know how these things work.'

Elizabeth picked up a bottle of red-coloured nail varnish — "Blood Red". People were starving; being tortured and sent to camps, yet here the privileged were wining and dining, swimming in the lake and having facials. What an unreal world it was. She wanted to scream at the injustice of it all.

'Where are you staying?' Amelie asked.

Elizabeth smiled. 'Surely you should know if you've been following me?'

Amelie ignored her reply but Elizabeth was left in no doubt that Amelie knew full well where she was living. 'We can't talk here. I have another appointment in ten minutes. Can you meet me tomorrow in Bonlieu? There's a bar next to the bus stop. It's quite safe. The owner is with the Resistance.' She gave her a coded sentence to give to him.

'What time?'

'Catch the midday bus from Clairvaux. I will tell you more then, but I'm asking you to keep this to yourself. Don't tell a soul where you've been or what you saw today.'

'Not even the Menouillards?'

'The few people who know, the better it is for them, but there is one thing you can tell them if they ask — that you're going away for a few days. Make some excuse.'

'Why?'

Amelie smiled. 'You want to meet Daniel, don't you?'

Elizabeth's heart skipped a beat. If only Amelie knew how much she had longed for this moment.

'Don't let what you have seen here today fool you,' Amelie added. 'The Grand Hôtel du Lac hides a lot of secrets that we wouldn't want the Germans to get wind of. The owner, Madame Sophie Martin is with the Resistance. It's a safe house.' She paused for a moment taking in Elizabeth's clothes. 'Wear something a little more ordinary tomorrow. I want you to blend in with the locals. What you have on now is far too stylish — and make sure you have sturdy shoes too. You'll be doing a lot of walking. One more thing: please don't refer to Odette as "a German's mistress". It's not as simple as that. She sleeps with him to find out information for us. She's a very brave woman.'

Elizabeth left the hotel feeling the best she'd felt since she landed in France. Persistence had finally paid off. She passed through the terrace on her way out. Most of the guests had gone, including Odette and her German friend, and the waiters were clearing the tables. Amelie had told her there was something important going on in Saint-Laurent-en-Grandvaux which was why there were more Germans there than usual, but she wasn't sure what.

Elizabeth looked at her watch. She had seven minutes to get to the main road or she'd miss the bus. She arrived just as the bus appeared around the corner. The bus driver didn't say a word when he picked her up, even though she was the only passenger, but she noticed him looking at her every now and again in his mirror. By the time they reached Clairvaux, the bus was half full. Judging by the jovial interaction between the driver and the passengers, she judged them to be regulars and was happy to remain anonymous at the back of the bus. In Clairvaux, she was the last to get off.

'Did you find who you were looking for?' he asked.

His question took her by surprise. 'No, I'm afraid I must have been mistaken, but I had a lovely walk by the lake.'

He gave her a cheeky smile which made her wonder just how much he knew of the area — in particular the Grand Hôtel du Lac. Rather than telephone Armand to pick her up, she walked back to the farm. Sabine was drawing water from the pump in the yard.

'Thank goodness you're back. How did it go?'

'No good I'm afraid. Because it was market day, the bus driver had more passengers than usual and couldn't recall exactly where the woman got off. I went to Saint-Laurent instead and had lunch.'

'I'm sorry,' Sabine replied.

'Never mind, there's always another day.'

Sabine asked if she wanted to come for dinner later but Elizabeth refused, saying she wanted to get an early night as she was thinking of going away for a few days.

Later that evening, she sent a coded message to London saying she had found agent Mireille and that she would be meeting up with Daniel in the next day or two. She finished off by saying she hoped the next call would be more informative. Sometime later, she received a message back. London congratulated her and wanted an update as soon as possible. Again they warned her to be careful. Another network was blown.

*

In Clairvaux, Elizabeth waited at the bus stop along with other passengers. She was relieved to see it was a different bus driver but not relieved to see a larger than normal amount of Milice hovering about. With their distinctive blue uniform jacket and trousers, brown shirt, wide blue beret and menacing attitude, they were easily recognisable. Some were plastering posters on the wall next to the bus stop with photographs of men and boys wanted for evading labour transport to Germany. Others checked everyone's papers and ration cards before allowing them on to the bus. The journey to Bonlieu took longer than expected as the bus was stopped at a wooded area just past Cogna and searched by the Milice again. When she arrived at Bonlieu, there were more Milice. This time they were pasting propaganda posters on the walls, but their constant presence worried her and she wondered if they were searching for someone in particular. It wasn't the best time to be meeting someone she hardly knew and she considered whether she should get back on the bus and continue to Saint-Laurent-en-Grandvaux. But the thought of seeing Daniel again was a lure too big to dismiss. At this time of the day the bar was quite full and no-one appeared to take any notice of her except the barman, who had been forewarned of her arrival. After giving the coded message, he ushered her into a backroom. Amelie was already there, sitting at a table waiting for her, drinking wine and reading a French propaganda magazine. On the wall behind her was a large photograph of Petain.

'What will you have to drink?' the barman asked. 'It's on the house.'

She ordered a beer which he brought with a slice of apple tart. When they were alone, Elizabeth asked Amelie to explain what was going on.

'It all began just before the parachute drop in December,' she said. 'You say you know what happened that night at the farm, but you

141

don't know the full story. Daniel told me he had a bad feeling but didn't say why — at least not to me at the time. Rather than cancel the drop, because that would mean waiting another month, and especially as it was winter, he decided to change the drop zone at the last minute. He wouldn't tell me why.'

Having worked with Daniel, Elizabeth knew him well and his instincts were usually right. 'Is that why he sent you away — before the drop I mean?'

'Yes. He wanted me out of the way in case he was right. Anyway, I never went with him to a drop zone. I usually met up with him afterwards.'

'Where did you go?' Elizabeth asked.

'To a safe house near Champagnole. It was a couple of days later when I heard what took place. André arrived and told me what happened. He said Daniel was still alive when he left him at the doctor's but because the Germans were raiding all the villages in the area, he had to flee. For a while we didn't know what happened to Daniel — whether he was alive or dead. Then we received a call to say he was safe, but the call was cut short and we had no idea where he was. After that we heard the doctor was taken away.'

'Why didn't you go back and find out what happened?'

'It was arranged that if anything did go wrong, I would lie low for a while. Daniel and I both knew that if the network had been blown, they would be searching for me too. Even the Menouillards, Mitzi, and Monique were under suspicion for a while, but it soon became clear they had nothing to do with it. André asked that I should stay put at the safe house until further notice.' Amelie reached for another cigarette, the third since she'd been there. Elizabeth said nothing but it was obvious to her she was a chain smoker. Whatever had happened had taken its toll on her nerves. At that moment they heard voices in the bar demanding to see everyone's papers.

'La vache!' Amelie hissed. 'It's the Milice! Damn them! The bastards are becoming a nuisance. That's the second time this week.'

The door opened and two of them entered. The older one with a thin moustache and slicked-back, light-coloured hair demanded to see their papers. The other, a younger, clean-shaven version of the first, stood behind him pointing a machine pistol at them. When he saw Amelie's occupation as a cosmetics saleswoman, he turned to his colleague, whispered what appeared to be a derogatory remark and handed it back with a smile. When he examined Elizabeth's, he asked where she was working as a nanny. Amelie didn't give her time to answer. Instead she answered for her.

'Monsieur, my friend has not had a job for a while. No-one can afford a nanny these days. She's looking for work around here. Perhaps you know of someone?' She flashed him a flirtatious smile.

The man thrust Elizabeth's identity card back in her hand without answering and left the room with the younger one hot on his heels. *Cheeky thing* they heard him mutter under his breath to his friend. When they'd left the bar, the two women looked at each other and burst out laughing.

'Bastards!' Amelie said, reaching for her glass. 'All the same, it doesn't pay to get on the wrong side of them. Anyway, drink up. We have to leave.'

Amelie called the bar-owner over and asked him to keep a look out and let her know when the Milice had gone or were otherwise occupied. After a few minutes he came back and told her they'd gone into another bar.

'Come on,' she said to Elizabeth, slipping on her jacket and covering her head with a scarf. 'There's a van waiting for us out the back.'

She ushered Elizabeth through the back door into a yard where a baker's van was waiting with its engine running.

'This is Robert,' Amelie said, introducing the driver as she pushed Elizabeth into the passenger side of the van. 'He's with us and he has an *Ausweis*.'

Amelie squeezed in the front seat next to her. A young man with a swarthy complexion, dark curly hair and wearing a beret, extended his hand.

'*Enchanté,* Mademoiselle.'

Elizabeth glanced over her shoulder towards the back of the van. Robert had finished his delivery of fresh bread; the racks of trays were empty, yet the wonderful aroma still filled the van.

They left the yard and the village of Bonlieu via a back road and then turned back onto the main road, heading towards Saint-Laurent-en-Grandvaux. At a certain point along the road it turned left, bypassing Lakes Ilay and Narley, until it reached the junction of the main Dijon/Geneva road which was heavily patrolled by the Germans. Two gendarmes waved the van aside and they were asked to show their papers. The first gendarme took a cursory glance at them while the second opened the back and had a quick look round. After a few seconds, he called out to the man checking the papers that all was fine. The man handed them back their papers, bid them a good day, and ushered them on their way. Elizabeth noticed through the side mirror that the second gendarme had a large bag with him which he didn't have when they were stopped. When she mentioned it to Robert, he smiled.

'It's a ritual,' he replied. 'I know the men on this route well and always keep a bag of fresh bread for them. I look after them; they look after me. No questions asked.'

Elizabeth had no idea where they were taking her, but she recognised the area they were driving through, as it was not far away from where she had lived with the Delatours. She did not mention this fact to Amelie. In fact, the three barely spoke at all. At a bend by the Gorges de la Langouette they were stopped again and the last bag of bread was retrieved. No-one said a word. At the next village — Fontaine-le-Bas — the van pulled up outside a car repair workshop. A middle-aged man with a thick-set face and neatly trimmed beard was in the garage bending over the bonnet of a battered car. He wiped his hands on a cloth and came over to greet them. He was introduced as "the mule" — a term Elizabeth knew the *passeurs* often used rather than give their real name. He locked the premises and they followed him to his house across the road. His wife was in the kitchen. She had been expecting them and laid the table with smoked sausage, cheese and bread. They sat around the table while the man poured them all glasses of wine.

'Is everything in order for tonight?' Amelie asked.

'We make a move after curfew,' the man said after cutting a large slice of cheese and tearing off a chunk of bread. 'I don't anticipate any problems.'

At first Elizabeth had no idea where the meeting place would be, but after taking the road here, it didn't take her long to realise where they were going — across the frontier into Switzerland. During her time with Belvedere, she had helped people escape via the network but had never made the trip herself. It was fraught with danger and not everyone made it. This wasn't exactly what she'd expected. After her conversation with Antoine Berger, she'd imagined Daniel to be somewhere closer to Moirans-en-Montagne or Saint-Claude. Now here she was preparing to follow in the footsteps of hundreds before

144

her, but for the moment she had put her trust in these people and her instincts told they were genuine. She had no option but to follow it through.

'I heard several escapees were killed last week,' Amelie said. 'Are you sure it's safe to move now? We can always wait a day or two until things quieten down?'

'Your information is correct. It was about ten kilometres north of my route. The *passeur* was inexperienced and was warned not to use that route. Six people died, including an old woman and a young child.' Amelie looked concerned. 'Don't worry, I know this area well. I've been using it since before the war.'

'How long will the journey take?' Elizabeth asked.

The weather's good so if all goes well, we'll be there before dawn — maybe eight hours. If it was winter, that would be another story. Possibly twelve hours, or even longer.'

CHAPTER 19

As soon as they'd eaten, Robert said goodbye. He was going back to Saint-Laurent and wished them the best of luck. After he left there was little to do but wait until dark. Amelie occupied herself reading magazines while Elizabeth offered to help the man's wife with the food. When the time came to leave, they set off in a car on a back road towards the border. After ten minutes, they arrived at a farmhouse belonging to the mule's brother-in-law. They left the car there and set off on the rest of the journey on foot.

Behind the farm, the footpath petered out into an area of cattle-grazing pastureland. Beyond was the Risoux Forest, one of the largest forests in Europe, lining the western edge of the Vallée de Joux for approximately fifteen kilometres. The Risoux formed a natural border between France and Switzerland and its density and geographical situation made it an ideal route for smugglers. The most dangerous part was to cross the pastureland as they were exposed until they reached the safety of the trees. Their guide was known as one of the best *passeurs du Risoux*. Even so, he made it clear that there was to be no talking at all until they reached the forest. All the men in his family were *passeurs* going back to the time of his grandfather. Nowadays, he made the trip once a week, usually bringing back tyres, car parts and fuel for the garage which were hard to come by these days. The fact that he now aided the Resistance was a bonus as they paid well, but he had seen too many people caught or shot while trying to escape to take any chances.

The ground was soft underfoot which cushioned their footsteps. Every now and again they stopped for a few minutes to crouch behind a large rock to gauge the terrain and check for any movement from the border guards. The *passeur* had acute senses of hearing and smell. Occasionally he would stop them in their tracks and tell them he could smell tobacco which meant the guards were nearby. There was no wind and neither Elizabeth nor Amelie could smell anything, but they trusted him. Another time, he was sure he heard the soft murmur of guards in conversation. Every snap of a twig, every scent in the air, did not go unnoticed. Elizabeth smiled when she thought of her SOE training in the Scottish highlands. This guide would have given her teachers a run for their money.

They reached the edge of the forest and breathed a sigh of relief. Since the occupation, the trees in the Risoux were witness to conspirators involved in acts of terrorism against the Resistance and fleeing escapees, and the Germans used every trick in the book to discover them. Every person killed or caught meant either money or the chance of a promotion. Now Elizabeth and Amelie had to make their way upwards towards the crest of the forest. It was steep and tiring but they were fit and wearing sturdy shoes. Even though the guide knew where the guards were, they could not afford to let their guard down. German and French patrols regularly moved about in the hope of catching less experienced smugglers. After five hours of criss-crossing endless networks of paths, they reached the border; a broken line of dry-stone walls in the heart of the forest making it easy to cross. Only a local would know these routes, as most areas were strung with barbed wire and a no-go zone which was guarded by searchlights with the likelihood of being shot on sight.

Even when they'd crossed the border, they still weren't safe. There was an area of several kilometres on the Swiss side which was considered out of bounds and any escapee found in this area was likely to be forced back over the border into the hands of the Germans by Swiss border guards. They stopped to rest in a forester's cabin and finished off the bread and smoked sausage prepared by the *passeur's* wife. When Amelie went outside to relieve herself, the *passeur* told Elizabeth he recognised her.

'You've changed a little but I never forget a face. You were at the Delatour Château last year, weren't you? I was there doing some repairs on one of their cars.'

Elizabeth knew there was no point lying to him.

'That's right, but as I have only just met Amelie I would rather not talk about that for the moment. It's a long story.'

'Don't worry. Your secret is safe with me. I am sure they would like to see you again though. They thought highly of you.'

'How are they?' she asked. 'And how are the children they looked after? I hope they're all safe and well. I aim to go and visit them when I've finished my assignment, but for the moment this is more important.'

The *passeur* sighed. 'I hate to tell you but they haven't had an easy time. There was a *rafle* in the middle of the night. Four Jewish children were caught and taken away. The others were French citizens and were safe. She still keeps in contact with the Swiss Red Cross and Swiss Children's Help Society but there was nothing they could do for the Jewish children as they were not deemed to be French. The youngest was only four.'

Elizabeth rubbed her head in her hands. This was terrible news. The Delatours were well-connected and resourceful but sometimes even that wasn't enough.

'Some of the villagers didn't take too kindly to her hiding Jews either, even though she tried to keep it quiet. There were a lot of deportations after August.'

They heard Amelie's footsteps outside the cabin and their conversation ended. It was time to get a move on if they wanted to reach their destination before dawn. The last few hours were less strenuous, but they still had to be on the lookout for Swiss guards patrolling the area. Eventually the forest petered out and they made their way down the beautiful flower-filled mountainside of the Vallée de Joux filled with the tinkling sounds of cow and goat-bells and bird calls. In the early dawn light, they approached their destination — the village of Le Pont, nestling against the lake. They stopped at a garage and workshop on the outskirts of the village where the *passeur* would collect his tyres.

'This is where I leave you,' he said. 'I will be here until tomorrow. If you want to return with me, be here before it gets dark. I won't hang around.'

The women thanked him and Amelie handed over a wad of money. They continued towards the village alone. It was still early, but already fishermen were preparing to go out onto the lake. They walked through the narrow streets with the aroma of freshly baked bread drifting through the air. How calm it seemed from the turmoil of France. Yet Elizabeth was far from calm. She was tired and her feet ached but all she could think of was that at any moment she would come face to face with the man she loved. She had no idea what to expect and it scared her.

'Come on,' Amelie said. 'We're almost there.'

Five minutes later they found themselves standing outside the door of a chalet set in a pretty garden. Amelie whistled a few bars of a French song and Elizabeth noticed the lace curtain in the window move slightly revealing a young woman's face, checking them out. Seconds later they heard the door being unlocked and the same woman appeared at the door. She greeted Amelie with a kiss on both cheeks and introduced herself to Elizabeth as Giselle.

'Is he here?' Amelie asked.

Giselle indicated the back of the house. 'He's waiting for you.'

As they walked down the hallway towards a back room, Elizabeth's heart pounded so hard she thought it would burst. Amelie knocked on the door three times and in a low voice, gave a coded sentence. A voice called out — Guy's voice. 'Come in!'

Amelie turned the doorknob, pushed the door ajar and stood back. 'Go on,' she said to Elizabeth. 'I'll wait for you in another room.'

She turned on her heel and walked back to join the other woman.

*

The man that sat in the chair facing her with a pistol by his side was not the one she had dreamt about night after night; he looked different. Even after she learnt what took place at the Ledoux Farm, she still envisioned the same handsome Guy she had fallen in love with If she saw him in the street she wouldn't have recognized him and at first she thought it was one of his disguises. Unfortunately, that was not the case. His injuries had been so severe it took her breath away and she had to force herself not to cry out in anguish.

'Hello, my darling,' Guy said. 'When they said someone was searching for me and told me the name, I knew it was you. Only you can be so tenacious.'

Even his voice had changed. The explosion had affected his larynx.

Elizabeth stood rooted to the spot. The shock was so great she could neither speak nor move. Guy stood up and slowly walked towards her. She saw that he had a slight limp and could no longer restrain herself. With tears streaming down her cheeks, she ran towards him, clasping him in her arms so tightly, his face distorted in pain. His hair was greyer and one side of his face was so scarred from the explosion, it was pulled into creases of reddened skin like folds of pale pink satin which stretched from his neck to his forehead, covering part of his eye.

'My darling, my love, my soul.' Elizabeth cupped his face in her hands and smothered it with kisses as if she could make it better.

Guy closed his eyes, inhaling her scent, sweet and womanly, allowing himself the pleasure of the touch of her soft lips on his injuries. When she kissed his eyelids, she tasted his tears, letting them mingle with hers. Eventually he pushed her from him, clasping her hand and bringing it to his mouth, brushing her fingertips with his lips.

'*Mon amour*, you're not wearing your wedding ring.'

'London's idea,' she replied with a huff.

'So here I am.' Even with all the scarring, he still had that same warm smile. 'Maybe it would have been better if you'd stayed in England. You see what a mess I am.'

Elizabeth swallowed hard. She knew this wasn't the real Guy speaking. The one she knew was stronger, someone who faced a challenge head-on. 'I am just thankful you are alive,' she replied. 'I don't care about your scars. I love you and to me you're still the man I married.'

He let her hand drop and walked to a couch by the window. By now it was light and beyond the garden they could see people going about their daily lives. He patted the seat for her to sit next to him.

She did as he asked and he reached for her hand.

'I never thought I would make it,' he said. 'There were times when the pain was too much to bear and I wanted to die. Yes, me, the man everyone thinks of as strong. I even thought of taking my cyanide tablet, but at times like that your face would appear before me, telling me it was going to be alright.'

Elizabeth squeezed his hand gently. 'There you are, it did turn out alright after all, and here I am, my love. But I can't understand why you never contacted London — or Amelie for that matter. Vera Atkins and Colonel Buckmaster were worried sick when they didn't hear from you. Not to mention the Menouillards, Pierre, and others in the Resistance. Thankfully, I was oblivious to all this until SOE called me in and asked if I'd heard from you. When I said no, they asked me to find you.' She paused for a moment. 'And you're a hard man to find Guy Maxwell.'

She leaned over and kissed him full on the lips.

'Now, my sweetheart, are you going to tell me what's going on or do I have to drag it out of you?'

He smiled. 'After I've made love to you.'

Elizabeth snuggled up next to him. 'You mean you are not so injured that you can make love?' she replied with a cheeky look in her eye.

'Let's see. It's been a long time.'

He stood up and led her to an adjoining room with a bed. He sat on the side of it and pulled her towards him. Slowly he unbuttoned her blouse and one by one, took off all her clothes dropping them in disarray around her feet on the floor. She found herself trembling like a young virgin anticipating her first sexual encounter. When he'd finished, she knelt on the floor in front of him and slowly undressed him as tenderly as he had her. With each piece of clothing she saw another scar. There was a small dent below his left lower shoulder blade where the bullet had penetrated but it had healed well. The worst part was down the right side of his torso where he'd suffered terrible burns. It was even worse than his face. As a nurse, she'd confronted such burns time and time again during the London Blitz and could only imagine the pain he suffered. A weaker man would never have pulled through. And then there was his leg. His femur had fractured and not healed well at all.

'It's not a pretty sight is it?' he said.

''Shush! Don't talk.' She pushed him back on the bed and caressed his body, kissing his scars in the same way as she had kissed his face. She smiled when she saw his erection.

'The most important part is fine,' she said in a soft voice. 'That's what counts.'

She straddled him carefully in the way she had done so many times when he was well. His hands moved over her body, feeling her buttocks moving slowly up and down as his mouth reached for her breasts, biting her nipples and pulling her over him, softly at first and more violently as their lovemaking quickened, culminating in a violent explosion of desire and pent-up emotion. She rolled off him, lit them both a cigarette and lay down next to him on his left side where there was hardly any scarring at all.

'If only you knew how much I dreamt of that!' he said, exhaling a thin cloud of cigarette smoke into the air.

'You know you can have surgery on those wounds?' Elizabeth said, 'when you get back to London. It's remarkable what they can do these days.'

He put one arm behind his head watching the smoke curl through the air. 'I'm not ready to go back yet.'

Elizabeth propped herself up on her side, resting on her arm. 'Tell me what's going on, darling — everything. London will want to know anyway as I've already told them you're alive.'

Over the next few hours, Guy told her the whole story. Every now and then, she saw tears well up in his eyes and could see how much the death of so many friends had scarred him even more than his physical scars. She already had her suspicions about what happened, but it was not as she thought. She cuddled up closer to him, pulled the covers over them and listened.

CHAPTER 20

'A few days before the airdrop, I felt something bad was going to happen,' Guy said. 'The drop was planned for a few days' time during the full moon period. It was important, as the Resistance was badly in need of supplies, so I was reluctant to cancel it.

'The thing is, I was told a few days earlier that someone had betrayed us — a *mouchard.*'

Elizabeth's eyes widened. She sat bolt upright, unable to take it in. 'You suspected a traitor in your midst and didn't cancel the drop. That's not like you.'

'Without evidence there was little I could do. A week before, I received a message that someone wanted to meet me in a bar just outside Lons-le-Saunier. It wasn't one of our normal meeting places and I was wary that it might be a trap.'

'Who told you this?'

'Someone at the German HQ. Pierre Dassin often goes there to see an acquaintance, Klaus Schubert, a thoroughly dislikeable man but one we put up with, because he passes on information to us.'

'Yes, Pierre told me about him. He doesn't sound like a man you'd want to cross.'

'On this particular day, I happened to go with him and waited outside the building in Pierre's van. He was making his usual delivery of wine to Schubert and unless he was trying to get information, he was only there a matter of minutes. It's not exactly a place you want to hang about. As I waited, I noticed a man in a Wehrmacht uniform staring at me from one of the first floor windows. It unnerved me and I was sure something bad was about to happen. Pierre was longer than usual and I almost got out of the car to do a runner but the man disappeared. A minute later, I saw him come out the door and head towards me. He tapped on the window and I wound it down, half-expecting him to point a gun at me and haul me inside. At the same time, I had one hand on my gun under a coat on the seat next to me, ready to shoot. To my surprise, nothing of the kind happened. He handed me a note, telling me not to show anyone, including Herr Dassin as he called Pierre. He immediately walked back inside before I could say anything.'

'What did it say?'

'That I was to meet him at a certain place at a certain time and to come alone. That was it. I'd only just read it when Pierre returned and I managed to stuff it in my pocket before he saw it. Thankfully he was too pre-occupied with cursing Schubert about wanting more wine to even notice my face. As we drove away, I saw the man looking at me from the window again.'

'And you didn't mention this to Pierre at all?'

'No. The note said I was to meet him in two days' time. I went back to Clairvaux and thought about it. Was it a trap? I didn't know but my instinct told me not. And I was curious. He obviously knew I was a friend of Pierre's and if he suspected I was someone important, he could have arrested me there and then — and probably got a promotion into the bargain.'

'Why didn't you tell Pierre, even though the man asked you not to? I mean, he does seem to know a few people there. He might know him.'

Guy sighed and kissed her cheek lovingly. '*Mon amour*, I thought it best not to involve him. From the moment Pierre joined the Resistance, he asked that we do nothing to endanger his family. If I could have protected you from all this, I would have done the same, but then Baker Street dragged you back into it again.' He lay back on the pillow and continued. 'Pierre is a good liaison man for the Resistance. He uses his wine contacts to get information, but that is as far as it goes. I know he's the Resistance leader there but if anything went wrong and they threatened Juliette and Angeline, I doubt he would stand up to it. Can you imagine what he would do if they dragged Juliette to Gestapo HQ and threatened to rape her — or worse?'

Elizabeth knitted her eyebrows together in a frown. 'I am not sure about that. He has just helped me with an important airdrop. Two of de Gaulle's men arrived from England and he liaised with Gavroche, Max, Brando, and Armand, to see that they were safely spirited away on their respective assignments. He also helped hide arms. And just in case you didn't hear, they now have another addition to the family — a son. All this took place around the time of Bloody Sunday.' She returned his kiss and smiled. 'So you see, you may have underestimated him, after all.'

Guy held her close. 'Perhaps it was your powers of persuasion that made him do these things.'

'Somehow I doubt it. Whatever you thought of him, he's certainly stepped up to the mark, especially with so many resistants being executed or deported.'

Guy's face dropped at the mention of those times.

'You remember all those tests we did during our training?' Elizabeth continued. 'How so many recruits had remarks on their files saying, *not mentally suitable under extreme measures; lacks focus; too timid; not cut out for this sort of work*, etc. Well, what a load of rot! How can you really tell until you are faced with the real thing? Fighting for your country *in* your country when your family and friends' lives depend on it is quite different to exercises in the Scottish countryside. War brings out something in us we never thought we had — survival. It's human nature, for better or for worse. Pierre is certainly such a person.'

Guy looked at her admiringly. 'Well, well, you could certainly teach those back in London a thing or two.'

'Don't mock me.' She prodded him, and smiled. 'I am quite serious you know, which is why I knew you must have had a good reason for going underground. So get on with the story. Why didn't you discuss such an important thing with someone you trusted?'

'I did. After much thought, I confided in André. We discussed it at length and agreed we would keep it to ourselves until we had more to go on. I decided to keep the rendezvous and he said he would have someone keep watch while I was there — someone he could trust who kept a low profile in the Resistance. I would recognise him by his rather unkempt dark hair and he would be wearing a dark brown sweater and scarf and reading a newspaper. If the newspaper was folded on the table, it would mean I was to get away as soon as possible. We'd done this sort of thing many times before.'

'Where was this meeting place?'

'Bistrot Papillon — about five kilometres outside Lons-le-Saunier on the Nogna/Clairvaux road.'

'I know it. It's a simple place where agricultural workers hang out,' Elizabeth said. 'I've passed it a few times. Didn't you suspect a set-up?'

'It was a chance I was prepared to take. I went there by bicycle a few hours earlier and cautiously surveyed the area in case it was indeed a set-up. When the bistro opened, I hid and waited until the man turned up to check he wasn't being followed. There were only a few customers, and you were right, they were agricultural workers. André's man was the first to arrive. He sat alone in a corner reading his newspaper over a beer. After about fifteen minutes, the German drove up in a car, only this time he was not wearing a uniform. He was, however, smartly dressed which hardly blended in with the clothes the agricultural workers were wearing. When I saw him seated at the table, I took my gun from underneath the bicycle basket, slipped it inside my jacket, and joined him. He ordered two glasses of wine and I waited for him to say something. He thanked me for coming.

'There was a choice of vegetable soup or rabbit with vegetables and we ordered the rabbit. It certainly wasn't the Ritz. Thankfully the man didn't waste time in telling me why he wanted to meet up. He spoke in a low voice so no-one could overhear.'

'"I've got some important information for you," he said. When I asked why he was doing this, he surprised me and said he was against the war; that he hated what Hitler and what the Nazis had done and wanted to help.'

Elizabeth looked sceptical. 'And you believed him — a man at Gestapo Headquarters?'

'I asked him to tell me more; who he was, etc. He said his name was Franz Wagner –*Oberstveterinär* Franz Wagner to be exact — a colonel in the Wehrmacht. As he was not wearing his uniform, he showed me his identity card to assure me he was indeed a Wehrmacht officer and not SS. He was from Hamburg and had just become a veterinarian when the war broke out. He claimed to be a pacifist and only joined the Nazi party because there was no other option. It was either that or be sent to a concentration camp, leaving his family to be ostracized. He then pulled out a photo of his wife and child — a beautiful woman called Hildegard and a son called Hans, about four years old. He said they were killed when the British bombed Hamburg. "They were living with my parents. I lost them all," he added.'

'A pacifist! If it wasn't so serious it would be funny.' Elizabeth replied, sarcastically.

'I actually believed him. I have looked enough men in the eyes to know when someone is faking that sort of thing. The Wehrmacht used his veterinary experience, not only with animals, but as a doctor as well and he quickly rose to the rank of colonel. I asked him why he chose to speak with me and not Pierre, who was a friend of Schubert's. He told me he'd seen me with Pierre once before and Pierre was already known to everyone at HQ. Naturally that comment perturbed me but he qualified it by adding that they liked Pierre as he brought them good wine, but he hated Schubert and considered him a troublemaker, so he couldn't risk speaking to someone associated with him in case they were ever interrogated.

'He went on to say he knew the Germans would lose the war and they expected the British to attack at any moment and he wanted to help hasten their defeat. When I said he could be shot for such a treacherous remark, he replied, "I don't care. I have lost everything I ever lived for. I never expected things to turn out like this. Hitler must be stopped before he wipes us out. He's a madman."

'I looked around hoping no-one heard. Thankfully, everyone was too preoccupied.'

'So what did he want then?' Elizabeth asked. 'To be exonerated when the Germans are eventually defeated?'

'Exactly. In exchange he wanted to give me information — important information as it turned out — and in return, if he was brought before a tribunal when the war ended, would I or anyone associated with me, testify on his behalf? Besides I needed to trust him in case he did have something on us.'

'Do you think he knew you are a British agent?'

'I believe he thought I was French and he knew I was with the Resistance because of the information he gave me, but obviously if he had asked me out right, I would have denied it.'

Elizabeth looked concerned. 'If he suspected you were with the Resistance, then surely he must suspect Pierre too.'

'It's highly likely.' Guy smiled. 'I can see your analytical mind is still as sharp as ever.'

'I should hope so.' Elizabeth answered. 'You trained me — remember!'

As if what Guy was telling her wasn't bad enough, the conversation quickly took an even darker turn.

'The thing is, the information which as we now know, was to have dire consequences for us all, came from Gestapo HQ at Besançon. As part of his work, Wagner moved around — Dole, Dijon, and Lyon. Lons-le-Saunier was the least important place for him. He was based in Besançon and had access to the Gestapo under Alfred Meissner.'

'Good God!' exclaimed Elizabeth. 'That bastard! It doesn't sound good.'

'My thoughts exactly, but although he was not SS, because of his work he did seem to know everything the Gestapo were up to in this region. I confess it did scare me and I almost thought about telling London I was pulling the plug on Belvedere completely for the moment. Yet until I knew more, what was there to tell them? All that effort we'd put in. SOE wouldn't have been too happy. Considering the predicament I was in, I gave him my word that should we both survive the war, I would testify on his behalf — *if* the information he was about to divulge proved trustworthy. We shook on it. He thanked me and then came the bombshell.'

Elizabeth felt the hair on the back of her neck stand on end. What was he going to tell her?

'We had a *mouchard* in our midst who was ready to blow our cover. My mind raced and I thought of those close to us who had access to important information. I still had not said I belonged to the Resistance but I could tell he wouldn't have believed me anyway. I asked for the name of the man and what the information was. That's when he told me the information did not come from a man. It was a woman.'

Elizabeth couldn't believe what she was hearing. 'The *mouchard* was a woman! I can't believe it!'

Guy shook his head. 'I found it hard to believe too. He told me the only thing he could say was that there was a file on her marked "S3964". I told him that meant nothing and I needed more than this before I would trust him. He assured me he didn't know her real name. I called the waiter over and asked for the bill, telling him we were finished. It was a tense moment as I was calling his bluff. Out of the corner of my eye I could see André's man watching me, ready to intervene should anything go wrong. Wagner grabbed my arm and urged me to sit down. The waiter asked if everything was alright. Wagner said it was a friendly dispute over who would pay for the meal and as I was his guest, he would pay.'

'"All I can tell you is that this woman went to see the Gestapo in Champagnole. She asked them not to use her real name as she knew she would be killed if word got out about what she was doing. She also asked for money in exchange for the information and signed a paper which awarded her 70,000 francs. This information was relayed to

Besançon and Dijon immediately. Meissner has the file, that's how I came to know about it. I saw it on his desk. It was marked, Top Secret — Informant "S3964". We have lots of informants, but this one attracted my attention because she was specific. She said the Resistance were due to receive a *parachutage* from England during the next moon period and it would take place near Saint-Claude." He added that Meissner also took this seriously and alerted everyone.'

Elizabeth was having a hard time taking it all in.

Guy checked the time. 'Come on, we'd better get dressed and go back into the other room before the others catch us like this. We'll continue later.'

Elizabeth slipped back into her trousers, did up her shirt and tidied her hair and applied lipstick. Guy kissed the nape of her neck. 'You have no idea how good it feels to have you with me again. There were many dark days, but now you are here and I feel better.'

She put her finger on his lips. 'I love you and we're going to get through this together. Now, can we get something to eat? I'm starving.'

He opened the door and called out to Giselle and asked if she would be kind enough to bring them some food. She soon appeared with a tray of fresh rolls, conserves and cheese, fresh fruit and real coffee.

'What a treat!' Elizabeth exclaimed. 'Are we going to ask Amelie to join us?'

Giselle said she'd gone out for a while to leave us to talk.

'Does she know about us?' Elizabeth asked when they were alone again.

'I couldn't even be sure it *was* you, until I actually saw you. When I heard someone called Marie-Élise was looking for me, I thought it might be a trap.'

'Before we go any further, tell me why you never contacted London to let them know you were safe, especially once you reached Switzerland?'

'There was a reason. Let me finish the story.'

Elizabeth wiped her mouth after finishing everything on her plate.

'Wagner had nothing else to say except that if I didn't heed his advice, there would be consequences. I asked him if he had a photo of this woman — anything at all — as what he told me meant little. He said no, but warned me to be careful. Then he got up to leave. I asked how I could get in touch with him again and he said that would be difficult as he never knew where he would be, but he'd given me his real name so if I really needed to contact him, he had no doubt I had the resources to do so. When I asked if he would get in touch with me again, he smiled.

'"If you heed my advice, you will not need to. If you don't, you will die. Let's leave it at that." We shook hands and as he left I noticed André's man leave at the same time. We both noted the car number plate. André confirmed it later.'

'And that was it?' Elizabeth said. 'So you still had nothing at all to go on?'

'Nothing! André came to the farm later that evening and we drew up a list of possible female suspects. One by one, we crossed them off the list. Sabine Menouillard knew about the drop but we ruled her out as she rarely went further than Clairvaux or Lons and hadn't been to Champagnole for a while. And if she did, Armand would have been with her. Monique Dumont was ruled out too because she wasn't privy to that aspect of our work. Then there was Mitzi. She and Amelie were close but I know Amelie never talked about her work, especially a drop. All the other women were wives, daughters, or girlfriends of maquisards and resistants and it was highly unlikely they knew anything about a drop. Only a handful knew about it, and they were men and we'd used them all before without any problems.'

Elizabeth looked at him thoughtfully.

'I know what you're thinking,' he said. 'What about Amelie?'

She nodded.

'I admit it did cross my mind — and André's for that matter. She was the only woman who knew when the drop would take place, but in the end neither of us could believe she would rat on us. It didn't add up. Amelie is a good courier and she has been loyal. She's smart and she's careful. Another thing, the whole time she worked with us, she never once came to a drop zone.'

'But she did travel around for you, making letter-drops and gathering information which would have given her a reason to be in Champagnole. Was she sent there during the time the information was passed on? And she was Paul-Emille's lover. I gather they were together quite a bit towards the end.'

Guy thought about it before answering. 'It's true, she was in Champagnole, but only for an hour or so before moving on.'

'It only needed half an hour to pass on information,' Elizabeth replied. 'A drink and a discreet conversation at the Hotel Ripotot,

160

Headquarters of the German Kommandant, is all it takes.'

Guy shook his head. 'No, Marie-Élise.' Elizabeth noted how this time he used her alias, even though they were alone. 'If she went there with such information *and* asking for money, she would have been interrogated for quite a while and someone would have spotted her and alerted us. We have informants at the Hotel Ripotot. It is not Amelie. As for your second hypothesis, Paul-Emille never made a transmission to London when she was around.'

'Are you quite sure?'

'That's what he told me and I believed him. I was often with him when he made a transmission.'

'Then who was it?'

In that moment Elizabeth saw that he suddenly appeared tired. He got up and went over to the drinks cabinet.

'The truth is we still don't know. In the end we had nothing to go on, but as a precaution I sent Amelie on an assignment so she was not around at the time, and I got Paul-Emille to let London know we were changing the drop zone at the last minute. I thought that was better than cancelling the whole operation because the Maquis were in desperate need of money and arms. Obviously, it proved to be a fatal decision.'

Elizabeth looked at him with pity as he poured them both a Scotch. The earlier happiness had dissipated and for the first time she realized just how much the guilt had consumed and aged him.

'It's a bit early to start drinking,' she said as he handed her a half-filled glass, 'but after what I've heard, I need something strong myself.' She noticed how quickly he drank his. He poured another but she didn't say anything.

'So you know what happened that evening then?' he said, moving on with the story.

'Yes, Pierre told me. He and Juliette were the first people I stayed with when I reached Lons-le-Saunier. The Menouillards told me more. Like you, I also listen to my gut instinct and I knew you were still alive. I told London so. They've given me a radio. It's safely hidden at the Menouillard's cottage. I also heard Amelie was not around when the Gestapo swooped so I gathered she was also alive. London's biggest worry was that Belvedere had been broken through transmissions. It's happened to so many networks lately.'

'After the Gestapo surrounded the Ledoux Farm, I didn't really understand what had happened myself. Caught in the crossfire and explosion, I was injured and in a coma for several days. When I did come out of it, I found myself alone in a forester's cabin deep in the woods. I had no idea how I got there. The first thing I remember was the excruciating pain and the cold. Temperatures had fallen below zero and the area was deep in snow. Added to that, the wolves appeared. Whether it was hunger or the scent of blood, I don't know, but it's not something I will forget in a hurry.'

Guy reached for a small bottle and took out a little white pill and swallowed it with the last drop of Scotch. Elizabeth looked alarmed.

'Pills and liquor don't mix,' she said, in the stern voice she often used as a nurse with difficult patients in the hospital.

Guy ignored the remark. 'You asked me why I didn't relay this precious information to the British Embassy and to the Swiss intelligence agency here. It was because I wanted people to think I was dead. I wouldn't rest until I found the traitor.'

CHAPTER 21

December 28 1943: Forester's Cabin. The Haute Jura, France.

Guy cocked his gun and stood behind the door waiting to see who the visitor was. He hadn't given a coded signal and it worried him. The door slowly opened and a voice called out to him not to shoot.

'Daniel, you're safe. I'm Raymond's son, Antoine.'

Guy lowered the gun. 'What's wrong? Where's your father?'

'He's been taken away. The Gestapo raided the house again and both of us were dragged away at gunpoint. I was released after being roughed up, but my father has been sent to Dijon. I fear he will either die during interrogation there or be sent to a concentration camp like the others.'

Antoine handed over a small parcel of food and a flask of water. 'You must be starving.' He also gave him a bottle of pills. 'More pain killers if you need them.'

Guy sat back on the floor and devoured his bread and cheese hungrily while looking at the bruises on Antoine's face. 'I'm sorry. It's all my fault.'

'No time for that kind of talk. How are the injuries?'

'I'm managing but it will be a while before I'm back to normal.'

'Let me take a look.' Antoine removed the bandages. '*Merde!* Not good but they'll heal.' He poured fresh water from his bottle, cleaned the wounds and applied fresh bandages.

'What's happening?' Guy asked.

'We need to get you away from here as soon as possible. The Germans are everywhere at the moment. This time they have really got it in for us. They've raided all the villages in the vicinity of the Ledoux Farm and arrested scores of people. My father and I would have been with them that first night if my mother hadn't covered for us. That's when we moved you. We knew they would be back. I helped my father get you here. He was right, they didn't let up. The day after he came to see you they came back again and took both of us to Moirans-en-Montagne. They interrogated my father because they said someone had seen André bring someone to the house and they were sure it was a resistant that was unaccounted for. My father denied everything, telling them they already searched the house. That's the last we heard before he was sent away. I was beaten up and sent back home. But I know they will be watching me so I have to be vigilant.'

Antoine told Guy that his father gave him instructions about what to do if anything happened. 'I was to move you straight away,' he told me. 'I believe my father gave you a map marked with safe houses and Maquis camps.'

'He did. I studied it and destroyed it.'

Antoine was relieved. Daniel's answer told him he wasn't letting his guard down.

'The thing is, it's not safe to take you to any of those places now. You would never survive in the Maquis camps in this weather with your injuries, not to mention their insanitary conditions. And as for the other safe houses, it's possible they're being monitored too. Except for one, which was not on the map, but it's quite a long way from here and you can't walk far at all at the moment. The weather is not going to improve any time soon.'

'What do you have in mind?' Guy asked.

'We have to get you across the border to Switzerland. There you can get proper medical attention and rest for a while. Whether you choose to return afterwards or get help from the Swiss authorities to return to London is up to you.'

'Who else knows I'm here?'

'No-one except my mother, but I will need to confide in a couple of maquisards to help me get you away from here. I can't do it alone. My father gave me a few names.'

'So what's the plan?'

'I will come back tomorrow evening and we'll move you. Remember I said there was one safe house. We'll take you there first. From there we'll use the *passeurs* to get you across the border.'

'Just one more thing,' Guy said. 'Any news about André?'

'Not yet.'

Antoine got up to leave. 'Be ready. I'll be back after dark tomorrow.'

After he'd left, Guy took two of the white pills, covered himself up with the warm blankets and fell asleep, but it was a sleep marred by nightmares of being incarcerated in a stinking cell and of hearing the cries of his friends being interrogated. This was his fault. If only he'd called off the drop, they would all be still alive.

The following night, Guy prepared to leave. He destroyed any incriminating evidence that anyone other than a forester or hunter had been in the hut, and waited. As promised, Antoine returned with three maquisards. Guy recognised one of them as Serge, *chef de cellule* of a Maquis group near Saint-Laurent-en-Grandvaux. The snow was still thick on the ground and the men had skis and a sled with two dogs. They wrapped Guy in a deer hide and strapped him onto the sled. Antoine handed him two more pills.

'Here, take these just in case you feel any pain. It's going to be a bumpy ride.'

One of the men gave a sharp whistle and the dogs moved forward, gathering momentum when they headed down the hillside or on flat ground. Serge was in front guiding them, with Antoine behind. It was one of the worst rides of Guy's life and he cursed them loudly as the sled rolled over several times and hit trees as they zigzagged through the forest. They made one stop at a Maquis camp where they were given venison stew, which Guy promptly threw up. After a few hours they arrived at the top of an escarpment with a view of a frozen lake below — Lac de Bonlieu. It was one of the smallest lakes in the region but it had the advantage of being situated next to the thickly forested Jura Mountains — the most inhospitable terrain between France and Switzerland during the winter months. At this point, they were met by two more men who transferred Guy to a donkey. The two men with the sled returned to the forest.

The group took the lower road along the frozen lake. By now, Guy was racked with pain and barely conscious and was relieved when Antoine told him they'd reached their safe house. Out of the shadows he saw the outline of a long building — the Grand Hôtel du Lac.

A lookout was waiting for them and led them around the back of the building. A woman came out of a doorway carrying a flashlight, giving orders to one man to put the donkey in the stable, and to the others to bring Guy inside.

'Lay him there,' she said, directing them to a makeshift bed in front of a log fire. She turned to a young woman and told her to bring him a large glass of cognac and some clean clothes.

The woman was in her mid-forties. She introduced herself as Madame Sophie, a member of the Resistance. The younger woman, who appeared to be not much older than twenty, was her daughter Hortense.

'You are in safe hands,' she said, handing him the glass. 'Everyone who works here is with us.'

Guy drank the cognac in one go. It slipped down his throat like nectar from the Gods.

'Let's get him out of these clothes,' she said to Hortense, 'before he catches pneumonia.'

The women started to undress him and Guy was too weak to protest. They peeled off his clothes carefully while he stared into the roaring fire in pain and embarrassment.

Madame Sophie smiled. 'We've seen it all before. You're not the first and you won't be the last.'

When it came to his underwear, she saw how it stuck to his bandages because of the journey and her smile disappeared.

'Maman, his injuries are too bad,' Hortense whispered. 'Maybe we should let him dry out first.'

Madame Sophie called Antoine over. They both agreed it was far too dangerous for the wet bandages to stay on.

She gestured to Hortense to refill Guy's glass. 'Drink this,' she ordered. 'It will numb the pain.'

Their words barely registered but Guy did as he was told. He was now shivering even though the fire was hot. All he wanted to do was sleep. Madame Sophie handed Antoine a pair of scissors and he began to cut away the cloth that adhered to the skin. Antoine had watched his father do this sort of thing numerous times and he was as gentle as could be. Bit by bit, the cloth came away and was thrown into the roaring fire. Madame Sophie was no nurse but Antoine was grateful for her presence. She'd helped enough injured maquisards in her time to know what to do. She brought over warm water and swabbed each section of skin gently as the layers of cloth were peeled off. By the time they'd finished, Guy lay in front of the warm fire as naked as the day he was born, with the two women gently massaging ointment onto his burns.

'He can sleep in my room until he's better,' Madame Sophie said to her daughter. 'I'll sleep with you.'

The men were directed to take him upstairs and for the first time in ages, Guy spent the night in a warm bed with a firm mattress and a cover filled with the softest eiderdown. The bedroom had a wood stove which was kept alight day and night during the winter. After a few days he was well enough to get out of bed and move around again. His wounds were beginning to heal quickly but he would still need another week before attempting to cross the border into Switzerland. It was during that time that he learnt about the Grand Hôtel du Lac.

Situated by Lake Bonlieu, the Martin family, who lived in Paris, bought it as a holiday home before the Great War. The family were all sports enthusiasts who spent their winters skiing in the Alps or hiking across the French countryside, and their summers in the South of France. In the early 1920s, their son, Philippe, married Sophie and they decided to leave Paris and turn the home into a hotel. With enough money behind them and Sophie's sophisticated upbringing, the hotel soon became a fashionable holiday place to enjoy the beautiful Jura countryside with its lakes and mountains and many outdoor sporting activities. When the war started, Saint-Laurent-en-Grandvaux was situated on the border between the occupied and unoccupied zones but because she had the hotel, the family was allowed a car and an *Ausweis* to travel between the areas. Being a pleasant hotel, the Germans did not requisition it because the Martins said they would cater for their new German clientele.

Because it was in such a strategic position, the Martins gathered information on the Germans, particularly troop movements between Champagnole and Swiss border near Geneva. Six months into the occupation, Sophie's husband died in an accident when a tree fell on the car as they were driving around one of the hazardous bends in the area. Rather than sell the hotel, she and her daughter decided to run it. It was Hortense who told Guy about their resistance work one day when she was changing his bandages.

'We had not intended to join the Resistance,' she said as she was tending his wounds. 'It just happened. Because we owned the hotel, people asked us to get them across the line. That's how it started.'

Guy recalled that was how Sabine and Armand began their resistance work too.

'Then I started to see someone who was in trouble with the Germans. He was from near here but was on the run, so we hid him. Afterwards he went to work in Champagnole. For a while it was just a few people who asked us for help, but after the occupied and unoccupied zones were united and the Germans came down hard on men with the *Service du travail obligatoire*, our work grew.'

'Didn't having the Germans coming here worry you?' Guy asked.

Hortense smiled. 'You don't know my mother. She can be most charming when she wants to. She's confident and there's very little that fazes her. She decided to use them from the very beginning and put on a front. I can't say that everyone likes her though. Obviously, there are many who really do think she panders to the Germans for her own ends. We can't exactly tell them what we're doing, can we? I just pray that after the war, those she's helped are ready to defend us before she's labelled a *mouchard* — and me as well.'

Guy told her they were brave. These were the risks people took and not everyone understood. Time would tell. Antoine came into the room and Hortense jumped up from her chair as if she'd been caught saying something she shouldn't have. He asked her if they could be alone for a while. Hortense picked up the bandages and ointments and left the room.

'A lovely girl,' Guy said to him when they were alone. 'She's looked after me well.'

Antoine pulled up a chair, took a few more bottles of tablets out and placed them on the bedside table.

'I'm leaving tonight,' he said. 'I've watched over you for a few days but I must get back before people start asking questions. In a few days you will be well enough to cross the border. It's all taken care of. Just look after yourself, *mon ami*.'

He was about to leave when Guy caught his arm. 'Have you any news about André?'

'All I can tell you is that he is alive and well and has gone underground. Like you, he wants to find out who sold you out. You'll hear from him when he is ready. Let sleeping dogs lie. Isn't that what you English say?' He smiled. 'We are all watching our backs at the moment.'

After Antoine left the room, Guy got out of bed, put on a dressing gown and paced the bedroom to get exercise. He was pleased with his progress. Tomorrow he would begin push-ups. There was no time to waste: the network was in ruins and he must save it.

There was a knock on the door and Madame Sophie entered.

'Tonight you will join us downstairs for a meal: we have much to talk about.' She placed a set of clean clothes on the bed for him. 'I think these should fit. They belonged to my husband. You are about the same size.'

Guy asked if there were any Germans in the hotel that night.

'No. We are closed until the weekend. You will be quite safe.' As she turned to leave, she added. 'By the way, we have another two guests joining us later.'

She left the room before Guy could ask who they were. He looked at the clothes. The trousers were beautifully tailored and the sports pullover an expensive navy blue cashmere with a cross-over collar. She'd also left a pair of shoes, one size bigger than his own to allow for the swelling from his injuries. After what he'd been through, he couldn't believe his luck.

Dinner was in the large kitchen and a rather grand affair after his earlier experiences in huts and rustic farmhouses. The aromas that filled the room were mouth-watering. The table was large enough to comfortably accommodate at least twelve people. It was laid with a crisp white tablecloth with an embroidered centre — also in white, fine china, cut-glass wine glasses and a variety of bowls and platters of food, but there were only three eating. Madame Sophie — dressed in a fine cream silk dress with a lace top and wearing a triple string of pearls and matching pair of earrings – was standing by the fire sipping a glass of champagne with Hortense when Guy appeared. She handed him a glass. The other two guests had been delayed and she suggested they start without them. The family had a live-in cook who was preparing the meal; an attractive young woman with dark brown hair and beautiful almond-shaped eyes. Over dinner, Madame Sophie proceeded to tell him about her work, much of which he'd already learnt from Hortense.

'The Grand Hôtel du Lac is not only a safe house, but we are also involved with the *passeurs* guiding people into Switzerland. I know you have been involved in this business yourself and it's likely we know the same people. When I heard what happened in Saint-Claude, I offered my assistance to André. I've known him a while although naturally he doesn't always tell me what he's involved in. I was also acquainted with the doctor who saved your life — Monsieur Raymond — and I was extremely saddened to hear what happened to him.' Madame Sophie offered Guy more food, telling him he needed to build up his strength. 'Do you have any idea who gave you away?'

'I've racked my brains, but as yet there's no-one I can really point the finger of suspicion at.'

The cook cleared away the dishes and placed a set of smaller dessert plates on the table and a freshly baked cake.

'The thing is,' Madame Sophie said, her voice taking on a serious tone, 'we really must get you away from here as soon as possible. André asked that I help you cross the border, but the decision is up to you as you know it's dangerous and you are not a fit man at the moment. If you do make it, you will have a better chance to access the right medical assistance.'

Guy deliberated over his reply. 'Thanks to your hospitality and care over the past few days, I will do what André has done — go underground for a while. I won't rest until I find the *mouchard* who did this. I still have contacts here that remain untouched by all this.'

Madame Sophie said she admired his courage. 'I confess that I'd already heard of you, but you don't have to worry, it came from a reliable source. I was told you are a brave man and now I see it for myself I think we are lucky to have you fighting for us. You can count on me to help in whatever capacity I am able to.' She looked across at her daughter. 'That goes for all of us here.'

The cook asked if there was anything else they needed. If not, she would retire for the evening.

'Thank you, Ruth. That will be all.'

When Ruth left the room Guy asked if it was wise to talk so openly in front of her.

'Let me tell you more about this hotel, Daniel. Every single person here is either in the Resistance or being helped by us. Ruth is Jewish. She was from Alsace and escaped. Her story is similar to many, but in her case, she survived. When the Germans occupied France, she was caught trying to flee and whilst being interred, was raped — repeatedly I might add. She ended up pregnant. When she came to us, she was too far gone to make the journey to Switzerland. The routes we use are difficult and not at all easy for a pregnant woman, the very young or old people. At the time, other routes were too hazardous. So we got her a false identity card and she had the child here. After that I offered her a job as my cook and she decided to stay on. The child lives here too.' She stood up. 'Come: let me take you on a little tour of the hotel.'

Guy followed her down a corridor to her office where she removed a large picture from the wall. Behind it was a safe in which were several dossiers. She took one out and placed it on her desk.

'This is the dossier for Ruth. I know everything about her: who her family were, their background, addresses — everything.' Then she unlocked a drawer in the writing bureau and pulled out another dossier. 'This is the new one — the false one we created for the Germans. It has her French identity papers with her certificate from a cooking school in Paris, her parents' Christian marriage certificate, and her own certificate of baptism. As for the child, his parentage is noted as a Frenchman who was killed.'

She snapped it shut. 'I vet everyone who works here. There is a dossier on all of them — the gardener, the woodsman, the man who rents out the boats to the tourists on the lake, the two cleaning ladies, the maitre d' and the chef who works here from Thursday to Sunday. They live in the area and all have a hatred of the Germans. Some have lost relatives, either through deportation or execution. In my own way, I am as efficient as the Gestapo.' She smiled. 'But less ruthless.'

Guy was impressed. He made a comment that the Gestapo would pay her handsomely for such diligent work. She took it in the spirit it was intended.

'I am not for sale.' She laughed. 'And I would not like to be in someone's shoes who dared to cross me.'

Guy didn't doubt that for one minute.

'Now I will show you something else.'

She grabbed a thick woollen shawl and this time they went outside via a back door that led to the *potager* and the far side of the house. At a certain point were a series of low windows along the back of the house, barely a foot above the ground. Next to them was a heavy wooden door with a large iron handle. She knocked several times and someone inside holding a lantern pushed it open. Madame Sophie gestured to Guy to go down the flight of steps. After a few seconds he became accustomed to the soft light and found himself in a huge cellar with lots of smaller side rooms. It was cold, damp, and uninviting.

'This is where we hide those escaping across the border. I know it's not the best of conditions, but at least it's safe.'

Madame Sophie called out a coded sentence and several "cell" doors opened and one by one, people appeared. Guy was astounded. He counted ten people from the ages of ten to fifty.

'We feed them well while they are here, but it's vital that they remain hidden and make no noise. The rooms have fresh straw beds and blankets so they are warmer than you think. I can't risk them being in the hotel.'

171

She chatted to several of them, telling them the visitor was a friend and they needn't be alarmed. At the far side of the cellar was a set of dusty shelves filled with tools, tins, and what looked like general rubbish. It stood on a set of small rollers which were not visible unless you knew what to look for. Madame Sophie pushed it aside revealing an old wooden door which opened into a dark, narrow tunnel hewn out of the limestone rock that glistened with moisture. A blast of cold air chilled his bones.

'This tunnel was here when we bought the property,' she said. 'I have no idea why. When the war started, my husband and I decided to cover it up and use it as an escape route. It leads to a cave high up in the escarpment at the back of the house. If we are ever raided and there is no time to use the cellar door to escape to the forest, then we would use this.' She closed the door and slid the shelves back in place.

When they were back outside, Madame Sophie told Guy the people he'd just met would leave the following night. She pointed to a large fir tree jutting out at the base of the rocks at the end of the garden. 'From there, where the track winds up towards the escarpment into the forest. Believe me, the Germans would never find our route. You need to know this area well to venture up there. It's dangerous if you don't have a guide.'

From where they were standing, Guy looked up at the escarpment looming vertically in the darkness. He wondered if he was in a fit state to make it himself.

Madame Sophie pulled her shawl tightly around her. 'Come on, let's get back inside, it's freezing out here.'

When they entered the kitchen, Guy got an even bigger shock. Standing in front of the warm fire was Amelie. With her was someone else he knew; Belvedere's forger from Chaux-du-Dombief, known to them as Bernard "the artist" because he was so good at his work, and who now worked near Champagnole. Amelie threw her arms around Guy and showered him with kisses.

'My dear friend, you have no idea how I've worried about you.' She stood back and looked him up and down. 'I have to say, you're looking better than I expected though.'

Guy smiled, even though it still hurt. 'You should have seen me a week ago!'

'Well at least you're alive and in one piece.'

Guy looked at Bernard and then at Amelie. 'What on earth are you two doing here anyway?'

Hortense spoke first. 'This is my friend... the one I was telling you about earlier.'

'Well I never!' So Bernard was Hortense's boyfriend. He looked at Amelie. 'And you?'

'You told me to make myself scarce until after the drop. I did just that. I went to a safe house and then ended up staying with Bernard. When I found out about the Gestapo raids, I was worried sick and Bernard told me about Madame Sophie and suggested that perhaps she could help. That's when I knew we could pull our resources together. Not knowing at that point whether Belvedere was finished, I jumped at the chance.' Amelie's eyes welled up with tears. 'I couldn't believe what had happened. I kept going over and over it in my mind. It didn't seem real. All had gone well up to that point.'

Guy knew she was affected by the loss of all concerned, especially Paul-Emille who had confided in him only days before the drop how he intended to marry her when it was all over — just as he had with Elizabeth.

'I'm sorry. I know how much he meant to you.' His words sounded lame.

Madame Sophie had no idea about Amelie and Paul-Emille's relationship, but she had been around long enough to know it was an *affaire de cœur*. Her response was to offer everyone more champagne and they settled back around the table to talk business.

'Tell me what I can do to help.' Madame Sophie said. 'Both my daughter and I are offering our services to you and the Grand Hôtel du Lac as a safe house for your network. I hope you will accept this offer in the spirit it is intended.'

Guy extended his hand. 'I cannot thank you enough.'

'Now we have established our alliance,' Madame Sophie said matter-of-factly. 'Let's get down to work. You have the choice of running your network from here or recuperating in Switzerland. Which will be easier? Or will you notify London and return?'

Madame Sophie's enthusiasm and clarity of thought was impressive and, with André still in hiding, Guy thought she would make a good Resistance chief herself.

'How well do you know André?' he asked.

Madame Sophie grinned cheekily. 'I know him very well.' She had a twinkle in her eye which made him think she was referring to an *affaire de cœur*. They were of a similar age although maybe André was a few years older, and they both had a similar character — strong, independent, and with a passion for life which probably entailed grabbing happiness whenever and wherever you could, although both were too astute to admit to such a thing. It was also highly likely that with André moving between Maquis camps in the area, their paths would have crossed.

'Do you know where he is?' Guy tried to push the point.

Again, Madame Sophie smiled. 'You and I have just declared a trust for each other. *If* I knew where he was — and I'm not saying I do — then I would not be at liberty to say. You yourself have chosen to reveal your whereabouts to a select few for a good reason. If André chooses to do the same, then we must respect his reasons for doing so. Patience, Daniel, is a virtue. Back to the question: what do you intend to do?'

'I will run Belvedere from across the border.' He looked at Amelie. 'You will be my go between.'

Amelie's face beamed with pride. 'I am honoured.'

Guy was quick to point out that rather than it being an honour, it was dangerous. He wanted everyone to think he might be dead, and that included London.

'Is that wise?' she asked. 'If we don't come clean, we could be putting other networks at risk.'

'I doubt it. They have their own liaison teams in place. Someone betrayed us and I won't rest until I find out who the bastard is.'

Madame Sophie announced that she was going to bed and would leave the two of them to talk alone. Bernard bid them goodnight too and Hortense saw him out. When they were alone, Amelie put her elbows on the table and held her head in her hands. The tears she had been holding back started to flow.

'Oh, Daniel, what a nightmare we've got ourselves into.'

'You can bloody well say that again,' he replied. 'I never expected all this. It's a mess and I blame myself. I was warned something was going to go wrong. I should have postponed the drop.'

Amelie glared at him. 'What!' she exclaimed. 'You mean you *knew* this was going to happen?' She got up and paced the room. 'All the bloody time you knew and did nothing about it. I can't believe what I'm hearing.'

174

'Calm down.' He got up and attempted to put his arm on her shoulder but she shook it away. 'You knew! You bloody well knew!'

'For Christ's sake calm down and let me explain.'

Reluctantly she sat back down and he explained about the meeting with Franz Wagner but he omitted to say a woman was involved and that even she had been considered a suspect. 'So put yourself in my position,' he said, as he concluded the story. 'I had nothing to go on but a stranger's warning about a *mouchard*– and someone who I met at Gestapo HQ too, even though he was not SS.'

Amelie shook her head. 'How do you know he wasn't with the SS? You know the sort of games they play.'

'He wasn't. Let's leave it at that. I feel bad enough as it is. But I *did* change the drop zone at the last minute. The new one was at least ten kilometres away in the opposite direction and I thought that would be enough.' He could see the anxiousness on her beautiful face. 'It's one reason I sent you away. To be sure you would be safe.'

Amelie apologised. 'I'm sorry for my outburst. I shouldn't doubt you. Please forgive me.'

He put an arm around her shoulder. 'There's nothing to forgive. You were right to be angry. If I could turn back the clock, I would.'

It was then that Amelie picked up on something he hadn't thought about, maybe because he'd been in severe pain and on drugs most of the time and it had clouded his thinking.

'You changed the drop zone *but...*'

Guy looked at her anxiously. 'But what?'

'You didn't change *where* you would all meet up afterwards — the Ledoux Farm.'

'Good God! That didn't occur to me. It was kilometres away from both drop zones.' He rubbed his temples. 'Maybe it wasn't the drop zone they had in mind at all, but the actual farm. What a fool I am. I know we were caught there, but I imagined it was because the Germans were searching the whole area.'

They talked long into the night trying to figure out who would have betrayed them. They went over and over Paul-Emille's transmissions and Amelie assured him he was always careful.

'Even I wasn't there when he radioed London,' she said. 'So what do you suggest we do now?'

'We lie low until we find out the truth. Madame Sophie has been kind enough to work with us. Use here and your other safe houses and we'll continue looking for the *mouchard* until we find him. Sooner or later, the name will be revealed.'

Guy was careful to say "him" and not "her", but Amelie noticed.

'What if it's a "her"?' she said thoughtfully.

Her quickness surprised him but it shouldn't have. Amelie was a good operator.

'Maybe,' he replied, somewhat thrown by her remark. 'All options are on the table. The thing is, it's important we don't involve our good friends, in case they are being monitored. That means Sabine and Armand Menouillard. Stay away from their farm and sawmill — and Pierre and Juliette Dassin too.'

'What about those in Clairvaux — Mitzi and Monique?'

'The Gestapo will be watching them, especially Mitzi. Play it by ear, but if you do go anywhere near there, make sure no-one recognizes you.'

'Okay. You have my word. Now let's get you to Switzerland and on the mend and I will stay here and work with Madame Sophie.' She lowered her voice to a whisper. 'Talking about Madame Sophie, did you spot the twinkle in her eye when you asked if she knew André?'

'You couldn't miss it, could you? She's a very attractive woman and from what I know of André –and I've spent many a night with him — he likes the women, especially feisty ones. He's married you know, but from what I gather it's a bit of an open marriage. Good luck to him.'

They both laughed. 'I'm sure wherever André is, he's safe. He'll resurface when the time is right.'

'If they're still in contact with each other, she might well tell him what's going on.'

'I trust them both. I think we're in safe hands so let's wait and see. No doubt we will find out what's going on soon enough. Now I think we'd both better get some sleep, don't you?'

Guy returned to his warm bed, took another little white pill and lay back watching the last embers of the fire flickering in the grate. It had been an enlightening evening and for the first time in ages, he felt a sense of positivity, but the danger was far from over.

The following night, after the people hidden in the cellar had started on the final leg of their escape, Ruth prepared another tasty meal. It was on this occasion that Madame Sophie learned of Amelie's job as a cosmetics saleswoman and offered her work in the hotel as a beautician.

'My guests bring glamorous women and like to spoil them,' she said. 'I think you could do well. Not only would you be able to make a little extra money, but we would be able to find out about the sort of women who collaborate with the Germans. They might have loose lips and we could learn a thing or two. What do you say? The hotel opens from Thursday to Sunday. It's the weekend that's the busiest so that would leave you plenty of time to do other things. If you're away for longer, that's fine too.'

Amelie liked the idea and agreed. She gave Madame Sophie a list of things she would need and two weeks later, with the help of two local handymen sympathetic to the Resistance, the beauty salon opened.

'For the purposes of the business, we will call you Claudette — a lovely name which suits you. What do you think?'

They all laughed. 'Claudette it is then,' replied Amelie. 'Claudette's Beauty Salon: I like the idea.'

Madame Sophie was the first to have a treatment, followed by Ruth. Amelie had asked for a radio and played music while she gave her massages, facials, manicures and pedicures. They loved it so much they booked themselves a session every week. Now Amelie had a legitimate reason to be at the hotel and was able to accompany Madame Sophie in her car to places that otherwise she would have had a problem getting to.

It soon became popular with the Germans' "fancy women" as Madame Sophie referred to them.

A few days later, Guy said goodbye to them and left the comfort and relative safety of the Grand Hôtel du Lac for the Swiss border. This time he had no sled but with the aid of two *passeurs,* he eventually made it through the rugged snow-capped Jura forest to the Vallée de Joux. It wasn't an easy route as they went via the town of Morez and the ski village of Bellefontaine. The town of Morez, situated right in the heart of the Upper Jura had been an important glasses manufacturing centre since the end of the 18th century and, being on the main route to Geneva from Champagnole, was heavily monitored by the Germans. Nevertheless, the *passeurs* had families who lived in the area and utilized their farms and huts to aid the escapees. Clambering up and down the heavily forested mountains, often with little to cling on to but the roots of trees, slithering down the hard Jurassic rock formations, encrusted with ice, were some of the hardest things Guy had ever done in his life. His physical fitness and period of recuperation stood him in good stead, but he could well understand how difficult it was for ordinary escapees who were not used to such hardships, and why many of the *passeurs* refused to take the very young, the old, and pregnant women. For those, they tried to take the easier routes into Switzerland, but that meant facing more German sentries and a higher chance of being shot on sight.

CHAPTER 22

The weeks and months of not knowing what happened were all beginning to make sense to Elizabeth now and Guy agreed that she should report back to London and put their minds at rest.

'As we are together again, don't you think we should disclose the fact that we are married to those closest to us, especially Amelie? It will soon become pretty obvious something is going on between us.' She gave him a kiss on the cheek. 'You know, I confess to being extremely jealous when Vera Atkins showed me a photo of her. I know the adrenalin that runs through you when you're in the field, and let's face it, she is extremely beautiful.'

Guy laughed. 'She most certainly is. Many men made a play for her, but she and Paul-Emille were besotted with each other. I'm sorry it ended up so badly for them.'

There was a knock on the door and Amelie entered. She addressed Guy.

'We've had a message. You have a visitor. He's waiting for you in the bar by the lake. He says it's urgent.'

Guy asked who it was but Amelie said she had no idea, except that he made it clear he would only speak with Daniel and no-one else.

He picked up his gun and prepared himself to go and meet up with the man. 'Wait here. I'll be back soon.'

'Do you want me to keep an eye on you — from a distance,' Amelie asked.

'No. That won't be necessary. Stay here with Marie-Élise.'

The two women watched him walk through the gate and head for the lake. They looked at each other, hoping all would be well. Elizabeth felt Amelie's eyes scrutinizing her and blushed. Whatever she was thinking she kept to herself. Half an hour later, Guy returned. The look on his face told them the meeting had gone better than expected.

'Finally, we have the news we've been waiting for.'

At first Elizabeth thought he meant the Allied invasion of France but quickly realised the whole town would have known if that was the case.

'The man was a messenger from "Uncle" André as he referred to him. André told me if ever he needed to pass on an important message the man would refer to him as Uncle.'

Elizabeth and Amelie waited anxiously to hear what it was.

'André has been in Besançon all this time keeping watch on the mysterious Herr Franz Wagner. He finally has a copy of Meissner's dossier on "S3964". He says it makes for eye-watering reading and we have to return to France as soon as possible.'

'Does he say who she is?' Elizabeth asked.

'No. The information was obviously too sensitive to give to the messenger.'

They all looked at each other in bewildered silence for a few minutes, trying to take it all in.

'Marie-Élise, I want you to return to France immediately. You too, Amelie. I will follow in a few days' time. Tell Madame Sophie what's going on, although somehow I expect she will already know. I will meet you at the Grand Hôtel du Lac.'

Guy asked Elizabeth to leave the room. He wanted to speak with Amelie alone. She went to find Giselle to prepare food for the journey. When they were alone, Guy confided in Amelie that Marie-Élise had been with him on his first mission in France.

'Out of respect, I need to tell you something. You already know Marie-Élise is with SOE, but what you probably don't know is that she was one of my original couriers, just like you. Together we expanded the Belvedere network. When our mission was over, we returned to England and married. Because of this, when I came back to France SOE thought our being married might compromise our safety — too emotionally involved and all that stuff — so they sent you instead. After the drop went wrong and they didn't hear from us, they knew she was their best bet to find me. That's why she's here. She also has a radio and can make transmissions for us once again.'

Amelie smiled. 'Thank you. I realised she was an SOE agent when she showed me the handkerchief, but knowing the rest explains a lot, especially the electricity between the two of you. I'm happy for you both. I will not breathe a word to anyone. It's your business who you choose to tell this to. Now, we'd better get a move on so we can meet our *passeur* before dark.'

The *passeur* was waiting for them at the garage. He warned them the weather report said there was going to be a heavy downpour. 'We'd better get a move on,' he added.

The journey proved to be a good one and they arrived back without any problems, even though the *passeur* carried three tyres on his back and two large bags of spare parts for vehicles which the two women took it in turn to carry. They arrived back at his brother-in-law's farm an hour before dawn, just as it started to rain. There they ate a hearty breakfast and continued on to the garage. By now the rain was pouring down and torrents of water gushed down the mountainside flooding the roads and filling the rivers and streams that wound through the villages. Because of this, Robert was late and they began to worry something had gone wrong, but it was only due to the downpour and the fact that one of the roads was blocked which caused him to take a round-about route to get there. The good news was that because of the bad weather the Germans were stopping fewer cars.

They arrived at the Grand Hôtel du Lac by late afternoon. Fortunately, the weather had also kept visitors away and the place was empty. Madame Sophie was in the kitchen going through a list of produce with the gardener and Ruth. Ruth's small boy was also with them. She suggested Ruth take a few hours off and take the boy for a walk by the lake. The gardener took this as his cue to leave as well. Madame Sophie was pleased to see them arrive back safely and asked if all had gone according to plan and if Daniel was well.

'His health has improved enormously. Better than we expected,' Amelie replied. 'You will be pleased to hear he's returning in the next few days. There's been a breakthrough in our investigations. He received word of it a few hours before we returned.'

Madame Sophie gave them a knowing smile. 'I heard. Let's hope it all works out for the best.'

Amelie glanced at Elizabeth. Guy was right. She did know and it could only have come from André.

Elizabeth told them she would return to Clairvaux for the time being, even though Madame Sophie offered her a room. She knew the Menouillards would be worried about her and she also had to update London on the recent events.

'I'll return when Daniel arrives,' she said. 'Telephone Monique at

Bistrot Jurassien and leave a coded message. Give it to her and no-one else.'

'What do you want it to be?' Amelie asked.

Elizabeth looked at the vegetables on the kitchen table. 'Just say *the vegetables are ready to be picked up.*'

They all laughed.

'How will you get back?' Madame Sophie asked. 'It's raining. I can drop you off in my car.'

Elizabeth looked at her watch. The bus would be along in fifteen minutes.

'Lend me an umbrella and I'll be fine.'

She left the hotel and made her way back along the lane to the main road and waited for the bus. It arrived on time and she was dismayed to see it was the same bus driver who'd dropped her off the first time.

'Not the best weather to be out walking,' he said, handing her the ticket.

She smiled sweetly and sat at the back of the bus hoping he'd forget all about her. By the time they reached Clairvaux, the rain had stopped and the sun was shining again. But the bus had also picked up several Milice going to Lons-le-Saunier who thankfully ignored her this time. As soon as she got off the bus, she went to Bistrot Jurassien to see Monique.

'I wondered where you'd got to,' Monique said. 'I haven't seen you for a while.'

'Business,' Elizabeth replied. She checked to see that no-one could hear them. 'Can you do something for me?'

'Of course: what is it?'

'I'm expecting a message from someone.' She told her what it would be. 'As soon as you get it, please let me know.'

Monique agreed. 'Any idea when as I'm not always here?'

'Sometime in the next few days. If you're not here, they will telephone again until they reach you.'

Back at the Menouillard's farm, the barking dogs alerted Sabine and Armand. They were listening to the French broadcast on the BBC and were happy to see her back safe and sound.

'Come in,' Sabine said. 'The General is telling us the Germans will soon be defeated. The Allied powers are gaining ground and morale is low in Germany.'

The news that the Soviets were gaining ground buoyed Elizabeth's already ebullient mood. When the broadcast was over, she left, retrieved the transmitter from between the logs and made the first really significant transmission since she had been in France — Daniel was alive and well and Belvedere was back in action. Her mission had not been in vain and during the next few weeks she would have much more to report. Shortly after came the reply that London was extremely pleased with the results. They also told her to prepare more drop zones urgently. Their coded reply left her in no doubt that the Allied invasion was about to happen.

She took off her earphones and let out a sigh of relief. The weeks of tension had taken more than their toll on her and the relief of knowing as she did now that Guy was alive and well suddenly came to a head and the tears streamed down her cheeks. They were all still in grave danger, but this time the tears were tears of joy rather than sadness.

Four days later, Elizabeth received the message from Monique. *The vegetables are ready to be picked up.* She went over to see Sabine and Armand. Armand was at the sawmill and wouldn't be back until later that evening.

'Sabine, I'm going away for a while again. Don't worry about me. All's fine and the next time I see you, I hope to have good news.'

Sabine gave her a hug. 'I won't ask any questions. Just take care. Remember we are here for you.'

Elizabeth knew that Belvedere would be calling on their help again, but it was not for her to tell them that. That would have to come from Daniel himself.

CHAPTER 23

Last week of April 1944: The Grand Hôtel du Lac

Guy finally made it back to France safe and sound and in his honour, Madame Sophie put on a splendid evening meal at the hotel. As it wasn't a weekend and there were no guests, she held it in the main dining room. She paid great attention to the smallest of details: swastikas were removed and replaced with vases of flowers, the table laid with her finest silverware and porcelain, and the best wine and champagne stood ready on the dresser. It was here that the high-ranking Germans liked to entertain their special guests. One evening she recalled a visit by Mussolini and two of his generals. All the guests drank too much and later in the evening decided they wanted someone to play the piano so they could sing Italian songs. As there was no-one who knew anything but a few French songs, she was forced to bring the pianist from the Hotel Ripotot in Champagnole and pay for it out of her own pocket, as no-one offered to pay her. When she complained to a German official in Saint-Laurent-en-Grandvaux, he paid her out of his own money and apologised for their ungentlemanly conduct. Naturally, she doubled the price and distributed the money to all her workers who had helped out that night.

Madame Sophie was beside herself with happiness and fussed about in the kitchen making sure the food was of the highest standard. Not only had Guy arrived back, but André was also there. He greeted Elizabeth like a long-lost friend.

'It's been a long time,' he said. 'So much has happened since you were last here — and not for the better.'

She responded by saying she was just happy to know he was alive and well. As were all at Baker Street. Guy came over, gave Elizabeth a kiss on the cheek and whispered in her ear that he loved her. Just to be near him set her heart on fire again but she followed his lead. For now, they would be cautious about their relationship. He commented on her pretty pink dress and the brooch she wore. When she said it was a parting gift from Vera Atkins, he took a closer look and guessed what was behind the deep-pink tourmaline.

The rest of the group consisted of Amelie, Hortense and Bernard. The gardener and several other maquisards had been put on watch just in case any Germans decided to call by. They were posted along the road between Bonlieu and Chaux-du-Dombief and were left in no doubt that this was an important meeting and should the hotel be raided, it would spell disaster for all of them.

The moment the entrée was served and Ruth returned to the kitchen, the meeting began. Madame Sophie made sure all their wine glasses were topped up, sat back and waited for André to start. All were desperate to know who the *mouchard* was who caused so many deaths and deportations in December.

'As some of you know,' he began, 'after the disaster, I went into hiding. I moved from safe house to safe house, but my intention was always to end up in Besançon. This was because of a conversation I'd had with Daniel prior to the airdrop in which we discussed a meeting that took place between himself and a German called Franz Wagner about the possibility of a *mouchard* in our midst. All we knew was that the leak came from the head of the SS there –*Haupsturmführer* Alfred Meissner. I changed my identity and installed myself in an apartment near the Gestapo Headquarters in rue Lecourbe. They had also taken over various hotels including l'Hôtel Voyageurs and l'Hôtel de Lorraine. So much was taking place in Besançon, it was hard to keep up with it all. For instance, several thousand people with British passports passed through, especially in the early part of the occupation. Many were sent to an internment camp in the Forbidden Zone, but quite a few were executed. Those executions haven't stopped. The citadel is awash with blood.

'Under a new alias, I got a job as a bartender at l'Hôtel Voyageurs during the evening and worked as an electrician during the day with a trusted friend in the Resistance. I already knew Wagner's car registration and soon located him. He used to wine and dine with various groups of Germans including the SS and their women at the hotel, and I kept my eyes and ears open for any useful information. It was common knowledge that several of the top Gestapo chiefs had mistresses, including Alfred Meissner himself. Another woman there was the mistress of Walter Menzel, who was also a cook for the SS.

'There was one woman however, who had more influence than others — Conchita — and she has appeared in numerous reports by the Resistance there. If anyone was well placed to know the mysteries of the SS in Besançon, it was her. The Resistance told me that she had been the mistress of Meissner's second in command, Herald Mauz, for several months and was on good terms with the Gestapo and the *Feldgendarmerie*. We had Conchita followed day and night. Mauz was besotted with her and there was little doubt that he would not have hidden much from her. We found out that she is a single mother of three children with a reputation for being an adventurer. She often met Mauz at l'Hôtel de Lorraine, next door to l'Hôtel Voyageurs.'

The group listened carefully without uttering a word. He had been exceptionally busy and they were amazed the Gestapo hadn't viewed him with suspicion, especially since there were wanted posters of him plastered on the walls everywhere from Clairvaux to Dijon and Dole. But he had foiled them by dying his hair and growing a beard. Even Elizabeth hardly recognized him.

'Knowing this, we needed access to the Gestapo HQ without compromising ourselves,' André continued. 'We wondered whether to pull Wagner in ourselves and offer him an amount of money he couldn't refuse, but decided against it because even though he had taken the chance of speaking with Daniel, he was in his principal place of residence — Besançon — with influential friends. Who knows what could have taken place during those months since the airdrop. Besides, it must have unnerved him to know that Daniel didn't act on the information he passed on.'

Guy's face gave little away. Amelie and Elizabeth knew the full story, but he wasn't sure about Madame Sophie or Hortense. They looked at each other trying to understand the importance of this man, Herr Wagner, and what it had to do with the events of December. Knowing they were confused and needing to gain their trust, he had to tell them the man had warned him the Germans had got wind of a *parachutage* from a *mouchard* and that he should cancel it. They were as shocked to hear this as Elizabeth and Amelie had been, but André was quick to come to Guy's aid.

'Daniel told me about this as soon as he knew and we both agreed to do nothing except change the drop zone as we had absolutely nothing to go on and thought it could be a hoax.'

'Go on,' Madame Sophie said, clearly upset at the latest revelation. 'What did you decide to do?'

'We thought about luring Conchita into becoming a double agent, but it takes immense composure and subtlety to be a double agent and we agreed Conchita would struggle to combine these two qualities. In the end, we planted another woman — one of our resistants — to become a close confidant of hers. Someone who would play up to the Germans in the same way Conchita does.'

'Odette?' asked Elizabeth in voice barely more than a whisper.

André looked at her. 'You've already met, then?'

This time it was Amelie who came to Elizabeth's rescue. 'The day Marie-Élise came here, Odette was here with Herr Krüger. She had no idea who Odette was until I told her she was working for us. In fact Marie-Élise had no idea at all what she'd stumbled on when she first came to the hotel. I'd even go as far as saying she thought poor Odette was a collaborator and almost killed her.'

Madame Sophie's eyes widened. 'Never mind this, what did you do?' she asked André irritably. 'Was it Odette who copied the contents of the file or not?'

'No. We told Odette we needed someone to do something for us and as she knows the Gestapo chiefs there, she suggested using another friend who worked as a high-class escort. She was familiar with all the Gestapo hotels in Besançon and she knew of Conchita too.'

'Who is this woman?' Madame Sophie asked.

'Let's just call her Madame X. She doesn't want anyone other than myself to know her name in case they come after her. I interviewed her and asked her if she would do it, knowing she would be executed if she was caught. She agreed and said she would photograph the file rather than try and memorise it or steal it. She thought it safer. I must say, she seemed an extremely cool character and I was of the opinion she'd done this sort of thing before. She never asked for any money but I agreed that it was only right we compensate her if we got what we wanted. I didn't give her my name either. She was to call me "uncle". It was arranged that I would be working at the hotel most nights and she would give me a message when she was likely to get access to the dossier. All I could tell her was it would be in Meissner's office. It was like looking for a needle in a haystack but she was brave enough to do it for us.'

'Did you tell Odette you were using her?' Amelie asked.

'Yes, but Odette didn't ask why we needed this woman's help and we didn't tell her. Only two trusted resistants in Besançon knew, because I wanted her covered in case she got into difficulties. We watched her for a few days. She got closer to Conchita and they seemed to hit it off. The weeks went by and as nothing was happening, I was beginning to think I'd made a mistake choosing her. Then she came to the bar one night, looking extremely glamorous and smelling of expensive perfume, and ordered a drink.'

'"Tomorrow you will have what you want," she said, and turned around and went to sit with a Gestapo official who I knew was a friend of Meissner and Mauz. Conchita joined them and they left in a Mercedes Benz in the direction of Gestapo HQ in rue Lecourbe. I made a call to one of my associates and he saw the car enter the gates. At sometime around two in the morning, the car left. Only Madame X was in it, and the driver. Conchita must have stayed behind with the other man. The informant arrived at my apartment to tell me this. I never got a wink of sleep that night and kept my gun with me at all times half expecting the Gestapo to turn up at any moment. The next day I admit I was still a nervous wreck wondering if she would turn up or not. She did. She ordered a drink and as she passed the money to me, slipped a roll of micro-film into my hand.

'"The contents of TOP SECRET file S3964." She grinned at me. "You look pale. Have a drink on me."'

'As she turned to leave, she said she'd also photographed a couple of other files which she was sure I would find enlightening. I told her I would study them and she would get her reward in a few days. She promised to return in three days' time. In the meantime, I checked the contents of the microfilm. Sure enough, it was all there. The other reports she'd recorded were of transports to Germany that occurred in January, and plans about more attacks on the Resistance in the next few weeks.'

At this point Ruth appeared with the next course — venison stew — which Madame Sophie knew was André's favourite. As soon as it was served, Guy asked the question on everyone's mind.

'Who was it?'

'Liliane — we know her as *"la simplette"*.'

Amelie's face went as white as a sheet and she dropped her fork with a clatter when she heard the name and the food splattered onto her dress and table.

'*Mon Dieu! Ce n'est pas possible.*' She kept repeating it. 'It's not possible. That crazy woman hasn't the wits to do such a thing. I don't believe it. There must be a mistake.'

She was shaking like a leaf. Guy got up and held her in his arms, trying to comfort her. She sobbed on his shoulder calling Paul-Emille's name over and over again. 'He died because of her; because she couldn't have him! They all died for nothing.'

Ruth heard the commotion and came rushing into the room. When she saw the mess on the table, she tried to clear it up but Madame Sophie stopped her.

'Not now, Ruth. Leave it. I'll do it myself. You go to bed.'

'Madame,' Ruth said, wringing her hands. 'Is everything alright?'

'We've had bad news, but nothing that can't be sorted out. Get an early night. I'll see you in the morning.'

After this revelation, no-one felt like eating. It was a sickening blow to think that the woman they classed as a simpleton had taken it upon herself to collaborate with the Germans because the man she loved wanted nothing to do with her. Elizabeth put her head in her hands and closed her eyes, trying to block Amelie's cries out. All she could think about was that she would feel the same if it had been Guy and not Paul-Emille. Madame Sophie wiped the table and fetched a bottle of cognac. After giving them all a half-filled glass, she glanced at André and saw tears streaking his cheeks. She picked up her napkin and wiped them away tenderly.

'I am sorry to be the bearer of bad news,' he said, his voice choking with emotion. 'But there's more.'

Amelie stopped crying and stared at him.

'Spit it out,' Guy said.

The tension in the room was unbearable.

'When she went to see the Gestapo in Champagnole, they interrogated her before giving her the money — 70,000 francs. They asked her about her family and that's when they learnt of her brother being with the Resistance.' He paused as if the name was too hard to mention. 'Claude Favre.'

A terrible silence filled the room and for a few minutes no-one could find words to speak. In the end Guy's temper exploded in a tirade of expletives.

'Obviously Lili had not expected this when she went to see them. Being the simpleton that she is, she probably expected Paul-Emille to be dragged before them...' He looked at Amelie, 'and maybe Amelie too, and given a dressing down. She had no idea who she was dealing with. The whole family was dragged to Gestapo HQ and interrogated. After the parents were beaten up, Claude Favre confessed and promised to co-operate if they would spare his family.' He paused to let this sink in to them all. 'So you see, in the end, it was Claude Favre who really gave them the details. He wasn't aware the drop zone had been changed until the last minute but he did know everyone would meet later at the Ledoux Farm.'

'The bastard!' Guy exclaimed. 'We trusted him. All the times we've worked together: all the meals we've shared, the laughs and sorrows...' He put his head in his hands, fighting back the tears. 'He was our brother.'

Madame Sophie commented sarcastically that he wasn't the first to give in to the Gestapo when his family were threatened, and he wouldn't be the last.

André continued. 'In return for this information, the Gestapo promised to let him live, even though he was a resistant.'

'But I thought he was caught and deported,' Guy said.

'It was a front. We all heard that he escaped as he was being transferred from Dijon but the Gestapo arranged it as a reward for "singing". He was given a new identity and told he was being watched. If he ever tried to contact the Resistance again, he would be shot. He was also told that if he had news of any other resistant or agent, he must contact them straight away. Naturally, as you, Amelie and myself disappeared, they kept bringing him into the Gestapo HQ at Dijon and questioning him about us. The Gestapo have had their collaborators looking for us everywhere, especially between Clairvaux and Lons-le-Saunier — even further.'

Guy's fist was still clenched in anger but by now, Amelie had stopped crying. Her beautiful face took on a look of intense hatred. Elizabeth reached out and held her hand in an effort to comfort her.

'Where are they now?' Guy asked.

This time Elizabeth spoke. 'Monique told me about *la simplette*. A few weeks ago she arrived back in Clairvaux to get her hair done with Mitzi. Afterwards Mitzi went to tell Monique and both thought it odd as no-one had seen her for a while. It seems that Mitzi was angry with her and refused to do her hair because she had left Clairvaux without paying her last bill. Apparently, it was quite a bit, but to Mitzi's surprise, Lili took enough money from of her purse to pay off her debt *and* for what she was about to have done. She also showed her a ring and said she was getting married to a garage mechanic from Dijon. Mitzi said she asked how everyone was, but she thought the only reason she'd returned, was to brag about her engagement rather than to see her old friends, as she could easily have had her hair done in Champagnole. The one thing that struck her as really odd was that she asked after Amelie. Mitzi knew she disliked her because of her relationship with Paul-Emille.'

'What was Mitzi's reply?' Guy asked.

'That no-one had seen her for ages.' Elizabeth looked at Amelie. 'But you seemed to know she'd been to Clairvaux didn't you? You were trying to find her?'

Amelie responded by saying she'd heard Lili was visiting Clairvaux and wanted to know why.

'Who told you?' Guy asked.

'Odette. She happened to be in a bakery and overheard her telling someone she was going back to Clairvaux to have her hair styled by her old hairdresser. Apparently, someone made a sharp remark about there being enough hairdressers in Champagnole who would be only too happy to do it for her. *La simplette's* reply was that she'd lived near there before moving to Champagnole and liked the way she did it, but stopped going because the place was now full of resistants. The bakery owner told her to keep her mouth shut and if she ever spoke like that again he would never serve her again. When Odette described her to me, I knew immediately who it was. That's when I thought I would try and check her out for myself. I'd also heard there was someone else asking after me. It turned out to be Marie-Élise.'

It didn't take much for them all to put two and two together. The Gestapo were putting pressure on Claude Favre and in turn, he'd contacted his sister to ask her to go back to Clairvaux and see what she could find out about more resistants.

'There's more,' André said. He passed his empty glass to Madame Sophie and she refilled it. The others wanted more too. This was going to be a long night.

'The evening Madame X was due to collect her money, I went to work at the hotel and found the place unusually quiet. I had the money in a brown paper bag and slipped it under the counter where I could get it easily without anyone seeing me, but the atmosphere was so thick you could cut it with a knife. I got scared. There were a couple of faces I didn't recognise — men in sharp suits reading newspapers as if they had all the time in the world. I went over to ask if they wanted a drink. Only one said yes and it was non-alcoholic. The others refused. When I looked at the clock, I thought Madame X was late: maybe she wasn't coming. As I cleaned up the glasses and wiped other tables, I looked out of the window. Several cars were parked nearby with men sitting in them. I knew then that this was a set-up. I needed to get away and warn the woman but I had to move the money from under the counter. If I left they would probably follow me and search me, so I slipped it in my pocket and hid it on a high ledge in a cubicle in the women's toilets.

'When I returned to the bar, Madame X was walking through the door. She saw the look on my face, looked around and turned to leave. It was too late. The men jumped up and called after her. "Halt! Halt or we shoot!"'

'She took a gun out of her pocket and fired at them. She was a good shot as she hit two men straight away before exiting the bar, but there were far too many and they fired. She was hit several times and fell to the ground. The other bartender and I rushed to the window to see what was going on. She wasn't dead, but there was no doubt she was critically injured. They picked her up and as they were bundling her into the car, she grabbed one of their guns and shot another in the face and then turned the gun on herself. I've been around too long to know the Gestapo would question us all in the hotel so without uttering a word to the manager, I walked out of the bar to the toilets, grabbed the money, left by the back door and ran as fast as I could down the alley.

'Over the loudspeakers I could hear them telling everyone to stay put. I knew the area would be surrounded so I made my way to the riverside. The road along there was also blocked off. Then I spotted a small houseboat and jumped onto it, the tarpaulin cover cushioning my fall. Unfortunately, a man heard me and popped his head out of the cabin. I had no choice but to hold him at gunpoint and ask him to take the boat down the river without attracting attention. After we'd passed the bridge and the river turned the bend. I told him to pull up by the bank. I apologised for frightening him, gave him some money and hoped he'd keep quiet. The poor devil was shaking like a leaf but he wished me luck.'

The clock chimed eleven. The group had listened to this story for several hours now. They were deflated and upset. Having got all this off his chest, André asked Madame Sophie if she could warm up the venison stew as he was now hungry. They discussed the situation between themselves for a while until Madame Sophie returned from the kitchen and ladled them all a huge helping of hot stew and told them to eat up. They needed a good square meal for what was ahead.

'One thing,' asked Guy. 'Do we know where Lili and her brother are living now?'

They all looked at each other knowing what this meant. Belvedere was now back in business and would seek restitution.

'Lili lives somewhere in Champagnole. She will be easy to find. But her brother is another matter. I believe he must be somewhere in or near Dijon, especially if they keep taking him to HQ there.'

'Fine,' Guy replied. 'Now let's eat. We can't let Madame Sophie's wonderful food go to waste. We will sleep on this information and tomorrow we'll decide what to do.'

After they'd eaten, the conversation turned to what had taken place in the area during early April. It was clear to the Resistance that the Germans were on the verge of starting a major offensive against them. With the melting of the winter snow it would be difficult for them to trace and locate the Maquis as the emergence of leaves on bushes and trees made concealment easier, and the advent of warmer weather made it feasible for the them to camp outside the forest region which had been their winter base. Now they were able to get closer to farmsteads and villages for supplies of food, but they had to be more cautious of collaborators.

When the evening was over, Madame Sophie showed them to their rooms. Elizabeth was in a room opposite Guy, Amelie at the end of the corridor, Bernard stayed with Hortense in her own bedroom, and Madame Sophie and André disappeared to a large luxurious bedroom, favoured by the top German officials.

Sometime after the lights went out, Guy knocked softly on Elizabeth's door. There was no intimacy that night: neither had an appetite for it. They were just happy to fall asleep in each other's arms.

CHAPTER 24

When Elizabeth woke up the next morning Guy was not in bed with her. Thinking he may have returned to his room, she knocked on his door but there was no answer. At that moment Ruth appeared. She was carrying her small son.

'If you're looking for Daniel, he's on the terrace with Monsieur André.'

She returned to her room and saw them from her bedroom window. They were sitting on the terrace talking. Knowing they had much to discuss, she decided to take a shower. It had been a terrible night with barely a wink of sleep. When she looked at her face in the mirror, it looked drawn and she saw fine lines under her eyes. The hot and steamy shower was a godsend: sheer luxury after the basic facilities of the Menouillard's cottage. She wrapped towels around her wet hair and body and sat on the tiny veranda taking in the beauty of the forest. It was so close she could smell the pungent scent of the fir trees. The air was invigorating and she closed her eyes, soaking it up to clear her mind. Below, she was aware of Guy and André deep in conversation but couldn't hear a word.

Her thoughts drifted back to the map Monique had shown her and she now came to the realisation that it all meant the area around the hotel. The upside down U's signified the mountains and what looked like a cross signified the hotel. The wavy lines must have denoted Lake Bonlieu. Everything else fitted — the train line going through Saint-Laurent-en-Grandvaux was in the right place as was the junction in the road. She heard a soft knock on her door which jolted her out of her tranquil mood. It was Amelie.

'Can I come in?'

Elizabeth noticed how much better she was looking and told her so.

'I took a pill,' she replied. 'Daniel gave it to me. It certainly helped.'

'I have no words to express how sad I feel for you,' Elizabeth said, taking a seat at the dressing table to fix her hair. 'I knew you and Paul-Emille were in love.'

Amelie lit a cigarette. 'Well we certainly underestimated that simpleton, didn't we?' she replied, her voice was full of anger.

Elizabeth didn't want to add fuel to the fire and she tried her best to enter into small talk: the beauty of the surroundings, maybe they should go for a walk around the lake to clear their heads, Ruth's food, etc., but it was in vain. Amelie wasn't the sort of person for small talk. She said very little and Elizabeth felt she just wanted another woman's company. No more, no less. All the same, the atmosphere was uncomfortable. As Elizabeth dried and styled her hair, she brought up the subject of the map.

'Monique showed the map to me you know. For a while I confess, I couldn't figure out where it was, but it was a map of here wasn't it?'

Through the mirror, Elizabeth noticed the look on Amelie's face. She shifted uncomfortably on the bed, drawing nervously on her cigarette — the same cigarette that the map smelt of. She didn't answer.

'The thing is.' Elizabeth continued, 'I couldn't understand why an agent like you — someone trained to be more cautious — could have dropped such an important thing and not realised it.' Amelie's face showed no sign of emotion but Elizabeth would not let up. 'You know what I think? I think you dropped it on purpose. Why? You didn't contact Monique again.'

Amelie gave her a half-smile. 'They always said you were a good agent.' Elizabeth didn't reply; she just waited for Amelie to respond. 'You are right. I did drop it on purpose. After what we'd just gone through, I was in fear of my life. I knew Monique would never show it to the Germans and I hoped it might get into the hands of someone who would put it to good use and help us. It did, didn't it — you. Was it that map that led you here, or the fact that you spotted me in the market?'

'Like you, I am trained to look at everyone with suspicion. Seeing you in Clairvaux certainly aroused my curiosity, but the map was always at the back of my mind. With so many lakes in the region, I thought of others, but not Bonlieu. In fact, it didn't even cross my mind as I'd never come across it when I was here before, even though I was often nearby. Does the small t signify the hotel?'

'No. It signifies a small religious marker at the entrance of the walkway around the lake. There used to be an abbey here hundreds of years ago. I have no idea what happened to it. As far as I know, it's the only thing that signifies there was an abbey on the spot. Maybe the stones were carted away to be used for other building. Who knows?'

Elizabeth hadn't walked as far as the lake so hadn't seen it.

'And G1 and G2, what do they signify?'

'Nothing: they were meant to throw anyone off the scent. Only the X's were significant. They were Maquis camps.' Amelie paused, watching Elizabeth's reaction. 'But the maquisards move about. They never stay in one place too long. All I cared about was if the right person looked further, they would unlock the secret of the Grand Hôtel du Lac and find out that it was used to help the *passeurs* smuggle people into Switzerland — and also to find out what happened to Daniel and André, and others in the Resistance.'

Elizabeth had to hand it to her; Amelie was one very clever agent.

'Thank you,' she said. 'I applaud your thinking. I only hope I would have had my wits about me and thought about all that if the boot had been on the other foot.'

'I have no doubt about that,' Amelie replied. She stubbed her cigarette out in the ashtray. 'Come on, let's go and get some breakfast.'

Hortense and Bernard had gone for a short walk by the lake and Ruth was preparing omelettes. Her son was playing with the cat on the rug and eating a small slice of chocolate that Guy had smuggled across the border for them all. André picked him up, wiped the chocolate smudges from around his mouth and his tiny fingers, and asked him how he was and what had he been doing since he last saw him. It was clear the child felt comfortable in his presence. Ruth smiled. It was good for her son to have a father figure around and these days, apart from the gardener, there were too few. She served the food and, knowing the group wanted to be alone, took her son by the hand and suggested to him that they go outside and help the gardener collect fruit from the orchard. After they'd gone, André commented on how lucky Ruth was to have found Madame Sophie. She made the comment that Ruth was like a second daughter and viewed the child like her own grandchild.

'You'll have grandchildren of your own one day,' Guy replied.

Madame Sophie raised one eyebrow as if to tell him not to think that far ahead. 'All I care about at this moment is that we're still alive by the time this war ends.'

The conversation quickly reverted back to the night before.

'André and I have been talking,' Guy said. 'There is no time to waste, so this is what will happen. André will get in touch with the Maquis groups to let them know we're ready to help them again. Marie-Élise, your first objective is to get in touch with London. The Allied invasion will take place soon and we already know the Maquis are still in desperate need of more arms and training, so more drops have to be arranged as soon as possible. The French are also sending their soldiers into France now and we need to meet up and arrange safe houses and liaise with them. You can do that with Amelie and Madame Sophie.

'At the same time, it's imperative we find out where Lili is living — and her brother too. As soon as we know where she lives, we'll determine what to do next.' He turned to Amelie and told her to get in touch with Odette. 'I want both of you to look for Lili.' He warned her not to take retribution without higher authority. All knew what that meant. 'In the meantime, André and I will use our own contacts to find out where Claude Favre is, but using his sister is our main bet.'

At that moment Hortense and Bernard returned.

'Just in time.' Guy addressed Bernard. 'It's highly likely you are in grave danger. I want you to move all your forgery equipment to a new place. Claude Favre knows where you're operating from and if the Gestapo are putting pressure on him, he'll turn everyone in.'

'Bernard can operate from here.' Madame Sophie declared. 'Either the cellar or the garden shed. No-one will think such things are going on under the eyes of the Germans. He can arrange for any meetings with those needing papers elsewhere. A relative has an unused office in Lons-le-Saunier. People can pick up their new papers there.'

'Perfect,' Guy replied. 'Get on to it immediately. Do you have a copy of Claude Favre's photograph? It's possible he's using an alias and may have changed his looks. Even so, it would be helpful for us.'

'I always keep duplicates of everyone's photographs and details of their identities.'

'Good. Make me a few copies.'

'What can I do?' Hortense asked.

André said he could use her as a courier between the Maquis groups. Bernard looked at her, his eyes full of concern. 'It's dangerous work, Hortense. Be sure before you commit.'

She gave him an indignant look. 'Do you think I can sit back and let you do all the dirty work? I *am* my mother's daughter you know.'

They all laughed, which helped to lighten the bleak atmosphere.

'Now, unless there are any more questions, I need to reconnect with certain people as soon as possible to let them know we're back in business. How about we meet here again on Monday evening? That way, any German guests in the hotel will hopefully have returned to work.' He paused for a moment. 'One important thing — who to contact should the need arise, which I am sure it will.'

Everyone had a suggestion. Making telephone calls was not easy at all. Conversations were monitored which was why couriers and letter-drops were preferred, but there were still occasions when they needed to use them. Sometimes speed was of the essence and a courier could not always get somewhere in time. The first and most obvious place was the Grand Hôtel du Lac. The code would be — *Can I make a reservation for two with dinner next weekend? It's a special occasion.* If the reply was guarded it would be, *I'm sorry Monsieur/Madame; we are fully booked.* If the answer was — *Certainly Monsieur/Madame; we have one last room available,* then they would know it was fine to meet.

The next place was Bistrot Jurassien but only after Elizabeth had cleared this with Monique as she had always been good at hiding people in and around the village. The problem was there were still quite a few Germans in Clairvaux, and the Milice and *Feldgendarmerie* were active. Elizabeth suggested the code would be — *We have an extra supply of vegetables, would you like to buy them?* If the reply was — *I'm sorry, we don't need any more,* this would signify it was too dangerous. If the reply was *how much are you asking for them?* Then the reply would depend on how many people were to be helped. *Twenty francs* signified one person needing help, *forty,* two people, etc.

Some of the suggestions for codes made them laugh, but they all knew this was not a laughing game at all. One wrong telephone call could bring down the network and with it, innocent victims. Ruth arrived to say that Robert was here. This time he would be escorting Bernard back to his house to collect the forgery equipment. It all had to be done as soon as possible and they wished him the best of luck. André was going to use the hotel as his base and Guy decided to return to Clairvaux and stay with Elizabeth in the cottage. Both he and André had changed their looks and identities since December and they hoped it was enough not to alert suspicion. Guy's papers now had him as a *cultivateur* — agricultural worker — but given that his age would have seen him called up for work service in Germany, he also carried a paper saying he had a weak heart and was of poor health due to a work explosion, which in a way, was true. Amelie was going back to her safe house near Champagnole.

When the time came to leave, Elizabeth caught the bus. Madame Sophie decided to drive Guy to Clairvaux herself later that evening as she had her *Ausweis*. The bus was filled with locals as it had been market day in Saint-Laurent-en-Grandvaux. There were also several rowdy schoolchildren onboard, and, as a consequence, the bus driver took no notice of her. By the time she reached the Menouillards, she couldn't wait to tell them to expect another visitor. They were beside themselves with anticipation.

Madame Sophie's black car turned into the driveway later that evening and Guy received such a welcome they were all reduced to tears. Sabine embraced him like a mother welcoming her long-lost son and was so overcome all she could do was repeat his name over and over again. Even the dogs remembered him and jumped up excitedly.

Armand asked Madame Sophie inside to celebrate with them.

'Just one drink,' she said. 'Then I must get back before the curfew.'

Sabine and Armand knew of Madame Sophie, but they were not aware of her activities.

'I heard about your hotel and that the Germans like to spend time there,' Armand said. 'We were always wary of your activities but now it all makes sense.'

Madame Sophie smiled. 'We do what we have to these days. It's not easy.' She finished her drink and left. 'I'm sure you have much to talk about so I'll leave you to it.'

That night Sabine and Armand brought out a fine Jura wine and served stew while Guy filled them in on what had taken place. Like everyone else, they had a hard time comprehending it was Lili and Claude Favre who had created all that damage. It was hard to believe, but there it was — the result of a jealous woman. Afterwards they listened to the BBC and a speech from de Gaulle. It was like old times. Sometime before midnight, Guy and Elizabeth left for the cottage. There was hardly any moon and even though they had a small flashlight, both knew the way by heart.

When they reached the cottage door, Guy pulled Elizabeth to him. 'I wish I was strong enough to pick you up and carry you over the threshold, my beautiful wife.'

Elizabeth laughed. 'There'll be time enough for that when you've fully recovered. We're alive and we're together; that's the most important thing.'

That night they lay together in the bed where they'd first made love over a year ago. The warm night air was invigorating and both wanted nothing more than to make love and savour each other's body, but they were both physically and mentally exhausted. So much had happened in a year which neither could have predicted, and the hours spent crossing the Swiss border, evading border guards, scrambling through the pine trees with their tangled web of slippery roots, sliding down embankments and scrambling along rocky outcrops, had taken its toll on them. Now, when they needed each other the most, they lay wrapped in each other's arms and quickly slipped into a deep sleep.

In the morning it was Elizabeth who was up bright and early. She kissed Guy on the forehead, careful not to wake him, and went outside to retrieve the transmitter from between the logs. She carefully timed her transmission, keeping an eye on her watch to see that she didn't go over the allotted time span which could be picked up by the Germans. She was always conscious of not giving German military intelligence, the *Abwehr,* ample time to find their quarry using their radio detection vans. Unbeknown to Elizabeth, London was becoming even more anxious about someone at 84 Avenue Foch, the *Sicherheitsdienst* in Paris, impersonating captured radio and codes and arranging parachute drops of supplies which they were sure would fall into German hands.

This time her news would allay those fears. Belvedere had not been infiltrated by German military intelligence, but was sabotaged due to an outsider — a woman. That woman, either advertently or inadvertently — something yet to be determined — managed to drag her brother, a maquisard, into the disaster. The most important news was that Daniel had been recuperating from his wounds in Switzerland liaising with agent Mireille and André based in the Jura and the Department of the Doubs. Now he had returned to France and Belvedere was back in operation again. She said he requested London to send over arms and aid as quickly as possible for the Maquis.

SITUATION DESPERATE SS PLANNING MAJOR ATTACKS.

She purposely left out the mention of Besançon for security reasons. By the time Guy woke up, she had received a coded reply.

200

SPUPPLIES AND FFI PACKAGES WILL BE SENT NEXT
MOON SEND COORDINATES CONGRATULATIONS VLF

She took off her earphones and saw him watching her.

'At this moment, my darling, Baker Street is celebrating your return.' She got up and kissed him. 'Maybe we should do the same.'

He smiled. 'Funny what a good night's sleep does for you isn't it?' He led her back towards the bed and pushed her gently on to it. 'You know, I think I am getting stronger by the minute.'

CHAPTER 25

Surprisingly, the group did not have to wait long to find out where *la simplette* lived. Knowing that both she and her brother had lived in a village not far from Clairvaux, Sabine and Monique decided to go there on market day. Under the pretence of looking for a bargain, they chatted with several of the stallholders. Some of the villagers were already familiar with the two women, but these days, people moved around the country for different reasons and there were plenty of unfamiliar faces.

They discovered that the Favre family had moved from the district soon after Claude was deported. According to villagers, they had nothing to do with their daughter, who by all accounts had inherited some money from a distant relative. The money had caused a rift in the family but no-one knew why. They said the family moved south — somewhere near Provence — but the daughter, Lili, bought herself a nice little apartment overlooking the river in Champagnole. It seems she came back to brag about that around about the time she visited Mitzi's hair salon. She also said she was engaged. Like Mitzi, the locals thought she only come back to brag about her engagement rather than to see them. She never mentioned her family at all. As they also thought her a simpleton, they didn't think any more of it.

Elizabeth arranged to meet with Amelie and Odette at Café des Amis near the Parc de Belle Frise in Champagnole. The town was situated around 130 km north-east of Lyon, around 90 km south-east of Dijon, and 60 km north of Geneva, which made it not only an important stopover for escapees, but for the Germans too. The River Ain passes below the lower edge of the park and along its bank are beautiful walks. She told the two women of Sabine and Monique's encounter with the locals in Patornay and asked if they'd also come up with anything. Amelie, who had now dyed her beautiful dark hair a reddish shade of chestnut and wore plain, rather ordinary clothes in order to downplay her natural beauty, said she had spent several days wandering the town and occasionally meeting up with Odette for a drink and an update on the situation. At one point, she spotted Lili walking along the riverbank and followed her. Lili crossed over the bridge, walked along a narrow winding road and entered a house on the edge of the town.

As there was nowhere to sit and watch the house without attracting attention, she hid for a while, noting details of the house. It was an attractive building but one which looked as if it had once seen better days. Because of the river, Champagnole had a lot of mills — iron and steel working — and was proud of its metalworking traditions and the area was full of homes which had once belonged to the bourgeoisie. Lili's house looked as if it might have been one of them. It had three storeys; if you counted the attic, stood alone, surrounded by a small garden, and had an elegant grandeur about it even though the roof and some of the woodwork clearly appeared in need of renovation. Amelie felt a strong urge to confront her and gun her down, but she controlled her anger. Now she had located her, the group needed to note her contacts and see if there really was a fiancé. Most importantly, they needed to know whether she was in touch with her brother and her links to the Gestapo. Amelie passed this information on to Odette who had her own apartment opposite the Hotel Ripotot and spent some of her time there when she wasn't with Krüger.

In the meantime, Amelie contacted Guy with this latest development and, after talking it over with André, they authorized certain members of the Champagnole Resistance to keep a twenty-four-hour watch on her. After several days, only one man visited the house. He was photographed on the doorstep as Lili gave him a kiss and asked him inside. The man appeared to be in his mid-forties, was clean-shaven, wore a plain suit, and was rather stout. All agreed he was quite an insignificant looking man and if he was her fiancé, they looked ill-suited. Lili was in her early twenties. The man's looks certainly contrasted with Paul-Emille, the handsome, fit young man *la simplette* had originally fallen in love with. Interestingly, he visited three times and only once did he stay overnight. That was the last time. Even then, he left early in the morning. Strange for someone she was supposed to be marrying.

The photograph was shown to all concerned. No-one knew him. He wasn't a local. When Elizabeth and Amelie showed Odette the photograph, she said she recognised him. She's seen him at the Hotel Ripotot but couldn't recall when. A few days later, she contacted Amelie and Guy and they met up again in the Café des Amis.

'The man you're after, he's from Dijon. I now recall he came to the Hotel Ripotot to see the Kommandant and at one time I saw a group of them together in the lounge. Hansi was with them.'

Odette often referred to Krüger as Hansi, her affectionate name for him.

Guy tutted. 'So it's a trap. The man Lili thinks of as her fiancé is actually a Gestapo agent.'

'It certainly looks that way,' Amelie replied.

'What else can you tell us?' Guy asked.

'I know that he passes for a Frenchman but is actually German. His mother was from Dijon which is why he has a perfect Dijonnais accent. In reality he is from Munich and was a member of the National Socialists from the early days of Hitler's rise to power.'

'How do you know that?' Amelie asked.

'I overheard Hansi talking with a friend in the bar. They laughed when the other man said he had fooled her. Now I know the story, I presume they meant this man was pretending to be Lili's fiancé.'

'Do you know his name?' Guy asked.

Odette shook her head. 'Sorry. And I can't ask now as it would look too suspicious. Hansi is always on guard and one of the reasons he keeps me as his mistress is because I don't ask too many questions. He once told me he doesn't trust French women.' She laughed. 'If only you knew how hard I have to work to keep him in a good mood.'

Neither Guy nor Amelie laughed, even though she did. What Odette was doing was dangerous. To everyone outside the Resistance, she was a horizontal collaborator and could be killed at any time.

'Okay,' Guy said. 'We've established he's from Dijon which means he must be working for the Gestapo there. We'll get on to it immediately. It's highly likely there's a link between him and Claude Favre too as André told us they kept taking him into the Gestapo HQ there. As we don't know this man's name, the only thing we have to help us is the photograph. If Claude Favre is still alive, he could also have a new identity, but Bernard gave us his photograph too, which is a help.'

Guy called the waiter over and paid for their drinks. The café owner belonged to the Resistance and refused to take his money. He had a soft spot for Odette and had come to her assistance once when two elderly women spat on her and shouted abuse. The women then hurled abuse at him and said he was helping a collaborator and his day would come. The incident had shaken Odette and she had been much more careful after that.

Guy and Elizabeth caught the train from Lons-le-Saunier to Dijon. They sat apart for the entire journey and both walked alone to their hotel, the same one Elizabeth had stayed in when she first arrived in France. At first Madame Genot had a hard time recognising Guy, but when she realized who he was, she was delighted to see him.

'I heard you were dead,' she said in a low voice, 'but I never believed it for one minute.' She smiled and winked at Elizabeth. 'He's too clever to get himself killed.'

Elizabeth agreed, but if Madame Genot only knew how he'd stared death in the face for days, she wouldn't have said that. Not realising they were now married she gave them a room next to each other on the first floor overlooking the park. At that minute another guest entered the lobby. She addressed him as Herr Müller, gave him his key and asked if he would be joining them for dinner that evening. He replied that he would be out with friends. The man bade Elizabeth and Guy a warm good-afternoon and went to his room. Guy looked quizzically at Madame Genot.

'He's the only German here at the moment, the rest are French,' she whispered. 'He's on the floor above you.' She then raised her voice to a normal tone. 'Is there anything else I can do for you?'

'Yes, Could you please bring a bottle of wine to my room?' Guy said. 'A good Côte de Beaune.'

'Certainly, Monsieur.'

Ten minutes later, Madame Genot knocked on the door with the wine. 'Here you are, Monsieur, a white *Clos des Mouches* from Maison Joseph Drouhin — a premier cru.'

Guy indicated for her to come into the room and close the door behind her. She noticed Elizabeth sitting on a chair by the side of the bed. Knowing he could trust her, Guy showed her the two photographs. The first was Claude Favre; the second was the German posing as a Frenchman.

Madame Genot put on her glasses and looked closely. 'This one I know,' she said referring to the unknown man. 'His name is George Malfroy. He says he's from around here but no-one seems to know him. He's friendly with the Milice. The people I know avoid him as he's often seen in the company of the Gestapo.' She turned to Elizabeth. 'Do you remember what I told you about Ludwig Kraemer whom the Dijonnais nicknamed "Stucka" who had replaced Willy Hülf?' Elizabeth nodded. 'I also told you that Kraemer has at his disposal, several officers and non-commissioned officers and recruited a large handful of French people who chose to collaborate. This man works with them. In fact, he's been with them from the beginning and has grown rich on his earnings from collaboration — if in fact he really is French.'

Guy said he was a German from Munich and he spoke French because apparently his mother was from Dijon. He went on to tell her his past with the National Socialist Party and that in all likelihood, that wasn't his real name at all.

Madame Genot shrugged her shoulders. 'Now it makes sense.'

'Do you know where he lives?' Guy asked

'No, but it won't be hard to find out.'

'And this other man, have you seen him before?'

'I'm afraid I can't help you there. Who is he?'

'He was in one of the Resistance groups in the Jura and disappeared. We believe he was compromised because of his sister. The last we heard, he was here in Dijon and visited the Gestapo HQ. We need to find him as soon as possible.'

Madame Genot said she would arrange a meeting with one of the Dijonnais Resistance. She left the room and returned an hour later.

'Be ready to leave at seven o'clock sharp. I will take you to visit someone who might know.'

After she left, Guy sat at a small table near the window cleaning his gun. Elizabeth sat opposite him. She relished the fact that they were together again even though it was an assignment. He'd been all over the place: everywhere from Saint-Claude to Lons-le-Saunier, where he'd stayed with the Dassins who were overjoyed to see him. From there he'd travelled with Pierre to meet up with Resistance members in Poligny, Arbois, and Château-Chalon. All of them were busy reconnecting and getting everything in place for armed resistance and sabotage when the invasion began which they knew was imminent.

'I hope we don't run into any trouble,' she said as she watched him. He was tense and she knew he wouldn't rest until they'd found both men.

He asked her to tell him how the preparations were coming along for the next drops.

'I gave London the list of everything we needed. And I've discussed it with Pierre and the others — Brando, Gavroche, and Max. De Gaulle is sending three more Frenchmen who were with the Foreign Legion. Navarre and Arbez already know them. They will use the same drop zone as before but I've also arranged for another drop zone between Clairvaux and Champagnole. That way, André can get arms to the Maquis in that area too.'

Guy asked where exactly it was.

'Between Billaude and Chevrotaine. There's an area of rolling farmland. I knew of it when I lived at the Delatour Château. I paid them a visit last week.'

'How are they?' Guy asked? 'What happened to the orphans Madame Delatour looked after?'

Elizabeth told him about the *rafle* in the middle of the night and the four Jewish children that were taken away. 'The others are French citizens and still safe and she still keeps in contact with the Swiss children's authorities. She's aged in the short time I saw her and she doesn't forgive herself for the fate of the Jewish children. The youngest was only four. Her husband was away at the time and she thinks that had he been there that night, it wouldn't have happened. Who knows? It could have been one of the villagers who ratted on them. Some didn't take too kindly to her hiding Jews. Apart from that they were glad to see me. They asked after you. I told them you were alive and well but that was all.'

At ten minutes to seven, Guy put his gun in his jacket pocket and the two prepared to meet with the member of the Resistance. It was a good walk to get there because Madame Genot took them via back streets in order to avoid random checks by the Milice and Germans. The man, who was introduced as René, was waiting for them. He was alone, having sent his wife out of the way for the evening so they could talk in private. When Guy showed him the photographs, he tapped on the first one. It was Claude Favre.

'He lives in Marsannay-la-Côte, a commune in the Côte-d'Or Department not far away. His name is Claude Favier.'

Guy glanced at Elizabeth. 'Thank you. Actually, his name is Claude Favre,' Guy replied, 'not Favier. How do you know him?'

'One of our men reports back to us on the itinerant workers used in the vineyards. Since many used to be Spanish and have either joined the Maquis or been deported, the Germans allow a percentage to keep the vineyards viable. He turned up one day with papers saying he was a *cultivateur* and had a permit to work. The vineyard took him on.' He noticed the look on Guy and Elizabeth's faces. 'Our men check everyone out, especially strangers. This man –Favre, Favier — whatever you say his name is, keeps to himself.'

Guy then showed him the next photograph.

'This bastard poses as a Frenchman but he's German.'

'His name?' Guy asked.

'He goes by the name of George Malfroy and works for the Gestapo here and in Lyon.'

'Do you know where he lives?'

'At the Hôtel La Cloche, as do quite a few of the *Abwehr* and Gestapo.'

'You cannot possibly know how much help you've been tonight. We really appreciate it.'

'What's he done that would bring you all the way here to look for him?' René asked.

'It's a long story but we think he's posing as the fiancé of a woman who now lives in Champagnole who betrayed the network. We've only recently found this out and we think this man could be putting pressure on her about the whereabouts of certain others in the Resistance.'

René studied him for a while before he spoke. 'Why don't you simply pull this woman in and interrogate her? Why come all the way to Dijon?'

'Good question,' Guy replied. 'If it was only her, we would. The problem is Claude Favre. He is her brother. If he found out anything untoward had happened to his sister, we're sure he would get revenge by telling the Gestapo everything. By *everything* that's exactly what I mean. He was a close member of our group. His sister knew nothing, but he knows too much: forgers, safe houses, other members in the Resistance and maquisards who were never deported.' Guy knitted his brows together. 'We trusted this man.'

René gave a heavy sigh. 'What a mess!'

'Exactly: a mess that will get worse if we don't eliminate it.'

Hearing this news about Malfroy, René went on to add more to his story. 'It seems to be rather a speciality of his,' he added, 'pretending to fall for unsuspecting women and using them. It's not the first time he's done it. We know of at least two others. I am presuming he has flattered this woman with a beautiful ring?'

Elizabeth answered this time. 'Yes. She went back to her old village to show it off to someone and was also well-dressed.'

'This follows his pattern.' René shook his head. 'These women believe he loves them and when he gets what he wants, he disappears. I bet this woman has no idea where he lives. He never gives his address. He is like a cat playing with a mouse.'

'An ugly cat,' Elizabeth said sarcastically. 'He's not exactly good-looking, is he?'

'That maybe so for you, but for many, he has money, and at this point when people have little, money speaks all languages. Besides, some women fall for flatterers. A lethal combination wouldn't you say?'

Elizabeth scoffed. 'A bastard is what I would say.'

'How do you know he's done this before?' Guy asked.

'Through the Dijonnais Resistance. One woman gave up a Jewish family in hiding. We shot her ourselves. Another gave him the address of a resistant later picked up on his way to a meeting and taken to Gestapo HQ. He died under interrogation. When we found this woman, she told us Malfroy had asked her to help him and that he had also promised to marry her.'

Guy, Elizabeth and Madame Genot looked at each other. They guessed she met the same fate as the first woman.

'We have no idea how many other women the man has lured into his trap,' René said.

Elizabeth made a comment that he'd evidently made it into an art form.

'The other thing is, we believe the jewellery he gives them — the rings, etc, are stolen from Jews. He would never have bought them himself.'

With this latest revelation, Guy and Elizabeth needed to think out their next move carefully. Who to go after first — Claude Favre or George Malfroy? They decided on Malfroy. As time was of the essence, they hatched a plan.

CHAPTER 26

The following morning, George Malfroy left the hotel to go to work at 9 rue Docteur Chausseur, the Gestapo HQ. He had just turned the corner when he passed a pretty woman looking at a map. It was not only her beauty that caught his eye but her brooch, a sterling silver flower with a deep pink tourmaline in the centre. It glinted in the bright morning sun. The woman appeared confused.

'Can I be of assistance?' Malfroy asked.

Elizabeth flashed a beautiful smile at him. 'Thank you so much. I'm looking for Rue Montpellier. I thought it was somewhere near here.'

Malfroy returned her smile. 'My dear, I am afraid it's nowhere near here.'

He reached for the map and offered to show her where it was.

At that same moment, a black van drew up alongside them. Malfroy was so taken by Elizabeth, he failed to notice it.

'Here it...'

He didn't have time to point it out when he was struck from behind with the butt of a revolver and quickly bundled into the back of the van by two men — Guy and René — where another waiting resistant taped his mouth and put a bag over his head. He was unconscious and blood trickled from the wound, but he would live. Elizabeth hastily jumped into the passenger seat next to René. The kidnapping had happened in broad daylight and even though it was swift, it was highly likely the Gestapo would hear about it sooner rather than later. The van was stolen and had false number plates from another Department, and an *Ausweis* displayed on the window. Even so, they had to act quickly.

Malfroy was taken to a disused mill on the outskirts of the city where he was tied to a chair. He was still unconscious when the bag was removed and the tape ripped away from his mouth. René's accomplice threw a bucket of icy cold water over him. The shock brought him to his senses. When he saw where he was, the fear in his eyes was clearly visible. Guy sat opposite him straddling a chair with his arms crossed over the back of the chair. The pair stared at each other in silence for a few minutes.

'Monsieur Malfroy, or should I say, Herr Malfroy,' Guy said, looking at the man's papers. 'It's a pleasure to meet you.'

Malfroy stared at him indignantly.

'I can see you don't know who I am?' Guy began taunting him. 'I'm probably someone who could make you very rich if you turned me in, as you have others.'

'You're right. I don't know who you are and whoever you think I am, you have the wrong man. I haven't done anything wrong.'

Guy mentioned one word — Belvedere — and Malfroy's face paled.

'Does it ring a bell?' Guy asked.

'No. I have no idea what you're talking about.'

René pistol-whipped him hard and the chair toppled over. Malfroy lay moaning on the floor. The other resistant pulled the chair back upright. The swelling on Malfroy's face was immediate. Guy repeated the name Belvedere again and still there was no response.

'Let's try another name — Lili — Lili from Champagnole.'

The man still kept a straight face.

Guy got out a packet of cigarettes and lit one. 'You're obviously finding all this hard, but don't worry, we have lots of time.'

'I'll mention another name. This time I expect an answer.' Guy blew cigarette smoke towards him. 'Sorry: how rude of me. Would you care for one? He got up and lit a cigarette for the man and allowed him to take a drag and then threw it on the floor and stubbed it out.

'Let's try again. Claude Favre. Surely you remember him?'

Malfroy shook his head. 'Never heard of him either.' He looked at Guy with steely cold eyes. 'I told you, you have the wrong man and you'll pay for this.'

Guy took his own cigarette and, without showing any emotion, bored it into Malfroy's cheek for a few seconds. He knew exactly how long to hold it for. The tip of a manufactured cigarette burns at around 400 degrees Celsius potentially resulting in serious injury and long enough to leave a permanent scar. Malfroy screamed in pain. When the cigarette was removed, the wound was deep and raw, and a smell of burnt flesh filled the air. It brought back memories of the explosion that night at the farm and of the burns Guy himself had endured. The memory made him do it again: this time a few centimetres away from the first blister.

René and his friend looked at Guy anxiously, as did Elizabeth who was watching from the next room through a hole in the wall. The mill was in a bad state of disrepair and she could see and hear what was going on quite clearly. This was getting ugly. Guy walked out of the room followed by the two men.

'It's going to be difficult to get him to speak and we can't let him go,' Guy said. 'A hardened Nazi like him would rather die.'

Elizabeth offered to take him a drink of water while they decided what to do. When she walked into the room, he smirked at her.

'You!'

She didn't reply. It was the first time he'd seen her since he looked at her map. She pulled up Guy's chair beside him and tried to get him to take a drink of water. The cigarette burns looked red raw. Malfroy took one sip and said it was enough. He noticed her brooch.

'You women are all the same,' he said with a look of hatred. 'You like your little trinkets, don't you? I wonder what you did to get that — No, don't answer, I can guess.'

Elizabeth put the cup down and slowly took off the brooch. All the time her eyes never left his. In the other room, Guy, René and the other resistant watched on. What did she intend to do with it? Only Guy knew it contained the cyanide tablet. *Surely she wasn't going to force him to take it?*

Malfroy watched her, somewhat bemused by her actions.

'It's beautiful isn't it?' Elizabeth said, bringing it close to his face and showing him slowly at different angles. 'Is this the sort of thing you gave your fiancées — little trinkets like this?'

The man sniggered.

Elizabeth had a smile on her face but it was a smile of contempt — like an actress playing a part.

The tips of her fingers slid down the long pin and she tapped the point onto her left index finger. 'It's very sharp,' she said. 'Would you like to know just how sharp?

The man stared at her. This woman was crazy.

His wrists were tied and she placed the end of the pin in the centre of the back of his hand.

He tried to move, his head jerking backwards. Elizabeth clasped the silver flower-head tightly in her hand and pressed — slowly. At first the man held his agony until the pain became too much. Elizabeth ignored his pleas and pressed harder until she hit bone. Even then she didn't stop. She stood up and with her left hand, pressed it over the right, the pressure forcing it through his hand and into the arm of the chair.

The man screamed even more than when Guy burnt him. When she was satisfied she'd penetrated to the wood, she pulled the pin out.

'That's for all the women you've deceived,' she said scornfully.

The man's head rocked backwards and forwards in pain. She turned to walk away just as Guy and René rushed into the room.

'Bitch! Whore!' the man screamed out. 'You're all the same.'

Elizabeth turned around to face him and filled with anger, kicked him with such force in the jaw that he toppled backwards. Guy ran towards her and pulled her away while René and the other resistant pulled him back up off the floor.

'What's got into you?' Guy said in a whisper.

She brushed past him angrily. When they were out of the man's sight, she collapsed into tears on his shoulder. All the months of pent-up emotions flooded out of her. Guy held her tightly, trying to calm her down.

René returned. 'Well that was a good kick! You broke his jaw and almost severed his tongue!'

'Serves the bastard right,' she said, wiping her tears. Then she apologised for her emotional outburst.

'This one's going to be a tough nut to crack,' René said grimly. 'He's stubborn: one of those who will stay true to Hitler till the last.'

'Maybe,' Elizabeth replied, 'but at least we know by his comment that he did use jewellery to buy the women's affections so he is definitely our man.'

'Well we haven't got time to hang around so let's get back and try and crack him.'

Elizabeth watched them return to the room and the questions started again. With each silence or smart comment, the man got a beating until after a short while he was only just hanging on to life by a thread. Bloodied, bruised, and with broken bones, he told them nothing. He knew they couldn't let him go and in the end it was left to Guy to finish him off. After putting a bullet through his head, they threw his body in the fast-flowing river as it gushed past the old waterwheel.

The next person on the list was Claude Favre. They got in the van and headed south. When they reached the first village, René stopped outside a bar known to be friendly to the Resistance, went inside and, seeing the place was empty, asked to use the telephone. He returned with the address of Claude Favre from the man who had first reported his presence in the wine-producing area. It was less than ten kilometres away near the village of Couchay in the Côte de Nuits area.

The owner's family had a farm frequented by the Milice which was why Favre had been put there in the first place. Like the Menouillards, they had itinerant workers working for them who lived in nearby rudimentary dwellings, most of which had no running water and heating was little more than a brazier. They worked long hours in their vegetable fields and the local vineyards for a pittance. René warned Guy that they should view all workers with suspicion. If Favre got wind the Resistance were after him, the Gestapo would be swarming the area in no time at all. It was 4:00 p.m. when they neared the village. The van veered off the main road down a rutted dirt road little more than a tractor track. They pulled up behind a thick hedgerow while they carefully planned their next move. A man appeared out of the bushes and René got out of the car to greet him. He belonged to the Resistance.

After greeting them, Guy showed him a photograph to make sure it was definitely Claude Favre.

'That's him,' he replied. 'He's been here since December.'

Guy glanced across at Elizabeth. After all this time, they'd caught up with him. He showed him Malfroy's photograph too. 'What about this man?'

The resistant looked carefully. 'I've seen him before but can't really say I know him. I think he comes here occasionally to check on some of the workers. Do you want me to find out?'

Guy said that wouldn't be necessary.

The man drew a map in the dirt. 'This is the vineyard where your man is working. He will be heading back home in half an hour. Be careful, everyone has their eyes on each other around here.' He drew a few lines representing rows of vines, a road, and a grand house whose family owned the vineyard.

'The vineyard owners are not pro-German, but they are aware that some of the workers from the farms are under the watchful eye of the Germans and Milice so they turn a blind eye. Please try not to involve them or their vineyard will be confiscated.'

214

Guy gave him his word. The man wished them good luck and left.

The van pulled out of the lane and drove slowly along the road as one by one the workers came out of the vineyard.

'There he is,' Guy said. 'That's him; the one with the striped shirt and cap.'

As he would recognise Elizabeth and Guy immediately, they stayed hidden in the back of the van. René offered to be the one to confront the man while his comrade drove the van. The van pulled up just as Favre was passing and René got out.

'Excuse me, Monsieur, are you Claude Favier?'

The man looked at him suspiciously. 'Why do you ask? What do you want?'

'I have a message from Monsieur Malfroy in Dijon. He asked to speak with you urgently.'

Favre looked scared. 'Why didn't he come himself?'

René could see the man was going to make a scene and took a gun out of his pocket, pointing it at Favre's chest. 'Shut up and get inside. One wrong move and you're dead.'

Favre was pushed into the van and René got in next to him, still pointing the gun at him. By this time, the other workers were walking along the road.

'Don't even think of alerting them,' René warned.

It all happened so fast that Favre had not seen Guy or Elizabeth in the back of the van. Within a few minutes the road was deserted and the van came to a stop. Before Favre could utter a word, Guy put his arm around Favre's neck while René taped his mouth. Elizabeth put the same bag over his head that they had used for Malfroy and they pulled him into the back of the van. Favre was struggling to free himself, but it was useless. A gun was pushed into his chest and he was told to behave or they would use it. The van returned to the disused mill, where Favre was taken into the same room as Malfroy.

When the bag was removed and Favre saw Guy's face, he looked terrified. Beads of sweat appeared on his brow. Both the floor and the chair were stained with dried blood and he must have known he would never get out alive. Guy sat in the same place where he'd questioned Malfroy. The others stood nearby, all waiting for him to speak. Favre's eyes darted between the blood on the floor and the scars on Guy's face. After a while, he began to talk. At first it was garbled. Words tumbled out in fear, making little sense to anyone in the room. Elizabeth gave him a drink of water.

'I had no choice,' he said, blurting it out wildly. 'I tell you, no choice at all.'

'Why did you do it?' Guy asked in a soft voice. 'We trusted you. Of all the people I worked with, you were the last person I expected to give us away.'

Tears of fear and frustration started to stream down Favre's cheeks. 'It was my sister who did it. She caused all this trouble. I swear on my father's grave.'

Elizabeth looked across at Guy. André's information had been correct.

'Go on,' Guy said. Elizabeth noticed he flexed his fingers, fighting back the anger.

'One night the Gestapo came to my house and dragged me away. They took me to Lons-le-Saunier and interrogated me. I was told that my sister had gone to the German High Command in Champagnole and sold us out. She signed a statement to say she'd overheard Paul-Emille talking with you and another resistant about a *parachutage* but she wasn't sure where, only that she'd heard they would all meet at the Ledoux Farm afterwards. When they asked her why she'd told them this, she said Paul-Emille had jilted her: that he'd fallen for Amelie who she suspected was a British agent and she wanted to get even. She wanted money for this and they paid her.'

Favre had difficulty breathing and Elizabeth gave him another drink. She looked at Guy as if to say he should take it easy, but Guy was in no mood for sympathy.

'The Germans asked her about her family. Who else knew, etc.? That's when she told them she had a brother — me. They pulled me in and asked me if I knew anything. Lili didn't know the extent of my involvement with the Resistance, but they told me they were going to kill her and my family if I didn't tell them where and when the *parachutage* would take place and the group I worked for. I told them she was simple-minded and had made the whole thing up. I even told them that Paul-Emille had no interest in her even though we all knew she was infatuated with him, but they didn't care. They wanted information and would stop at nothing to get it.' He paused for a moment to get his breath. 'They asked me where the drop zone would be but I said I wouldn't know until the actual night. They didn't believe me.'

Favre was shaking with terror, pleading for forgiveness. 'You never knew it, but they tortured me that night — where it couldn't be seen — *and* I was threatened with rape. In the end I agreed to give them information on the proviso that they didn't hurt my family. They agreed. At the same time they said they would arrange for me to disappear. So I told them we would be meeting at the farm. That was all I knew. They said if my information was correct, they would look after me. If not, both I and Lili would be executed. I escaped from the deportation train because the Gestapo arranged it for what I had done, but I was to be under their watch at all times and I was left in no doubt they might call on me again to help them out.'

By this time, Favre was shaking with terror and his face looked as white as a ghost.

'Where does George Malfroy fit into this story?' Guy asked.

'When the Germans realised that you, André, and Amelie had never been found, they suspected you'd gone underground. Malfroy kept an eye on me. He asked me if Lili might know and I told her she had nothing to do with any of you. That's when I found out he was planning to ask her to marry him. I knew it was a ploy because I'd had no contact with her for ages. He told me he'd arrange for her to speak with me on the telephone when he was in Champagnole and it would be in both our interests if I told her where to look for you all. I had no idea, but I also knew I had to play along or the Gestapo would kill us both if we were of no more use to them. Then a few weeks later I got a call from Lili. She told me that a Frenchman called George Malfroy had asked her to marry him. He was rich and well-connected. She sounded so happy. How could I tell her it was a set-up and they were trying to trick her? I knew the call was being monitored.'

Elizabeth could see he had got himself in a tight corner and almost felt sorry for him.

'Every time Lili telephoned I knew he was standing nearby. What could I say? Then she asked me if I knew where you were — and André and Amelie. I told her I had no idea but maybe she might find out in Clairvaux. That was the last time I spoke to her. I don't even know where she lives — or even if she's alive or dead. I haven't heard from her in weeks.'

Guy got up and walked out of the room gesturing to the others to follow.

Favre started crying like a baby, screaming out. 'I loved you all like my brothers! You know that. It was my sister's fault I tell you.'

Guy put his head in his hands and sighed. 'My God! That damn woman.'

It was René who quickly brought them to their senses. '*Merde*! The man could have warned you all and given you the chance to go into hiding — himself included — *connard!* Instead, he took the easy way out. I've known men endure torture and kill themselves for less. If you ask me, he's a coward.'

Guy knew he was right. He also knew there was no way they could let him go. He took out his pistol and cocked it. 'He has to die. We can't prolong this. It's doing my head in.'

René could see it was hard for Guy to kill someone who had been so loyal. He'd had to do it himself on occasions. They all looked at each other. All the while Favre was still shouting out for forgiveness.

'I'll do it,' René said.

Guy refused. 'No. I am the one who has to do it.'

He turned and walked back into the other room while the others watched on. It was like a scene in slow-motion. Guy walked over to him and put a hand on his shoulder in a last attempt to comfort him.

'You know I'd never hurt any of my brothers,' Favre blurted out through his tears, spittle drooling from his mouth.

'I know. Let's see if we can work this out.'

With a sigh of relief, Favre closed his eyes. 'Thank you, thank ...'

He never saw it coming. Guy moved behind him, quickly pulled out the gun and shot him through the back of the head. It was all over. The others rushed into the room.

'Get rid of him,' Guy said to them. His hand was still shaking when Elizabeth took the gun from him.

'You had no choice,' she whispered. 'Don't beat yourself up.'

Guy didn't respond. René and his comrade hastily took Favre's body and dumped it in the river as they had done with Malfroy.

'What are you going to do with his papers?' René asked. 'Shall I destroy them?'

Guy nodded. René took out his lighter and lit the corner. No-one said a word as they watched them slowly burn, the photograph of Favre's sepia-tinted face growing darker as it became consumed in fire until all there was left of the man Guy had once thought of as a friend, was a small pile of charred paper.

They headed back to Dijon in silence. After giving René and

Madame Genot money for their invaluable help and to help with other Resistance activities, Elizabeth and Guy returned to Lons-le-Saunier. The train was packed: German soldiers in the first-class carriages and French men and women carrying suitcases and mollifying frightened children in the others. They found a seat together opposite an elderly couple. Elizabeth wondered what their story was but no-one was in the mood to talk. At one point, she leaned over and gave Guy a kiss, but his face remained expressionless. Even her kiss could not get a smile from him.

Her thoughts wandered back to her SOE training in England. *We can only teach you so much*, someone had said, *but nothing will prepare you for the time when you're confronted with eliminating another human being, especially if that person is someone you thought you could trust.* How right he was. There was a divide as vast as the Verdon Gorge between the textbook scenario and the real thing. She shoved her hands in her pocket and stared out the window at the countryside with its undulating fields and small villages. Anyone who had not experienced it would never understand. She knew this was what Guy was thinking. He had trusted Claude Favre; they were brothers in arms. It would stay with him for the rest of his life.

CHAPTER 27

On the outskirts of Lons-le-Saunier, Elizabeth and Guy made their separate ways to the Dassin's villa where they would spend the night. Guy was there ahead of Elizabeth and was in the drawing room with Pierre when she arrived.

'My goodness,' Juliette said. 'What on earth's happened? Daniel looks awful.'

'It's a long story, but we're fine. Pierre can tell you when we've gone. For now, I need a stiff drink.'

Elizabeth knew Pierre would only tell her half the story, enough to satisfy her curiosity. She asked after the children while Juliette poured her a fine Jura brandy and prepared something to eat.

'They're fine. Angeline is always asking about you — her *Tante* Marie-Élise — and she adores her little brother. If it wasn't for the war, I'd be blessed. I try to protect them from what's happening but the increased bombing scares Angeline too much. These days it's far more intense. Pierre tells me it's because the Allies are about to land. I can only pray he's right.'

Elizabeth assured her that would definitely happen soon. The rest of the evening was taken up with small talk — what Juliette was knitting for the baby, the lack of food, etc. Elizabeth didn't mind. It took her mind off recent events. She slept well that night and in the morning was woken up by Guy. He looked in a better mood.

'Come on. Pierre's offered to take us back to Clairvaux. There's a lot to be done.'

Elizabeth gave a big hug to Angeline, who wanted her to stay longer, and a cuddle to baby Louis who was gurgling and smiling. Their innocence touched her and made her realise how much she missed the domestic bliss of normal households.

'You didn't say anything about your adventures in Dijon to Juliette, did you?' Pierre asked anxiously as they drove away. 'She's more scared than she lets on because of the more frequent bombing raids.'

Elizabeth frowned at him. 'I think she was only too happy to talk to a friend about domestic issues. I don't imagine she gets much of that from you these days.'

'Okay. I apologise. I know you better than that. We're all on edge at the moment. The Germans know the Allies intend to land soon and they're on edge too. I get pulled up and searched almost every day now, even by people I know.'

The conversation turned to the pressing issue of the upcoming airdrops and whether everything was in place.

'It's all going well. Let's hope there are no air raids on the night,' Guy replied.

Having spent most of the night talking about Belvedere with Guy, Pierre was up to date with the situation confronting them — namely what to do about Lili.

'What *are* you intending to do with her?' he asked.

Guy answered. 'We'll leave her be until after the drops. With her brother and Malfroy gone, she can't do much damage. She doesn't know anything and if we eliminate her beforehand, it could alert the Gestapo. You never know who's keeping an eye on her. Rest assured we'll have her watched at all times though.'

At the Menouillard Farm, they found Sabine. Armand was still at the sawmill. The Germans had put in orders for urgent truckloads of timber.

'Only God knows what they intend to do with it all,' she said bitterly. 'And they never pay, even though they go through the motions of signing contracts. It's all worthless so why do they bother? Those German bastards! Thieves, that's what they are.'

'Where's the timber being delivered to?' Guy asked.

'I don't know for sure. They've sent their own trucks. Armand thinks it's to fortify bridges and railways for when the Allies attack.'

She looked at Pierre expectantly as he usually gave them a few bottles of wine.

'Sorry, nothing today, Sabine. I'm going to Château-Chalon. Hopefully they won't have raided all the cellars by the time I get there. Even my uncle in Poligny has run out of stock except for that deemed undesirable which is now desirable.'

Elizabeth told them about her mother's parsnip and elderberry wine and jokingly said she should get London to send them a few bottles.

'All this talk about wine: are you trying to demoralize us? It will be the lack of wine that will finally force the French to kick out the Germans.' Sabine chuckled. 'I can see you're all in good spirits. Come inside and let me see if I can rustle up something — soup with smoked sausage. How does that sound?'

Pierre rubbed his stomach heartily. These days they were lucky to have any meat in their soup. They ate their meal and as Armand had still not returned, Pierre left for Château-Chalon. They wouldn't see him again until the night of the drops. Elizabeth and Guy headed to the cottage. When they got there the afternoon sun was streaming through the windows. They left the door open and collapsed on the bed for an afternoon siesta. Elizabeth started to talk about what would happen to Lili but when she looked at Guy, he was fast asleep. She stroked his face gently.

'My poor darling,' she whispered to him.

Guy slept until sunset. She was sitting on the doorstep with Armand and Sabine when he awoke and the look on Elizabeth's face told him something was wrong.

'I received a telephone call at the sawmill this afternoon,' Armand said. The tone in his voice told Guy it was serious. 'It was from Madame Sophie. Her exact words were — "Please tell the Monsieur we are fully booked this weekend." It was short and to the point. I didn't even have time to say a thing before the line went dead. Besides, two Germans officers were standing nearby watching the men loading wood on to the trucks. One of them asked me who the call was from. I told them I had no idea.'

Guy knitted his brows together and sighed. He asked if anyone else had called. Armand shook his head.

'I have to get to Bonlieu as soon as possible,' Guy said.

Elizabeth caught his arm. 'Surely she would have contacted André if it was anything really serious. Maybe the Germans are on the move in the area and she is just being cautious.'

'André may not be in the area and she wouldn't make a telephone call like that without a good reason.'

'No-one else has raised the alarm.' Elizabeth replied, trying to reassure him. 'Where's Amelie?'

'In Champagnole, liaising with Odette.'

'There's no bus to Bonlieu now,' Armand said. 'And it will soon be curfew. Can't you wait until tomorrow?' He didn't offer to let Guy use the telephone at the sawmill in case it was being monitored.

'No!' Guy was getting more anxious by the minute. 'I can't wait.' He asked if he could use Elizabeth's bicycle.

She looked anxious. 'I don't want you to go alone. Let me come with you.'

Armand said they had another bicycle he could use but it needed a new tyre.

'I have to contact London first,' Elizabeth added. 'They are expecting a transmission.'

She went to the woodshed to fetch the radio while Armand left to repair the bicycle. Sabine went with him, leaving Elizabeth and Guy to talk alone.

'Are you sure you really want to go now?' Elizabeth asked as she set up the radio. 'You can telephone Madame Sophie tomorrow morning from Clairvaux.'

He didn't answer. Instead he checked his gun and went outside to smoke a cigarette while she made the transmission. It was hard for her to concentrate as she could see his cigarette in the darkness as he paced up and down. She closed the door so she couldn't see him. This was not the time to make an error in her coding.

When the transmission had ended, she told him London had arranged for two drops to the same drop-zone as before, and one to a new location between Billaude and Chevrotaine. They were to expect three more important military men attached to de Gaulle's Free French and all the arms they asked for. It was to take place on the full moon in one week's time. The BBC would give the coded message that it was going ahead.

*

It took just over two hours to get to Bonlieu as they took several back roads or hid when the occasional car and truck passed. They were also slowed down by the fact that Guy was not as fit as he used to be. The Grand Hôtel du Lac was in darkness, but when they went around the back they saw a soft light in the cellar. Guy peered through the narrow window and saw Madame Sophie with Ruth. He tapped on the window and whistled the first line of *Cette chanson est pour vous*.

Madame Sophie looked distraught. 'I hoped you'd come. I couldn't say more to Armand as I could tell by his voice someone else was

223

with him. I've been notified that someone has told the Gestapo in Saint-Laurent they think I'm working with the Resistance and maybe hiding escapees. They also said that they suspected the cook — meaning Ruth — was Jewish, and that she has a son. They are planning a raid at any moment. I tried to contact André but I have no idea where he is.'

Guy saw a group of people huddled in the shadows of the cellar and asked how many there were.

'Five. I'm frantic. I have to get them away immediately but I can't get in touch with Robert or the *passeur*. Who will take them? Ruth and her son must get away too.' She put her head in her hands. '*C'est terrible*. I expected it would happen one day, but who could have told them? We've been so careful.'

'Who gave you this information? Guy asked.

'A policeman who lives in Saint-Pierre He pretends to be friendly with the Germans but it's a front.'

'When did he tell you?'

'He passed by on his way to Bonlieu after lunch. That's when I made the telephone call.'

Guy asked if they could talk in private. A woman started to cry when she saw Madame Sophie leave the cellar. She tried to console her saying she would be back soon. She was quite safe. Ruth offered to stay with them. Her son was not with them.

In the kitchen the three sat around the table deciding what to do. The clock struck 11:30 p.m.

'If the Gestapo are going to raid, it's highly likely they'll do it in the middle of the night. Maybe we have two hours at the most. Who are these people? Where did they come from?'

'Four were sent via the Delatours. They've been moved from house to house since the beginning of the occupation but the Delatours cannot accept any more; it's too dangerous. They are still being watched. They are all Jewish: a middle-aged couple and three teenagers, one a fourteen-year-old girl and her sixteen-year-old brother, and a seventeen-year-old — Isaac — who was found by the gardener wandering the forest. He had made his way from an orphanage in the Loire region by himself and tried to cross the border but was quickly discovered and sent back by the Swiss border guards.' She paused while Guy absorbed all this. 'Then there's Ruth and her son. How they found that out is beyond me.'

'No time to go through that now. We have to get them away. The problem is that we have important work in the next week which cannot be put off.' He was referring to the airdrops from London.

Elizabeth could see he was in a dilemma. 'I'll do it,' she said. 'I'll take them.'

This was the last thing Guy wanted. After everything they'd gone through, now was not the time for them to separate again.

'You have to stay here,' Elizabeth said to him. 'You're needed now more than ever. The Allies will land soon and the Resistance must be ready.'

'I can't let you do this,' he replied, raising his voice. 'Without the help of the *passeurs*, it's too dangerous. You won't get past the Forbidden Zone.'

'You are no longer my boss, *Daniel*,' Elizabeth replied matter-of-factly, using his code name to stress the point that this was work. 'I came here to find you. My job is done. Now I can do what I want and right now those people down there will be sent to a concentration camp if we don't do something.'

Guy turned to Madame Sophie and asked her to give them a few minutes alone. When she'd closed the door, he pulled her to him. 'What are you trying to do, for God's sake? These people are not your responsibility. We need you here. *I* need you here.'

Elizabeth took his hands and squeezed them as she looked into his eyes. All she wanted was this damn war to be over so they could live in peace and do the things married couples were supposed to do — have children and live together until a ripe old age, but no, that would not happen if they did things they would never forgive themselves for.

'My darling, you have everyone else to think of now, and they are all here to help you: Pierre, André, Amelie, Madame Sophie, Monique, Sabine and Armand — and the maquisards. Do you want me to go on?'

'What about the transmissions? You are the only one who can transmit. You took the place of Paul-Emille.'

'No. Everything is in place for the drops now. All you have to do is listen to the BBC and make sure it's on.' She smiled and kissed him on the lips. 'You see, you don't even need me for that any longer. I told you, my mission was to find you and Amelie and I've done that — more to be exact. Belvedere is alive and active again. In fact, you don't need me at all now.'

225

He pulled her into his arms. 'My sweet love, it's too dangerous, especially with a small child.'

'My mind is made up. Think of those poor people in the cellar, of Ruth and her child. Neither of us could live with ourselves if we didn't act. There's no time to wait to contact a *passeur*. It's now or never.'

She looked into his eyes. The love they had for each other was evident but both of them were as stubborn as each other. At the same time, they knew their work in the field came first.

Reluctantly, Guy agreed. He went outside and told Madame Sophie. Their voices were too low for Elizabeth to hear what they were saying. He asked her to fetch Ruth.

'How are they?' Guy asked, referring to the people in the cellar.

'Terrified — how do you think?'

'Ruth, I want you to go and get your son,' Elizabeth said. 'Put him in warm clothes and sturdy shoes. The same goes for you too. We are leaving straight away. I will be taking you all across the border.'

Ruth stared at her as if she hadn't quite heard correctly. 'Sorry! *You* are taking us?' She looked at Guy as if he should be the one to take them.

'Marie-Élise knows the terrain well and she's used to this sort of thing. She'll keep you safe. You don't have to worry,' he replied. 'Do as she says, and you'll be fine.'

'Madame Sophie...' Ruth blurted out. 'Is this true? I thought my papers were in order.'

'Yes, my dear, they are, but we can't risk the Germans taking you in for questioning. We're all at risk here. Please do as you're told and get ready.'

Ruth ran out of the room with tears in her eyes. While she was preparing herself and her son for the journey, Guy scribbled out a map. Elizabeth was familiar with most of the terrain and the towns and villages along the border even though she hadn't been to some of them. He marked several spots where they would find foresters' huts and two farmhouses belonging to *passeurs*. She had several options where to cross the border, and none would be easy as they had a three-year-old child. She chose the area nearest to Bellefontaine, thinking that it would have the fewest patrols.

Madame Sophie gave her a thick pullover and scarf and told her to exchange her lighter shoes for a pair of heavy boots. Guy asked her to find a few metres of rope too. After preparing everyone a small bag of food which could be carried on their backs, Madame Sophie went back to the cellar to prepare the others for the journey while Guy gave Elizabeth a compass, flashlight, and his gun and made sure she had enough rounds of ammunition. She told him she already had her own gun, safely tucked away where no-one would find it, and a knife.

'All the same, I'd feel better if you took this too. I can get another.'

Ten minutes later, Ruth returned carrying her sleepy son in her arms. Elizabeth looked at Guy. He was right. Taking a small child was dangerous, but she couldn't leave him behind. No wonder most of the *passeurs* refused to do it. Madame Sophie returned with the rope. All was in place and the escapees were waiting to enter the tunnel. Elizabeth pulled her aside.

'I need something in case the child cries. I will have to sedate him. Do you have anything — drugs, alcohol; anything at all?'

Madame Sophie nodded. She went to her bedroom and returned with a small bottle of pills.

'I think it's called Paraldehyde — some sort of drug that will make him sleepy,' she whispered. 'It was prescribed for some of the children to help calm them down during the escape. Use it wisely and it's safe'

Elizabeth had used such things before, especially during the Blitz. She slipped it into her pocket.

It was almost one o'clock in the morning when the group gathered at the entrance to the tunnel. Guy gave Elizabeth a long, lingering kiss and she promised to contact both him and London as soon as she reached Le Pont. Fighting back her emotions, she turned and told the group to follow her. They were to keep together and stay silent.

'The only time you are allowed to say anything is if you need help,' she told them sternly. 'Even then you must speak in a whisper. This is a matter of life and death. Is that understood?' She looked at each one and waited for them to say yes. 'Good. Now let's get going.'

Within minutes their muffled footsteps in the tunnel faded and the dim light from the flashlight disappeared. It was eerily quiet. Guy helped Madame Sophie slide the shelves back into position and they checked the cellar for any evidence that could betray them. Then they went upstairs and stood on the terrace staring into the darkness of the forest beyond. Above them, the Milky Way swirled beautifully in the night sky. Madame Sophie noticed Guy's eyes were moist with tears. She reached out and clasped his hand.

'They'll be fine, Daniel. You'll see.'

CHAPTER 28

First week of May, 1944 Le Pont, Switzerland.

They had finally made it to safety but it had been a harrowing experience. From the moment they left Bonlieu, the escape was not without difficulties. The first happened as they left the tunnel and had to clamber along a narrow ridge towards the first cave where they would rest for a short while before continuing. The exit from the tunnel was slippery due to moss on the limestone. Ruth was carrying her son in a child's sling on her back and thankfully the boy was so tired he was asleep at this point. It was the middle-aged woman who became the problem. Unbeknown to Elizabeth, she had lost her spectacles during one of their escapes and her eyesight had deteriorated. She was so short-sighted she couldn't see clearly and slipped. It wasn't a bad fall, but it was the first of many and with each fall, she acquired bruises and cuts and slowed them all down. Her husband anxiously helped her as best he could. The teenagers also took it in turns to help. After a while, seventeen-year-old Isaac took Ruth's child and carried him. They agreed that they would all take it in turns to carry the boy. The climb gradually became steeper and there were many times when the rope was needed. Elizabeth, aided by Isaac, managed to pull them all to safety every time.

By dawn they had covered several kilometres but decided to stay hidden until the evening rather than risk being spotted by Germans. Elizabeth walked on alone until she found the first hut for them to take refuge. She returned to the group and they started out again at night. This same pattern went on for three nights until they found the last forester's hut near the border. By this time, the group, especially the married couple, Ruth, and the young girl, were tired and racked with pain from struggling to climb the mountains. Their feet were swollen and covered with blisters, as were their hands from grasping on to rocks and branches. At this point, Elizabeth decided it was best for them to rest for at least one or two full days. The problem was they were almost out of food and they were getting weaker. To make things worse, it began to rain and the forest floor became even muddier and slipperier. Not to mention the gushing waterfalls that poured down the mountainside, blocking their path and forcing them to make detours.

Elizabeth knew the Maquis were also hiding out in the forests and had hoped they might come across one of their camps, but they were too well hidden and she'd been extremely cautious in only moving the group at night. She also knew there were plenty of deer in the forest. Maybe if she could shoot one, they would have something to eat. She was a good shot but even so, a shot ringing through the woods might alert the Germans. In the end she decided the best thing to do was to leave the group to rest in the hut and go on alone to the nearest safe house — a farm near the border. Alone, she could make it within a day. If all went well, she would return with food the next day or the day after and by then the group would have recovered enough to continue. When she told them what she was going to do, they looked fearful.

'What if you something happens to you?' someone asked.

'Nothing will happen.' She sounded more reassuring than she felt.

She pulled Ruth and Isaac aside. 'Ruth, I want you to continue to give your son one of these with a bite of food. It will keep him sleepy.' She handed her the bottle. 'Only one a day and he will remain sleepy but that's fine.' She turned to Isaac and gave him her own gun. He stared at it in fright.

'I am putting you in charge so I want you to have this. I don't expect you'll need to use it if everyone stays inside the hut, but just in case.'

'I don't know how to use a gun,' he blurted out.

Elizabeth sent Ruth back inside and took Isaac behind a tree where the group couldn't see what they were doing. There she showed him how to use it and made him load and reload several times until she felt sure he would be fine.

'There are wolves in these parts you know,' he said. 'I've heard them in the night.'

Elizabeth thought about Guy's experience after the raid and assured him they would be fine if they stayed in the hut.

'Under no circumstances are you to go outside. The rain has cleared and the sun is shining again, but don't be deceived into thinking you can wander around. You could be killed.' She turned to Isaac. 'Keep the door locked. The only time someone goes out is to relieve themselves.'

She slipped on her backpack and left wondering if she'd done the right thing. Almost six hours later, as the sun sank over the mountain ridge near the Swiss border, she saw the farm in the distance. She hid for a while watching to see if there was anyone around. A young auburn-haired woman in her early twenties came out of a shed wearing wellington boots and carrying a large basket. She went towards a nearby field calling and whistling to the goats until one by one they ran towards her. From her hiding place, Elizabeth could hear her talking to them. She whistled *Cette chanson est pour vous, Madame,* and immediately the woman looked in Elizabeth's direction. When Elizabeth received the reply she came out of hiding calling the woman's name.

'Solange Lehmann! I am a friend.'

Solange put down the basket and cautiously walked towards her.

'My name is Marie-Élise. I am a courier for Daniel and friend of André, chief of the Saint-Claude Maquis. I need your help.'

Solange could see Elizabeth was exhausted and invited her into the house. In the kitchen were the rest of the family: her parents and six children ranging from ten to thirty years of age. Just like the Menouillards, the farm dogs growled at the stranger in their midst, ready to pounce at any minute. Solange's father shouted at them and they stopped immediately, retreating like lambs to their blankets by the door.

'I need your help,' Elizabeth said. 'I am trying to help six Jews across the border. There was about to be a raid. Daniel said I could trust you.'

Monsieur Lehmann pulled out a chair. 'Sit down and eat first before you collapse. Then take your time and tell us what happened.'

Solange's mother gave her a plate of potatoes and sausage slathered in melted Swiss cheese while the rest of the family sat around waiting for an explanation. She was ravenous and ate it so fast, she almost made herself sick.

'Where are these people now? Solange asked.

'Hidden in a forester's hut,' Elizabeth replied. She drew a detailed map of the area and retraced her tracks. She had used her compass and knew within a radius of a few hundred metres where they were. 'The thing is, are you able to get us across the border? I don't have much money now, but I can certainly get more later.'

Monsieur Lehmann waved his hand in the air. 'Don't worry about that. Get some sleep and we'll fetch them tomorrow.'

The next day, Solange and three of her brothers returned with Elizabeth through the forest. She'd had the foresight to make marks in certain places to guide her back and they made it well before dusk. When they reached the hut, the group were still locked inside. They had hardly slept because of a pack of wolves that surrounded the hut during the night. Isaac could see them through a crack in the door and kept the gun aimed should they attempt to get in. The biggest worry was the cracked window pane with a piece of glass missing. The middle-aged man sat next to it armed with a big stick. After a while the wolves disappeared but it didn't stop them being terrified.

The men gave the group something to eat and drink before starting out again. When they reached the farm, Madame Lehmann had prepared the barn for them to sleep in for the night. They were only ten kilometres from the Swiss border but the area was heavily patrolled. This was the most dangerous part of the escape and it was suggested that the group divide into two to make things easier. The two elder brothers would take the elderly couple, the girl and her brother, while Solange and another brother would cross with Elizabeth and the others.

The Lehmanns asked Elizabeth if she wanted to stay in the farm. She could sleep in Solange's room. She was only too happy because it meant she could listen to the BBC broadcasts. The stay ended up lasting two days longer than expected as a neighbour told them the Germans had caught several people trying to cross the line and they'd all been killed whilst making a dash for freedom. While this was disheartening, Elizabeth looked forward to listening to the radio. Every night she had watched the moon until it now became a beautiful silver ball hanging in the clear night sky. It told her the drops would be taking place that very night. She also knew they were happening because she'd heard the coded message on the radio. That night she lay on her bed, unable to sleep. All she could think about was Guy and the others congregating at the allocated drop points, welcoming de Gaulle's men and checking the arms and ammunition. Despite not being religious, she put her hands together and said a little prayer. *Dear God, look over them and protect them all.*

When the time came to make the crossing, Monsieur Lehmann took his cart along the border road where he knew the Germans and French border police were. He made this trip frequently to and from the nearest town and they knew him. He stopped to talk to them and asked them if the rumours he'd heard about escapees being caught were true. While he kept them occupied, smoking a cigarette and chatting, the two groups crossed the road at a designated area and disappeared through the barbed wire into the woods. Later that afternoon, they exited the forest and saw lac de Joux shimmering in the sunshine in the distance. A few kilometres further on was Le Pont. They had made it.

The Lehmann brothers had made the crossing first and were waiting for them behind a stone wall. They returned back across the border leaving Solange to go on with Elizabeth to Giselle's house to make sure all was well. That night the group celebrated their success in style — wine, a good fondue, and lots of music. It was a moment they thought would never happen. Elizabeth and Ruth, however, would have to wait until they could celebrate. Elizabeth was worried about the amount of sedative they'd given Ruth's son and wanted a doctor to check him out. Giselle fetched the same doctor who had treated Guy. He assured them the boy would be fine and it would only be a few days until he was back to his normal self.

Solange returned to France and Elizabeth stayed with the escapees making sure that they could find a Swiss family willing to sponsor them in order to get a "tolerance or residence permit" that would allow them to live in the canton but not work. Often the families claimed these people were distant relatives. This was their best option. Otherwise there was a chance they would be put into an internment camp. As refugees in Switzerland, they still had to be careful. When things had settled down, Elizabeth travelled to Bern and contacted the British Embassy. There were other SOE contacts there too. It was in Bern that she was able to let London know she was safe and had crossed into Switzerland with her "children" as she referred to them, without any trouble. However, she was unable to get any information on the recent events in the Jura. On the positive side, there was a buzz in the air that the Allies would land in France very soon. Rather than return to London as Guy had wanted, she went back to Le Pont for a few days and then decided to go back into France.

'What!' Ruth declared when she heard this. 'Are you crazy? You're safe here and you told us the Allies will attack soon. Wait until it's all over.'

'I am more use there than here,' Elizabeth replied.

She contacted the *passeur's* friend at the garage outside Le Pont and told him to let her know when he was in town. She would return with him.

A few days later, Giselle received a telephone call. 'The *passeur* is here,' she said. 'I'll prepare you some food for the journey.'

The next evening, Elizabeth headed back into France.

CHAPTER 29

Last week of May, 1944, Fontaine-le-Bas, Jura.

It had been a slow and tiring journey through the forêt du Risoux. This time the *passeur* zigzagged through the more inaccessible parts of the forest and Elizabeth was glad she'd had the chance to rest for a couple of weeks. They spent two nights in a forester's home due to German activity in the area. From the very beginning of the occupation it was not uncommon for unscrupulous smugglers to take advantage of the dire situation for the Jews and other people whose lives were in danger in the occupied zone. Scandalous sums of money changed hands. Some estimated it was anything between 2,000 — 8,000 francs for the passage through the Jura forests, and even more if the journey was from Paris. Anywhere between 30,000 to 40,000 francs for the whole journey, and quite often the unsuspecting escapees were handed over to the Germans at the last minute. Finding the right person to trust was extremely difficult. Fortunately, Belvedere had excellent *passeurs*. Even so, a lot of luck was needed. It was there that Elizabeth learned of further mass arrests, executions and deportations in the Jura and Franche-Comté.

Around the time she was leading the group over the mountains, the Germans, aided by the Milice and anonymous whistleblowers, executed more *rafles*. The major one was in Poligny using the same tactics as Saint-Claude. They waited until it was market day and surrounded the town early in the morning.

'Fifty-seven people between the ages of eighteen and sixty were deported,' the forester told her. 'After a stop at Gestapo HQ in Lons-le-Saunier, they went to Clairvaux-les-Lacs and spent the night there. All the men, women, and children were forced to watch on as they were kept in the school without food along with others arrested in the vicinity.'

Elizabeth felt sick and wondered if the drops had gone wrong and the men caught.

'Men were also rounded up from Saint-Laurent. All were later transferred to Montluc prison in Lyon. On April 27, 1,500 prisoners were loaded onto cattle trains and although it's thought there were no Jews, it left the next day for Auschwitz-Birkenau. Word had it that some were to be transferred to Buchenwald.'

Elizabeth wondered if the information given to Madame Sophie had anything to do with these impending raids. It was obviously a well-planned attack and if it was meant to demoralize the people, it succeeded.

The following evening, they arrived at the *passeur*'s brother-in-law's farm outside Fontaine-la-Bas. There the news was even worse. When they neared the house, the *passeur* saw his brother-in-law had left a signal that all was not well. A pitchfork was propped up against the wall near the door. It was their private code. The *passeur* asked Elizabeth to stay well-hidden while he went to check what was going on. After half an hour he returned.

'The Germans came sniffing around yesterday checking on everyone in the area. When they couldn't find me at home they came here and questioned by brother-in-law. *Putain!* Fuck! *My* house is now being watched.'

This was the first time she'd heard the *passeur* swear like this. 'What are we going to do?' she asked. 'I can't go back with you.'

The *passeur* said his brother-in-law had offered to let her stay in his barn overnight.

'I'll come back tomorrow and we'll figure out what to do. Don't worry.' He swore again.

Elizabeth did worry. Since hearing the bad news at the forester's house, she would have to be extremely cautious. The brother-in-law came out and pointed to the barn. She clambered up a ladder and lay on the straw watching the two men talking outside. He gave the *passeur* three rabbits caught in a snare and told him to tell the Germans he'd been hunting.

The next day the *passeur* returned. He looked pale and anxious.

'Thank God the Germans believed me when I said I'd been out catching rabbits. They've gone, but knowing them, they'll be back.'

She noticed he was agitated and avoided looking into her eyes.

'For God's sake, what's wrong? Tell me.'

'It's worse than we thought.' His brother-in-law hovered in the background smoking a cigarette and staring into the fields beyond. 'There's been a series of well-organized attacks in the region. Many homes have been burnt down and most of the residents either shot, deported or left homeless. A team from Gestapo HQ in Besançon arrived in Saint-Laurent-en-Grandvaux. It included some of the most despicable men from there. It is also thought that Menzel was here himself. Maurice Gehin, a Frenchman, was seen in the company of another German lieutenant from Besançon named Raderscheid. They were recognised because they drove around in a big grey car — a Chrysler or Chevrolet. The locals refer to this group as "the killers".'

Elizabeth felt a chill run down her spine and her throat constricted with fear. *People killed, houses burned down, many more deported. Please God, don't let it be Guy or anyone I know personally.*

'This small group were here for six days with a detachment from Besançon. They were sent to Saint-Laurent-en-Grandvaux with two objectives — military and psychological — to put fear into the Resistance. The reason they stayed there was to secure the national route between Champagnole and Morez because of sabotage activities against German convoys. A group led by an FFI chief from the area of Lons-le-Saunier was one such group, but the attackers withdrew after the arrival of German reinforcements from Champagnole. The Germans then withdrew to Saint-Laurent but the FFI suffered significant losses, as did the Germans.'

The *passeur* could see Elizabeth's distress and could offer few words of comfort. She knew the Germans were not going to allow such a setback to go unpunished. It was clear they wanted to terrorize the population in order to isolate them from the Maquis who they were sure were being supported morally and materially by the locals.

'A week ago, a German convoy left Saint-Laurent-en-Grandvaux for the nearby village of Chaux-du-Dombief. No-one was allowed to use bicycles or any other vehicles, even if they had a permit. Everyone was stopped and searched. If they ran, they were shot on sight. From Chaux-du-Dombief, they continued to Bonlieu.'

By now, Elizabeth's legs were about to give way and the two men took her into the house.

The *passeur* continued. 'At Bonlieu, the Germans came across a group of seven FFIs and killed them. The soldiers made their way to a local farm and after telling the farmer to let his animals go free, set fire to the farm. Their servant, who had been hiding, ran away and the Germans shot him on the spot. The next day, more German trucks from Morez and Champagnole arrived at Saint-Laurent. They were obviously looking for the ringleaders who were being denounced and it had to be of great importance to send their top Gestapo men. Needless to say, there are strong rumours of torture, and machine gun sounds could be heard throughout this time. Wherever the grey car went, travelling through hamlets and villages, it put the fear of God into people. They were relentless.'

'What about Bonlieu?' Elizabeth tried to conceal the fear in her voice. 'What about the Grand Hôtel du Lac, Madame Sophie, Amelie — everyone else?'

The *passeur* went quiet. By now, all were chain smoking.

'You'd better tell her,' his brother-in-law replied.

'*Merde!*' the *passeur* answered, angrily. It was clear he didn't want to impart this last bit of news to Elizabeth. After the assassination of one of the maquisards, a German convoy headed to Bonlieu. They burnt down the abbey and looted several houses before setting fire to them.' Elizabeth had a strong feeling how this was going to end and prepared herself for the worst. 'Finally they arrived at the hotel and...'

'And what?' Elizabeth asked, raising her voice.

'It was burned to the ground.'

Elizabeth put her head in her hands. She found it hard to believe but she didn't doubt him.

Seeing the *passeur* was also deeply affected, his brother-in-law continued the story.

'Then they continued to the village of Ilay by the lake. News travelled fast and when the troops returned to Saint-Laurent, they were attacked by FFI. The Germans sustained some losses and at least one SS officer was seriously injured and taken back to Saint-Laurent in a car stolen from the Resistance. Saint-Pierre was also raided and people taken away at gunpoint. Much of the looting and burning was because the locals were suspected of housing maquisards. According to what we heard, it was so bad, even neighbours were denouncing each other.' The brother-in-law paused to offer Elizabeth another cigarette. 'All these atrocities were committed during one short week and at least some of the men helping them were French. They are still finding bodies — in fields, in the woods...'

'And what of Madame Sophie?' Elizabeth asked again.

'She was spared. After being taken to Saint-Laurent, someone higher up came to her defence. A car came for her and she was taken to Gestapo HQ in Besançon where she awaits deportation.'

'Good God! Everything she did for those damn Germans and no-one saves her.' Elizabeth was filled with disgust. 'What about her daughter — and Amelie?'

'We don't know. They weren't there at the time of the raids.'

'And the gardener?'

'Shot as he tried to escape.'

Elizabeth let out a deep sigh. 'No doubt they looted the place first.'

The *passeur* shrugged his shoulders. For a while they sat around without saying a word but that was a luxury Elizabeth could not afford. She had to get away but going anywhere near Saint-Laurent, Bonlieu, and Clairvaux was out of the question. Neither could she risk making a telephone call from the *passeur*'s garage. She knew she had to get to Champagnole as soon as possible. At least there she had a chance of finding Amelie. The *passeur* said that although bicycles were confiscated in some parts, namely, where the raids had taken place, she could take his wife's and head to Champagnole. It was the opposite direction but it would also give her a chance to visit the Delatours.

'Come on then,' she said, stubbing her cigarette in the dirt with her foot. 'I'd best get going.'

*

The iron gates to the Delatour Château stood wide open. She cycled along the tree-lined driveway with a sense of dread. Placing her bicycle against a large urn filled with geraniums, she ran up the ornate curved steps that led to the front entrance and banged on the door. There was no answer. She ran back down the stairs and around the back. One of the servants came out.

'If you're looking for Madam and Monsieur Delatour, you're too late. They were taken away to Champagnole.'

'Where are the children?' Elizabeth asked.

'Gone! They were smuggled away a week before. Don't ask me where because I don't know. The Germans say they will return, so you'd better not hang around.'

Elizabeth left straight away and used the back roads to Champagnole.

The place was teeming with Germans in armoured convoys and on motorcycles. She hid the bicycle behind thick bushes near the river and walked into the town towards the Café des Amis. The place was full but the owner recognised her and waved her over.

'I need to get in touch with Amelie or Odette as soon as possible,' she whispered.

'Take a seat. I'll see what I can do.'

He brought her an aperitif and whispered to a waiter that he was going out for a while and he was to take care of her. Elizabeth scanned her eyes around the room while flicking through a magazine and trying to look at ease. The customers appeared to be French and were talking in low voices about the events taking place in the area. It was sometime before the owner reappeared. He called her over to the bar and whispered an address.

'Apartment 2 — the first floor. Three blocks away. Knock and whistle a tune — NOT the *Marseillaise* or the Partisan's Song!' He winked at her.

Elizabeth reached the apartment block and found the ground floor door ajar. There was no-one around and she slipped upstairs. Outside apartment 2, she knocked three times but didn't have time to whistle the first few notes when the door swung open and Amelie appeared.

'Come inside, quickly. Did anyone see you?'

'No, I took great care.'

Amelie told her the apartment belonged to Odette but she had purposely moved to the Hotel Ripotot to share a suite with Krüger so she could stay there. Whenever she could, Odette called by to impart any snippets of information under the pretext of collecting jewellery and clothing. The neighbours deemed her a horizontal collaborator so she was careful when she came back — usually when it was dark.

'That means the neighbours will be watching us too,' Amelie added, 'so please take care. When did you arrive back in France?'

'A few days ago. The *passeur* and his brother-in-law told me what happed in Bonlieu. I came here via the Delatours, but was too late, they've been taken away. My God, Amelie, the news is devastating. Please tell me Daniel and the others are safe.'

Elizabeth was venting her emotions which, as an agent in the field, she'd had to bottle up.

Amelie put her arms around her. 'My dear Marie-Élise, Daniel is safe.'

Elizabeth remained strong. '*Merci*. Thank God. And the others?'

'Come on, *cherie*. Sit down and I'll tell you everything I know.'

Odette's apartment was well-appointed. The French windows opened onto a balcony which overlooked a square with Linden trees and a fountain. Light streamed through them highlighting the beautiful period furniture and carpets. They sat near the window, careful not to be seen by anyone passing by. Amelie held Elizabeth's hand as she told her what happened.

'The drops went according to plan. De Gaulle's men landed safely and all the arms we asked for. Everything was distributed to the Resistance. It was only afterwards that the *rafles* began and we don't know why. Daniel left to help train the maquisards near Saint-Claude and André went to help the maquisards near Saint-Laurent.' Elizabeth slumped back into the softness of the sofa, breathing a sigh of relief. 'Everyone else is safe. Monique was forced to watch the deportees being herded in to the school — something they've all become used to now — and Sabine and Armand are fine too. They have arms hidden around the farm and the logging area — right under the noses of the Germans, but they are safe.'

This time it was Amelie's turn to show emotion. Elizabeth felt the tension as she squeezed her hand tighter.

'The night you left Bonlieu, the Germans arrived and the hotel was raided and searched. Daniel had left by then. They found nothing and left, but someone must have had it in for Madame Sophie because they came back again later — as you've heard, took her away and burned the hotel down.' She paused and took a deep breath. 'I heard that she was tortured before being taken by car — a big grey Chevrolet, someone said — to Besançon. One of the top Gestapo men accompanied her.'

'What about Hortense and Bernard?'

'Hortense is hiding here in Champagnole. Bernard is in Lons-le-Saunier using the new premises that Madame Sophie told him about.'

'What about all the forgery equipment? Didn't he move that to the hotel?'

'He did, but he had the good sense to bury everything near the lake and as soon as he heard there'd been a raid, he went back and managed to salvage it all.'

The questions poured out. 'Have you been back to the hotel since?'

Amelie shook her head. 'No. I can't bring myself to go there yet.'

She looked out of the window, her thoughts far away. 'We have to look forward, Marie-Élise. You know that as well as I. There's still work to be done. We need you to get back to the Menouillards and transmit for us. From what I've been hearing on the BBC, the invasion is imminent and we still have much to do.'

'What about *la simplette*?' Elizabeth asked.

'She's still under surveillance. Every now and again, she wanders around the town, seemingly in a dream. I think the fact that she's heard nothing from Malfroy has frightened her.'

'Then she's dangerous,' Elizabeth replied. 'She could just denounce someone in a rage.'

'Both Daniel and André want her brought to trial as soon as the Germans leave. It was one thing to kill the other two, but maybe it's because she's a simpleton — and a woman — I don't know. I don't agree but we can't go against their wishes.' Elizabeth was angry and Amelie sympathized with her. 'For the time being, let's see how this plays out. Those watching her have been told not to allow her anywhere near Clairvaux.'

'How can I get in touch with Daniel?' Elizabeth asked.

'If we can get you back to the Menouillards, he'll get to hear of it.'

'Then I must leave as soon as possible.'

At that point they heard a key being turned in the door. Amelie snatched her gun from the table and aimed it at the door. It was Odette. Seeing Elizabeth safe and sound made her extremely happy.

'Marie-Élise! What a wonderful surprise. You have no idea how much we've been worried about you.' She gave her a big hug.

Amelie looked on. 'It's true. We never thought you'd make it and if you did, we certainly didn't think you'd want to come back to France.'

'What! And leave my friends in a mess. What sort of an agent would I be then?'

They laughed. Odette went to the drinks cabinet and pulled out a bottle of the best champagne.

'Here, drink this tonight. Hansi bought it for me but I think you both deserve it.'

'Odette, why didn't Krüger put a stop to the burning of the hotel and the deportation of Madame Sophie?'

'The truth is, when he heard what was going on it was too late. He went to see her himself when she was held in Saint-Laurent and if it hadn't have been for him, they might have killed her. It was he who sent her to Besançon. It was out of his hands what happened then. All I know is he put in a good report for her and said he found her to be a woman of good character. I know it's not good enough and I'm just as distressed about all this as you.' She started to change her clothes. 'There's an important function on tonight, and he wants me to look my best. Apparently, the top brass are coming from Lyon and Besançon.'

Amelie and Elizabeth looked at each other. 'Is there any way you could get me into the hotel?' Elizabeth asked.

Odette stared at her as if she had gone mad. 'Are you crazy? The Hotel Ripotot is highly monitored at the best of times. Tonight, it will be even more tightly controlled.'

'I'm serious,' Elizabeth said. 'I want to see who's there. It's important.'

Odette stood half naked in a beautiful silk slip with lace edging staring at her with her mouth open. 'They'd spot you a mile away. No. It's out of the question. Just stay here and enjoy your champagne before you get us all shot!' Odette was getting angry.

Elizabeth refused to give up. 'Find me a menial job. I promise not to put any of us in danger.'

Odette finished dressing. She dabbed a little Chanel No 5 on her wrists and behind her ears and put on a diamond necklace. '*Merde!* You are a damn nuisance. Okay. I will find a way. Ever been a cloakroom attendant?'

'No,' replied Elizabeth, 'but I'm sure it can't be as hard as helping people cross the Swiss border.'

Odette opened a safe behind a gilt-framed portrait of her, given to her by Krüger as a gift, took out a wad of money and stuffed it in her purse with her lipstick, powder compact, and cigarette case.

'I have a good friend who works as a cloakroom attendant who will gladly exchange places with you for the evening, but I need to make it worth her while. For this amount of money, she will suddenly take ill and I will come to the rescue. You, my dear Marie-Élise, will be my cousin who has been out of work looking for a job. There's a uniform you must wear. I will ask her to drop it off here. She can leave it on top of the letterbox downstairs in the hallway. Keep a lookout for her and pick it up immediately. Don't let her see you though. When I give you a signal later in the night, you will leave the hotel and come back here. Is that understood? I don't want you hanging about after the function finishes.'

Elizabeth smiled. 'Bossy little thing, isn't she?' she said to Amelie.

Odette picked up a cushion and threw it at her. 'Just be careful.'

An hour later, Amelie noticed a woman carrying a brown parcel cross the square and enter the building. She left seconds later without it. Elizabeth went downstairs, retrieved the package and opened it to find a navy pencil skirt, a crisp white blouse buttoned down the front, and a pair of flat neat-looking shoes. They fitted perfectly.

'How do I look?' Elizabeth asked Amelie.

'Not bad. You'll pass.' She looked at her watch. 'You'd better get a move on. 'I'll wait up for you.' She gave her the outside door key.

Elizabeth made her way to the Hotel Ripotot, lined with luxurious cars emblazoned with Nazi flags, and entered by the back entrance as she'd been told. She asked for the manager and introduced herself as Madame Lombard's cousin who would be standing in for the cloakroom attendant who'd taken ill. The manager looked her up and down, asked her a couple of questions, and then showed her to the place she'd be working. Another young woman also worked there. The Hotel Ripotot was the epitome of refined elegance. Before being taken over by the German Kommandant as their headquarters in Champagnole, it had been an important stopover on the Grand Tour from London through to Switzerland. Every room was filled with plush carpets, potted palms and elegant decor that belonged to the bygone days of the Belle Époque. It had a faded grandeur about it and was a far cry from the rustic dwellings Elizabeth had been living in for the last few months. Apart from the decor, the first things that stood out were the red and black Nazi flags and two enormous portraits; one of Adolf Hitler and the other, Marshall Petain, which had been hung in pride of place in the grandiose hotel lobby.

Elizabeth settled herself behind the counter and prepared for an interesting evening ahead. The other cloakroom attendant showed her what to do. It wasn't complicated. She took their articles of clothing, gave them a numbered ticket and hung them up. What could be simpler? The girl told her it was going to be a busy night. The tables in the dining room were set for fifty people and elevated with a sophisticated touch required for a special occasion. Each table was decked out with starched white tablecloths, beautiful floral arrangements, and fine silverware and crystal. Three enormous crystal chandeliers hung in a row from the decorative ceiling, glittering like beautiful spiders' webs. At the end of the dining room was a small orchestra playing classical music. There were already quite a few guests milling around, talking in small groups. Elizabeth had never seen so many Nazi uniforms under one roof and she was taken aback at how smart they all looked. Even those wearing civilian clothes were smartly groomed. If it hadn't been a gathering of the Nazi elite, she would have thought it enchanting.

Elizabeth prided herself on her good memory and set about checking all the faces that passed by. There was little doubt as to the importance of the occasion. Instantly she recognised Alfred Meissner himself. With him was Maurice Gehin, who had taken part in the *rafles* around Saint-Laurent-en-Grandvaux, Louis Chetelat, a *passeur* working for the Germans and Robert Gervais, a French agent working for the *Abwehr*, well-known for chasing down resistants. There were also two important people from Dijon and to her greatest dismay, the Butcher of Lyon, Klaus Barbie. It was a veritable who's who of the worst of the Gestapo. Several of them were accompanied by attractive women dressed in fine clothes with matching hairdos that the local village women could only dream of emulating.

After cocktails, the group moved into the dining room. Elizabeth had just placed a finely embroidered jacket on a hanger when she saw Odette appear on the arm of Herr *Obergruppenführer* Hans Krüger. She excused herself and came over to hand over her mink stole.

'Is everything going fine?' Odette asked in a whisper, putting her ticket into her bag.

Elizabeth nodded but didn't say a word. She noticed Krüger looking at her and quickly turned away to hang up Odette's stole.

'Haven't I seen that woman somewhere before?' Krüger asked Odette when she returned.

'I doubt it,' Odette replied.

They made their way to the dining room. Before entering, Krüger turned to take another look. This time Elizabeth had kept out of sight but Krüger was one for details.

'I'm sure I've seen her before,' he reiterated. 'It will come to me.'

'Maybe,' Odette replied, 'but for the moment can we just enjoy ourselves?'

'*Habe ich Dir gesagt, wie hinreißend Du aussiehst, mein Schatz?*' He put her hand to his lips and kissed it, breathing in her perfume which he'd given her when they first met. 'Have I told you how ravishing you look tonight my darling?'

He could be the perfect gentleman and Odette would have loved to believe the endearing words were genuine, but she knew he was playing the same game as her.

'*Viele Male. Du bist doch der größte Schmeichler.*' She gave him one of her beguiling smiles, 'You are the biggest flirt,' she replied playfully, but his earlier comment worried her. She knew Krüger only too well. He would not let it rest and they would have to be careful.

After the first course had been served, someone got up and gave a speech. It was to do with gaining more information on the Resistance and reprisals. Odette spoke perfect German and understood there were to be more raids. This time they were going to cast their net wider. Lons-le-Saunier was among those places mentioned. Information had come to light about a "nest of vipers" operating under their noses and that certain Resistance chiefs were still at large. He finished with the fact that many of SOE's operatives had been caught through the *Funkspiel* — the radio game as he referred to it. Orders had come from Berlin that putting a stop to these agents and resistants were a priority. Operation *Frühling* — Operation Spring — the German offensive that began on April 7 in the south of the Jura and the north of the Department of Ain was still ongoing.. Despite the vast amount of divisions and secret police thrown at this operation, there was still much to be done. He mentioned one network in particular that still needed to be broken — Belvedere.

'The Führer is losing patience,' the speaker said as his speech drew to a close. He gave the Hitler salute '*Heil* Hitler.'

In the cloakroom, Elizabeth could hear the resounding voices of the men repeating *Heil* Hitler. Her companion looked at her and made a derogatory comment. After the speech, Odette excused herself to powder her nose. Krüger was busy talking to a colleague and barely heard her. She hurried to the cloakroom and indicated to Elizabeth to meet her in the Powder Room. There, she told her about the speech.

'You've got to get word to Amelie and the others as soon as possible,' Odette said. 'They could strike at any minute. The other thing is, Krüger thinks he recognised you. Thankfully he can't recall where. All the same, can you try and leave early just before everyone leaves. I will try and keep him in the dining room as long as possible. Just go. Don't say a word to the other woman. She will be fine on her own.' Odette looked anxious. Her hands shook. 'This was a bad idea,' she added.

Elizabeth clasped her hand. 'No it wasn't. I recognised so many here tonight. It's been crucial for us, but just to be on the safe side, I will leave for Lons-le-Saunier as soon as possible. I'll get the first train out of here.'

'No! You can't do that. The place will be teeming with Germans. You must leave tonight.' Odette was getting more anxious by the minute. 'Take Amelie with you. There's another bike in the back yard a block away. No-one will notice you take it.'

Elizabeth knew it would be difficult as there was hardly any moon.

'Okay. I will do as you ask.'

Odette turned to leave but something made Elizabeth pull her back. She put her arms around her, kissed her cheek and thanked her for everything. Odette pulled away and left, leaving behind the lingering perfume of Chanel No 5. Elizabeth returned to the cloakroom just as the waiters were about to serve dessert. Around 10:00 p.m. the dining room began to empty. Several men, including Klaus Barbie and his entourage, went into the drawing room. Odette managed to keep Krüger back by engaging with other couples they already knew. In the end, she couldn't keep him back any longer and they left.

'I've just realised where I saw that woman,' Krüger said as they left the dining room. 'She was at the Grand Hôtel du Lac the last time we were there. Don't you remember? She sat alone.'

Odette was alarmed. 'No I don't recall her. You must be mistaken.'

'*Mein Schatz*, when it comes to a pretty woman's face, I am *never* mistaken.'

Odette laughed, but inside she felt a chill run through her bones. When she went to collect her stole, Krüger came with her. Thankfully, Elizabeth had gone.

'Where's the other young lady who was with you?' he asked the cloakroom attendant.

'She's finished for the night, *Mein Herr*,' she replied.

Odette breathed a sigh of relief. She took her stole and Krüger told her to go to bed. He would be up later. He turned on his heels and went to join his associates in the drawing room. Instead of going to her bedroom, Odette left the hotel by a side door and went to her apartment. She breathed a sigh of relief when she found it empty. She looked around. Should Krüger or anyone else come to the apartment tomorrow, there was no sign that Amelie and Elizabeth had been there. She noticed the champagne bottle was almost empty and hoped the alcohol wouldn't affect them. Feeling secure, Odette returned to the Hotel Ripotot.

CHAPTER 30

Elizabeth and Amelie wasted no time in leaving Champagnole. Elizabeth decided to go to Lons-le-Saunier while Amelie decided on a safe house in Clairvaux. Both places were about 35 kilometres from Champagnole and easy enough to get to in a couple of hours except that with hardly any moonlight it could be dangerous and slow them down. Amelie couldn't risk going south or anywhere near Bonlieu, so they headed out of Champagnole together and parted company at the village of Pont-du-Navoy. Through a combination of fear and the cool night air, the effects of the champagne soon disappeared. Both had their guns hidden on them and Elizabeth still kept her knife hidden in her shoe. She also wore her brooch with the cyanide pill. In fact, it didn't matter which clothes she wore, the brooch was worn at all times. She had no idea whether Amelie carried her cyanide pill with her, or even if she had one at all, as some agents had refused them. They arranged to meet up at the Menouillard's as soon as possible.

It was pitch dark when Elizabeth arrived at the Dassin's home. Knowing which bedroom Juliette and Pierre slept in she threw small stones at the window. Pierre opened the door.

'Marie-Élise! You gave us a fright. What on earth's happened?'

She told him what had transpired at the Hotel Ripotot and that he needed to alert his contacts as soon as possible. She asked him if he knew where Guy was and he assured her he was safe.

'He's hiding out with the Maquis. Don't worry. We'll put you back in contact as soon as possible.'

They spoke about the raids around Saint-Laurent-en-Grandvaux, the burning of the Grand Hôtel du Lac, and the fate of Madame Sophie. He knew about it all. Juliette came downstairs to see what was going on. Pierre told her he had to go out. It was urgent.

'What! In the middle of the night? I demand that you tell me what's happening.'

'Tell her,' Elizabeth said. 'This is important.'

'Tell me what?'

Pierre told her Elizabeth had risked her life cycling from Champagnole to alert the Resistance of more raids which could take place at any moment. This time Pierre knew his luck might be running out and his family were in danger.

'My darling, I want you to go and pack a suitcase and get the children ready to leave as soon as possible. You will catch the first train to Dijon.'

Juliette looked terrified. 'I don't know anyone in Dijon. Why can't I go to one of our relatives?'

'Because if they come looking for me, they will contact them too. In Dijon there is a woman who will keep you safe.'

He was referring to Madame Genot. He pulled Juliette into his arms. 'Things are going to become dangerous here. I want you to be strong and trust me.' He kissed her tenderly.

'He's right,' Elizabeth said. 'You must get the first train out of here. You shouldn't be harassed being a woman alone with two children. I'll go to the station with you.'

Pierre kissed his wife and left immediately to inform various local members of the Resistance in Lons-le-Saunier, including Father Henri. In the meantime, Elizabeth helped Juliette prepare the children for the journey, assuring Angeline they were going on a holiday and she was to take care of her brother. She put her favourite book in her little backpack for her and at dawn they headed to the station. After making sure they boarded the train without any trouble, Elizabeth returned to the Dassin villa. Pierre had returned and was trying hard to put on a brave face in an empty house that normally was filled with love and happiness. He was going to see Brando at his office in the water department and then visit the German High Command to see if he could get any information out of Schubert. After that he would leave for Saint-Amour to meet with Gavroche. Elizabeth left for Clairvaux.

As usual, the barking dogs alerted Sabine. She was so relieved to see her she couldn't stop crying. 'When Daniel told us what happened, we thought we'd never see you again,' she said, her voice choking with emotion. 'And when we heard what happened to the hotel we couldn't believe it.'

Armand was still at the sawmill, and Elizabeth filled her in on what had transpired and that they had to alert the Maquis to keep a lookout for the Germans.

'From what I heard, the raids will be as bad as the ones around the lakes. There's no time to lose. Make sure the Germans don't find anything that will link you both with the Resistance.'

'Don't worry,' Sabine replied. 'Everything is well-hidden. I will let Armand know straight away.'

'Good, but be careful. Now I have to send a message to London straight away.' She started to walk towards the cottage when Sabine shouted out. 'You will come over later, won't you?'

Elizabeth hurriedly set up ready to transmit to London. It had been a while since her last transmission and she took time to make sure her coding was accurate. She could only let them know the barest of details as the radio frequency vans were still posing a great danger. After a short while, she received a reply informing her that more help was on its way. She was to listen for the signals on the BBC. The invasion was imminent.

She packed the radio away, boiled some water and stripped off all her clothes to have a good wash. The door was open and a warm afternoon breeze drifted through the door, carrying with it the fragrance of wild flowers. She soaped her body and at the same time looked across the fields. Cows grazed peacefully and the air was filled with birdsong. She couldn't believe she was still alive. If she had made it this far, she could make it to the end of the war.

That evening, refreshed and wearing her pale pink dress, Elizabeth walked through the dark winding pathway to the farmhouse and was greeted with the tantalizing aroma of roast pork and the sound of an Edith Piaf song through the half-open door. She walked in and to her great surprise and happiness, saw Guy standing there waiting for her with a beaming smile and holding a large bunch of wildflowers. He opened his arms and she ran across the kitchen into his embrace. Sabine and Armand clapped loudly. For the next minute or so, all they could do was kiss and whisper how much they loved each other. It was such an emotional reunion that both Sabine and Elizabeth were crying tears of joy.

'This calls for a celebration,' Armand said and promptly produced one of his last bottles of a particularly good *vin jaune* while Sabine put the flowers in a vase for her.

Their happiness soon disappeared when they started to discuss the raids and deportations of the last few weeks. She discussed the meeting at the Hotel Ripotot and together they implemented further plans to protect the Resistance. The only good news was that André had gone back to Besançon with Hortense to try and save Madame Sophie. They heard she was locked up in the citadel with others awaiting deportation. Their contacts in the Resistance who worked at the railway station there were shown a copy of her photo and identity which Bernard had made for them. A large sum of money was promised to anyone who passed on any information which would aid in her release. As a consequence, all trains departing Besançon were checked and double-checked. Elizabeth told them Pierre had sent his family away in case the Gestapo took them hostage and was trying to find out what he could from Klaus Schubert at the German High Command. They ended the night listening to the BBC. The increased heavy bombing on the continent meant the invasion was imminent: probably only a matter of days.

That night Guy stayed in the cottage but left early in the morning to return to the Maquis. If she needed him, Armand would contact him. She stood on the doorstep and watched him until he disappeared into the woods and then set off for Clairvaux to find Amelie. There was hardly anyone around. Bistrot Jurassien was closed so she went to Monique's house thinking that is where Amelie would have headed. She was right.

Monique checked to see no-one was watching and quickly pulled Elizabeth inside. What she wasn't expecting to hear was that soon after Amelie arrived, Monique received a coded telephone call from the owner of Café des Amis in Champagnole for Amelie.

'She'd only just finished telling me what took place at the hotel when we got the call. She looked terrified saying the message meant Odette was in trouble. I hope she's going to be alright.'

This was the last thing Elizabeth needed. 'When's the next bus to Champagnole?'

Monique gave her an anxious look. 'Not you too! Please stay here, my dear. Don't push your luck.'

No amount of begging had any effect on her either. Elizabeth had ten minutes to get to the bus stop. The bus seemed to take forever to get to Champagnole. It was market day, but already the Germans and Milice were out putting up more notices. The people gathered round to look and, as usual, large sums of money were being offered to those who came forward with information. She headed straight to the Café des Amis. As soon as the owner saw her, he indicated she should go through to the back. He locked the door and sat her down.

'The news is bad. Odette is dead.'

Elizabeth felt numb. Odette — dead! When the enormity of his words sank in, she almost burst into tears.

'What happened?'

'From what we gather, her lover, *Obergruppenführer* Hans Krüger, asked the manager who the new cloakroom attendant was. When he told her she was Odette's cousin who'd replaced the usual attendant because she was ill, he flew into a rage and stormed off to their room. Apparently, Odette was asleep when he entered. He dragged her out of bed and seeing that she had no clothes on, threw her nightdress at her and told her to cover herself. When he confronted her with his findings, she denied it, but Krüger had someone bring the manager to the room. He pointed a gun at his head and said he would shoot him if he was lying. He asked her again. By now, almost everyone in the hotel knew something was wrong and staff started to disappear in case they too were pulled into the fray. The manager told me afterwards what took place. He was terrified for Odette. She was his friend but there was little to help her.'

'This woman,' Krüger said to Odette, pulling at her hair while still pointing his gun at the manager. 'I will ask you again. Who is she?' He clicked his gun ready to fire.

'Alright,' Odette replied calmly. 'She's not my cousin. I met her in the street. She asked me if I could get her a job. I only wanted to help as she seemed desperate.'

Krüger asked the manager for the address of the woman whose place Elizabeth had taken and sent two of his men to get her. Twenty minutes later, the confused and distraught woman was pushed into the room and asked to tell them what happened. Immediately she began to tell them what transpired — that Odette had paid her to say she was ill. The woman was hysterical, saying she had no idea why, she just wanted to help her friend. Krüger indicated for his men to take her away and lock her up. Her screams could be heard through the hotel until she was knocked out by one of Krüger's men. Krüger told the manager to wait outside while two more were sent to search Odette's apartment. The manager could hear Odette pleading with Krüger.

'Hansi — *Liebling*. There was nothing in it,' Odette said in an endearing voice. 'This is a mistake.'

Only Krüger and his trusted lieutenant stayed in the room. The lieutenant was told to tie her hands to the back of the chair while Krüger sat opposite her and waited until the men returned from searching the apartment. One of them showed him the cloakroom attendant's uniform. His face was cold and unemotional. Whatever had gone on between them was long gone. Except for the lieutenant, the other men were told to leave. Krüger gestured to his lieutenant to start on her.

The first blow knocked her to the ground. She lay on the floor groaning in agony. Her face was swelling and blood trickled from her mouth. The lieutenant picked her up. Krüger lit a cigarette and after taking a long drag, pulled her nightdress away and pressed the burning end into her breast. The pain was unbearable. Her screams could be heard along the corridor and in the nearby rooms. Then he did it again — and again — six times in all until she fainted. A sickly smell of burning flesh mixed with Chanel No 5. Even the lieutenant was forced to pull himself together. Krüger threw a glass of cold water in her face to bring her to. She knew he no longer trusted her and faced death. There was no other way out.

'I have nothing to say,' Odette said, defiantly.

Krüger aimed his gun at her and told her she had one last chance to redeem herself.

'Who are you working for?' he asked, coldly.

She stared into his eyes as he aimed at her forehead.

'*Vive La France*, you bastard!' she shouted out defiantly, and spat at him.

The gun went off and Odette slumped backwards. Krüger walked out of the room and as he brushed pass the manager, told him to get a doctor. A German doctor was called to pronounce Odette dead and her body was taken to the church. For most of the German officials at the hotel, this was all in a day's work, but for the staff, they were deeply affected. The manger was advised by Krüger's lieutenant to call a priest and arrange a burial as soon as possible so as not to scare the rest of the population. Even though the lieutenant was with the Gestapo, he had been brought up a strict Catholic and apologised to the priest for what had taken place.

The café owner gave Elizabeth a strong drink. Odette had not wanted her to go there. How could she ever live with herself?

'They are burying her today,' he said, 'without fuss. Unfortunately we cannot let the truth out yet that she was one of us.'

Elizabeth asked about Amelie and was told she left the café when she heard.

'I have no idea where she is,' the owner said. 'If I were you, I would leave too. She will turn up when the time is right. Trust me. She's a clever girl.'

Elizabeth caught the next bus back to Clairvaux. The drive and the emotional turmoil made her feel sick and she vomited as soon as she got off the bus. She headed to Bistrot Jurassien and broke the news to Monique before going back to the Menouillards.

CHAPTER 31

09:32 a.m. Tuesday, June 6 1944

Elizabeth sat in the kitchen with Sabine and Arnaud listening to the BBC radio broadcast.

> *This is London. London calling in the home, overseas, and European service of the BBC, and through United Nations radio, Mediterranean, and this is John Snagge speaking. Supreme Headquarters, Allied Expeditionary Forces, have just issued a communiqué Number 1......*
> *Communiqué Number 1:*
> *Under the command of General Eisenhower, Allied naval forces, supported by strong air forces, began landing Allied armies on the Northern coast of France. This ends the reading of communiqué Number 1 from Supreme Headquarters Allied Expeditionary Force.*

The elation at hearing this was so emotional that for a few minutes the three sat in silence trying to take it in. They all had tears in their eyes and there was great jubilation, yet, at the same time, a feeling of dread. The Germans would not take this lying down and they knew they would unleash a terror campaign. Everywhere else, this was the moment SOE and the Resistance — now known to many as the FFI under the control of de Gaulle and the men he had sent into France — had been waiting for. It was the moment to put their months of training into action. Within twenty-four hours, up to 1,000 acts of sabotage were carried out. Bridges were blown up, trains derailed, bringing the rail network almost to a standstill, Nazi communications disrupted, and convoys attacked. Many of those who had stayed on the sidelines now came out, put on FFI armbands and openly aided the Resistance.

As Elizabeth knew, the Normandy landings would only exacerbate the terror in the Jura. She prayed that Guy and his men would be safe. She didn't see him for a while but knew he was somewhere between Clairvaux and Saint-Claude working with an officer from the Foreign Legion in charge of the maquisards, but she still hadn't received any contact from Amelie and was extremely worried about her. Every day she listened to the radio with Sabine and Armand. Armand's connections with the rough lumberjacks obstructed the roads with enormous fir trees from the forests which only served to anger the Germans even more.

Throughout all this, heavy bombing had little effect on Hitler and deportations continued from the Jura to Germany. Every few days, Elizabeth reported back to London but radio traffic was intense and it often took ages to get through. After the first week, they received their first bad news. Bernard the forger's new office in Lons-le-Saunier had been raided. He had a family with him at the time trying to get new identity cards. All were taken to the Gestapo HQ along with some of his equipment. He had hidden most of it and only Hortense knew where he'd stored the rest but she was still in Besançon. Bernard refused to reveal names despite severe torture. After two days, he tried to jump out the window but was caught and executed by firing squad. The news affected them all enormously.

On the June 13 the BBC announced that Germany had deployed a V1 Flying Bomb attack on London. Both sides dug in. In Lons-le-Saunier, they heard Pierre had been to visit Klaus Schubert to try and save Bernard, but Schubert now wanted nothing to do with him, not only because good wine was in short supply, but because he was angered at the Resistance for venting their anger on the Germans and sabotaging important infrastructure. 'If I were you, I'd get out while you can before you end up like your friends,' Schubert advised Pierre with a smirk. 'There's little I can do for you, now.' He pointed to the door. 'Out! I don't want to see you here again. *Damit Basta! Verzieh Dich jetzt!*'

Pierre left the building and decided enough was enough. With his family gone and the Germans confiscating vehicles that had previously been allowed a permit, he headed to Orgelet to work with the maquisards, headed by Max.

'The Germans are concentrating their troops in Normandy,'

Armand said, 'This makes them weaker in the south. We won't have to wait much longer until the Allies land there too. Then they will soon reach the Jura.'

Guy returned to Clairvaux at the beginning of July and stayed two nights. He never told Elizabeth where or what he had been doing; only that it was still dangerous. On July 11 a tragedy occurred just a few kilometres from Armand's sawmill. Sixteen men between the ages of thirty-one and sixty-two were caught by a German patrol and executed at the edge of a quiet thicket in Charchilla, just metres from the main road to Moirans-en-Montagne. They had all passed this spot many times. That day there were more executions and on July 12 German planes bombed the town of Moirans-en-Montagne, destroying houses, factories and shops, including the bar and the pharmacy where Antoine had worked. The Germans were relentless and executions and the burning of homes and farms recurred regularly for the next three weeks. Few dared venture outdoors for fear of being shot on sight. The beautiful and peaceful Jura landscape became soaked in blood. Throughout all this, the deportations continued.

Elizabeth was still in contact with London but, by the end of July, they asked her to return to England. Unlike some of the other networks, Belvedere was still operating. The Resistance and agent Daniel were doing a fine job. Elizabeth was reluctant to leave. She made the excuse to them that she was working as a courier again because agent Mireille — Amelie — could not be found, it was feared she had fallen foul of the Germans. However, Elizabeth wasn't convinced of this. Like Guy, she was a chameleon and she was in possession of various identity cards so could be working under another alias.

Guy returned to Clairvaux again during the first week of August. They discussed the latest news. Rumours were circulating of a failed assassination attempt on Hitler at his Headquarters in East Prussia and of an uprising in Warsaw by the Polish Resistance. He told her he was intending to help the Maquis near Saint-Laurent-en-Grandvaux. This time he had news from André. His contacts had given him a list of deportees about to leave Besançon. Unlike most of the earlier deportations, this convoy was no longer going via Compiegne to concentration camps in Germany, but would be heading straight for the camp in Alsace — Natzweiler-Struthof. Madame Sophie's name was on the list. He planned to free her. How he was going to do that, he didn't say. This time, Guy stayed for a couple of weeks, often disappearing one day and returning the next. She asked him if he'd been back to the Grand Hôtel du Lac. He said yes but there was nothing left. The building had been burnt to the ground. The only thing he did tell her was that the building had caved in on itself and completely covered the entrance to the escape route. He hoped it would remain a secret. The sight had obviously distressed him because he asked her not to speak of it again. Every night they listened to the radio at the Menouillards and then went back to the cottage. It was the middle of summer, the weather was hot, and despite what had happened, they were as deeply in love as they'd ever been. Guy's body and face was still disfigured but he had regained his strength and they made love every night.

On August 15 the Allies landed in the South of France intending to make their way northwards to join the Allies from Normandy. Four days later, the Resistance began an uprising in Paris. This time Guy informed her that he was going away and would not return until they had chased the Germans out of France. She told him London wanted her to return but she wanted to go with him. They argued all night. She was a good shot and trained in sabotage as much as any other agent and could be useful, not to mention the fact that she was his radio operator, but her pleas were met with a resounding no. It was still too dangerous and he didn't want to lose her again. When she mentioned Amelie, he told her to forget her. She was no longer her problem. He would keep a lookout for her.

He pulled her into his arms. *'Je t'aime tellement, ma cherie,'* he said, running his fingers through her hair. 'I love you so much, my darling, it hurts. I couldn't bear it if anything happened to you. I want you to go back as soon as you can. Wait for me at home.'

Elizabeth tried hard to be strong, but inside she felt crushed. Knowing she couldn't burden him with more anguish, she agreed. However, the decision was now out of her hands. That night during a radio transmission to London, they told her she had achieved what she had set out to do and as she had been in the field for six months they were recalling her back to London and sending someone to replace her.

AGENT D MOVING NORTH NEW RADIO OPERATOR ARRIVING ASSIGNMENT COMPLETED WE AWAIT YOUR RETURN.

The next day he left Clairvaux. That night, she went alone to the Menouillards. They could tell something was wrong and tried to comfort her.

'I have a strange feeling I won't see him again,' Elizabeth said, choking back the tears.

Sabine chastised her. 'Where is the feisty Marie-Élise we have come to know?' She waved her hand in the air like a mother berating a child. 'He will be safe, you mark my words.'

By the end of August, much had changed. Paris had been liberated and the Free French Forces, working with the Allies, were gaining ground. Lons-le-Saunier was liberated at the beginning of September. The Menouillards, along with Monique and Mitzi were there to welcome the U.S. Third Infantry Division into the town. They met up with Pierre again and were overjoyed to see him, however he was still worried about his family because of German resistance.

One week later, Elizabeth was informed of the date and place she would leave France. This time it was from an airfield near Lons-le-Saunier itself. The day before, she said goodbye to her friends. In Clairvaux, she took one last walk with Monique to the cemetery and put flowers on the grave of her son.

'What was it all for?' Monique asked sadly.

Elizabeth tried hard to find the right words but they seemed meaningless.

'Every act of defiance led to this day,' she replied. 'Freedom comes at a cost.'

'I will miss you,' Monique said. 'Come back one day and see us.' Elizabeth put an arm around her and assured her she would. 'With Daniel.' She gave her a knowing smile. 'Yes, the two of you.'

The following day, Elizabeth was taken to the airfield by the Menouillards. Pierre was also there to say goodbye. Before leaving, she met Belvedere's new radio operator, a young man who looked as if he'd only just left university.

'Take care of agent Daniel,' she told him.

Elizabeth hugged each one in turn and headed out across the tarmac without looking back. This time she was travelling in relative luxury on a Douglas C-47 Skytrain with half a dozen military officials.

CHAPTER 32

September 1944 London.

Elizabeth was summoned to a debriefing at 64 Baker Street with Vera Atkins and Colonel Buckmaster. They wasted no time in conveying their greatest admiration for her work. She had taken enormous risks but, at the same time, she had kept her head down. More importantly, Belvedere was doing a fine job in the field again and much of that was down to her tenacity as an agent. They told her nothing of the networks that had been blown by the Germans or of her other friends in the field.

'You will keep me updated about Guy won't you?' she said to them.

Vera, sitting at her desk smoking a Senior Service and looking as smart as ever in her uniform replied that they would do their best. For now, she should go home and relax. That was easier said than done. London was still suffering from bombing raids but at least her flat was still there. As the weather was still warm, she was wearing her pretty pink dress. She took off the brooch that she had worn night and day and handed it to her.

'Thankfully, I never needed it,' she said.

Vera said she had something for her too. It was her wedding ring.

On the way out, she saw her old friend Andy coming out of another office. 'I don't believe it,' he said with a smile. 'When did you get back?'

'A week ago — and you?'

'I was injured just before the Normandy landings and flown back. How about we meet up for a drink again? Like old times.' Elizabeth was happy to see him but she wasn't really in the mood. 'I won't take no for an answer. Meet me in The Flying Horse at six. The Red Lion was bombed.' He turned to go into another room. 'Don't let me down.'

Elizabeth walked back to her apartment. London was in a mess.

The shells of burnt-out buildings had changed the landscape and the permanent smell of smoke filled her lungs, yet everywhere people were getting on with their lives. How she longed for the pure air of the Jura. It seemed a lifetime ago now. In her apartment she kicked off her shoes and listened to the radio, picked up a wedding photo and touched Guy's face through the glass. Even though he now had a scarred face, he was still her handsome husband. The program on the radio changed: *Uncle Sam Presents: A broadcast by the Army Air Force Band, under the direction of Captain Glenn Miller.* The first tune to play was *Speak Low*. She got up and dusted off her melancholia and decided to meet Andy for a drink. It would do her good.

'I'm glad you came. How was France?' he asked.

'Oh you know, highs and lows. What about you?'

'Our network was blown and I had to make my way alone. Eventually, I joined up with another, headed by a woman. Boy was she tough — and effective. She reminded me a bit of you.'

'I'm not tough, Andy. I'm just as vulnerable as anyone else.'

'What will you have to drink,' he asked. 'A pint or something stronger?'

She patted her belly. 'Ginger beer.'

Andy stared at her for a few seconds and then burst out laughing. 'My God — you're not...'

'Pregnant,' she replied. 'Yes. It's due in May.'

Andy grinned. 'Who's the lucky father?' he asked cheekily.

Elizabeth smacked his leg playfully.

'We heard Guy was still alive,' he said to her. 'Baker Street was very happy and celebrated when they heard the news. Agent Lisette is famous, you know.'

Elizabeth raised an eyebrow and smiled. 'They celebrated did they? They never told me that.'

'Does he know?' Andy asked. 'About the baby, I mean.'

Elizabeth shook her head. 'I didn't even know myself when I left France.'

'Well, well! As you are not drinking, I'll have a double Scotch to toast the lucky couple.'

He went to the bar to buy the drinks. When the air-raid siren started again, he rushed back and grabbed her. 'Come on. Let's go.'

They hurried to the nearest air-raid shelter just in time. A woman with a small child of about two or three sat next to them. The child was crying and nothing the mother could do would silence her. Elizabeth pulled the child to her and started to tell her a story she used to tell Angeline — *La Belle au bois dormant* — The Sleeping Beauty. After a while the girl fell asleep. Andy put an arm around her shoulder.

'You'll make a great mother,' he said.

After her last miscarriage Elizabeth had been careful, but this pregnancy was presenting no problems at all. In fact, she felt the best she'd felt in a while. It gave her cause for optimism and she soon returned to her old job as a nurse at the hospital. Her shifts were long but the work kept her occupied. After each shift, she returned to the apartment and listened to the radio, always expecting Guy to walk through the door at any time. By Christmas she had not heard anything from him but Vera Atkins called round one evening to assure her he was well. Besançon had been liberated and he was now in Alsace. She promised he would be home soon.

At the end of April 1945 the BBC announced that Hitler and his wife had committed suicide. The child she was carrying kicked violently. *Yes, I know my darling*, she said stroking her swollen belly. *It will soon be over and you will be born into a free world.*

She made herself a cup of tea before preparing to go to bed. There was a knock at the door. Thinking it was the landlady coming to tell her she'd also heard the news, Elizabeth opened the door and there stood Guy.

'*Bonsoir,* my darling. Remember me?'

She clutched the door to stop herself from passing out. When Guy saw her belly, neither of them knew who'd got the biggest shock. It was a reunion both had thought about every single day and it was what had sustained them both. After everything they'd endured, they were united once again.

'What do you think?' he asked with a smile while stroking her belly. 'A boy or a girl?'

'I think a girl, but she'll be a fighter, I can tell.'

Guy took her in her his arms. 'Then she will take after her mother.'

When the euphoria of having her husband back safe and well subsided, Guy told Elizabeth what transpired after she left. Monique, the Menouillards, and Pierre, were all safe. Pierre's family rejoined him after the liberation of Dijon and they set about rebuilding their villa which had been destroyed in an air-raid. Pierre went back into the wine business again. He also added that a third child was on the way. Elizabeth couldn't have been happier for them.

'And André and Madame Sophie?'

'Having been notified that a transport was leaving Besançon for Natzweiler-Struthof and that Madame Sophie's name was on the list, André and a friend acquired forged documents and German uniforms and posed as soldiers overseeing the transport. When the convoy of trucks arrived at the train station from the citadel, the prisoners were herded onto the platform. The Resistance working for the rail network had managed to delay the train's arrival, but only by an hour. Any longer and it would have aroused suspicion. Madame Sophie was spotted in the crowd and the men, aided by a French guard working for the Resistance, pulled her aside under the pretext of checking her name against a list. André was with them. He was a wanted man and photos of him were plastered on buildings all over the Jura but he had changed his appearance. Not enough to fool Madame Sophie though. As soon as she saw him, she feared for them all. The Germans would soon realise something was wrong, but before she'd had time to acknowledge him, she was whisked away by his comrade to a waiting car stolen from the Gestapo themselves only hours prior to the arrival of the train — enough time to change the number plates. With more Germans entering the station, the Resistance melted away. It had taken less than ten minutes, but Madame Sophie was safe.

Elizabeth heaved a sigh of relief. 'Thank God. What happened then?'

'Besançon was liberated on September 8 but by that time Madame Sophie was in hiding with Hortense. André and I continued fighting. There were pockets of German resistance everywhere. They laid mines, and snipers hid in deserted buildings. After France was finally liberated, he joined her and they went back to Bonlieu. The burnt-out shell of the hotel and the local farmhouses caused them both distress. The Maquis fought bravely to the very end and they paid a huge price for it.'

'What happened to them — as a couple I mean?' asked Elizabeth. 'Wasn't he married?'

Guy grinned and gave her a kiss. 'Theirs was a love match like ours, my darling. His wife agreed to a divorce. As a wedding present, André promised to rebuild the hotel for her. What's more, they would run it together, and as André told her, it would be a tribute to the men, women and children they'd helped to freedom.'

Elizabeth was very happy for them. She knew it would not be an easy task, but she also knew they would achieve that dream and do it well. Guy promised her that one day, when the war was over, they would return for a holiday. 'This time as a family,' he added.

'And Amelie — what happened to her?' Elizabeth asked, almost afraid to mention her name.

'You're not going to believe this,' he said. Elizabeth prepared herself to hear something terrible. 'When she heard what happened to Odette, she left for Champagnole. It was too late to save Odette, but by then she had become obsessed with *la simplette*. She was convinced the woman would realise something bad had happened to Malfroy and her brother and would retaliate so she stayed in the house opposite and watched her day and night.'

Elizabeth couldn't believe what she was hearing.

'The house belonged to an elderly couple and their son who belonged to the Champagnole Resistance — a friend of the owner who ran the café we all frequented. The son and Amelie took it in turns to watch the house. By the time you left, *la simplette* rarely left the place except to buy food. She'd lost weight and by all accounts was steadily losing her mind. Sometimes she would wander by the river talking to herself. There was a time when Amelie would have shot her for what she did, but the more she saw of her, the more she felt sorry for her. The week Champagnole was liberated was like elsewhere: people retaliating against collaborators and shooting them in the streets and in their homes — it was mayhem. *La simplette* was in danger of being shot too, and Amelie and her friend decided to kidnap her and hide her until they could bring her to a tribunal. These tribunals are happening everywhere and in many cases are complete farces. People still want retribution. When it was *la simplette's* turn and knowledge about her collaboration came out, the jury wanted to execute her. At this point Amelie got up and gave a rousing speech. She told them they had not fought a war to end up acting like animals. What Lili had done was unforgiveable, but after having watched her for weeks in order to bring her to justice, saw she was clearly descending into madness. Even the people in the courtroom could see that. She pleaded for her to be put into a sanatorium.

'The judges deliberated and came to the same conclusion. There was uproar in the courtroom when Lili was led out to a cell to await transfer to an institution for the insane.'

263

Elizabeth could imagine it all; anger and hatred from all sides. When Guy first started to tell her Amelie's story, she feared Amelie herself might be losing her mind and was glad she rose to the occasion.

'Where did they send her?' Elizabeth asked, referring to Lili.

Guy could not look at her when he replied. 'They didn't get the chance. She hung herself in her cell that night. No one knows for sure if she acted alone or the guards did it.'

The room fell silent. The world they had lived in for so long flooded through their minds. They had found each other, but they had also lost so much.

'Did Amelie return with you?' Elizabeth asked.

'No. She decided to stay in France. Monique offered her a partnership in Bistrot Jurassien and she jumped at the opportunity. I have a feeling she will live out the rest of her life in Clairvaux, keeping the memory of Paul-Emille and others like him alive.'

'She was a very brave woman,' Elizabeth said, her voice choking with emotion.

Guy pulled her close. 'They all were, my darling.'

POSTSCRIPT

The Secret of the Grand Hôtel du Lac is based on real events which took place in the Jura/Franche-Comté Region of France during 1943-1944.

Between 2019-2020 I was fortunate enough to spend some time there researching WWII. The region is one of beauty and peacefulness: from the rolling, cultivated hills, filled with vineyards between Poligny, Château-Chalon, and Arbois, the region of the scenic lakes around which Clairvaux is centred, to the forest-cloaked alpine mountains bordering Switzerland. Yet this beauty hides what took place during the German Occupation. Not only do the hamlets and market towns bear witness to the atrocities which occurred, so do the quiet country lanes, fields and woodlands. It is impossible to drive more than twenty kilometres without coming across monuments to the maquisards and resistants. Everywhere, there are *tombs* to these brave men – and in some cases women. Their ages range between sixteen and fifty-six. Often there would be a marker for only one or two, occasionally sixteen or twenty. It is also noticeable that many are young men, due mainly to them fleeing to join the Maquis after the introduction of the compulsory *Service du travail obligatoire* (Compulsory Work Service) of 16 February 1943 – the forced deportation of thousands of French workers to Germany to work as forced labour for the German war effort.

Many of the events in the book actually took place – Bloody Sunday in Saint-Claude and the raids and deportations in the towns mentioned. As the Resistance gathered strength, early in April 1944, the Germans started a major offensive against them. Resistance confidence remained high, however. With the melting of the winter snow it would be difficult for the Germans to trace and locate the Maquis which had become, in the preceding month, the *Forces Françaises de l'Intérieur* (French forces of the interior). In response, the spring offensive – Operation

Frühling (Spring) – was instigated by the Germans, who managed to create a large and successful counter-network of covert collaborators, which succeeded in infiltrating many Resistance cells. The first major German military operation against the French Resistance took place in early 1944 in the mountainous region of the French Alps and Jura. The Resistance forces reorganized soon after the German operation ended, but knowing that the Allies intended to land in Normandy sometime soon, German countermeasures became particularly harsh. The deportations and raids that I described actually occurred. Many deportees from the area ended up in the Nazi concentration camp of Mittelbau-Dora, which was established in late summer 1943 as a sub-camp of Buchenwald, supplying slave labour from many Eastern countries occupied by Germany. Many inmates worked in the nearby tunnels, manufacturing the V-2 rocket and the V-1 flying bomb.

The raids which took place from Saint-Laurent-en-Grandvaux actually occurred at the beginning of August 1944, but for the purpose of the story, I brought them forward by a few months.

When France was occupied by the Germans in 1940, it was divided into the Occupied Zone, the Non-Occupied Zone, and the Forbidden Zone near the Swiss border. During my time there, I lived in a residence overlooking Lake Bonlieu, fifteen kilometres from Saint-Laurent-en-Grandvaux. The train line going through Saint-Laurent marked the demarcation line between the Occupied and Non-Occupied Zone from Champagnole to Morez.

While the main characters are fictional, the Gestapo chiefs mentioned in Dijon and Besançon are real. As was Conchita, the mistress of Mauz. The main headquarters of the Gestapo in the region were at Besançon, Dijon and Lyon. All these places became notorious for torture, executions and as deportation centres. Despite being despised by the majority of the population, the Gestapo recruited hundreds, if not thousands of collaborators and Milice. It is a fact that such terror in the region could not have been achieved without the co-operation of those people.

My characters are a composite of a several SOE agents. The betrayal of the Belvedere network by a woman was inspired by what happened to Noor Inayat Khan, alias 'Madeleine'. Noor was betrayed to the Germans, either by Henri Déricourt (codename Gilbert) or Renée Garry. Déricourt was an SOE officer and former French Air Force pilot who had been suspected of working as a double agent for the *Sicherheitsdienst*. But most likely it was Renée Garry, the sister of Émile Henri Garry, the head agent of the 'Cinema' network, and Noor's organiser. Renée Garry was allegedly paid 100,000 francs (some sources state 500 pounds). Her actions have been attributed to Garry's suspicion that she had lost the affections of SOE agent France Antelme to Noor. After the war, she was tried, but escaped conviction. Noor was also an excellent radio operator.

The Character of Guy — agent 'Daniel' — was inspired by SOE agent Harry Rée. He was parachuted into France in April 1943 and joined the 'Acrobat' network around Montbéliard. Later he became active in the 'Stockbroker' network around Belfort and was responsible for organising sabotage attacks on the Peugeot factory at Sochaux. He also managed to share tactical information on the Wehrmacht projects they had become involved in, especially the V1 rocket. The Germans tried to capture Rée, and after being shot four times, he managed to reach Switzerland where he continued to operate with the Resistance. He returned to Britain in May 1944.

South of Bonlieu, towards Lons-le-Saunier, is the pretty village of Clairvaux-les-Lacs, a mere ten-minute drive away and a place I visited frequently. Clairvaux was the place where not only Harry Rée frequented, but also SOE agent Diana Rowden. Her name in the field among fellow agents was 'Paulette' and her primary role was as a courier delivering messages to other agents and members of the underground. She would travel constantly, mostly by bicycle, and she worked with wireless operator John Young. Barely a month after her arrival, an SOE agent was arrested, betrayed by a double agent who had infiltrated the circuit, so Young and Rowden were on the run. After three weeks in hiding, she joined Young in what would be their last hideout with a family who owned a local sawmill outside Clairvaux-les-Lacs. Since it was likely the Gestapo had a description of her, she dyed her hair and wore different clothes to blend in with the locals. In November 1943 Young received a message that a new agent, named Benoit, would arrive. Unfortunately the man who turned up was an imposter and they were caught by the Gestapo. Diana was taken to Lons-le-Saunier, and then to the Gestapo headquarters in the Avenue Foch in Paris. After being moved to Karlsruhe in Germany, she was again moved to the infamous Natzweiler-Struthof concentration camp in France with three other female SOE agents, Andrée Borrel, Vera Leigh and Sonia Olschanezky, in July 1944. This was part of the

Nacht und Nebel – Night and Fog Policy – ensuring that agents and resistants should simply "disappear" without trace.

Orders were quickly given that they were to be executed immediately.

Inside the building housing the crematorium, each woman in turn was told to undress for a medical check and a doctor gave her an injection for what he told one of them was a vaccination against typhus, but was in fact a 10cc dose of phenol which the doctor believed was lethal. When the women became unconscious after the injection, they were inserted into the crematorium oven.

Writing The Secret of the Grand Hôtel du Lac, it was purely co-incidental that much of the story is based in Clairvaux-les-Lacs as it was a central point for SOE agents and close to where I was living, but I was aware that I had walked in the footsteps of one of SOE's bravest female agents, and it still gives me goosebumps to think I walked along the same streets, drove along those quiet country roads, and most likely stopped to take in the same beautiful scenery. It is also coincidental that my protagonist, Elizabeth, alias Marie-Élise Lacroix – SOE agent 'Lisette' – lived at a farm where there was a sawmill, as did Diana, but sawmills are everywhere in this area due to the forests and logging.

I would also like to mention the bravery of the *passeurs* who aided many fugitives, especially Jews, over the border into Switzerland, escapees who would otherwise have been executed or deported to Germany. The Risoux Forest is the largest forest in Europe. Lining the western edge of the Vallée de Joux for approximately 15km, it forms a natural border between France and Switzerland. Its vast surface area, its density and its geographical situation meant it was the setting for numerous escape routes by French and Swiss friends known as the *Passeurs du Risoux.*

On September 13, 2014, a monument was unveiled at Le Pont in Switzerland in memory of the *passeurs*. Some 200 people took part, honouring those who made transit during the Second World War from France to Switzerland – individuals pursued by the Nazis, resistance fighters as well as Jewish children.

"The emotion was intense on the shores of Lake Joux, in the middle of the day, when the last surviving ferryman, the Frenchman Bernard Bouveret (90 years old in October), and a former child saved from deportation, Walter Reed (born Werner Rindsberg in 1924 in Bavaria), unveiled the monument."

The monument is in six languages, (French, German, Italian, English, Hebrew and Chinese), and the hollow hexagonal column carries a brief text.

"To the smugglers of the Risoux forest who risked their lives to help take refuge in Switzerland, resistance fighters, intelligence agents and Jews threatened with death in France occupied during World War II, 1944-2014. The grateful Vallée de Joux."

What is important to remember is that it is only now that the courage and bravery of these smugglers have emerged. For decades, "they have not been appreciated and recognized at their true value", noted Laurent Nydegger, president of the *Association of Passeurs de Mémoire et Municipal de l'Abbaye* (VD), at the event.

The Swiss initiative is being carried out in full collaboration with their French neighbours. The same text will be put on the place of the church of Chappelle-des-Bois (F), on the other side of the border, thanks to the Association du Mur-aux-Fleurs-de-Lys. The Risoux smugglers numbered about fifteen people, in Switzerland as in France, four of whom received the Medal of the Just. About two hundred people owe them their lives. Another place of remembrance was inaugurated at the end of August at a place called Gy-de-l'Echelle on the Franco-Swiss border.

The Grand Hotel Ripotot in Champagnole was indeed the Headquarters of the German Kommandant and played an important role as a meeting point for the Gestapo in the area, particularly in light of it being on the main route between Dijon and the Swiss border. It was once a plush and luxurious establishment but ceased to operate quite a few years ago. The SOE agents also frequented the area around Saint-Amour and had access to the Château d'Andelot in the Jura. The Château d'Angerville is based on this.

As for the story itself and the hotel at the centre of the novel – the Grand Hôtel du Lac – it is based on a hotel which once stood a few hundred metres away from where I was living. I lived in the ground floor apartment of what is now the Residence du Lac and it was there that I discovered it had once been a hotel, built by the same owners of the original Hôtel du Lac which had indeed been burnt down by the Gestapo during the raids mentioned in the book. The original hotel was much closer to the escarpment and, from what I gather, was certainly used to aid escapees to flee into the forest and on to safety. Unfortunately, little of what took place at that time is known today, and the whereabouts of their escape route and caves remain unknown. Like all stories, they fade over time. For me it was a powerful story and one that I could not let go. One thing is for sure, it was like walking through the countryside accompanied by ghosts, and I hope that in my own small way, I have brought the bravery of those ghosts alive again.

ALSO BY THE AUTHOR

Conspiracy of Lies
The Poseidon Network
Code Name Camille (USA TODAY Bestseller)
The Embroiderer
The Carpet Weaver of Uşak
Seraphina's Song

WEBSITE:
https://www.kathryngauci.com/

To sign up to my newsletter,
please visit my website and fill out the form.

AUTHOR BIOGRAPHY

Kathryn Gauci was born in Leicestershire, England, and studied textile design at Loughborough College of Art and later at Kidderminster College of Art and Design where she specialised in carpet design and technology. After graduating, Kathryn spent a year in Vienna, Austria before moving to Greece where she worked as a carpet designer in Athens for six years. There followed another brief period in New Zealand before eventually settling in Melbourne, Australia.

Before turning to writing full-time, Kathryn ran her own textile design studio in Melbourne for over fifteen years, work which she enjoyed tremendously as it allowed her the luxury of travelling worldwide, often taking her off the beaten track and exploring other cultures. *The Embroiderer* is her first novel; a culmination of those wonderful years of design and travel, and especially of those glorious years in her youth living and working in Greece.

Since then, she has gone on to become an international bestselling author. *Code Name Camille*, written as part of *The Darkest Hour Anthology: WWII Tales of Resistance*, became a *USA TODAY* **Bestseller** in the first week of publication.

Made in the USA
Monee, IL
06 April 2021

64947904R00163